Paperback: 978-1-7375919-3-1
First paperback edition July 2025
Edited by Eleanor Leiva
Cover by Bookfly Design
Published by Guillermo Leiva
Printed in the USA.

APOCALYPSE

THE BEGINNING OF THE END

PART ONE

Eleanor Leiva

Hide. Run. Fight.

For Charlotte, who always told me to keep writing

Allen Richmond speaking.

"This nation and its people can believe what they want to believe. Believe what your eyes see, or believe what you hear from your peers, friends, and family. But you have all heard the rumors that a plague is circulating this globe, starting in many different places at different times. Do what you need to do; you've all seen the news; you have seen the disappearances. I warn you away from the time periods of night. Believe me when I tell you I don't know more than you do. I don't know where it started or how it started, but as a nation, as a world, we're facing a zombie apocalypse."

PROLOGUE

Four years ago

Celeste screamed out in pain as the sharp metal bullet pierced her arm, sending a wave of white-hot pain over the rest of her body that made her crumpled to the ground, her head spinning.

Dark snow was underneath her, stained with blood. Her vision was swimming in and out as she heaved a breath, trying to summon the energy to heal herself.

When she was called onto the field as a medic, she thought she would be entering a battlefield and was *prepared* to do so. Not this bloodbath.

The Ice people were battling with all the magic and fight they had in them, and with their allies in the Shadow realm and the Earth realm, they had one of the largest armies. But for the first time, it looked like they were losing.

Celeste wasn't sure who they were battling; the snow was stained red as the wind rippled through, but that didn't make sense. Ice, Shadow, and Earth.

Blue, Black, and Brown. They didn't have red blood.

Who were they fighting?

They were small men, completely covered in odd clothing that resembled the earth and was patterned with green.

They held large pieces of metal that gave off loud bangs whenever the trigger was pulled, and they had the words **"The US Army"** printed in large, bold letters on the side of their arms.

The metal objects seemed to work because every time they pulled the trigger, an Ice, Shadow, or Earth person would collapse.

She was supposed to stay out of it, but now, one of the metal bullets had pierced her arm, and through a haze of pain, she could hardly see where she was going.

The realms where she lived were in chaos from these men, these men with odd clothing and odd customs. They had come one day through a portal in the sky. They had come with fire in their hands and with unbending will. They had come to destroy them. She didn't know why, but they had come.

She and her sister were supposed to be staying out of it, but Indigo had been called to battle.

And Celeste had been left behind.

Celeste could hardly make a forest grow, and according to her teachers, she was supposed to be able to create whole mountains by now.
Her parents hardly cared; dark expressions and stony words were all they had for their daughter. Indigo. Indigo cared.

Celeste desperately scanned the battle for signs of her sister, but she saw no trace of her; the last she had heard of her was a desperate mental scream that only close-blood relatives could make. She needed help, Celeste's mind was hazed with pain, but she sent her magic into her body, unable to move the metal but able to dull the pain and clear her head. Was Indigo one of the bodies lying motionless in the snow? Celeste pushed away nausea and fear. Indigo had just called to her! Where was she? Celeste wished more than ever to be able to communicate. She wasn't strong enough. She never would be.

Then she saw her.

Her beautiful sister was sprawled out in the snow.

Her long strawberry-colored hair was singed with black, all her limbs were twisted in awkward angles, and her face was contorted in an expression of pain. Her beautiful hazel-green eyes were filled with tears.

"Indigo," murmured Celeste. Her worry for her sister was the only thing that could beat back her growing fear. On shaking feet, Celeste threw herself forward, stumbling across the snow as she fell to her knees beside her sister's limp body.

"He's coming," she whispered. Her breath came out in short gasps. "Run."

"I'm not leaving you. You're going to be fine." Celeste cupped her sister's head in her hands. She felt her power flicker under her skin and tried to concentrate against the pain pulsing in her arm.

Indigo coughed again, her eyelids flickering. "Save your strength, sister. I'm already gone."

"Stop talking, Indigo." croaked Celeste. She had to be. Celeste pressed her shivering hands against her sister's side, trying to stem the staunch of blood, but it was no use.

When Indigo spoke again, her voice was distant, like it was being stretched over a very thin wire. "I love you."

"Indigo, please! Don't leave me," whispered Celeste. "No..."

Indigo heaved a choked breath. Her eyes began to lose focus, and then, suddenly, the light drained out of them. The rosy glow that always seemed to surround her sister faded, and the rasping gasps that Indigo had been heaving in and out of her lungs... disappeared.

"No!" Celeste let out a raw scream, not caring that she was on a battlefield, not caring who could hear. Tears streamed down her face as she clutched her sister's lifeless body. Indigo was gone, and she was never coming back. Never. Never.

8

Indigo was dead.

Her home was days away from being invaded and destroyed.

Celeste had lost the battle and the war.

 EARTH

Present day

"Beijing has its first case. We've nearly lost India, and Russia is locking down. We have our first case in Canada-"

"I don't know what's happening-"

"Never seen anything like it-"

"Won't respond-"

"Night-"

"Zombies-"

He could hear their scrambling from halfway across the facility. They were scrambling for answers, and he sure as hell wasn't going to give them.

They would be gone soon anyway; things were clicking into place. Nobody knew but him and a close ring of advisors. He was safe. He was *better* than safe. He was thriving.

Already, as he neared the room, he could hear their frenzied voices, their panic, their confusion.

Of course, he didn't blame them for the confusion. He was sure he'd be just as confused as they were, but he wasn't the one being confused and scrambling; he was on the top and calling the shots.

The doors were opened before him. The green and blue map of the countries was spinning with red before his eyes, and his peers and colleagues were pouring over maps and satellite images, papers in hand.

Already, as he stared at the map, the red increased, and little by little, the dots grew. One by one, the population was decreasing.

One by one until they were all gone.

Perfect.

10

They would all pay for what they did to him.

1

The sun was gone. No more blue skies. Dark rolling gray clouds as far as the eye could see. The darkness sang of danger; if the sun didn't come back soon, they would all die. She didn't know when she began to hear them, but once she did, she couldn't not listen to them. And then she began to run, sprinting away from monsters. But it didn't matter- it wouldn't work-
She was going to die.

Opal Kermerna jerked herself from the dream. Her body was sweat-stained, and her fingers were twisted tightly into the starch fabric of her sheets.

For a second, reality and dream swirled together in one great pit. The lines blurred, and Opal felt a desperate scream tear out of her throat.

But gradually, the panic loosened its iron grip on her body, and her heart stopped beating like a caged bird.

This was real life; she didn't have to live in her nightmares. She *wouldn't* live in her nightmares.

Opal sometimes dreaded going to bed; she knew what was in store for her. She had terrible dreams, so vivid they woke her screaming on many occasions. No medicine helped. She'd never told anyone about the dreams, not even when they kept her up; she didn't want to sound like a child.

Dreams were just dreams.

Suddenly, a bright crackle of a radio voice rippled through the silent house and punctured the morning air.

"President Richmond reports that the supposed 'zombie apocalypse' is a hoax and the violators shall be punished. The disappearances are no more than gangs running through the streets, the president advises caution for these gangs are armed and dangerous and uniting across the globe-"

The radio had been playing nonstop for a week now from Opal's younger sister Amelia's room. It was driving everyone mad - someone was going to step in at any second.

"Shut it off!" Opal heard her older sister call down the hallway. There was the sound of a door slamming, followed by quiet, as the radio was switched off.

And than-

"The murders include young children and old alike. Obviously, these killers have no moral standards for who their next victim will be."

"AMELIA!"

"Alright! Alright!!"

Opal sighed; getting dressed quickly, she slipped out of her room and into her sisters.

Amelia was twelve, the youngest in the family, with Opal at sixteen and Gina turning eighteen next month.

Amelia was short for her age, with brown eyes and short brown hair that was darker than Opal's. In this case, she looked even smaller than she was, clutching the old radio to her chest and perched upon her bed.

"Are you alright?" Opal asked tentatively, unsure of what to say.

Amelia glanced up, looking mournfully at Opal, her eyes wide and questioning, questioning for answers Opal didn't have. Nobody in the world did. "I'm fine," she mumbled. "J-just want to be informed. Y-you know?"

Opal would have believed Amelia's strong words if she was anyone else, but she could tell in her sister's hunched posture, quivering lips, and glassy eyes that she was *anything* but okay.

Pity flushed through Opal. She was angry. Angry that her sister would be scared by the liars out there. But still, it was scary; gangs were prowling the streets. An uprising of sorts, the adults called it. An uprising against what Opal didn't know. The United States had been in a semi-peaceful state ever since Allen Richmond was elected and cooled a lot of the fire that people had started to direct at the government.

Opal hurried across the room, pressing the radio out of Amelia's hands and pulling her sister into a hug, smoothing her hair and whispering into her ear. "It's a lie. It all is, but even if it wasn't, I'll always be there to protect you." Opal smiled. "And come on, let's go down to breakfast. We'll be late for school."

Amelia nodded quickly, though she didn't meet her sister's eyes, and gently placed the radio down on her bedspread.

Opal smiled, stood up, and carefully left the room.

As she closed the door, she came face-to-face with her mother. Linea was a gentle woman, most unlike her three very strongly spirited daughters. Her hair was graying (probably from the stress of being a single parent with three teenage daughters). Linea's eyes were clouded slightly but still the trademark blue of the Kermana family.

"Is she doing alright?" Linea asked gently.

Opal let her hand drift from the doorknob. "Of course. Just spooked. Like we all are."

"But she's the only one making a big deal out of it."

14

Opal turned to the sound of a slamming door as her older sister, Gina, shut the door to her bedroom behind her. Gina always looked hostile and angry these days, but somehow, she seemed worse today. Her dark blue eyes were clouded, and her mascara was smudged under her eyelids. Her perfect, heart-shaped lips were twisted into a pout, and she idly twisted her blonde hair between her fingers.

"Gina!" Linea rebuked. "Don't talk about your sister like that."

"What, Mom?" Gina snapped. "We're all scared, but she's just making it about her. As usual. And you're not doing anything to help her; you're just leaving it up to us."

"Gina!" Linea protested. "I'm doing my best."

"Well, your best isn't *good enough*." Gina hissed. She paused as if contemplating before spitting out. "Dad would have known what to do."

Then, a second later, she was slamming the door behind her in a whirl of blonde hair.

Linea's face creased with hurt, her face folding into a frown, but she quickly tried to correct it for her own daughter's sake. "Well, that's that."

Opal nodded stiffly, forcing a smile on her face.

Her father had died when she was seven. Opal could hardly remember him because she had bloated him out of her mind, unable to handle the grief. It was easier to forget than to hurt; Gina had always taken it hardest of all because she was the one who remembered him the most.

She did have one clear memory of him, though, and it was impossible to get out of her mind. It resurfaced, coming back again and again. No matter how many times she buried it. When her mind was wandering, when it was buried in sleep. This memory came.

Even though the memory had happened nearly twelve years ago, she remembered it clear as day:

"Hylight. My moonbeam." Opal's father had a soft, serious smile on his face as he addressed his daughter with the nickname Hylight, another name for the opal gem.

He was twirling something in his hand; over and over, he moved his fingers over the hard stone he clutched. "This, Hylight, is the gem that we named you after; I want you to remember this forever, remember how strong and beautiful an opal jem is." with the most delicate of care, he had reached out, taking Opal's tiny child fingers and wrapping them around the hem.

"Take it, Opal, and always remember."

She would remember his smile forever.

And then he was gone.

She'd lost the gem he gave her, but the memory she feared would never be lost.

Her family hadn't exactly seen him die, but Opal still remembered when they got the call late at night. Her mother had already been going crazy wondering where he was, why he wasn't answering his phone, and why he had skipped dinner. And then they got the call that they'd found his old station wagon lodged under a tree after it had skidded off the highway. Just like that, in one second, he was gone.

Opal would never see her father again.

"Look." Linea's face suddenly softened. "I know this is all so crazy, but I want you to understand it's going to be alright-"

16

Opal felt a lurch in her stomach. She didn't want to think about it. "Can you stop? We're late for school anyway." Opal snapped. "Thanks, Mom, but I'm not hungry. I think I'll walk to the bus stop and take the bus." Opal stood. She didn't feel like driving with Gina today.

Linea looked annoyed for a second but then wiped the expression from her face. "Of course. Bye, dear!" Linea hugged her daughter quickly, a sort of awkward one-armed hug that Opal pulled away from probably quicker than she should have. A wave of guilt stung her, but she pushed it away. She would apologize later.

"Come on, Amelia!" Opal called her sister. Opal waited, somewhat impatiently, as Amelia moved around the house, half in a daze before they left together.

As they left, a cold breeze drifted through the trees, and Opal sighed. She didn't know why, but her whole body ached today. She missed her father more than she had in a while. Perhaps the dream had rattled her more than she realized.

Amelia was still quiet. Opal felt a pang of worry. Her sister was never this quiet.

"Amelia-" Opal began.

"I know what you're going to say!" Amelia snapped. "I'm fine. I'm just worried. That's all."

"I know you are." Opal sighed. "Come on. We're going to miss the bus."

Amelia seemed a little downcast, but Opal didn't press. It was a normal day. The leaves swirled around Opal, the wind tugging at her clothes, and Opal's cheeks burned from the biting wind. Her shoes scuffed on the pavement as she watched the clouds swirl across a once-blue sky, promising a day of nothing but dark gray clouds.

Something large suddenly came hurtling from the woods on the other side of the sidewalk; loud slapped footsteps echoed across the street as a woman hurtled into Opal's arms.

Opal yelped in surprise, staggering back and pushing the middle-aged woman with dirty blonde hair and wild, scared blue eyes out of her arms and letting her collapse against the sidewalk.

She was filthy; her clothes were in tatters and stained with mud. Splats of dirt and mud coated her arms. Something sickeningly red was on her leg. It was a giant gash, and it made Opal's stomach want to hurl; it oozed beads of blood.

The woman was clawing and groping at Opal, staining her clothes with mud as she tried to haul herself to her feet, but she kept stumbling over, falling onto her knees.

"They're coming! They got me. THEY GOT ME!" her voice was garbled, making no sense. Her mouth was spitting blood, and bits of foam and blood speckled the pavement in front of her.

"What?" Opal caught the woman by the shoulders as her head lolled around, her eyes shaking. "What's going on?" Opal demanded. Her heart was pounding, and she was terrified. What was this? Was this woman sick? Should she not be touching her?

"They're coming..." the woman's voice trailed off, her body becoming limp.

Opal turned, bewildered and terrified, to her sister. Her heart was racing.

"Get away from her!" Amelia suddenly screamed, grabbing Opal's arms. "She's infected!"

18

Opal staggered back, feet tripping over rock and soil. "What's going on!?"

"Richmond was wrong. I was right. *They're coming.* If she means who I think she means, then we need to get back to the house."

The wet grass was slick under Opal's feet as Amelia grabbed her arm and yanked her forward, away from the crying woman on the pavement, forcing Opal's stumbling, numb feet to break into a run.

"Wait!" Opal cried, twisting in her sister's grip as she craned her neck to see behind her. "S-shouldn't we help her?"

Amelia's face was hard with fear. "No. She's already gone."

Opal felt a bile rise in her throat; her pulse skittered wildly all over the place at her sister's words. "Amelia." Opal hissed; she stalled her feet, twisting to face her sister. "What's going on?"

Amelia didn't move; she didn't give any hint that she had heard Opal at all; instead, her eyes were glassy and frozen as she stared beyond Opal at a spot behind her.

Opal swiveled around, following her sister's gaze, and immediately, she wished she hadn't.

The world was burning. Orange and yellow tongues of flame shot through the air and engulfed the town Opal called home. The flames licked hungrily at the wood of Opal's pretty little blue house right in front of the town; the whole structure creaked and groaned under the blackening support beams. The air was hazy with smoke and heat.

"MOM!" Amelia screamed, releasing Opal's hand as she sprinted forward.

"No!" Something else took over Opal if her mother was in there... But she couldn't let Amelia get hurt. She flung her arms around her sister, hugging her to her chest as she held her back. Amelia fought against her grip, scrabbling with her fingers to get free, but Opal held her tight, fighting the pain in her heart as she stared at the hungry flames lapping up her home.

"Let me go!" Amelia half screamed half sobbed as they watched their house burn.

"What's going on?!" Opal could see other people, other neighbors standing horrified at their own houses that were ablaze. What was this? Some arson attack? Stray bit of lightning?

The woman on the pavement was pushed to the far back of Opal's mind as she wove through her neighbors and friends, trying to coax information out of any of them.

"I've been telling you! I've been telling you!" Amelia shrieked. "Something is wrong! And nobody wants to do anything about it! We need to hide- or find Mom-" Amelia was teetering now, just like the beams of the burning houses- rambling endlessly in what was likely an attempt to hide her terrible fear.

The whole world tinted slightly darker as the sun slid behind the clouds; the sky was acrid with smoke, sparks flying through the air and mixing into Opal's hair. Bonfire gone wrong.

Somebody screamed, and Opal jerked around.

In Opal's mind, the world froze. It just stopped. In a split second, everything was suspended in a moment, in one last beat of normalcy before everything changed and normal became a thing of the past.

She would never forget as her heart seized and adrenaline rushed through her, a clear message that she was in danger and she needed to run.

At first, it looked like a whole crowd of people were slowly walking out of the trees. Sure, they were walking a bit strangely, but maybe it was because they were injured.

And then they came closer.

Everybody in the crowd hung at an awkward angle as if they had broken their back but never healed and walked anyway. The arms were extended, and misshapen feet were dragged against the floor. Every creature's body was slashed like someone had run through it with a sword, but the person had never fallen and instead just kept running.

Their eyes were probably the scariest; the white irises were stained a violent shade of red. Red veins stretched across the rolling pupils, and no spark of life or emotion shone in them. The soul was gone. Sucked dry. A sack of bones and marrow.

Opal's body reacted faster than her mind, a primitive survival instinct that suddenly slashed through her. An electric pulse ran through her legs; seizing Amelia's hand, she yanked her sister forward, and suddenly, they were stumbling over the ground, racing away from the crackling fire that was spitting sparks into the air and away from the growing horde of monsters that were pouring out from the forest.

Something was wrong.

Those weren't people.

Other people were screaming and running as they realized what was happening; they abandoned attempts to save their homes and any loved ones or pets left behind, instead bolting away toward the distant horizon, set against blazing fires, toward trees, toward roads, toward other towns. But Opal had a sickening suspicion that no matter how far they ran, it wouldn't matter. They were never going to get away.

Opal was hyperventilating, her mind racing and her heart racing along just as hard.

Her mother.

Her sister.

Opal almost crumpled to the ground, her knees shaking as she tried to suck in air through her rapidly closing lungs.

The blazing houses were in the distance; they were running back towards the bus stop when Amelia suddenly jerked Opal's hand. And abruptly yanked her towards the forest, catching Opal by surprise. Amelia had the strength to haul her over, so the dark canopy of trees covered her head.

"Are you crazy !?" Opal hissed; anger and frustration that was wrongly directed at Amelia began to leak into her voice. "Those- those *creatures* came from here! You want to go into where they came from?! We can't go back into the woods-"

"Opal, I don't know!" Amelia cried. "J-just-" Amelia's voice broke mournfully on the last syllable, her eyes watered as she bit back tears.

Opal's stomach turned uneasily as guilt washed through her. "I'm so sorry," she whispered. "I-I didn't mean that. We're going to find a way out of this, I promise."

Amelia looked upwards through her eyelashes; she rolled her lip in between her teeth; for a second, she looked so young and innocent, but her following words were anything but that. "Don't make promises you can't keep, Opal."

Opal tried to ignore the pang of hurt that attacked her heart as she ducked her head, searching for some sort of response that didn't sound like a sugar-coated lie.

23

Suddenly, a twig snapped, and Opal jerked her head so fast she must have pulled a million muscles in her neck; every nerve on her body jerked to attention, and her breath came in jagged rasps.

Something was rustling in the bushes, coming nearer and nearer.

"Get behind me!" Opal screamed, grabbing Amelia's arm and pushing her behind her back.

What are you doing, Opal? Like you can protect her-

Opal staggered back a few steps as the bushes rustled some more, and the sound of footsteps echoed through the trees. Fear stirred in her stomach like she'd never felt before. She felt like she was in a dream- in that moment, in a nightmare right before she was going to be eaten and killed.

But she couldn't wake up.

Amelia was whimpering now, and Opal didn't know how to help her; she didn't know how to do *anything*. What could they do?

"MOM!" Amelia suddenly tore herself from Opal and flung herself forward as two bedraggled figures emerged from the bushes.

Opal gasped, hands flying to her mouth and fighting back tears as the adrenaline coursing through her body faded in a rush.

Linea looked as though she had been torn through a shredder; her body was unharmed, but she looked thirty years older, her eyes were wild, and her shoulders were as taut as a bowstring.

Gina looked terrified. That was almost scarier than the zombies themselves. Gina was able to turn literally any emotion into anger or annoyance. So, being terrified... that wasn't on the list.

Linea's eyes slid from her youngest daughter, where she had been smoothing Amelia's hair, to Opal's. "We're in trouble, girls. I don't know what's going on, but literally, the entire town is burning, and there are these *creatures* everywhere. All around the world, they suddenly attacked. It started with buildings suddenly just going ablaze, and then they all just started coming from the shadows. Even with all the rumors... I never expected...." Linea's voice shook as she broke off, clearing her voice of the stress before she continued. "Remember that place by the water tower that everybody talked about that would be used for a hurricane? Or a tornado? I think it's time to go there."

Now, standing in this shadowy forest, mist circling their legs and creeping up their bodies, it seemed like the best idea in the world.

But Opal didn't want to leave their safe little bubble. She felt like she was in one of those video games. She was in the safe zone, but then, once she stepped outside, *they* closed in from all angles, and she was dead.

Linea must have seen the hesitation and fear in all of her daughter's expressions because her face hardened, and her gaze zeroed in on each of her daughters in turn.

"Look at me. It's. Not. Safe. Here. We need to go. We have one of the strongest governments in the world, and I know they are instructing people to go to this... safe room for a bit while they sort this business out." Linea's voice was firm. Commanding even. "We're going to run, ok?"

Linea grabbed Gina's hand, extending her other hand to Opal, who grabbed on, and Amelia took Opal's hand.

Linea gave both Gina and Opal's hands a little squeeze. "No matter what, we're going to get through this in one piece."

They walked out of the forest, simple as that. When Amelia and Opal had run in, they had done a large loop around the burning town and headed into the forest that way. But now they were coming out directly into town, closer to where this supposed safe house was, but also closer to where Opal had seen the zombies.

The flames were still roaring angrily; they'd gobbled up all the fuel in sight and were greedily searching the rest of the countryside for more; it wouldn't be long before this entire forest would be up in flames. Nobody was in sight.

And there were no creatures. It was strange and eerie as if the world were hanging on the very edge. Something drastic had just happened, but now it had faded. But it felt so strange. There was no way that it had all just disappeared.

Was the wave over? Could things go back to normal?

What had happened?

Could it *ever* go back to normal?

Opal glanced sideways at Linea. Her mother's posture relaxed the slightest bit as she looked around at the deserted landscape.

Linea let out a small breath. "Alright, girls. Perhaps the worst is already over. I knew the government would take care of this." Linea turned her bright smile on her daughters. "It's a little eerie, I know. But I'm certain those monsters are under control. We just need to find some sort of television broadcast, and we'll find out all about what's happening."

Opal was taken aback. Was it that easy? But she desperately wanted to believe it. Why couldn't it be true? The monsters were gone, and nobody was hurt.

Was it that easy?

Could it be?

Or did something much, much worse happen to everyone else, and Opal's family was only seconds away from reaching the same fate?

"What!!?" Amelia suddenly screeched, wrenching her hand from her mothers. "Are you all that gullible?!"

"Amelia!" Linea snapped. "Control yourself; this is a blessing that those monsters are gone!"

"No, it's a trap. We live in the middle of nowhere in a town that most people don't even know exists. And honestly, I don't care if it exists. This is too coordinated. The burning buildings and then the zombies? Zombies are *afraid* of fire. They don't create it. So the whole world was attacked, right? So, if I were the government, who would I decide to save? London? Beijing? Paris? New York City? Or would I save the small town in the middle of nowhere?" Amelia snapped.

Gina went pale. "Oh my god. We're going to die."

Opal sealed her lips, trying to suck in the gasps that threatened to escape. What was she going to do? The second the word die had slipped from Gina's lips, everything just became a bit more real. *Death* became more real.

Linea's brow furrowed. "It doesn't matter, girls. We just need to get to a safe house."

Linea folded her hand, pressing it against her forehead to keep out the glaring sun that had finally come out from the clouds. "Alright, it's right under the water tower, only a few minutes walk. We're fortunate." Linea pointed to the large metal structure, set in the close distance with a few flames of dying orange surrounding it.

Opal shivered as the sun dipped back below the clouds once more, and the whole earth was thrust into an eerie sort of cold and darkness.

Amelia's eyes suddenly bulged. "RUN!" she screamed, tearing at her family's hands and pulling them along. "The sun!"

"What?!" Linea snapped, grabbing her daughter's arm and holding her fast. "Calm down, Amelia! Nothing is happening-"

Movement caught Opal's eye, and she jumped, ready to run, only to find it was more people coming out from the wrecks of houses and buildings, alerted by the sound of Amelia's desperate screams.

"RUN!" Amelia screamed again, struggling against her mother's grip. There was something wild-looking about Amelia; her eyes widened in horror, and Opal could tell that she was on the verge of tears.

"We need to go," Opal whispered, her gaze trained on her little sister. Amelia had been right before; she would be right again.

"Opal-" Linea turned on her daughter with an exasperated look in her eyes. "Don't you start as well-"

Another shrill shriek suddenly pierced the air, and the whole family jolted, looking around in different directions, but then another scream split the air. And another. And another.

Pouring from the trees, eliciting screams as they went, were the horrible creatures.

Opal's whole body was filled with shivers, her mind momentarily paralyzed as she gaped, open-mouthed, at the scene before her.

It wasn't a dream.

It wasn't a hallucination.

It was *real*.

Opal's legs jerked into action; she didn't even think to look back as she bolted up the hill.

28

Jolts of terror mixed with adrenaline were the only thing keeping her going as she scaled the hill, not daring to look back, her eyes fixed on the distant point of the water tower; that was the only safe point right now.

Trees over her. Dirt beneath her. Air whipping her face

She was running, tearing through the forest; she wanted to scream, to cry.

Tree root below her.

Opal let out a gasp as she tumbled onto the ground, leg caught in the root. Panic quickly set in, numbing her thoughts and delaying her actions as she realized how vulnerable she was.

Someone grabbed Opal's arms.

She screamed just to have Linea clamp her hand over her mouth and yank her up.

"We need to stay together!" she hissed.

Despite it all, a flash of guilt seared through Opal's body. What was she thinking, leaving her family like that?

"Come on!" Opal snapped, struggling to her feet.

Amelia, white-faced with terror, locked hands with Opal. And they were close, so close Opal could see the doors of a bunker underneath the belly of the massive water tower, see people moving around the entrance in a funnel, shoving to get in. Would there even be space?

She risked a glance back, her hair whipping over her eyes in the growing wind. She watched as the sun disappeared behind the thick covering of clouds; any hint of the blue sky was gone on this cloudy day. If Amelia was right and the sun was what kept the zombies away, then they were in trouble.

29

Just like that, the first zombies appeared over the crest of the hill, moving at an unhuman pace; one became two, which became three, which became hundreds. And any human left on the hill...

Opal threw every last bit of strength she had towards her legs and pulled Amelia forward. They couldn't fail now when they were so close! But the unrelenting mass was coming ever so closer-

"Opal!"

The scream chilled Opal's blood as she whirled around. One particularly large zombie, perhaps the body of a jacked-up athlete, had wrapped a grimy hand around Amelia's ankle, pulling her backward.

"No!" Opal screamed, yanking her sister forward by the arms. Tears fell in streams down the side of her face, blinding her.

"Opal!" Amelia was crying too, the cries like little arrows to Opal's heart.

"Hold on!" Opal cried, pulling with all of her strength. Still, Amelia's sweaty hand suddenly slipped through Opal's grip, and Opal was flung backward, falling onto the hard-packed dirt. "No!" Opal scrambled forward, moving on her hands and knees to get back to her sister. Still, she watched instead as the mass of zombies encircled Amelia. She emitted one last desperate cry and then disappeared. Just like that. Gone.

"Amelia." Opal wheezed. How could this be happening?! Not her sister-

The screams around her were the very thing that woke Opal from her trance of grief; a far-buried survival instinct roared to the surface of Opal's body, and she summoned her last ounce of strength to scramble to her feet and run. Run away.

"OPAL! HELP!"

30

Opal turned a heartbeat too late; Gina screamed as the zombies caught up with her; their pale hands reached out and yanked her into their midsts.

No. Not her. Not her to.

"GINA!" The scream tore from Opal's throat, and she made a move to run forward, but the mass of survivors were pushing her towards the bunker in their own desperate haze to escape. Pushing Opal away from her sisters, from where she had failed. She stumbled as the doors of the bunker were upon her; she fell, scraping her hands and face against a cold concrete floor, but didn't feel the sting of the cut.

What did it matter? Her sisters were dead.

Something hit her head, and she was in darkness.

3

"Is she ok?"

"Should we move her?"

"Is she dead?"

"No, look, she's breathing."

"Let me *through*!"

Voices swam through Opal's head; blurry shapes flitted around her vision, but she couldn't make them out.

Opal was lying on something hard; she could feel it digging into her back. For a second, she couldn't remember at all. Why was she here? Why wasn't she at school?

"*Opal!*" someone suddenly screamed.

Opal tried to sit up, but more hands pushed her back. Just as she had managed to prop herself up on her elbows and her eyes were adjusting to the dim lighting that she had found herself in, she felt someone fling their arms around her.

"Mom?" gasped Opal disbelievingly.

"Yes, honey, it's me! I'm so glad you're safe!" cried Linea; she sounded on the verge of tears.

Safe.

And it all came back.

The zombies.

Amelia was right.

She was right about everything.

But she was gone.

They were gone.

32

"Now, where are your sisters?" Linea asked, her relieved tone of voice fading to a brisk, businesslike one; she raised a hand to brush away the tears leaking from her eyes as if Opal wouldn't notice.

Opal's throat seized; it closed up. How could she tell her mother that she watched her siblings be taken right before her eyes? And that she stood and did nothing?

It's not your fault. You had to keep yourself safe. There was nothing you could do. Opal thought firmly. And they weren't gone. They *couldn't* be. If they had just become zombies, couldn't they come back to life if they were somehow cured of the disease?

But even in her hopeful thoughts, the idea seemed far-fetched and impossible.

"Opal? Where are your sisters?" Linea asked more firmly this time, a hint of fear twisting into her tone, color draining from her tear-stained cheeks.

"M-Mom. I-I couldn't do anything, I swear. The zombies were just too fast, and there were too many of them." Opal's voice was splintering; how could she explain?

The light died from Linea's eyes. "No." She whispered, stumbling backward as if she had forgotten how to walk.

"Mom." Opal tried, her voice quivered. How could she explain that she needed her mom to be strong? How selfish was she? After the death of both of her daughters, Opal wanted her mom to be strong for her, to tell her that everything was going to be alright even when it wasn't? Linea had taken their little family through so much. Through the death of her husband, she'd raised them alone. Perhaps this was finally too much for her to bear.

"I- Opal- I can't. Come find me in a bit- you'll be safe here... I just need some time alone." Linea backed up rapidly now, disappearing into the crowd of people that were surrounding them, leaving her one and only living, breathing daughter behind.

Opal could hardly breathe. *No.* Her mother couldn't leave now! She needed her! They needed each other- they were all they had left now, and-

Opal staggered to her feet; someone had laid her down on a pile of empty sacks when she had lost consciousness getting into the bunker. She blinked back tears and the pounding headache in her temples that was making her stomach heave.

She had to find her mother.

The bunker was smaller than she had thought, or perhaps it was just the low ceilings and masses of people packed together within its cement walls, cowering in fear, many nursing injuries, and crying over lost ones. It was a room full of broken people. With a jolt, Opal realized she was one of them; she knew that the empty feeling in her chest had nothing to do with physical injuries.

Opal struggled forward into the mass of people. She knew it would be no use trying to stop the tears, and she wasn't the only one stumbling around, looking lost and crying.

Where was her mother?

How could she just leave?

Opal scanned the room, and all over, she saw people she had grown up with, families slumped on the ground, arms wrapped around each other. She saw her neighbors and classmates. And every person she didn't see was like a jolt to her numb heart. She told herself they could have been out of town when the fire started; maybe they were in

34

another safe house. But she couldn't let the other possibility creep into her mind.

What was *happening?*

Here they were, a hundred or so survivors cramped into a bunker while who knows what raged outside.

She wasn't going to find Linea in this mess. Opal felt her legs buckle underneath her, and she was sinking to the hard stone floor, utterly alone.

And she cried; she cried for Gina, for Amelia, for her mother, and for herself. For the situation she was in with no escape.

A loud siren suddenly burst to life, jolting Opal out of her stupor. Screams split the air, and a few children burst into tears, clapping their hands over their ears.

The siren was awful. It felt like it was cleaving straight to Opal's soul, burning into her mind. But worst of all was what it entailed. And nobody knew.

"Get us out!" a man burst forward, pushing aside people who reached out to pull him backward. His eyes were wide; something unhinged lay in their depths. Madness.

He didn't get far; two men in dark blue jackets seemingly melted out of the shadows from where they had been lurking and pushed him away from the exit, their faces grim and hands raised.

The siren hadn't relented, and it was doing nothing to stop her pounding headache. The people on the floor were beginning to stir and get agitated, some arguing with the men guarding the ladder, which must be the exit.

Suddenly, the fresh night air pierced the bunker as the door was opened, and the men in blue jackets started leading people out. It was organized for a split second until someone pushed someone, and the carefully controlled atmosphere of fear boiled over, and the sounds of screams overpowered the siren.

It was like the entrance all over again; the bigger groups of people managed to hold their own, but Opal felt herself being buffeted from one side to the other, struggling to gain a footing.

"Mom!" she screamed.

Linea's face was suddenly visible through the crowd; her face, still tear-stained, was suddenly alight with desperation as she clawed forward for her daughter. "Opal!" she yelled. "*Stay there.* I'm coming!"

Opal tried not to move; she tried to plant her feet and fight the onslaught, but she was only one teenage girl, and suddenly, her neighbors and peers became the people trampling her underfoot in their own desperation.

All this is going to attract the zombies, and we'll all be dead. Opal thought miserably. She couldn't hold on for much longer; she struggled to the far wall and clung on as people rushed past her. Linea had disappeared. Any second now, Opal was going to be overcome, fall to the ground, and be trampled.

Another sound suddenly split through the din. Two loud bangs.

Gunshots.

Opal wasn't the only one who screamed; she fell to her knees and covered her head. That was the only chance of surviving now. She didn't know who was shooting at who. Maybe the police were shooting at zombies- maybe at people who were fighting a little too hard to get out, but Opal didn't risk it.

She wasn't strong enough.

36

The ground thundered with moving feet, but Opal didn't dare move as more gunshots pierced the air. The siren was the only sound that was constant now, ringing in her ears and making her head spin.

All she could see out of her blurring eyes were flashes of clothes and bodies. She was knocked to the ground by someone who she couldn't see, and panic bloomed across her body. She didn't have enough strength to haul herself to her feet again; she wasn't strong enough.

She cried out as feet slammed down on her fingers- her back- she couldn't move- they were everywhere- any second now, she would be trampled. All she could do was curl up, hands over her head, screaming out for people to notice her-

Opal didn't know how long it went on like that. No one stopped, no one tried to help the scared teenager on the ground. Opal's mother was nowhere to be seen. Gunshots peeled through the air, the siren wailed, and kids and adults alike sobbed and screamed.

And slowly, the sounds faded only a few feet thundered across the bunker floor. Opal raised her head. The bunker was deserted; this time, a whole new feeling of panic came over her, and she forced herself to her feet, ignoring the aches from where countless people had stepped on her.

And she was running, running towards the ladder where the men with guns had been standing moments before but were now gone.

SLAM.

The hatch closed, and the light that had been filtering in was shut out.

A lock clicked.

The siren stopped.

No.
Mom, where are you?

4

"NO!" the scream split the dull air; a bundle of movement, much of which was red, danced before Opal's vision, and she staggered back.

Someone shoved past Opal, and she realized the whirl of red was actually a young girl with a mess of curly red hair and tears streaming from her large, erratic blue eyes. The silent air was split with desperate sobs as she pounded against the metal that was sealed shut.

Opal wasn't alone.

The panic that had started to close around her chest eased the slightest bit; in grave danger, yes. But alone? No.

Opal turned her gaze from the red-headed girl, looking for real, this time around the bunker.

A few people were lying on the ground, picking themselves up as if they, too, had been trampled and left behind. The whole bunker had left in such a hurry; what was going on out there? Why were they ordered to evacuate? And what had happened to her mother?

Linea wasn't in the bunker.

There was only one adult in the bunker, an old woman who was hunched against the wall, her mangled head of silver-white hair slumped against her chest. She might as well have been dead for how much she was moving.

There was another girl, probably a few years younger than Opal, with long, curly black hair, dark brown eyes, and overalls; her skin was so pale in the dim light that it almost seemed like she was glowing faintly.

A boy suddenly moved past Opal without a glance in her direction and rushed to comfort the crying girl by the sealed exit, taking her into his arms. He had dark skin, black hair, and a startling birthmark stretching from his eye to his jawline.

Opal's eyes caught what she had dismissed for a pile of clothes or stone, which was actually a boy. His head on his knees, he didn't look up, but Opal caught a glimpse of his sparklingly dark eyes matched with purple sleep bags under them. The tips of his black hair were dyed a cold silver as if he had dipped it in metallic paint, and his skin was deathly pale, as if he hadn't seen the sun in months. He also hadn't moved.

There was one more girl; even in tattered clothes, she was quite pretty with long, wavy blonde hair that framed her petite oval face, bright blue eyes, and heart-shaped pursed lips. She carried herself with an air that she knew what effect her looks could have and took pleasure in them.

She was holding hands with another boy who could have been her twin with sandy blonde hair, a strong build, and kind blue eyes; by Opal's standards, he was pretty cute.

"What are we going to do?" the red-headed girl asked quietly, her eyes dripping with tears.

"We're going to get out of this." the boy with his arms around the girl murmured. "I promise."

"I don't know, Nolan." the teary girl sighed.

"We're here too, you know." the pretty girl snapped. "You're not the only ones trapped."

Nolan scowled. "Hi," he muttered sarcastically. "Name's Nolan."

40

"I'm Miranda." the red-headed- girl sniffed.

"I'm Sasha." The girl said with curly black hair. "And that's Casper." she pointed to the boy slumped on the ground.

"I'm Cora." Cora flipped her shiny sheet of blonde hair across her shoulder, fixing Opal with a sharp glare.

"My name's Tyler; nice to meet you." The cute boy smiled sweetly at all of them. His blue eyes caught Opal's for a moment, and despite herself, she felt a flash of a blush cross over her cheeks.

"It's nice to meet you too; I'm Opal," Opal whispered a little breathlessly.

A crash made Opal jump; the old woman with the angry face, who had been slumped against the wall, had knocked over one of the buckets lining the bunker walls; a strange liquid was dripping from it.

"Ignore her. She's my mom. Irene." Cora sighed, flipping her hair again. "She does just as much as a rock. But she's still family. Speaking of which, why aren't *you* guys with your families? Left behind? Or dead?"

The blunt words pierced Opal like an arrow, and a swell of dislike rushed over her, followed by near-crushing sorrow. First her father, and now this? That one little hope Opal had harbored that perhaps her sister could be cured felt far and distant now. All she had was a mother who abandoned her.

"Miranda and I-" Nolan broke off and glanced at Miranda, but she shook her head fiercely, more tears welling in her large eyes. "We ran as hard as we could, but both our parents and siblings didn't make it."

"Tyler and I have been family friends for years, well, his family. He has a brother and parents. I just have my mom, Irene. Irene was no

41

help when we were getting trampled trying to get out." Cora's face twisted in a scowl. "She never is any help. Tyler's family-"

"I can explain for myself, thanks." Tyler cut Cora off, his voice cool. Opal felt a flash of admiration for his easy assertiveness. "My family didn't even make it out of the car. We were blown off the roads by the fire."

"My sister and father got out in the crowd, I saw her calling me, but I was swept back," Sasha explained quietly, her voice dark.

A few people glanced half heartedly at the unmoving form of Casper, but he didn't offer an explanation of where he was from.

"Well, *I* know Casper." Sasha's voice suddenly dropped with disdain. "He just appeared in my town one day. I think he was let out of prison or something. He's violent and unpredictable, and he didn't even try to get out of here. Just sat there while we were being trampled. He's a danger, really."

"You don't know anything about me."

Casper spoke, his head still in his hands, his voice quiet and raspy. His words edged with a crisp British accent.

An odd silence took over the bunker; it felt like it was eating away at Opal.

"And yours?" Miranda asked, nodding at Opal.

Opal's throat caught. How could she explain? She didn't want to. How was everyone just *okay?* Casually stating that their families were dead? It wasn't as simple as all the others. *It wasn't.* Her mother hadn't left her because she had died. It was because she was *broken.* And she lost her sisters. She'd failed.

42

Her voice was cracking when she finally spoke. "I'm Opal. My family and I ran, but my two sisters were taken, and I lost my mom in the bunker."

Opal looked up from the ground, and when her eyes caught Cora's, a blistering pain shot through her skull like nothing she had ever felt before. A cry split from her lips, and she stumbled backward, hands pressed up against her skull in a desperate plea to make the pain stop.

And then she was falling, far, far away. Her vision blurred, and shapes swam before her eyes until everything suddenly went dark.

"Please! NO! PLEASE!" a girl suddenly screamed out of the blackness.

The voice felt like electricity through Opal's veins. She knew that voice. The knowledge came with a rush of hope, but then more shapes took form from the darkness, and the hope quickly melted to despair.

Amelia was strapped to a metal bed attached to a large metal crane that disappeared into the darkness. The bed was hovering over a large pit on the floor. As far as Opal could see, there were no windows or doors in this cell-like room Amelia was imprisoned in.

Dark cords stretched across her skin, so tight they looked painful. She shrieked again. Opal wanted to scream; she tried to run forward and demand what was going on, to stop this horror. But she couldn't move, she couldn't speak. She was paralyzed, a helpless bystander.

"I'll ask you again. Where. Is. The. Sightseerer?" hissed a voice, echoing across the metal chamber. Seemingly to melt from the corner shadows, a woman stalked forward, edging around the dark pit, her cruel gaze fixed on Amelia. She wore a long black cloak that brushed the floor, raised just enough to reveal strappy-heeled black boots. A dark mask

covered her face, sparing slits for her mouth, nose and eyes. A dark wave of black hair rippled out from behind it.

Amelia started to whimper, her eyes widening at the sight of the woman in black.

Amelia! *Opal cried, but of course, no sound left her mouth.*

The woman suddenly plunged a gloved hand into her pocket and withdrew a match; it sparkled to life with seemingly no fuel, but Opal didn't dwell on that. Instead, she watched, transfixed, as the woman threw the lit match into the pit, illuminating the walls.

Opal's stomach heaved. Hundreds of bodies were crammed into the narrow space, but not any bodies. These bodies were alive; these corpses were alive. They twitched and flailed, desperate to claw out of their prison. Bloodthirsty zombies. The match flickered and died, but it almost made it worse not to be able to see them.

The woman could drop her. She could drop Opal's little sister into them. The zombies would rip Amelia apart.

"I'll ask you again: Where. Is. The. Sightseer?!" *repeated the woman, her voice laced with a deadly impatience.*

"I don't know!" *sobbed Amelia, her head bobbed forward; she looked exhausted as if she had been suspended in that horrid state for hours.*

The woman flicked her wrist. Several cords that had been holding Amelia snapped until she was dangerously close to slipping from the bed. Amelia let out a cry of fear, scrambling in her bonds to try and get a better grip.

"My patience is thinning. I hope you answer my questions soon. For your own sake." *the woman swore darkly; she turned on her heel and left, leaving Amelia alone in the dark room, hanging on for dear life.*

Amelia. You're alive. *Opal's mind whispered as the scene began to dissolve.*

For now. *A darker part of her mind whispered.*

5

Opal gasped, the fear carrying through from her dream to reality.

What the hell?

The strangers in the bunker were staring at her with mild curiosity, and she tried to act normal even though her heart was pounding.

But how was it just a dream? Why would she collapse if it was just a dream?

Slowly, Opal's heart rate slowed, but her mind didn't.

Amelia. Are you alive? It was too much to hope for. If her little sister was alive, then maybe Gina was too. Alive and, if her dream was correct, in grave danger.

She needed help.

She needed to help *them.*

"You have to help me." Opal gasped as she pushed herself to her feet, facing the people crowded around her, faces creased with concern.

"We have to help each other," Nolan added firmly. "Of course we do. Most of our families are dead. We don't know what to do. We need to work together and *stop* this."

Cora suddenly scoffed. "*Stop* this? Are you crazy? This isn't up to us! It's up to the government, the people who have power. We are *stuck* here." And there's nothing we can do. Nobody will ever listen to us."

"Well, I'm not going to die here," Sasha said in a quiet but firm voice.

"I need to find my sisters," Opal murmured.

46

"I need to find my family." Sasha nodded along.

Opal's gaze caught on Sasha's. "They're not dead," Opal said. A silent sentiment passed between them, a silent bond of hope. "They're not." Sasha agreed quietly.

Cora, Tyler, Nolan, and Miranda exchanged looks.

"We have nothing," Tyler said mournfully.

"No," Nolan said fiercely. "We have our lives."

Opal sunk to the ground, her heart beating fiercely, the adrenaline from her dream still attacking her system. "Is this air-tight?" Opal asked offhandedly.

Cora shrugged. "If it is, then I'd rather run out of oxygen and die here than outside where those creatures could get me."

There was an awkward pause, nobody really knowing what to say after that.

Finally, Sasha rushed to fill the silence. "Tell me more about your family." Sasha sank to the ground next to Opal, nodding in Miranda's direction.

A ghost of a smile flitted across Miranda's face, replacing her tears. "They were amazing. My little sister was so annoying."

"Well, she's dead, so what's the point?" Casper's drawling voice suddenly cut across Miranda's face, and she bristled fiercely, her eyes flaring.

"How dare y-" she began, her eyes blazing.

"What did she do?" Sasha asked quickly.

And they faded into a quick and calm conversation, all of them. It was a brief distraction from the horrors that were unfolding in the real world. Opal caught Sasha's eye again, and she knew the same thought was going through their minds. The longer they delayed, the further their families were traveling, if they were even still alive.

"I can't wait to get out of h-" Cora began but was suddenly cut off.

"CORA!" It was so sharp and harsh that the scream that came from the hunched-over shape of Cora's mother, Irene, shocked Opal. But as the shout filled the stagnant air, the same pain that had come over Opal only minutes before attacked her again, like a hammer to her head.

Horror filled her like a quick, hot lead. No. What was happening?

She wanted to see Amelia; she wanted to know how to find her- If this was real. If she could even imagine it to be real... *she wanted to know more.* But she couldn't take the nightmare; it was too horrifying. And she couldn't collapse again. What would everyone else think?

But even as she fought to stay present, to stay in the scene in front of her, she felt her consciousness fading even more until she was drifting away into blackness.

"CORA!"

"Mother! Please!" It was the sound of pure terror that escaped a young girl. She loomed out of the darkness, cowering against a filthy floor, with short, tangled blonde hair and blue eyes that were alight with fear as a woman loomed over her.

With a jolt, Opal realized she was staring at a younger version of Cora, except without the easy confidence and witty remarks.

The woman looming over young Cora didn't seem imposing to Opal; she was stout, wearing a filthy gray dress, and she was swaying uneasily on her feet as if she might collapse at any moment. But it was

48

her eccentric blue eyes, much like Cora's, that made Opal pause in her judgment. Those eyes, so filled with rage, were unlike anything Opal had ever seen. And it scared her.

This old woman pulled back her hand and slapped the younger Cora across the face; from the dirty red marks on Cora's cheeks, it wasn't the first time this had happened. Opal's heart twisted; why was she seeing this? She knew in an instant that this woman must be Irene, that somehow this dream had been triggered by Irene's shout. And.... Well, this was how Cora grew up.

"I TOLD YOU TO MOP THE FLOOR!" the woman screamed, words slurring into each other with every syllable.

Cora sank further into the floor, hands coming up to cover her head.

The woman dropped the mob on younger Cora's lap and hobbled away. Cora slowly raised her head, and in those same blue eyes, Opal watched fear melt into humiliation, then anger, and finally to hate. Pure, undeniable hate.

Cora hated her mother. And rightfully so.

Opal blinked, her mind pulled from the darkness as quickly as it had come. She hadn't collapsed this time; it seemed like she had only been out for a moment. She glanced sideways at Tyler. Did he notice she'd just blinked out? But then her gaze slid towards Cora, whose hand was still grasped tightly around Tyler's; the sight made Opal's stomach clench, and she didn't know why. It didn't make sense. Cora had no idea what Opal had seen. Even with the mixed first impressions that Opal had formed around Cora, she couldn't help but feel a large swell of pity, swiftly followed by an even stronger swell of admiration. Cora wasn't just a pretty face; she was able to pull off this calm façade

49

and strong exterior. But then- how much did this façade hide? How much was Cora broken inside?

Opal's train of thought was cut off by a much more pressing idea- *she was assuming these dreams were real. What was happening?*

Irene suddenly moved, with an angry swipe of her hand, knocking over a whole rack of bins; the contents tumbled out.

Opal glanced at Cora, and she wasn't the only one.

"Um, Mother, you know we need those supplies," mumbled Cora. Her words were strong, but Opal could sense the tremor beneath them, and she wasn't surprised after seeing that dream.

The old woman, Irene, suddenly froze, her head whipping around as she glared at her daughter. "Don't tell me what to do, or I swear you'll regret it." Her words were icy, and though spoken quietly, Opal could hear the danger in them.

Cora didn't respond, some of the color leaching from her face as she exchanged a glance with Tyler.

"Er- Ms. Irene..." Sasha started to protest.

Irene let out a harsh bark of a laugh. "Ms, am I?" Suddenly, she grabbed one of the glass water containers and hurled it at Sasha.

Sasha let out a scream as it smashed by her feet, a flood of water coming over her shoes.

Nolan jumped forward, bundling Sasha away before Irene could so much as glance in her way.

Irene lunged forward, her fingers grasping Cora's ear as she shook her fiercely, dragging her forward.

"See?! SEE! Your friends don't care about you! Like they never have!!! HE HATES YOU!!!!" she bellowed in Cora's ear as Cora covered her ears to block out her mother's horrible screaming and tried to twist away.

Opal was dumbfounded; she'd only met these people, she'd only just met Cora... but the pity that swelled inside of her was as if they had known each other their whole lives. How did she survive living like this? Did Irene care?

Opal hoped one of the teenagers would step forward, but they were too scared, and so was Opal; there was no way she was going to step into the way of an angry woman.

I'm sorry.

I wish I was different.

Opal didn't realize she was shying away until she almost backed into Tyler, who was watching Irene speak in a hushed voice to Cora. Cora responded every few sentences by nodding miserably and giving a mumbled response back.

Opal's heart jumped to her throat as she found herself next to Tyler, their arms brushing, and then beat those feelings down instantly because this was *not* the time.

"I don't know what to do," Tyler muttered, blinking quickly as if only then realizing that Opal was so close.

"We-we've been friends forever, but I've never seen Irene so angry before. I guess- everything going on finally got to her?" Tyler continued.

"I-I well- I g-guess." Opal's words were jumbled, twisted. She kept getting distracted by Tyler's sparkling blue eyes.

Great. Now, she sounded like an idiot.

Opal twisted away; she couldn't look at him anymore, or she would turn redder than she already was.

51

And she looked around, Miranda crouching over Sasha, Casper slumped against the wall, but his eyes watching Irene and Cora's hushed conversation. Nolan watching Miranda, and Tyler watching Irene. They just met each other, all of them did. But how could Opal leave them? She didn't want to go alone.

She didn't want to *be* alone.

Would they come with her?

Nolan, Miranda, Cora, and Tyler had nowhere to go.

Her heart jumped at the thought of traveling with Tyler but sank just as quickly when she realized that a journey with Tyler meant a journey with Cora.

What am I thinking? When have I been this cruel? I can't just judge Cora on first impressions- and who am I to judge her while her mother abuses her like that?

Irene suddenly released her daughter from her grip by the ear and dropped her to the ground, not gently in any way.

What had they talked about? What had they whispered in hushed voices?

Irene abruptly kicked her daughter in the back, causing her to stumble on all fours as she tried to twist away from her mother.

Tyler's hands twitched forward. "Irene!" Tyler started, his tone was tinged with anger.

Irene turned to him, her eyes flashing. "Come here, boy!" she bellowed, her hand twisted in a half-claw sort of shape.

Tyler held up his chin as he stalked over to Irene, his eyes narrowed before flicking to Cora, who was watching him with a mixture of fright and admiration.

For a moment, neither Irene nor Tyler moved in a silent standoff. But in the blink of an eye, Irene surged forward and struck Tyler across the face. "Don't you *dare* tell ME how to be a parent!"

Opal almost screamed, and Sasha did. Tyler let out a cry of shock and pain, doubling backward and cradling his injured cheek.

After a brief, tense moment, Tyler straightened up, his eyes burning with a fierce defiance that Opal so rarely saw. He started forward as if to hit back, but he glanced at Cora for the briefest second and deflated.

He did that for her. He's brave. He did it to protect her. A flash of admiration ran through Opal's body, and the butterflies started flying again, even if it was at the most impromptu moment.

Irene did the same, stumbling backward until she hit the wall of the bunker and sank down, sprawled against the floor.

Irene had ducked her head against her chest, hunching over a mirror of Casper as grizzly snores began to emit from her mouth.

Tyler straightened up, eyes passing scornfully over Irene before landing on Cora and opening his arms.

Cora practically flew into them; Opal could hear her muffled sobs as she whispered words Opal could barely make out. "I'm so sorry," Cora whispered, and though Opal tried, she couldn't make out what Tyler responded.

Opal stood awkwardly for a second, emotions prickling across her skin. Something just didn't sit right with her as she watched Cora and Tyler embrace. It wasn't... jealousy? No- that was too cruel. Opal couldn't be jealous! The mere suggestion of that was fatally unfair.

Opal pushed the thought away, and it wasn't hard. Exhaustion threatened to overwhelm her limbs and body; after the day's events, her head was spinning, and she wanted nothing more than to collapse and forget about the world.

Opal wished that she was at home, in bed, with the sound of Amelia's radio from across the hall. She wished that she had been smart enough to at least bring her school bag and not have left it stranded on the sidewalk after she ran into the crazed woman. She desperately wanted anything that was her own, not just the clothes off her back that were falling apart. Some sort of comfort.

Amelia.

I hope you're alive.

"What are we going to do about Irene?" Nolan whispered, his gaze flicking to Irene's slumbering shape. "If we get out... Can we bring her with us?"

Cora, who placed herself between Tyler and Opal, bristled angrily.

"When did everyone here become a we?!" she snapped angrily.

Nolan, taken aback, was at a loss for words.

Thankfully, Sasha jumped in. "We became we when all of us were stranded here together. We became a we when everybody left us. We need to stick together."

A murmur of ascent rose through the bedraggled group.

Cora's face darkened. "That's a bunch of junk right there. I don't care about anybody here but Tyler. The only reason you're saying that is because you have nobody."

Sasha gaped at her, open-mouthed.

"Hey. That's not true." Tyler protested. "Sasha's just trying to be kind."
Sasha smiled gratefully at him. Cora narrowed her eyes and flipped her sheet of shiny hair over her shoulder but didn't respond.

"Right. So...?" Miranda asked slowly, tentatively trying to bring back the conversation.

"I think it's obvious, don't you?" Cora asked, her voice dripping with contempt.

Even after the events of today, Opal couldn't squash the flash of dislike aimed toward Cora that surged through her.

"What is?" Miranda sighed, clearly as frustrated as Opal.

"We're not getting out of here until someone comes and gets us, so really, it's not up to us," Cora responded in the same superior tone.

"Us." Sasha suddenly breathed beside Opal. "She used the word us!"

Opal suppressed a giggle, and Sasha winked at her.

Opal looked up, and her gaze caught on Tyler's; he gave her a half-hearted smile before glancing away and leaving Opal's heart thundering.

"Well, I don't care what we do later. All I want to do is sleep." Nolan said loudly.

There were a few muted mumbles of agreement, and the inhabitants of the bunker began to spread out, everyone keeping a wide berth around both Irene and Casper as if they were a dangerous disease.

Nolan and Miranda moved away, talking in low tones, to the other side of the bunker.

Tyler hovered for a moment until awkwardness overwhelmed them, and he moved away with Cora. Something ached in Opal's chest when she watched them go. Something deep and lonely.

"Erm. Hey, Opal." Sasha said quietly. Opal jumped; she had been so absorbed with Tyler and Cora that she forgot about the gentle girl beside her. "Should we stay together?" Sasha asked.

"Yeah, that'd be great," Opal responded gratefully. Sleeping in the bunker was undoubtedly uncomfortable; the mob of people who had left seemed to have taken almost everything with them. A few bottles of water and dried packs of food remained, but it wouldn't hold off the group for long. The thought was added to Opal's pile of growing fears.

Nonetheless, she was grateful for Sasha as they curled up together by the wall. Opal didn't think she would ever be able to sleep, not with the horrors of the day's events painted into the back of her eyelids.

But her body was truly exhausted, and in a moment, she found herself slipping into the unknowing bliss of sleep.

Gina was strapped to a dark, cold bed, her eyes closed and her chest rising and falling; dark straps held her hands and legs down, but she didn't thrash; she didn't move.

Opal's eyes flared wide in horror; why wasn't her sister fighting back? Why wasn't she struggling?

There was somebody else lying in the bed next to Gina, somebody just as still and just as quiet.

Opal went closer, her heart pounding.

It was Linea.

And her eyes were open, staring into the distance, glassy in death.

Because she was dead, cold, and still like a statue.

Opal screamed, terrified as she staggered back, ramming into the cold table that held her sister. And suddenly, she saw them all. All of them. Rows and rows of cold tables in a field that seemed endless.

Amelia.

Sasha.

Miranda.

Nolan.

A boy with a gaping mouth staring right at her.

A girl with an eye missing.

57

Cora.

Tyler.

What was this?

Opal surged up, her heart pounding fiercely, her hands shaking just as hard. Where was she? Her eyes re-adjusted to the dim lighting of the bunker.

The dusty bunker was beginning to smell even worse with the reek of stale air and unwashed clothes; she missed sunlight. She missed the daytime. Severe claustrophobia mixed in with the tendrils of the dream she couldn't shake jolted her to her feet. It didn't help when she pushed herself to her feet and saw Cora and Tyler's hands entwined, even in sleep.

A flash of loneliness made tears prick in Opal's eyes.

"Opal?" A quiet voice echoed out, and Opal jumped, hastily wiping her eyes.

Tyler, rubbing his eyes, got up and walked over, glancing quickly back at Cora to make sure she was still fast asleep.

Cora looked so beautiful in sleep, her limbs spread eagle, so much more peaceful than awake. Opal couldn't stop a pang of undeserved jealousy.

"You alright?" he asked, his brow wrinkled in concern.

Opal's eyes prickled. She couldn't start crying, not now, and *definitely* not in front of Tyler.

"I-I'm fine." Opal began; she turned away, desperately trying to keep her eyes from streaming. She didn't want Tyler to see her this way. For *anyone* to see her this way.

"Bad dreams?" Tyler asked sympathetically, his eyes kind.

That's when Opal lost it; choking sobs wracked her shoulders as tears streamed down her cheeks. "I'm sorry." she gasped. "My family, I saw them all. They were all dead, I don't know."

The cold, helpless feeling that had washed over Opal disappeared as Tyler wrapped his arms around her, pulling her close to him.

Opal jumped and resisted the urge to push him away. She barely knew him. This felt... odd.

Odd and nice. A hug was more than Opal's mother had given her before she stumbled away.

"It's alright," he muttered. "It's not fair we were left behind like we were. And now all we can do is keep going. They're just dreams. We're in the real world now. And we're safe."

"That's not true, and you know it. Of course, we're not safe." Opal blurted out, words muffled by her sobbing.

Tyler glanced at her, taken aback. "Well. Yes. But is it strange to say that we're much safer here, in this bunker, than whatever hellscape appeared in your dreams?"

"Fair." Opal stopped, considering. "I guess you're right."

The conversation lapsed for a moment; it didn't take long to become awkward. Tyler cleared his throat as he realized they still had their arms wrapped around each other, and he pulled away.

"So you have sisters?" Tyler asked, clearly in an effort to stoke up conversation.

"Yeah. I have two, older and younger. Uh- my dad died when I was younger, so it's just been us and my mom. The news reports and everything were always hard on my little sister, but she paid so much attention I think she knew what was going on." Opal heaved a sigh,

59

what she wouldn't give with even a few more seconds with them. "How about you?"

"I have- had-" Tyler stumbled, and his face crumpled, but he managed to regain his composure. "I had a little brother, and my parents were amazing. But it was really Cora I grew up with. It was almost unfair, I had this great family, and she was stuck with no one but Irene." Tyler glanced over at his friend's sleeping form. "I know she comes off a little prickly when you first meet her. But she's been through a lot, and if there is anyone I'm happy to be stuck here with, it's her."

Opal had to bite back a sharp retort. *A little?* Opal felt a sharp pinch of jealousy like her insides were too squirmy.

"So you grew up in Duxbury?" Opal asked after a beat.

"I'm from New Jersey but moved here a while back; it's great. Beautiful, huh? Have you ever been down to The Cape?"

Opal smiled; the light conversation felt better than anything in the last twenty-four hours. "Yeah, I went down with my family a couple years ago. The sunsets are amazing."

Tyler's eyes lit up. "My favorite part! I like sunrises too, but at that time of day, I'm too exhausted to enjoy it."

Opal couldn't help but laugh. "How late do you get up? They're at like 6am."

"Yeah. That's *early*." Tyler rolled his eyes with a smirk. "Anyway-"

"Tyler?"

Opal's head jerked back to where Cora was stretching, her arms moving frantically when she couldn't find Tyler next to her.

Ugh. Look at her; she can't go a minute without him. Opal couldn't help the thought full of bitterness and resentment from slipping through. *Stop thinking like that, Opal. How can you be so cruel?*

Cora's eyes narrowed ever so slightly as she took in Tyler and Opal's paused conversation.

"Hey, do you want to wake everyone else up? It can't have been that long, but I think we should get some food and try to get the day started." Tyler glanced awkwardly from Cora to Opal.

Cora wasn't going to give a response, so Opal nodded, if only a little stiffly.

"I'm starving," muttered Miranda as soon as she woke. Opal's own stomach was in knots; it felt like it was being torn up. She hadn't eaten since breakfast that morning.

Tyler cracked open one barrel filled with bottled jugs of water; passing them out, Opal felt her stomach jump as he turned to smile at her.

"I wonder how much oxygen there is in this place," Miranda grumbled, looking around at the ceiling. "It smells so much worse than before. It's stuffier too, like if you put your head under a blanket for too long."

The thought left a blanket of uneasiness around the group, one that nobody wanted to explore further.

"I'm sure it's fine," Sasha commented somewhat uneasily.

Tyler cracked open one barrel filled with bottled jugs of water; passing them out, Opal felt her stomach jump as he turned to smile at her. He cracked open the next one, which contained blankets, clothes, and fabric.

"Wish we'd seen these earlier," Tyler muttered.

The next two were full of packets. Packets of freeze-dried food, chicken, ice cream sandwiches, potatoes, everything you could possibly imagine.

"Lovely. Astronaut food." Casper muttered from behind, making them all jump.

"Wow. The walking dead boy actually wants to eat." Cora sneered, cocking her head mockingly.

"Wow. I'm surprised the princess is five feet away from her prince." Casper snapped back, cocking his head right back.

Opal looked away as Cora reached to kiss Tyler on the cheek, ignoring the twisty feeling she had in her stomach.

The food was disgusting, tasting of nothing but a vague scent of pickles, but Opal could feel it moving through her body, lifting some of the haze that had settled.

Opal walked away to change, moving to a more enclosed part of the bunker. Her heart was still pounding, her mind spinning with what to do next with Cora, Tyler, and her family. But it was a new sense of peace, being alone for only a bit. Her heart ached as she threw down her dirty clothes, the one and only thing she brought from home, and put on the basic change of clothes found in the barrel. The fabric was starchy and rubbed against her skin, making her itch immediately, but at least it was clean.

But when she came back, the little bit of peace evaporated in a second.

Irene had Cora backed against the wall, her limbs spread eagle. She raised a hand, and like Tyler, she struck Cora across the face.

Miranda, Sasha, and Tyler stared open-mouthed at Irene, shocked into silence.

"This has to stop," Miranda whispered. "What is this?"

Tyler took a hesitant step forward but didn't go any farther, perhaps the memory of last night flashing in his mind.

"*You useless excuse for a daughter!*" snarled Irene.

"Mother, *Stop*!!!!" howled Cora.

Irene didn't listen.

"Toughen up!!!!" she screeched, her face in a sneer, half laughing. "This is your payback."

"Irene!" protested Tyler, somewhat weakly. Opal had never seen or heard him so helpless.

"What is she talking about?" Opal whispered to him. "Payback?"

Tyler glanced backward at Opal, a little surprised to see her, but it quickly faded from his face as he swept a hand through his hair. "Irene blames Cora for how her father left."

"What?" Opal gaped. "That's terrible. Who was her father?"

Tyler shrugged. "Dunno. I don't remember him; he left when I was young, but that's what tipped Irene off the edge."

Irene ignored Tyler's protest. She hauled her daughter away from the wall and shoved her against the floor. "This is your fault! This whole thing- trying to get me to leave the house. *Ridiculous.* I wish the fire had burned you."

Everyone was silent for a second, the words ringing in the air. Cora let out a muffled sob from the ground, and Opal's heart ached with pity.

A vein pulsed in Irene's eye as she stayed still for a moment before she suddenly snapped and pulled back her leg as if to kick her daughter.

63

To Opal's surprise, Casper was the first one to jump up and move in front of Cora. Straightened to his full height, he towered over Irene. "Stop it," he said, his voice was low and dangerous.

Tyler quickly joined him, followed by Miranda and then Nolan. Opal moved quickly, followed by Sasha. "You're unstable, we all get that, but Cora is my friend. *Our* friend and I'm not standing for this anymore. I'm not afraid of you, Irene. None of us are. Stop this, or we'll fight you."

Irene suddenly cackled. "Fight me? We're good as dead already. If this place is air-tight, we only have a little more oxygen; it's been so long already. I might as well execute my revenge before I'm dead."

Opal hearts seized. She didn't want to believe it, but it made so much sense. *So much sense.* Is this why her head was pounding and she felt so lightheaded? Why the musty air seemed to hang around them like a real tangible thing?

"G-guys?" Sasha gasped.

Opal turned quickly to see the quiet girl's body swaying.

"I-is this why I feel so weird?" Sasha suddenly doubled over, coughing. "I-I feel weird," she muttered again, and suddenly, her knees buckled, and she fell to the ground.

Opal might've screamed. Miranda did.

"Shallow breaths!" Nolan suddenly cried. "It's alright."

Tyler pushed forward, knocking back Irene, who was cackling, nearly falling over with the laughter bursting from her body. Delusional laughter.

Tyler reached down, hauling Cora to her feet and pulling her into a protective cage of his arms. "Shallow breaths," he muttered.

"Get to the door!" Nolan cried. "Find something to hit it with; it doesn't matter what, we can't wait for anything."

Miranda crouched over Sasha, feeling her pulse as she tried to shake her awake.

Claustrophobia was setting in hard and cold now as Tyler led Cora to the door, with Nolan joining in, banging and banging with anything they could find: barrels, hands, and lanterns.

Nothing was happening.

It was happening so fast now, Opal didn't know how she hadn't seen it before, how her head was throbbing, and she hardly understood a thought coming across her mind.

And the world was fading beneath her eyes as she started to crumble, her knees buckling; she stumbled away, her heart thundering. She couldn't take it anymore, and she collapsed, her hand hitting something cold, metal, and red.

Her eyes closed, her chest heaving for air that never came.

She needed to get up. She needed to- breathe-

But her legs were so weak her body felt like it was shaking.

How did this happen so fast?

But she had to get up; Opal pushed herself forward, grabbing on that metal thing to pull herself up.

Opal collapsed again, her body shaking.

I can't die.

No.

Terror was all she could do to keep her eyes open just to see Tyler, sweet, kind Tyler, run towards her, falling down on one knee in front of her.

65

Suddenly, she felt her hands pressed against his; the feel of his skin against hers would have been such a happy feeling for her at any other time.

"Opal. Opal."

Why did his voice seem so far away?

And yet, it was getting easier to breathe. Suddenly, the air started to lose its dank heaviness, and little by little, fresher air began to rush in.

"It's alright, you opened it. An emergency lock." he was whispering words that hardly had any meaning to her, but slowly, she felt herself coming back.

Oxygen, sweet, clean oxygen filled her lungs.

She was alive.

But she was too tired to do anything, and with Tyler's arms still around her, she drifted off into sleep.

7

Actual sunlight! Streaming into the bunker, which had smelled so bad a few minutes ago, which was now bringing the scent of grass and flowers.

"Opal." someone whispered. "I swore you were dead."

"I thought I was, too," Opal muttered, and a smile curved over her lips as she realized who it was.

"See, it's not so bad." Tyler laughed.

But it was.

It was so much worse.

The blackness pressed around on the edges of her vision- pain flashing through her body- the claustrophobia threatening to swallow and squash her.

She felt as if she had been drifting towards the edge —and if she toppled over, she would fall and fall. She would never find herself again. She would be lost in the blackness.

But she couldn't tell Tyler that.

"Thanks." Opal sighed.

Opal pushed herself to her feet, helped by Tyler. She brushed her hair out of her eyes and looked around; the sunlight streaming through the open bunker door was amazing. It was startling how bright it was and how much she had missed the clean, fresh air, in stark contrast to the dank air she had grown accustomed to.

The metal object she had fallen against was apparently an emergency lever they had never seen before, hidden behind one of the barrels. They had a lot less oxygen than what they had assumed; it had been a few minutes later, and perhaps they all would have passed out and then died.

Irene had passed out cackling, the same cackling that had turned into choking and caused her to double over, wheezing until she crumpled to the ground. Sasha was still out.

Opal's body ached, but she couldn't stay in this place any longer, not when she saw Linea in every corner. Amelia in every shadow.

Her fingers slipped against the rusted rungs of the ladder as she pulled herself up, one rung at a time, into brilliant sunlight.

After hours in darkness, the brilliance shocked her, and the clean, sweet air flooded through her lungs; it wasn't for a few minutes that she opened her eyes, for it had been too bright for her to see anything.

Was it really just this morning she'd walked to school with Amelia?

Or that she ran through the woods?

And now, with the greenage of Duxbury below her, the craggy snowy peaks of the New Hampshire mountains all around her, the stone water tower above her, the distant valleys and ominous peaks behind her, it was beautiful. Beautiful but deadly. This was the view that Opal had been staring at her whole life, the view she thought would always be comforting now with the memories of the zombies lurking in her mind... every shadow seemed to conceal a deadly threat.

Again, Opal wished she had brought *something* with her to remind her of her home and where she was trying to get to. But there was nothing. If she turned around and didn't look back, closing the doors on the memories inside of her head, then she would have no proof of her past life. If she left Duxbury, this view...

"It's beautiful," Nolan muttered, tightening the straps of his backpack. "I can almost forget-" he trailed off.

"Yet you can't forget." Miranda sighed, coming up on his shoulder.

"The sun is going to set soon. We only slept for a couple hours." Tyler muttered. "What are we going to do?"

"I'm staying in the bunker," Cora muttered stubbornly.

"They can only travel in the shadows," Nolan whispered. "We shouldn't be out at night."

Opal rubbed her hands over her arms, trying to ignore the goosebumps popping up all around her skin.

They.

Nobody needed to clarify what they *were*.

Outside, in the sunshine that was waning, it was suddenly so much more prudent.

"The government will take care of us," Sasha whispered, her eyes still hollow from fainting. Her whole body was shivering weakly.

Good grief, I hope I don't look like that. Opal thought quietly, glancing at Tyler, but he didn't notice Cora had her arms wrapped around his waist, pulling him close to her.

Opal had to resist the urge to go over there and pry them apart.

Suddenly, he turned his gaze to meet hers; butterflies erupted in Opal's stomach as he shrugged at her in a half grimace, looking awkward.

"No, they won't. Not if this is happening all over the world."
Miranda replied to Sasha quite bitterly. "Who cares about a small town
in the middle of the US?"

"We do," Cora muttered.

"Yeah, but nobody cares about us." Nolan snapped.

Cora opened her mouth again, her eyes darkening.

"Guys! Stop fighting." Tyler said quickly. "It's only going to
make things worse."

"Guys," Sasha whispered.

"What's that noise?" Nolan asked suddenly, cocking his head
to one side as he glanced at Sasha.

The sun. It was waning, slowly disappearing bit by bit behind
the mountains as the day wound away. Slowly, the sky darkened, and a
mix of colors swarmed across the sky. Violets, pinks, reds. Twilight had
come.

And soon-

The night.

Opal was sure that not all of them would survive.

And now she could hear it, the rumbling coming from behind
them, coming straight for them.

The sunlight was gone.

Cora was the first to react. She screamed loudly, pulling herself
from Tyler. "Get to the bunker!" she screamed, darting forward to the
ladder, which was a distance away.

But Opal already knew it was too late. They had been too
drunk in the sunlight to realize how close it was to waning.

The trees seemed to bend forward as the creatures emerged,
dozens upon dozens of them.

71

Opal staggered back, half dragged by Tyler as fear paralyzed her limbs.

Nightmares come to life.

They were slow, the only advantage being that they walked awkwardly, as if they were dragging themselves forward. But not slow enough.

Opal's lungs closed off. What could she do? How could she escape? Would she have the courage to jump off the cliff- even though it probably meant death with the steep drop below her?... But better than the undead, surely? They would rip you apart. But she knew; she knew in her heart that she would never have the courage to do that.

Tyler was squeezing her arm; she probably looked as though she was faint. He was whispering in her ear, but she didn't hear him.

Cora let out an ear-splitting shriek as zombies skidded across the bunker, slamming the hatch shut and cutting off Cora.

Well, there goes Casper and Irene.

All six of them were back-to-back, the zombies preventing them from moving any farther.

The zombies were running in a circle around them, circling closer and closer; every time they circled, a little bit of space was lost.

"They're not stopping!" Cora was sobbing now, tears streaming down her face.

"We're dead."

Opal didn't know who had said it; she was too focused on the zombies, on the foe in front of her —and around her, the air was echoing down. It was becoming increasingly difficult to find space.

Suddenly, they broke the line and lunged forward, hands outstretched; Opal screamed and fell backward into her friends, scrambling against the dirt as she tried to get away-

They were everywhere, on everyone.

The circle was closed. It was gone.

Opal squeezed herself into a ball, trying to hide herself as best she could. She closed her eyes and pretended she didn't hear the feet thundering around her or the screams.

Something was pressing against her body; something was pushing her forward.

Something hurt; something was digging into her back, into her arm, into her leg. And she couldn't breathe, she couldn't smell anything but blood and sweat and tears- she didn't know how much longer she could hold on for. How much longer could she fight against the black dimming the corners of her eyes? But she had to fight- she had to.

And then it was all gone.

The sky, now a twilight color, was sparkling up in front of Opal's eyes.

Her clothes were ripped, torn in places, and she was covered in blood.

Blood!

Who's blood?

Opal frantically patted herself down; she felt multiple cuts, but nothing serious. She got the feeling that the cuts were from rocks and hard bits of the ground, not the monsters.

She was safe. Hiding at the bottom like a coward, taking being trampled over certain death at the zombies hands.

73

Where were her friends?

For a moment, Opal's heart seized with terror when she thought her friends were gone. Or worse. But she forced herself to look around and breathed a sigh of relief.

Scattered around on the cliff face, Tyler, still in arms reach, Cora not too far away. Nolan and Miranda were wrapped in each other's arms, and Miranda bleeding from a heavy cut on her forehead. The zombies had backed away, forming a protective semicircle that closed them off from the mountains, the forest, the valleys, and the open land, herding them against the steep cliff face.

They had backed away; the sun was not out. *The zombies had backed away.* What did that mean? Opal braced herself, waiting for them to lunge and attack, but they didn't move. They waited like puppy dogs for their master.

Their master.

Who? Was something controlling the zombies? Or some*one*?

But what drew her eyes next were the dark trails of blood on the sandy, grassy floor, leading all the way to...

Opal found out why she and none of her friends were hurt by the zombies.

Somebody else had taken the blows.

It was a broken, mangled body, the limbs askew, the neck bent at an awkward angle, blood trickling from many wounds...

And the eyes, the eyes staring off into the distance, glassy and never seeing because they would never see again. It was a corpse.

It was Sasha.

Sasha was dead.

"NO!" Miranda suddenly cried, breaking from Nolan's grasp to lurch forward, hands against the sand as tears streamed down her cheeks.

The zombies suddenly growled threateningly, closing ranks around the mangled body.

Miranda let out large, choked sobs. "No..." she whispered again.

"*Monsters!*" Nolan cried, his face vicious.

Sasha.

Sweet, disarming Sasha.

Then came the grief, but it was a different grief; there was no hope. No hope. She could see Sasha's glassy eyes staring up to the sky she would never see, her body mangled beyond repair.

Gone.

She would never talk.

Never walk.

Never smile.

Never *feel* again.

Because they were all alone, Sasha was the only one who had a family. A family that would cry for her death. Opal had only known her for a few hours, but all of them had bonded so quickly. How could they have not, in the face of such a disaster?

"How very, very touching."

It felt like ice was seeping through Opal's veins because she recognized that voice. It was the voice of the woman in Opal's dream. The one that had been torturing Amelia.

And the zombies parted, some crawling on all fours as they dragged themselves out of her way.

A woman with sharp red lips and a permanently arched eyebrow, giving her face a deep scowl look, walked confidently out of the mass of zombies as if they were nothing more than insects. She wore black mascara as dark as night. She wore high-laced, deep black boots that wound around her like a snake. She had dark, black hair that swirled around her shoulders and eyes, eyes with colors Opal couldn't place —sometimes green, brown, magenta, and sometimes even the flicker of red. She smiled, her tongue flicking out ever so briefly to lick her lips as she stared around.

A surge of hatred filled Opal's body, hatred that she couldn't even begin to explain. This was no petty schoolgirl grudge. Opal wanted nothing more than to *hurt* this woman in front of her.

"What's going on? Who the hell are *you*?" demanded Tyler.

The woman laughed a high, cold laugh. "Someone who's going to haunt your dreams, dear boy." Her voice was ringing with deep, suppressed anger and grief as she dipped her head to look down at Tyler.

"You killed her!!" Miranda suddenly burst forward, her eyes wild as she ran at the woman.

"I did." the woman whispered quietly. "And I'll kill many more." she brandished a finger at Miranda, and as if a wind had emerged from nowhere, Miranda was blasted back, mere inches from the cliff face.

Miranda half screamed, scrambling back on the palms of her hands, sending rocks skidding down as she regained her balance.

Something suddenly clicked in Opal's mind as she stared straight at that woman with her ever-changing eyes.

Something.... *Familiar.*

76

Familiarly evil.

Opal gasped. She had heard that laugh before. *"Irene?!"* shrieked Opal.

The woman snapped her head up, staring straight at Opal. "Irene?" she snarled. "Who is Irene? My name is Delphina." The bitterness scoring through *Delphina's* voice was prudent as Opal stared at her.

Something was wrong.

Opal tried to stamp the shiver of fear passing over her as the threat became ever so more alive. The shadow woman had a name.

Delphina.

And she sounded like Irene.

Perhaps evil had a sound.

"Sasha. I-is she dead?" Miranda whispered quietly from her sprawled position on the floor.

"We're quite thorough. Your little friend is dead." Delphina regarded Sasha's falling body for a moment before tearing away her eyes.

We?

Miranda let out a sob and turned away.

"We?!" shrieked Cora, catching it too. "What do you mean *we?"*

"Some secrets are only for adults, child," Delphina smirked.

"What do you want then?" Tyler hissed.

Delphina glared at Tyler, making him shrink back a little. Opal admired Tyler for his courage, but Delphina looked ready to knock him aside. Or feed him to her zombie pets.

Delphina rolled her eyes "You would never understand what I want." The anger rolling from Delphina's voice sounded like poison.

Opal tried to contain the flashes that were happening before her eyes —the flashes of Amelia from her dream, the cloaked *woman* screaming at her.

Perhaps.

Perhaps.

"You want The Sightseerer," Opal whispered, more to herself than to anyone, but it was no use; Delphina's head snapped towards her.

Delphina's eyes widened. "How did you know that name?" She demanded.

Opal opened her mouth, but no words came out. She didn't want to say anything, not when zombies prowled closer to her every second, and Delphina had her gaze trained on Opal.

Delphina leaned closer.

"*Nobody* knows about The Sightseerer except for me and a few others. HOW exactly did you get this information?" snarled Delphina even more sharply.

"Do you have my family? Where are they?" Opal asked quietly, her voice shaking.

Delphina looked even more surprised as she leaned back.

"Somewhere safe," Delphina growled. "Now, if you know so much about The Sightseerer, could you tell me where he is?"

Opal looked down at her feet in horror; they were being dragged through the sand, bringing Opal with them, getting closer and closer to Delphina's outstretched hand as Opal, against her will and her body's will, was dragged until she was meer inches from Delphina's face.

"Tell me. How do you know?" Delphina hissed, her long, jagged fingernails suddenly clenched around the back of Opal's head, dragging her ever so closer until her perfect lips were whispering in Opal's ear.

Opal whimpered and tried to drag her head away just to catch a glimpse of Sasha's mangled body lying in the dust, being stamped on by millions of feet and hands.

She couldn't move her hands or her feet; no matter how much she willed her body to twist and thrash, they were held in place by an invisible force.

"Tell me, Opal. You see, I know. I know what you see in your dreams, and I know your secrets, your cowardice. Your friends will die. They all will. Now, why don't you tell me what you saw in that helpful dream of yours-" Delphina's hissed remarks were suddenly cut off by a yelp as the invisible strands holding Opal were wrenched away. She found herself toppling to the sandy floor, her cheek slamming into the ground.

Hands clenched around her shoulders and dragged her away from Delphina as Opal thrashed her head to see what had knocked her from Delphina's grasp.

It was Tyler; he had tackled Delphina and was holding her down. "Run, Opal!" he suddenly cried, turning to face her, his face red with exertion. "Run," he whispered again.

Opal felt a massive surge of affection for the boy who had just as likely saved her life; she wanted to run and hug him so badly, but-

But Nolan grabbed her hands, hauling her to her feet, and pushed her forward. The zombies were still circling Delphina, who was still too incapacitated to call them. Opal was able to slip around them with Nolan, Miranda, and Cora hard on her heels.

Delphina suddenly screeched, ripping her hand away from Tyler, who had wrestled her to the ground, and raking her fingernails over the side of Tyler's face.

Opal winced as she watched a bright bead of blood leak over Tyler's handsome features.

"GET THEM." Delphina suddenly screeched with ferocity, her eyes flashing.

Opal's heart shot with adrenaline as she burst forward, terror giving her speed. She didn't wait for anyone, darting towards where the zombies had come from, towards the trees and mountains.

Please be somewhere I can hide.

Please.

Opal prayed desperately in her mind, hoping the zombies would be too distracted by the others and not notice she was gone.

Opal felt horrible as she imagined Tyler lying, broken, and bleeding in the dust. But she had to keep going.

She had to.

And she was almost to the tree line, so close she could see the misty paths stretching up towards mountains full of caves she could hide in and eat the dried food in her backpack until the Apocalypse was over...

She could disappear; the fog would swallow her up, never to be seen again.

She just had to run a little longer.

80

But a root tripped her up.

Literally.

The first second she saw it, jutting rudely out of the moss and dirt in front of her. The next second, it was there, twisting her legs until she was sprawled out on the mossy floor.

Her vision dimmed; she couldn't stop it; she couldn't stop herself from fading out even though she knew she was exposed right on the brink of the forest—not yet under the cover of the trees, not yet swallowed by the fog.

If the undead came upon her....

Nothing would stop them from ripping her apart.

But the vision wouldn't stop. It never would.

She closed her eyes, and the darkness took her suddenly-

"Run, Cora!!!!" screamed Tyler. His body heaved with the effort to keep running as he and Cora sprinted over rocks and roots. They pushed their way into the forest just beyond where Opal lay. Tyler, with his handsome face smeared with dirt and blood dripping from the scratch Delphina had ripped in his face. He looked back once, terror lighting his shining eyes; Cora was hand in hand with him, both of them barreling past where Opal was lying, running from something, from something that Opal was running from just as well.

Cora suddenly stumbled, just as Opal had. She fell to the ground, dragging Tyler down with her as they both crouched in the ground; Cora's face twisted with pain, tears trickling down her face as she closed her eyes.

Tyler fell to his knees in front of her, his gaze on the rumbling horde in the distance.

And suddenly, Cora turned to him, cupping his cheek in her hands; her eyes shone with tears.

81

"I love you." She whispered quietly and pulled her face to meet his, kissing him softly and holding him close.

Opal felt a surge of hatred, unlike anything she had ever experienced before. Everything went wrong at that moment. She didn't care how happy both of them seemed. She didn't care that she had run into their already unfolding story. She just wanted to stop it.

The vision cut off to Opal's immense relief.

But the emotions stayed.

What was that? It felt so random, so unneeded, and yet... So wrong.

Why did she care so suddenly? So fiercely? In just a few hours, she had completely and irrevocably inserted herself into two people's lives. Two people who were destined to meet on the road, ultimately finding each other.

Suddenly, she felt as if she had scrambled it all.

Tyler suddenly burst through the trees, dragging along a terrified Cora as Cora tripped on the ground, bringing Tyler down with her.

"Run, Cora!!!!" he cried, mirroring the vision with careful precision.

That was no nightmare.

That vision was *real.*

"Tyler!" she cried. "Cora!"

Tyler suddenly swiveled toward her, and Opal couldn't help it; she dove into his arms as he staggered back with a surprised yelp. Opal clung to him, her heart thundering. "I'm so sorry I just left you with her. I'm so glad you're alright."

Cora's face was murderous behind Opal's back, angry at her for disrupting their perfect moment.

Opal disentangled herself guiltily; what was she thinking?

Miranda and Nolan suddenly burst through the same trees as a rumbling filled the air, and Tyler pushed himself to his feet, helping Opal up; Cora was at his shoulder now.

"Guys." Nolan panted. "She's coming."

And she was there.

Delphina stood firm, her arms outstretched as she walked towards them; the zombies obediently followed behind her.

"My friends." she laughed. "You can't get away from me that easily."

With horror, Opal found that Delphina was staring straight at her. "And that one." she snarled. "Is *mine*."

Opal let out a strangled gasp as she felt herself being dragged forward, just like before, unable to stop it, her feet dragging through the mossy ground.

"Nobody will be tackling anybody today," Delphina growled; the semicircle of zombies suddenly grew, closing Opal alone with Delphina; Opal caught one last glimpse of her friends' terrified expressions as she was suddenly lost alone, lost with furious monsters and a woman who had taken half of her family.

No...

Delphina suddenly released the invisible grip she had on Opal, and Opal tumbled to the ground, landing in a heap on the sandy floor.

"Little Opal. You will become mine. Those little powers were never enough to stop me." Delphina suddenly crouched down beside

Opal, murmuring the words into her ear. "Your mind is no match for mine."

And that's when the pain started.

It was black before anything came.

Opal screamed into a silent void that she knew in her heart would not hear her. She was alone in the pain. Pain that attacked every fiber in her body, stretching over her bones.

Suddenly, images like ink spooling over a page ballooned in front of Opal's eyes, appearing edged in black.

It was a young woman hunched over a fallen shape. The two beings were alone with Opal in the darkness.

"H-Hello?" Opal stuttered.

The woman jerked her head around, and Opal stumbled back, letting out a shriek of surprise. "Why did you leave me to die?" crooned Gina, tears tracking down her face. Opal realized the shape on the ground was Gina's broken body; one eye was ripped out, leaving only a bloody socket behind. "I loved you, and in return, you let me die." she snarled as her form disappeared. Opal cried out and tried to grab onto her sister as she faded away, trying to scream that she wasn't dead. That Opal would come back for her. But she turned to smoke and was no more.

Opal sank to the ground and wept as more voices whispered in her ear, crowding her head, always there, but not there. She was alone in the darkness.

Suddenly, Cora was there in her mind's eye. Or was it her mind? "You aren't loved," Cora whispered suddenly. "A coward. How could anyone love you?"

"Why were you born at all?" cackled Irene.

"You are nothing. I will make you nothing." Delphina's ever-changing eyes loomed up in front of her.

And suddenly, it was Linea. "You failed me. You will fail everyone."

And suddenly, it was Cora again, but this time she had Tyler snared her arms; she turned her leering face to Opal. "You're foolish if you ever think he can be yours. He will always be mine."

"Sasha's death was your fault; you could have saved her; you failed," leered Irene from the shadows.

"Your friends will hate you."

"This is your fault."

"Your sister's death was your fault."

"You will never be loved, never."

"Your fault."

"Your fault."

"Coward."

"Coward."

The voices joined together. They wouldn't stop.

"Your father left so he could get away from you."

"Your friends will reject you."

"You will die alone, helpless, friendless, a coward."

"You will die."

No.

No, I can't.

Opal's heart twisted; fear started to hollow out a spark of resilience, a spark of fight deep inside her.

That spark was something that had been growing inside her. She could survive; she could pull herself out of this pit of tar. She could do it.

She had to. She had to endure for her sisters; she had to fight to get them back.

Suddenly, new images spilled over the blackness, the dark voices being pushed away to the edge.

"You're the best sister in the whole wide world!" it was Amelia, just like Gina, her image bloomed out of the darkness. Her smile was like a ray of sunshine; she was walking hand in hand with a younger version of Opal and playfully swung her sister's hand.

Opal cried out, begging for the scene not to disappear, but in a swirl of smoke, it was gone.

"I'll always believe in you," Linea whispered. There was no scene this time, only the quiet voice whispered from the darkness.

"I love you, Hylight." her dad.

"I love you, Opal." Gina.

Beams of warmth seemed to be seeping through the coldness, pushing it back.

Another scene appeared before her eyes. It was Tyler, standing there in the darkness, a slow grin spilling over his face.

Opal's heart jumped, but he was already gone and replaced by a much happier version of Gina, standing by her sister as she braided her hair.

But it was still there; it had always been there. The darkness pushed on the edges of the light, trying to seep into her heart.

Gina, holes appearing in her body as she screamed for help that would never appear.

Linea pulled away from her, disappointment lighting her gaze.

Sasha's mangled body lying in the dirt.

"You will never be loved..."

"You are useless."

Tyler smiling.

"You will die alone......"

"Come on, it's not so hard! You can do it!"

"The world will celebrate your death....."

"I love you!"

"Your friends will reject you...."

Amelia, terrified as she screamed over a pit of zombies.

Tyler whirled her around, and she fell into his arms.

Zombies filtering into her town......

"You will never be loved,"

"You're the best!"

"You're a coward."

Their house going up in flames....

Opal let out a scream as her body writhed in pain; a monster inside her seemed to be crying to be let free. She screamed again, and the pain filled her and went through her. She crawled on all fours and saw her reflection in the inky darkness around her, but it wasn't her face staring back at her.

Opal's face was half rotten, holes poking through to her bone, the flesh peeling away.

Pain surged through her again, the dark voices clustering in her mind.

The undead surged forward, determined to rip her apart.

Gina dying.

Tyler dying.

Linea dying.

Amelia dying.

87

It was her fault; it was all her fault. It was too much, between the voices and the pain. Opal couldn't keep going; she couldn't. She just wanted to give up.

"Hold on," whispered a voice. Instead of dripping with menace, this voice was soft and wonderful. It was inviting. It was helping her.

Opal blearily tried to get up. But the voices pushed her back, pushing her to the ground.

"You will never find love!"

"You. Are. Nothing!"

"Never wanted, never loved,"

"Tyler doesn't deserve you!"

And then Tyler's face swam out of the haze. His golden hair was tossed to the side, causing him to fall into a sort of glow. As he stared at her, his eyes twinkled, and he reached out his arms; she reached to take them. But the voices beat her back.

"You don't deserve him!" screeched Cora.

"He will never love you! No one could ever love you!" screamed Irene.

Opal screamed again as the pain consumed her, and she collapsed to the ground.

Much like Tyler, another softer voice whispered in her ear.

A voice she hadn't heard in years.

A person she missed.

He was there in the shadows, fighting them back, his outline hallowed in a light.

That's when the realization struck her. Opal would keep fighting.

For him.

For her father.

88

He wouldn't want her to give up. So she wouldn't

Like glass, the darkness broke away into millions of pieces, raining down. With a yell, Opal broke free from the voices and gasped awake.

Delphina's cry of shock was enough to make Opal smile when she pushed herself to her feet to face Delphina.

"W-Why didn't it work? Y-You should be under my control by now-" gasped Delphina. "Who are you?"

Opal gasped for air, craning her neck to catch a glimpse of Tyler or any of her friends' faces through the smog of zombie bodies around her.

"Don't try to run. It's impossible." Delphina suddenly hissed; her arms were out, her hands to the sky. Suddenly, she was lifted high into the air as if by invisible strings.

Opal's breath caught with terror. Delphina was flying. *She was flying.*

Suddenly, the whole air seemed to flicker with heat, and the stench of smoke reached Opal's nose.

She gagged and fell to the ground on her knees as the acrid stench stung the back of her throat.

And she saw, beyond the barrier of zombies, tall flames flickered, flickering and shooting puffs of smoke into the air. Opal felt a flash of fear, but this time, it wasn't for her own life.

Tyler.

Nolan.

Miranda.

Her heart cried with fear as she imagined her friends trapped with smoke and flames on all sides.

NO!

90

Opal slammed a brick wall on her thoughts as she watched Delphina. "Let me go!" Opal shrieked at the woman in the sky. "I have nothing! I know nothing! *I am nothing.*"

Delphina suddenly snapped her eyes open, the color a sharp green as she floated down from the sky, anger filling her gaze as she landed only inches from Opal.

"You have everything." She hissed. "And I'm going to take it."

Her clawed hand was suddenly at Opal's forehead, and Opal let out a shriek of surprise.

It felt like ice was crawling through her veins, paralyzing her in a place that she couldn't get out of, pushing her to the limit from which she couldn't escape.

She would never escape.

And then the ice was crawling faster; it was crawling deeper, and she couldn't seem to find an end.

The paralyzing feeling stretched over her body, and Opal struggled to keep her eyes open, but she knew it was no use; consciousness was fading from her body like water slipping through outstretched hands.

The last thought that made it through her numb mind was how everything had gone so terribly wrong.

Opal awoke to blaring lights flashing in her eyes. Her vision was snatched away by the brightness, and she squeezed her eyes shut.

The air had a sweet metallic taste, nothing like the smoky air she had just tasted moments before.

Where was she?

Slowly, her eyes adjusted to the light, and she opened them a crack. She reached up to brush the hair out of her eyes but then realized she couldn't.

She was tied to a thick metal chair with large restraints that dug into her wrists and ankles as they bound her in place.

Opal jumped, well, as much as she could with the restraints. There was something about the way panic consumed the body when you couldn't move; it seemed to dig into every fiber of her being. Never had she been tied back, never like this.

Who did this? There was only one answer, *Delphina*.

What did she want from her?

Her visions?

No. Her *dreams?*

But they didn't come true.

The thing with Cora and Tyler-

It wasn't *real.*

And that was the only remarkable thing about her.

But...

But did they not come true because she stopped them? She stopped Cora. But- the vision of Cora when she was younger likely came true- who knows, Amelia could have been getting tortured- she dreamed of zombies the night before it happened...

No.

It wasn't possible.

Opal banged her head against the metal bed in desperation. She was alone; her bed was in the middle of a stone-cold room lined with metal walls, and the light was fixed on her face, so blinding she couldn't see any farther.

But if she squinted... There was a door, the same color as the walls, and with no doorknob.

It looked like a prison.

Am I in prison? Opal thought, terrified for a second. *By whose authority?*

But why would the police go around arresting random teenage girls when they had an apocalypse on their hands?

If there even are any police left. Opal thought.

"Terrifying, isn't it?" asked a slow voice snidely. "The loss of control. I could do anything I want to you right now, and you would never be able to do anything about it, like a nightmare. But yet when the time comes for you to die... you won't wake up."

Opal gasped, Delphina's voice rang through the stone-cold chamber, but Opal couldn't find any trace of her. Delphina's words sank deep into her soul. They terrified her.

"Where am I? What happened to Tyler and the others?" stuttered Opal, her words echoing strangely in the metal room.

"Tell me what I want, and you can go scampering back to your friends." hissed Delphina's voice again. "Like the kicked *dog* you are."

"I don't know anything," Opal immediately promised, almost automatically. She didn't.

"No, not now, you don't. Your head is useless. All full of thoughts of a pretty little boy you can kiss- nothing of use." Delphina snarled.

Opal blushed scarlet, anger lighting her mind. How dare Delphina say that!? How dare she dig through her own thoughts-

Opal squeezed her eyes shut, wishing to be anywhere but here. She didn't know anything! She didn't know why Delphina was dogging her like this. Why *any* of this was happening. It wasn't fair.

Opal squinted one eye open and yelped in shock.

She hadn't heard a door open, and yet, Delphina was staring at her, standing right at her elbow as she glared down at Opal.

Opal shrieked, twisting away from Delphina's glower to no avail.

Opal began to sweat. And that's when the pain started.

It felt like a thousand white hot knives were pressing into her skull.

The darkness was back; it pressed into her, stopping any light or happiness that would try to peek through.

Delphina was right. She could do anything to Opal in that chair, and she wouldn't be able to wake up. Or to run.

Opal grunted in pain as if a hand was pressing into her as if she could never escape.

But Delphina was straining, too. Her hand began to quiver as she pushed forward. Opal began to scream.

Veins dotted her temples as she strained against the invisible magic puncturing her mind. A quiet voice suddenly spoke in her mind: *hang on, Opal, the Acana Magic only lasts a bit; hang on, hang on.* It was strangely familiar, and the word *Acana* sounded odd in her mind, but the pain pushed away any further thoughts.

Yes. Opal whispered back to the voice inside her head. She was going to hold on.

White flitted in Opal's eyes as Delphina added more power to her attack. The pain lanced farther and seemed to enter her, letting the darkness settle into her soul and fill her with doubt.

Straining against Delphina's hold, Opal felt something inside her stir that she had never felt before.

A deep voice in Opal's mind was saying, *"Opal, the key is- the zombie apocalypse was c-ca-ca-caused b-by-"* The voice was cut off, and the pain from Delphina stopped abruptly.

Opal lay there, chained, letting her heartbeat slow and the sweat around her cool, trying to look anywhere but Delphina's leering gaze, all too aware that she was trapped for more torture.

Her mind was racing. Her body was racing- trying to recover from the trauma it just endured.

Just hold on. Until you can get back to Tyler.

In her weakened state, with no way to filter her thoughts, Opal found herself longing to be back in the bunker, no matter how scary it had seemed at the time. Nothing could be worse than this.

"Please. Tell me." Opal gasped, her voice rough. "Who are you, and where am I? Do you know where my family is?"

Delphina's face suddenly contorted in an expression of pity; her eyes were flashing, and Opal could have imagined it, but she swore she saw flashes of deep sadness in them. "I'm an experiment. I used to be like you, Opal. I used to be just a girl with visions. Until he found me. I have powers now; my Acana Magic was amplified. I'm strong now, but I can see in your eyes and in your mind that you are just as strong as me. You can change the fate of our world, Opal."

Strong? That's an interesting way to describe me. Opal thought, disgruntled. But as more of Delphina's words sunk into her mind, more of the terror of what was also done.

It had a name.

Her strange visions, her hallucinations, she called them.

The blackness pressed down upon her, bringing her to places she would never go.

Future.

Past.

Acana Magic.

It had a name.

"Magic? There's no such thing as magic-" Opal began.

"There's no such thing as zombies either? Or seeing the future? Or levitating?" Delphina snapped back. "And all of those things you just saw. Grow up, Opal. Open your eyes already."

Opal couldn't. She didn't want to be special. She didn't want to be the one with the powers.

Why? Why her?

Delphina snorted. "You'll see. In time, Opal. In time, in this facility, you'll be begging for a little power."

"N-Never," Opal whispered.

"We'll see." In the blink of an eye, Delphina was gone. The light that had blared so sharply in her eyes was also gone, and Opal was plunged into darkness.

Alone in the dark.

The darkness scared her; she felt as if spiders were crawling all over her body. Monsters waiting with their jaws open.

Opal squeezed her eyes shut.

The dry sobs that had attacked her body and her mind ever since she opened her eyes to see Delphina glaring at her came back. The desire to cry was stronger now, and she couldn't help it as she broke out in tears yet again.

What am I going to do? The sad, mournful cry rang in her mind, and for the first time in a long time, Opal truly had no idea what would happen next.

Opal awoke to the strange sound of beeping; she gasped in shock, as she hadn't remembered blacking out or falling asleep at that. Her memories were a little foggy, but she swore she hadn't fallen asleep.

And that's when her memories rushed back.

Acana Magic.

It was real.

And she hated it.

She didn't want it.

No more visions.

The realization was strong as it blazed through Opal. This was how she was going to be; she wasn't going to have any more weird visions; if she had one, she would wake herself up. She wanted to be normal, to fade into the background. That's what she was going to have to do. If she wanted to survive.

She tried to move her arms, and they slowly, slowly responded. She twitched her fingers, and they reacted just as slowly; she wasn't bound, but everything seemed... *weird.*

She felt like she was encased in something.

Like a bug.

Snagged in a trap.

Opal blearily opened her eyes. Trying to keep the panic down. Everything was tinged orange. It was so strange.

But beyond the orange, the weird tinge of eyes that would hopefully fade... she was in a room out of the horror movies.

The horror movies with the mad scientist trapped in their labs while they experimented, going crazy while they were at it.

The lab had solid metal walls that gleamed and sparkled, casting harsh light over the rest of the materials in the metal room. The room was about as big as the bunker where Opal had first met her friends.

Lining the walls were large tanks about the size of a full-grown man; they were round, like an enlarged tube, and filled with odd, thick-looking liquids that bubbled and popped. With the consistency of corn syrup.

People in large coats hustled around with strange, large tools to a different array of tables filling the rooms, tables like the one Opal had been lying on, with their open cuffs waiting for someone to jump in and be imprisoned. Each table had a sort of bedside table filled with pinchers and metal tools that gleamed in the odd light.

It looked like an odd, grotesque dentist chair.

But they would be doing a lot worse than pulling out teeth. Opal reckoned.

They.

There were so many scientists in white cloaks bustling around. So many *people.* Under whose authority?

Delphina had spoken of a he.

Delphina wasn't the head of a snake.

She was an *experiment.*

This was a lab.

A lab.

A *facility.*

Opal's breathing quickened when she saw what was on the far end of the room, strapped to the tables with at least three of the white-cloaked people running around with sharp-looking tools was a zombie with dank sunken eyes and pale skin; it thrashed against the people who were fighting it.

Will that be me?

Will I turn into a red-eyed monster like Delphina?

No.

Please.

Is this what my sisters are being forced through?

WHERE AM I?

Opal struck out in her confusion, and that is when she realized she had hit stone-cold glass.

Opal fumbled with her hands as she realized with terror that *she* was in one of those tanks with odd liquid; that orange haze was *liquid.*

How was she alive?!

Opal fumbled with her mouth, trying to feel the flood of oxygen where the oxygen that was whistling cleanly in and out of her mouth was coming from. Her hands found plastic, and a diver mask was strapped around her face, protecting her eyes and giving her oxygen.

But it was a prison.

She was a prisoner.

"HELP!" Opal screamed, fumbling to hit the glass as hard as she could but to no avail; she didn't even know if the words escaped her mouth or if it was just a stream of bubbles.

But someone was there, messing with the control panel at the bottom of the tank Opal was ensnared in; it was a squat woman with graying hair, beady brown eyes, and a large lab coat on with a name tag that read: Hi! I am Delsea!

Too cheerful for a place like this. Opal thought bitterly.

Claustrophobia was setting in now. Opal felt her breath quicken in her chest as she tried to escape in any way possible, but she was too terrified. Fear made her hands clumsy, and her lungs struggled as she began to hyperventilate.

"Please!" Opal was half sobbing now as she pressed her body as close to the glass as she could get, glaring down at the squat woman with no emotion on her deeply lined face. "Please." Opal sobbed again. "I've never done anything to you. Or to anyone. Just release me."

"Sorry, little friend. I'm not the boss here." Delsea muttered, no sympathy in her voice, her mouth twisted into a cruel smile.

Then who is?! Opal cried silently.

Opal pushed with her arms, trying to reach the surface- the bubbles had to pop somewhere, didn't they? Didn't they? She knew she had to find a way to get out.

But she couldn't; she raised her hand to find cold metal waiting for her, metal and glass on every side.

Just breathe. Opal whispered to herself, trying to concentrate on breath whistling in and out, even if it had the strange claustrophobic tint that she was breathing underwater. *Breathe.* She whispered. She would survive. It was what she was good at.

And somehow. I'm going to escape.

I'm not going to be a pawn, an experiment like Delphina claims she was.

I'm going to find a way out of this hellhole.

I have to.

10

TYLER

The zombies were gone. Delphina and Opal had disappeared into thin air; the zombies had scattered afterward, running deeper and deeper into the forest and towards the mountain until they were gone, seemingly uninterested with the rest of the group.

Tyler's heart ached with every step as the undead ran farther and farther away.

Away from where Opal had disappeared in a puff of smoke.

The four of them couldn't speak as they moved on unsteady legs, staggering forward, tree branches scraping their faces as they moved a little farther into the forest.

And they collapsed, where the trees opened up slightly to reveal a clearing surrounded by the outcrop of mountains on all sides, creating a valley. This valley was sheltered by trees and revealed a network of caves that stretched far above their heads, deep into the mountains.

Miranda sank to the grassy floor, panting wildly, sharp tears welling up in her eyes, and it wasn't long before she began sobbing wildly.

"I can't believe we lost them." Nolan gasped. "*Two.*"

"Tyler."

Tyler's heart immediately quickened. It'd been years, but his crush on Cora had never faded; it never faded throughout their childhood when she slowly started to lean on him like he leaned on her.

Her determination, her courage, and, of course, she was *gorgeous*. It was impossible not to look at her. But recently, Tyler almost wanted to hold back; it was before he met Opal, which was a whole other thing. Perhaps it was the way Cora treated some people, or maybe the way her sass could just go a little far. It was simply that Tyler almost didn't know who she was anymore; she'd changed since the little girl who rolled around in the mud with him when they were younger.

And recently...

She'd been throwing herself at him, being fake and controlling, always stuck to his elbow.

And though Tyler had dreamed about it, he wasn't sure he liked it. But he still loved her; he couldn't stand it when Irene was on top of her, and when she was in pain, he had to step in. Of course, he did!

He just didn't know what to feel.

When Opal walked into the room, her whole mind was blank; it was perhaps her quiet and shy demeanor or her worried eyes. She made him want to walk over and just wrap his arms around her.

Oh, what was he thinking?

Opal, sweet, innocent Opal, was taken by that *witch*. And Sasha was dead. And his family was dead.

Cora was all he had left, really.

Tyler slammed another wall of ice on his emotions; he *would* find Opal. He had to.

He couldn't leave her.

She wasn't dead.

Not like his family.

103

There was still hope.

Tyler tried to stop the wave of sadness that crashed onto him, just as powerful as before. *He couldn't stop them.*

He and Cora had come from the village across the short line of mountains; they had crossed or run to the bunker through the long valley shadowed by the mountains on all sides- Tyler grew up running in the caves that they now sheltered in. He used to hide and play with his brother all day long, but that was before.

Before it all came crashing down.

Just like that, the memories enveloped him, and he closed his eyes as they washed across his mind.

Irene had been particularly nasty the night before.

Tyler had seen her wild eyes from his window as he watched her crash around, screaming at everything but especially at Cora.

He'd watched, terrified that something was going to happen, something worse. That she was going to get hurt. He'd watched for years, and that night, he was worried that she had finally been pushed off the edge.

He was worried she would finally kill Cora.

Tyler watched as Irene lobbed around, Cora running to hide somewhere as her mother smashed a window with her angry hands, glass sprinkling and breaking all over the ground.

He'd gone to sleep, worried sick about his friend, and the next morning, he didn't hesitate to run over to find her, packing food and extra clothes in case he would stay over at Cora's. He didn't know that that backpack would be the last thing he would have from home.

Tyler had found her in their usual spot, the boulder on the highest point in their town, a hill shadowed by the mountains looming over it. That was one of the reasons he loved this particular spot. Perspective. Because above them were the mountains, but below them was their entire village.

Cora had sat there, her back curled, when he slid into the seat next to hers.

"You alright?" he muttered, sliding his arm around her shoulders.

She turned to him; her eyes were puffy and red as another tear slipped out. "No," she whispered back. "I hate her."

And he let her cry there for a while, the two of them perched on that rock. Cora's face was buried in her hands as she struggled to contain her sobs, and Tyler urged her to let them out.

"She's getting worse. She's drinking too much, and she won't listen, yelling at me for things she sees in her head..." Cora trailed away, gulping for air. "B-Bout my f-father."

Tyler was at a loss for words; he didn't know what to say. He couldn't say he related or even reassure her because he knew. He knew how dangerous Irene was, nothing like his perfect parents, who he loved.

"Tyler-" Cora whispered. "Tyler, I'm scared she's going to kill me." Cora buried her head in her hands again as she let out another muffled sob.

Tyler felt a jab of fear, of pity as he pulled her closer, smoothing her hair. "It's alright," he muttered. "I won't let her do anything to you. I promise."

"I know. But what if you're not there? When the nights get cold and dark, you leave. She comes at me... What do I do then?" Cora half wheezed, her face coloring from the shame of the confession.

105

Tyler felt his heart seize as he stared at his lifelong friend and lifelong crush. Tyler grabbed both of Cora's hands in his. "Cora, you run. Run, alright? And I'll come. I'll always, always come."

"I know. I know you will." Cora wiped her nose and hugged him tightly. "I'll come to if you need me; I doubt you will, though. Don't think this is me being weak, Ty, I'll still destroy you in any game we play."

Tyler smiled at her joke and hugged her back. "Right, we'll see about that. Hey, you know what? This is wrong; how about we go to my parents, and we stop Irene once and for all? The way she treats you... she should be in prison, Cora, prison."

Cora looked up at him, her eyes wide. "I-I know." she breathed shakily. "But I'm scared."

"It's going to be okay. My family is going to protect you, and we're going to make sure Irene is sent far, far away from you." Tyler swore quietly, hope blooming in his chest. This was something they should have done long ago when Irene's words turned violent. Cora didn't deserve to live like this; nobody did.

It was the sharp scent of smoke in the air and the crackle of something ominous that had jolted them both up. Tyler jumped up, pulling Cora with him as they wildly looked down at their home.

It was flames, the flames that licked the houses hungrily, enveloping everything in a canopy of smoke and flames. A uniform line of fire and destruction destroyed their home.

But what was worse were the flickering shapes around the fire, the ones darting in and out, hazed by smoke as they chased the humans sprinting for safety that would not come.

Creatures.

Creatures of the night, ones only whispered of on the news.

106

One claimed to be a hoax.

Dead, listless, and empty eyes. No soul there.

Dragging limbs.

Moaning.

Zombies.

Cora shrieked, her eyes wide. "My mother- your family-" *she choked- crying out now. Her body was paralyzed with shock.* "I-I t-thought it was f-fake- they said- they promised-."

Tyler didn't care that the president had spent the last several months assuring everyone the outbreaks of deaths and supposed zombie *sightings were nothing more than a fearsome gang in the area. He cared about his family. His family was probably still sleeping- sleeping in a house covered in flames.*

They needed to move.

Tyler seized the still-paralyzed Cora's hand and half dragged her down the slope, his heart pounding as the ground flattened out and they reached the town.

And it really was a helltown.

The zombies were everywhere, leaving no rock unturned as they crawled on the edges of the flames, lunging at everyone in sight. All around the flames, people succumbed to their tearing hands.

And he was screaming with Cora as he saw these zombie creatures move closer to him- he saw their hands reach for him. All he could do was elbow and fight, hold Cora to his side, and push his way around.

And he fought his way to where his house was. The house he had grown up living in, with its dark red door and pleasant white paint. The house of safety.

Instead, it was an inferno, broken and blistering; roof beams crashed down as flames licked hungrily at the frame of his house. He tried not to look back at the zombie dragging someone by the leg who was long gone. Or his neighbor yelling for help as teeth closed around his shoulder.

"No," Tyler whispered; he couldn't help himself, even though he knew it was stupid, even though he knew he could die... His family was there. He spared one last glance at Cora. "Stay here! I'll be right back; keep out of sight!"

Tyler didn't have time to consider his choice or to try and get Cora to safety. All he could do was shrug off his backpack and run headfirst into his old home, the flames licking around him as he tried to swerve and avoid them.

The only thought was for his family.

His mother.

His father.

His little brother Calico.

He loved them.

And he couldn't see them dead.

"Mom!" Tyler cried into the haze. "Dad! Calico!"

The smoke was billowing fast from the flames that were encroaching into the house; Tyler paused on the threshold, unsure whether to go deeper in, especially when a wooden chunk of their mantel fell, sparking all the way.

Flames sent columns of heat spiraling up his body until he began to sweat uncontrollably as his shirt stuck to his skin. His eyes were burning from the smoke, and he struggled for a breath of fresh oxygen in the smoky air. Fear was setting in, just like the heat.

But the thought of Calico, his mother, and his father was the only thing that enabled him to push forward. Immediately, the smoke attacked his lungs, forcing him nearly to the ground in his hacking coughs. He tried not to look around, to realize what the fire had done to wreck his perfect home. But he couldn't see anyway—the haze was too strong and the flames too numerous.

His skin was blistering.

"Calico?" Tyler coughed. "Mom?!"

He pushed forward, one foot after another, into the house, dodging flames and holding a hand over his mouth.

"T-Tyler?!" Tyler's heart spiked, and he gasped; swirling around, he fell to his knees, ignoring the heat licking at his body as he crawled forward to find his mother and father crouched on the floor, one of the gigantic beams from the ceiling pinning them to the ground.

"Dad! Mom!" Tyler cried, reaching out his hand to his mother, her brown hair stained with ash and her large blue eyes sparking with fear.

Her skin felt hot. Too hot. Feverish.

Dad was crouched beside his wife, both of their bodies pinned to the floor by the fiery wreckage all around them.

"Tyler-" Dad was coughing now. "Go find your brother."

"No! Wait! I can get you out," Tyler gasped, pulling harder on Mom's hand, ripping and breaking his nails as he pulled at the burning wood on top of them.

"No!" Dad responded quickly and firmly. "No time, go find Calico."

"Go!" Mom repeated, squeezing his hand before yanking it out of Tyler's grip.

109

Tears sprung to Tyler's eyes as the smoke stung him; he could imagine his terrified black-haired brother cowering in his room- hiding as the flames circled him.

But he couldn't leave his parents. He couldn't. "Please." Tyler gasped.

"Do you want your brother to die?!" Dad growled harshly. "GO! NOW!"

Tyler backed away, shaking his head.

"We love you." Mom gasped.

"I love you," Tyler whispered back before turning head on his heel and running as fast as he could up the falling staircase as the smoke put iron claws around his chest, his body sweating from the heat.

But then Tyler saw him on the landing, his little brother curled up from the heat. The air was hazy from the smoke, but even from here, Tyler saw that he wasn't moving.

A bolt of fear and pain sent Tyler lurching forward. "Calico!" he cried, reaching forward to shake his brother, but he recoiled; his brother was white hot.

"Calico!" Tyler cried again, ignoring the blistering hot pain in his hands. Tyler pushed Calico over, trying to ignore the heat singing his clothes. "Calico," he whispered again.

But he knew it was too late. For when he turned his brother's limp body over, no fluttering of breath rattled in his chest, no light in his eyes. He was only a limp, hot corpse; the burns covering his arms and legs were a deathly black. He had probably died right here, running to find his parents.

It felt like real, tangible pain that pursued him next. It felt like his chest was being ripped open. He couldn't even cry; any tears would

110

evaporate, after all. It was just hot, real pain that crawled through his body.

White hot pain as he tried to drag his brother's body down the stairs, but it was simply too hot, too hot. His hands felt like they were bleeding.

He had to run, he couldn't take it. His chest was heaving, and his mind was spinning. His body was shaking, threatening to keel over, and Tyler knew that if he fell here with his brother.... He would never leave again.

Tyler let out a scream of pure anger and hate and let his head fall down until it hit his brother's chest.

Would it be so bad to die here with them? Let the flames consume him, the pain in his heart making him numb to the pain from his body?

It was the thought of Cora that got him standing; he couldn't just leave her. He couldn't.

So he ran. He ran past his parent's limp forms, their chests no longer rising and falling.

Dead.

He ran towards the last flickering light, not even thinking of the creatures that waited outside for him. He ran to outrun the burning in his chest that didn't come from the fire. He tried to outrun the flames.

He ran from his hurt.

And he ran from his family.

With a cry, he barreled through the door just as the flames reached their maximum and just as the house exploded.

The heat and power of the explosion threw Tyler off; as the flames licked his body, he tried to ignore the needle-like sensation and scurry as fast away as he could as the heat and smoke blew out all over him. He crashed headfirst into the dirt and grass.

His family was gone. He was alone again.
Alone in the dirt, his heart slowly broke for the people he had left behind in the smoke and flames.

There was a ringing in his ears. There was pain in his body. Tyler groaned. Through slitted and watering eyes, he watched Cora rush to his side, tears already in her eyes as she collapsed next to him.

"Ty- you're burning." her fingers raced across his body- pouring water from his discarded bag over his clothes.

Tyler shuddered; he could almost see steam rising from him. As he cried out in pain, once before, his eyelids grew heavy.

His head crashed down onto the ground, and the world went dark.

And the rest was history; they'd packed up his backpack, Cora, and a disgruntled Irene and ran for the mountains and for safety.

His body had long since recovered from the effects of the smoke and flame—he hadn't been in there long enough for any real damage... But he worried the damage it had done to his heart was beyond healing.

And his heart still felt like it was splitting in two when he thought of that fire.

"Tyler!" Cora repeated, and suddenly, she was at his side, and Tyler could smell her sweet flower scent. "My mother. Casper. They're still back in the bunker. With it sealed. They don't know where the escape hatch is; they could die. They *will* die if we don't get them out soon."

"So?" Miranda sneered. "They wouldn't help us when Sasha was getting k-killed and Opal kidnapped!? Why would we help them?"

Cora bristled. "Because she's my mother!"

Nolan was suddenly at Miranda's shoulder. "Miranda's sort of right. Wasn't she horrible to you?"

Cora suddenly looked away, her face darkening. "Sure. Yes. But she's my mother? Don't you understand? Tyler. Please, you must understand." She suddenly turned on him, her eyes wide as she placed a hand on his chest, so close he could practically feel her heartbeat.

Did she know the effect that she had on him? The way he almost stopped breathing when she was around? But that wasn't the point. Tyler couldn't help but admit that he was torn. Just this morning, they had agreed that it was time to leave Irene behind... and now, in this new world, she would be an even bigger liability. Who knows what she would do and how she would react? But something inside of Tyler knew that Cora wouldn't leave her behind; just like how she had brought Irene to the bunker, Cora would bring her to the next stage of their journey. Because she was her mother, the last standing member of Cora's family, Tyler knew that some part of her always hoped that Irene would love her like a mother should.

"Cora's right," Tyler grunted firmly. "That bunker can't be trusted, not when we nearly all died in there. I suggest we stay in one of these caves; I know them well, and if we go deep enough, nobody could hurt us. Well, until we come back out."

Tyler wasn't going to give up on Opal. He couldn't. He'd left people he'd loved to die before, and he swore never to do it again. Not after seeing Sasha's broken and mangled body before him... however short he had known both of them... it didn't feel right to just abandon

113

her. And she had no family; nobody knew how she had been kidnapped. In the mess of the zombies... nobody would bother to look for her. Except them.

But for some reason, he didn't want to tell Cora that. He knew how she was. He could even imagine how her eyes would flash as she stared at him as if he had committed some act of betrayal.

But it *wasn't* betrayal. Tyler found himself annoyed with Cora, even though she hadn't done or said anything yet, but he still felt as if Opal and him could be friends. Good friends. And good friends rescued each other from zombies no matter what other friends said. *Cora isn't just your friend, idiot.*

They'd been best friends since they were three. Still, over the last year, things had evolved, perhaps because boys were beginning to look at Cora, and Cora was starting to look at Tyler. Still, really, it was the crackdown Irene had. She got even more unstable, even more brutal; she stopped just occasionally lashing out at Cora. She stopped ignoring her daughter most of the time and started hitting her instead.

And it pushed them closer together. Suddenly, Tyler found himself staying late nights with Cora as they huddled together in her room, wrapped in blankets, while Irene crashed around. Or they sat on their rock all day, sometimes swimming in the lake or making dandelion crowns.

Suddenly, Cora stopped laughing about him with her girlfriends and started laughing *with* him. Suddenly, she began to lean on him like a crutch.

So he did understand; he understood how Irene was really the one who had given Cora a lifelong friend and made them both rely on each other.

114

"We need food. Supplies." Miranda whispered, her face softening. "But I don't want to go back-"

Tyler knew what she meant. He imagined trekking back to the place where they all had almost died of suffocation and, beyond that, the place where Sasha's life had been ripped away. And, of course, where an even bigger villain was revealed. *Delphina.* The name was whispered in his mind- like a snake had hissed it.

But Tyler needed sleep; his body ached, and the night was wearing on, twilight fading away into a pitch-black sky.

Nolan shivered, rubbing his arms with his hands. "I don't care what we do; I just want to find somewhere warm and with some food. I don't want to know what's looming out there."

Tyler used to love to play at night, hunting frogs or watching the stars, but now it felt as if an invisible threat was hanging over them.

"I don't know if we'll be finding anything warm tonight, Nolan," Tyler muttered darkly.

"C-can they smell us?" Cora whispered.

"As far as every zombie movie I've seen. Yes. They can." Nolan muttered.

"Then what are we waiting for? Let's go!" Miranda snapped, stalking through the trees.

Nolan hovered for a minute before rushing after her.

Cora slipped her fingers into Tyler's, holding him tight; there was nothing romantic about it; they had done it hundreds if not thousands of times before, but Tyler couldn't help but feel glad Opal wasn't there to watch it.

Tyler tried to push away any foreboding as the dark trees loomed in front of him; he felt vulnerable. Exposed. Like anything could reach out and grab him or Cora.

Tendrils of fog seemed to be stretching out from the tree's roots, pulling themselves around Tyler's feet. He stumbled a couple times but somehow found the strength to keep going, trying to ignore the desperate fear tugging at his chest. The fear and the hopelessness.

They were just trying to survive.

But how long could they survive for?

Tyler tried not to shiver as they entered the empty clearing. And there she was.

Sasha.

Just as Delphina had left her mangled. Broken.

The spark in her eyes was gone. Nothing but flat stormy disks- staring off into a dark sky that she would never see.

Tyler didn't want to get any closer, but they *had* to. Surely they had to bury her or something-?

He took a step forward-

"*Stop!*" Nolan's shriek sent Tyler scurrying backward as he turned to stare at Nolan.

"What?" he demanded. "Come on, we should at least bury her or something... I know it's strange, but I don't just want to leave her."

"No." Nolan burst forward. "It's not that. She was bitten by a zombie. She's going to change; she's going to get dangerous."

Tyler blanched. Is that why she looked strange? Was it just his imagination, or was her skin looking paler? Her open eyes looking redder?

116

"H-how do we stop it?" Tyler whispered. "How do we stop the... process?"

"Well, typically-" Nolan's face was stony. "You chop up the body and then burn it."

Tyler couldn't help the little gasp of horror that escaped his mouth as he stared- open-mouthed at Nolan. "No way," he spoke firmly. "No way am I letting you *chop her up*."

Nolan shrugged. "She's already dead."

"But isn't there a way to turn zombies back into people?" Tyler whispered. He didn't want Nolan to know, to know that he wasn't a hundred percent condemning Sasha to be dead. He didn't want to give anyone false hope, not when it was burning in his heart. There must be a cure out there, a cure to turn zombies back into people. It had to work somewhere... Wasn't that how all the movies ended?

This isn't a movie, Tyler.

"If there is, we won't be the people to find it," Nolan responded quickly. "Tyler. She's already gone; look at her. Even if there was a cure, there was no way to put her body back to the way it was. All her bones are probably broken."

Tyler swallowed, bile collecting thick and heavy inside of his throat as he stared at Sasha's mangled body. The parallels between his brother's lifeless body and hers were all too similar... "I just wish..." he croaked.

"I know. We all wish it was different, but it isn't." Nolan sighed.

"Got it!" Miranda smiled ear to ear- unaware of the grim conversation springing up between Tyler and Nolan. She'd managed to

117

throw her weight against the bunker door, and with a hiss and a click, it sprung open.

Immediately, Casper popped his head up as if he had been waiting. His expression slid quickly from delight as he took deep breaths of the fresh night air to a scowl when he saw his audience.

But Tyler saw his flushed face and desperate, wild eyes; he knew Casper had been trying to open that door with all his might.

He hasn't given up on the world yet.

He still wants to live.

Casper's face darkened as he stared around at Miranda's bewildered face, Cora's concerned one, and Nolan's annoyed face.

"Hi," he grunted after a while. "Uh, thanks."

"We didn't do it for *you*." Cora snapped, flipping her hair.

Oh, come on. Let him be happy for once. Tyler thought, annoyed.

Miranda, undaunted by Cora's harsh words, reached down a hand to haul up Casper and then climbed down the ladder herself.

Cora followed soon after,

Tyler tried to squish down the unease in his stomach; he didn't want to go back there. To where they all almost died, where the panic had nearly consumed him when he watched Opal collapse, sure she was dead.

But the thought of Cora going down that ladder where she would be with Irene without Tyler to jump in if things got too out of hand... Tyler didn't want that to happen. He *couldn't* let that happen.

That was the only thought that drove him as he slid down the ladder and back into the gloom he hoped never to come across again.

Though the air didn't smell nearly as bad, with moonlight pouring in through the open hatch, Tyler still shivered at the long shadows. He worked as quickly as he could, opening up the sacks and buckets and pushing food and clothes into his backpack. Nolan, Miranda, Cora, and, surprisingly, Casper did the same.

Tyler kept a watchful eye on the hatch door; he didn't want it to close again.

When the bunker had been picked clean and it was time to leave, Tyler was surprised to find that he felt a prick of regret. Despite his trepidation about returning. He almost wanted to stay here; it seemed safer than the caves. With man-made steel surrounding him, buried underground where no monster could reach...

But what if the emergency lever was a one-time use thing? The door sealed far too easily...

It was impossible to get in.

And it was impossible to get out.

"So. My idiot daughter returns." Her voice was cracked. Garbled. Tinged with anger and sounding half insane.

Tyler stiffened instantly, his whole body going on edge.

Irene stalked out of the gloom.

Cora was standing tall, her chin raised, but Tyler could see her hands; they were quivering and balled into fists as if she was waiting for the perfect moment to run.

"You don't sound very grateful, Irene." Cora snapped.

"What happened to calling me mommy, little girl?" Irene sneered.

Tyler flinched; Cora hadn't called her mother by any name except Irene in years, ever since Irene first laid a hand on her.

Nolan, Miranda, and Casper were shrinking around the edges of the mother and daughter, quietly picking things up and throwing

119

them out the hatch. Tyler moved closer to stand protectively by Cora's shoulder.

He could feel her relaxing in his presence, and she sank into the arm he wound around her shoulders.

Irene suddenly snapped her gaze to Tyler's, her eyes burning.

"Oh, so *now* you stand by my daughter?!" Irene sneered. Her gaze was malevolent.

Tyler felt a flash of foreboding. Where was she going with this? He never knew what Irene would say next.

Irene suddenly canceled. "He's never going to be yours, little girl." she snarled. "He already chose the other one. If not already. He will."

A flash of lightning-like horror flared over Tyler. D-Did she mean Opal? Did she know what he had been feeling?

Cora's face was also filled with horror, her gaze fixed on her mother's.

Tyler couldn't see her hurt; no matter what he felt for Opal, he didn't want to see her like this.

He just wanted Irene to shut up.

But he wasn't that lucky.

"You should know that while you were still sleeping, little princess, he had already woken up with *her*." Irene leered, slowly moving towards Cora. "Comforting her, hugging her. While you slept soundly."

"Stay away from her!" Tyler snapped, but he was paralyzed. They had been doing nothing wrong when he had hugged Opal after she had had nightmares, but he didn't think anyone had known about it; he'd thought it was a secret. Their little secret.

120

He hadn't imagined or seen Irene leering at them from the shadows.

Irene was *wrong.* Twisting his actions into something they weren't. He was being ridiculous. He had known Opal for hours. Why was he thinking about her like that?

"Enough!" he snapped at Irene. "You're horrible, alright? She just had a bad dream, and I hugged her. We are *friends.*" He didn't dare look at Cora; everything he said seemed wrong. He was digging himself a grave already. All he could do was keep his eyes on Irene, hating how he felt so guilty when he shouldn't have. "Now we're leaving and sealing this door; either you can come with us or die." Tyler didn't care how harsh his voice sounded; at this moment, he honestly did want Irene to die.

Irene stopped laughing. "You won't get rid of me that easily, pretty boy," Irene murmured darkly, her eyes narrowing with a thinly veiled threat.

She stomped forward, glaring darkly at Nolan and Miranda as she passed. She paused as she came face to face with Casper, standing by the entrance to the ladder and the exit.

Casper's face was impassive, but his mask slipped slightly to reveal confusion when Irene continued to stare at him. He shifted his grasp on his packs and held her gaze. Irene's face twisted into a scowl, worse than usual, as her beady eyes filled with unprecedented hatred.

They didn't move for a second, and then Irene feinted forward, jumping at him and then stopping inches before slamming him to the wall.

Tyler could hear Casper's cry of shock as he stumbled backward.

121

Irene's heavy breathing dissolved into fits of laughter. Sending one last glowering look at Casper, she crawled up the ladder with heavy footsteps.

"Right. She's a maniac. I'm in a bunker with maniacs." Casper mumbled, shaking his silver-tipped black hair out of his eyes as he followed Irene up the ladder.

Miranda and Nolan exchanged a loaded glance of laughter before following. Tyler didn't know what to make of the instantaneous loathing Irene seemed to covet for Casper, but at this moment, it was the least of his worries.

And suddenly, as Tyler and Cora were left alone, the air became charged with tension. He could feel the dynamic shift as if it was an actual switch.

He couldn't take the silence.

"Cora?" Tyler whispered to her; she seemed frozen, alone, scared. Eyes staring off into the distance. She was standing a few feet away from him, rubbing her hands up and down her bare arms. He resisted the urge to go over and put his arms around her in case she was mad at him.

This was only Irene's fault, making him feel all guilty for nothing. He wasn't doing anything wrong.

Cora caught Tyler's gaze, and her large blue eyes were brimming with hurt. She turned on her heel, ignoring his signs and calls of protest, and fled up the ladder.

Tyler felt a flash of annoyance. This was overreacting! Why did Cora have to be like this?

Their friendship was important to him; why couldn't she see that? He didn't want to lose it for anything.

122

Tyler sighed, pulling himself up the ladder, casting one last dark glance at the bunker where he had been trapped; he slammed it shut, hopefully for the last ever time.

It was a quiet, jumpy walk back to the caves; Tyler felt on edge like every nerve in his body was a live wire as he watched the shadows.

Cora wasn't talking to him; she wasn't even looking at him; her walk was quick and purposeful, marching ahead and avoiding both him and Irene.

The turmoil and anger were stamped clear across Cora's face. And it was making Irene smile.

She's sick. Enjoying watching her daughter suffer like that. Tyler thought, worried.

The bedraggled group of six finally came into the clearing. The wind whistled through the trees, and the clouds began to pull back in the sky, revealing a brilliant moon and a full coat of stars.

The moon won't keep anything away.

Tyler paused by the sheer entranceway to the cliffs. With Nolan's help, he started chucking their bags and supplies over the edge and into the dark entrance. When everything was over, Tyler turned to Nolan.

"Boost me up?"

Nolan braced his back against the sheer stone, and Tyler jumped up on his shoulders- hauling himself over the top by the tips of his fingers.

Tyler straightened up. Inside the cave. Safe.

But it didn't feel safe.

He stood in the large cave entranceway. Stalactites sprung down from the ceiling, and the sound of small creatures scuttling around the stone sent shivers down his skin.

The shadows were long. The crevices deep.

The air was cold and dank, and suddenly, he longed for the cold wind once more.

He wanted light.

Tyler ignored the shivering down his body, and he turned back to the entrance of the cave.

He bent down to his knees and hauled up Miranda, Casper (who refused his hand), and Irene.

His stomach twisted a little as he turned down to Cora and offered his hand. It was all he could do.

She took it, much to his delight, and he pulled her up. His other hand reached to grab her shoulder as she stumbled a little, and for the briefest of moments, their faces were only inches from each other. Tyler almost couldn't breathe as he watched her eyes find his. They stayed still for a moment, time frozen. Before Cora blinked and looked away, biting her lip.

Tyler tried to push back frustration at Cora's pettiness. It was nothing, really, between him and Opal; it was only her perception. But he didn't expect she would be too happy when, in the morning, he would announce that he planned to go find Opal and rescue her. Tyler shivered as the night air blew through stones, puffing out his shirt.

"Let's go deeper," Miranda whispered, shivering. "I-I don't want to sleep with the thought of *them* only feet away from me."

124

They walked deeper, past the large cave they had climbed into. The moment they stepped a bit farther into the darkness, it seemed to explode. Tiny black bodies surged from every crevice and shadow- shrieking and whirling until the air was nothing but flapping wings and the shrill cries of hundreds of bats.

Cora screamed, and Tyler jerked towards her.

But the next second, the mass of bats swirled and flooded out of the cave. In one big body, they were gone just as quickly as they had come.

Tyler faded back away from Cora and took a deep breath as he stared around the cave, letting his heartbeat return to normal.

This second cave was just as big, if not a little bigger than the first cave, but with a small entranceway. Dotted around the far side of the cave were smaller jagged entrance holes and tunnels leading to different-sized caves.

Cora didn't say anything; she didn't ask for clothes to change into or food. She just picked up a blanket and practically ran into one of the smaller caves.

Tyler sighed dejectedly as Casper and Irene did the same, leaving him with Miranda and Nolan. He didn't bother protesting about how they should check the caves first to make sure there were no lingering bats or creatures.

Already, their 'group' was dispersing and unraveling. Frail hopes of sticking together started to fade in Tyler's mind.

"Give her time, man." Nolan patted Tyler on the back sympathetically.

"Just tell her how you feel," Miranda added softly. "Talk to her in the morning when she's cooled off."

125

"Go get some sleep. We'll keep watch tonight and camp out here. You prepare for the morning." Nolan smiled.

Tyler sighed again, too tired to take any food. "Thanks guys." At least he had two people to count on. After everything that day, he was glad he had met them. Them and Opal. And Sasha.

He walked away, slipping into the cave next to Cora's before turning once to see both of them huddled together, their heads touching. Even from his far vantage point, he could hear their hushed voices and gentle laughs.

He envied them how easily they could forget about everything that had happened today. How could they forget about their family?

The cave was cold and small. There was not even enough room to fully stretch out. It was claustrophobic, all the cold bits of stone pressing into every part of his body. He hated it instantly. Was he supposed to *sleep* there?

But what else could he do? He was lucky to be alive. He should stop complaining. Half of the people he had grown up with were probably dead. The thought sobered him, a dull cloud shifting over his mind.

Tyler curled up on the ground, trying to shift into a comfortable position. He missed sleeping beside Cora, the two of them facing out the world together. He tried to ignore the sound of the wind whistling through the cave. He tried to ignore the images flashing in his mind of an army waiting outside, his family in the forefront. Their eyes were dead and lifeless, skin-pasty, and arms stretched out to rip him apart.

Zombies.

126

Tyler shivered more. He tried to tell himself he was safe. Tried to tell himself that they could never get to him.

But he knew.

He knew since that first spark of the fire had fallen.

This was a zombie apocalypse, and he would never ever be safe.

11

TYLER

Tyler slipped in and out of sleep, the darkness fragmented by sounds from outside and by his own worried thoughts. But at one point, he did dream. And he wished he hadn't.

He was running in the hallways. The hallways of... He didn't know where or how he got there, but he was there. These hallways were endless. An endless row of a rosy red carpet underneath his feet. Thousands of doors lined the walls on either side of them. In between each door was a brass candle.

And suddenly, it all cut off. The space in front of him started to bend. The carpet began to melt forward. The walls started to splinter and break as if a child had stretched puddy; the scenery began to stretch.

Tyler screamed as he found himself on a downward slant. The hallways were burnt away, revealing nothing but blackness in front of him. An endless void that he would soon succumb to.

He was going to fall. He was going to die. Zombies were waiting for him in the darkness. Swimming in the lava that was consuming the hallway. He was going to fall. The zombies would suck him up like quicksand.

Just when Tyler couldn't hold on any longer, when his arms began to ache from keeping himself from tumbling into the void, one of the last remaining doorways swung open.

Standing on the threshold, haloed in light, was Opal, her hand reaching out to grasp his and pull him to safety. He didn't hesitate as he grabbed her hand, their fingers locking, and she pulled him out, out of the dissolving hallway and the zombies that were waiting for him on the other side.

He could see everything in that void.

The zombies reached their hands out to tear him apart, and he saw his family, their burning, tortured faces, as he ran out of the house.

He saw Sasha, her eyes closed as she drifted into blackness....

But it was Opal who was in front of him and led him away from the blistering lava as the door slammed shut, and they were safe, safe in the empty hallway once again as if nothing had happened.

Opal smiled up at him, her eyes shining. "I'm glad you're here, Tyler," she whispered, brushing his hair with her hand.

"Me too," Tyler muttered. Something felt strange about the rosiness of this dream, as if, for some reason, he didn't have Opal safe with him in the hallway—as if she was gone.

And then she was gone.

Tyler gasped in shock as he found Opal turning to smoke in his hands, horror gripping his heart as he tried to keep Opal with him. Trying desperately to grab onto those last strands of her essence that were drifting away.

But it was no use; she was gone.

"Opal!" he cried, struggling to keep the desperation out of his voice as he screamed into an empty hallway.

"Tyler." It was a different voice this time.

A softer one, one he knew quite well and always made his heart race.

Cora appeared, her soft blue eyes shining as she took Tyler's hands. "Forget about Opal. I'm the one with you now." She whispered.

129

Her face shone with such delight and happiness. How could Tyler not give her what she wanted? So he slowly nodded, thoughts of Opal gone from his mind. Cora was with him now. How could he think about Opal when she was shining so brightly in his arms?

But suddenly, her face twisted; the happy smile was gone from her face, melting into an expression of pure, undeniable pain. She let out the softest of moans, becoming limp in Tyler's arms as she slid down on her knees to the carpeted floor, bringing Tyler down with her.

"Cora?" he whispered, his heart thundering. What was wrong with her?

She gave no response.

That's when Tyler saw the spear in her back, through her stomach, as the dark stain of red slowly spread through her clothes.

"T- Tyler." she gasped, clutching his hands.

"Cora!" Tyler cried; she was dying in his arms, and he could feel it. What would he do without her? How would he survive? How could he help her? "No!" he whispered as slowly the life drained out of her body right in front of him. And her eyes flickered shut.

She was dead.

Cora Irene was dead.

Tyler awoke screaming; his head throbbed as he jolted upright. Cora.

She was mad at him, and he couldn't stand it any longer. Why hadn't he ended their silence earlier? Now, during this apocalypse, when every day could be their last, every minute could be the last spent together, and he'd simply thrown it away? What was he thinking?

Sunlight was pouring into his cave; this should have relaxed him, but his heart was still thundering from his dream.

130

He flung off the blankets he was clutching and ran out of his cave, nearly skidding and falling into Cora's.

Her cave was empty, her blankets tossed in a hurry as if she had jumped awake just like him. Tyler tried not to let the disappointment flood through him. Where was she? She hadn't *left*.... had she?

No.

She *couldn't* have.

She *wouldn't*.

Tyler almost sprinted into the main cave, seeing Miranda and Nolan passed out in a heap, their fingers clutching each other.

"Nolan!" Tyler hissed. He didn't want to wake them up, especially when sleep seemed so hard to come by with the nightmares he knew would be plaguing all of them.

But the panic of not being able to find Cora was enough for him to roughly shake his friend's shoulder until Nolan stretched up, rubbing his eyes.

"Geez, Tyler. What do you want?" he grumbled.

"Where's Cora?" Tyler demanded, his voice sounding too desperate. He took a deep breath, trying to take the edge off.

"Relax! She just went to the river to wash off. You can go find her if you want." Nolan sighed, rolling his eyes.

He knew it was irrational to think- after all, it was just a dream- but it was so vivid- for a moment, he had been scared Cora was dying somewhere.

"Good luck. She has a tongue like claws, that one." Nolan muttered. "I don't envy you."

"Thanks, man." Tyler grinned, his mood instantly lighter, even if he did have to face Cora. But he was done tip-toeing around her.

131

"Be careful! I know there's not a cloud in the sky, but don't let your guard down! People get desperate, you know. Some survivors might attack you." Nolan called after him, his words chilling Tyler to the bone, but he forced himself onward.

He slid down the rock face, hardly feeling the sharp stings as the rock dug through his shirt and into his skin.

The grass outside was completely trampled as if hundreds of people had passed by last night.

Or hundreds of monsters. The thought was uneasy in his mind. Perhaps he hadn't imagined the groaning last night. Or the sound of thousands of feet.

But it meant their cave was safe for now.

He was tempted to go check if Sasha's body was still there, but the thought of Cora overruled the thought. He set off at a brisk pace down the ravine towards the outcropping of pine trees and the river.

The river was known for the herring runs; it was far from any town, but normally, people would gather to watch the herring make their long journey to their breeding grounds.

It was a beautiful river, one of the longest in New Hampshire and certainly in Duxbury. It stretched all the way from its source up in the mountains down to one of the lakes down east.

It was only a short walk before Tyler was there, at the riverside. It was truly one of the most gorgeous places Tyler had ever been. The river sparkled in the morning sunlight, sending beams of sunlight off the rocks sticking out of the sparkling, clear water. Dark pine trees lined the banks on the opposite side, with the snowy white peaks of the mountains rising behind them, making the view seem straight out of a postcard.

Tyler smiled, watching the herring jump out of the water briefly before diving back in with a splash, sending sparkles of water across the sunbaked rocks, turning them black with water.

Tyler walked closer, his eyes on the lapping crystal-clear water on the sides of the bank. A sense of peace descended on him as he glanced around. Even if the peace was all fake and it was about to be shattered... he enjoyed it nonetheless.

And then he saw her, a couple hundred yards down the bank, washing her hair in the tidal pools, sending sparkles of water down her back as she tossed back her golden hair.

Tyler couldn't help but smile a little bit as he started down the riverside towards her.

She looked up, too. And for a second, they stood there. And she smiled. Just a little bit to let him know that it was fine; whatever weird tension between them had disappeared in the sunlight. And he was happy to stand there for a second, soaking in the peace of nature and the presence of his best friend.

That was before the people emerged from the trees on the opposite bank.

At first, Tyler felt a surge of hope, adults! Other *people*! Perhaps they could help them-

But the hope faded almost as quickly as it had come when he examined this bedraggled group more closely. There were around four of them, all in their early twenties and all men. Though not zombies, Tyler could tell they weren't doing much better. Many of their eyes were sunken in and hollow with hunger, missing the spark of life and almost mirroring the zombie's unblinking stare. Their clothes were in tatters and stained with mud and dirt, and all of them were armed to

133

the teeth, daggers clutched in their hands, and thick clubs strapped to their backs. The only comfort Tyler could see was that at least no visible guns were shown.

In a flash, Nolan's words from this morning rang in Tyler's ears, and he cursed himself for his stupidity.

The last fragile hope that the group hadn't seen the two of them yet was dashed when the leader (Tyler assumed he was the leader because he was standing in the front and looked the least starved as if he was stealing all the food for himself) fixed his dark green eyes on Tyler, his mouth twisting into a sneer beneath his mop of a black beard and his hands twitched towards one of the knives bolted to his belt. But then his gaze slid from Tyler to reach hungrily toward Cora.

Tyler's stomach clenched; he didn't want this man to look at Cora like that or ever look at her. He wanted to cross the distance between them in one big leap and stretch his arms out to shield her from the world and protect her. Protect her like he failed to protect Opal. And Calico. And his parents. And Sasha.

Tyler pushed the thoughts away and quickly moved down the riverside to stand by Cora; she seemed to straighten up a bit in his presence, and though no words were exchanged, he could feel her lean on him, and he was grateful for her closeness.

The gang of men stalked closer, staying on their side of the river, but with the lack of rain, the river was low enough that they could easily cross on the stones jutting out from the current.

"Hey hey hey, pretty girl! What are you doing all the way out here?" one of the men called out, his voice jeering. Another one cat called.

Tyler felt Cora flinch. He leaned down to twine their fingers together, holding on tightly as his heart pounded against his rib cage.

"We're just passing through," Tyler called feebly, his voice echoing over the water.

The leader turned his mocking eyes from Cora to Tyler, narrowing in contempt. "Where are your parents, little boy?" he called, his voice booming.

The damning truth almost slipped from his lips, weakened by his own grief, but thankfully, Cora saved him in the nick of time.

"They are just over the trees; they'll be coming to check on us in moments." She said smoothly, without an ounce of fear, and Tyler had to admire both her courage and the calm mask she wore.

The leader's smug expression faltered for a moment, taking in Cora's lie and wondering how much of easy prey they would be. Tyler's heart soured with hope, but then one of the men stepped out from the crowd, whispering something into his leader's ear that seemed to sedate him.

"In that case, give us all you have, and we'll be on our way." the leader demanded threateningly, hand twitching closer to the knife on his belt.

"We don't have anything." Tyler protested, taking a step backward and pushing Cora with him.

The leader curled his lip. "I doubt it. Boys, go get 'em." He nodded his head, and the group surged forward, crossing the river at a rapid pace.

Tyler barely had time to process before they were on him. Three full-grown men surrounded him and Cora, eyes empty of any sort of mercy.

135

"Stop!" Tyler protested weakly as hopes of escape became smaller and smaller as the men closed ranks around them. "I promise we don't have anything!"

Cora was whimpering beside him, shaking like a leaf, and Tyler knew he wasn't the aspect of bravery either.

And then they attacked; grubby and rough hands closed around Tyler's shoulders and yanked him away from Cora.

"No!" he cried, fighting to get away. "Cora!"

Cora was disappearing behind a mass of moving bodies; he could hear her screams and their laughs but couldn't even get a glimpse of her golden hair.

Someone struck him hard over the head, and he let out a cry of pain, reeling from the blow. It took all of his strength to slam his foot into one of his captors' feet.

With a yell of anger, he felt the grip on his shoulders slacken ever so slightly, and he pulled free.

He didn't stop to see what their reactions would be. Instead, he jumped forward to try and throw some of the men off Cora. They were going after her earrings, pretty gold ones that would have been worth a good amount if they weren't in an apocalypse.

She was fending them off as best as she could, biting any that got too close and kicking fiercely, even as one of the men grabbed her arms and tried to hold her back.

Someone pulled at Tyler, and he stumbled. "Cora!" he yelled.

Cora's wide blue eyes caught his for the briefest of moments, bright with panic, but in the next moment, they widened even more with pain.

Cora let out a scream as one of the men lunged forward with his knife and slashed Cora across the stomach.

To Tyler's horror, he watched dark red blood seep from the wound and stain Cora's dress, spreading rapidly.

One of the men laughed. It was like a dull red haze that swept over Tyler's eyes; it was just too much; he couldn't watch his best friend in pain like that.

The knife came down again, slashing another gash through Cora's stomach, and Tyler felt as if the blade was cutting his own flesh as well.

The red haze in front of Tyler's vision cut everything else out, and with all his might, he shoved forward; his hands collided with one of the men. Caught off balance, the man let out a shout and toppled backward into the river. Tyler didn't even pause to watch the man splutter as he was pulled downstream. Instead, he marveled at his new freedom before turning to Cora.

His heart sank, however, at the sight before him. One of the men had his arms secured around Cora's, holding her back, while the other held his grimy dagger towards Cora's pale throat.

"One more move, boy, and we'll all see how she bleeds!" the man growled, eyes narrowed.

Tyler was frozen; he didn't know what to do. All he could do was stand there helplessly.

The man's gaze was suddenly drawn away from Tyler's, narrowing in suspicion as he fixated on something over Tyler's shoulder.

And then a dagger whizzed through the air. Tyler felt it beside his ear, missing him by an inch before burying itself inside the man's chest.

Tyler watched as his eyes widened in surprise, drifting down slowly, almost comically, to the intruder inside his body. And then his eyes widened, finding their way back to Tyler before his knees buckled and he crumpled to the ground. Blood spilled out in a pool around him, and the dagger dropped off to the side.

The last remaining man shouted out in surprise at his companion's sudden death, and Cora took advantage of it; she whirled around and pushed him as hard as she could until he careened into the water and was swept away in the current.

Tyler stared, dumbfounded at the gore around him, his heart thundering. Did that really happen? His heart lurched at the sight of the motionless body on the ground, of the unnamed man who was suddenly gone. And those men that had been swept into the river...

But all thoughts and remorse were driven from his mind when he caught eye with Cora. She opened her mouth in a soundless cry before her legs buckled, and she fell to the ground, blood pooling from the wounds in her stomach.

"Cora!" he cried, jumping forward to fall to his knees beside her. He tucked his hands under her head and pulled her forward onto his lap. She was deathly pale. "Cora, please." he gasped. "Wake up."

"That's not going to help." someone suddenly snapped from behind him.

Tyler nearly jumped out of his skin, shielding Cora as best as he could. He craned his neck. His heart dropped in relief when he saw Casper walk calmly out of the trees; putting two and two together, he realized that Casper must have been the one to throw the dagger to save both Tyler and Cora's life.

But gratitude would be saved for later.

"Please, Casper." Tyler gasped. "We need to do something."

For a terrifying moment, Tyler thought Casper was going to shrug and offer no help and move on. But instead, he nodded stiffly and bent down, pulling Cora up into his arms.

"Come on," he said brusquely. "Let's go to the caves, Miranda and Nolan have a first aid kit."

Tyler was too shocked for words, eyes fixed right on Cora. Blood was flowing even more freely from when Casper had picked her up. Every step felt like an eternity.

How bad was their luck to have Cora injured like this?

And I couldn't protect her.

I failed.

The trip back felt like a blur; Casper silently passed Cora into Tyler's arms when they reached the entrance to the caves. Casper pushed himself into the entrance and came back to carry Cora.

Tyler watched as he laid Cora gently down on the rock; she looked horrible; blood was pumping too fast from her chest, and his hands were doing little to nothing to stop it.

Suddenly, Cora's eyelids flickered briefly. "T-Tyler-" she muttered softly.

Tyler felt a flash of fear like never before. He couldn't lose her. Not after his family. Not after Opal.

Please don't die. Come on.

Come on, Cora!

She lifted her hand weakly, and Tyler didn't hesitate to grip it, holding his blood-soaked hand with hers as he pressed her hand to his cheek.

"I-I'm sorry," whispered Tyler.

Cora's eyes flicked weakly one more time.

Don't die, Cora.

I can't live without you.

If you live.

I promise.

I'll choose you.

12

OPAL

An old man in a stained white lab coat was crouching over a hard metal floor, his shaking hands riddled with arthritis, tearing through his tangled, erratic white hair. His head suddenly jerked up, and Opal caught a glance of eerily familiar deep brown eyes that gave a hint they could radiate kindness and warmth. But today, his eyes had a faraway look. His eyes darted around his grim surroundings, a cell that looked like a metal box with no windows. He muttered words, some unintelligible, but some Opal was able to make out. "No. If I eat the food, timeline seventy thousand will sift through timeline thirty-seven hundred; no, no, timeline seventy-nine is shifting! Wait! Wait! They are coming!" the man screamed. Suddenly, he launched himself onto the floor and lay there, hardly moving.

They? *Opal peered closer.* Zombies? How would they get into a cell? *She thought, bewildered.* What an odd dream.

The door across the small cell suddenly rattled fiercely and burst open; six men crowded into the small place, filling every crevice with their bulk.

Their gazes were dark and forbidding as they stared coldly down at the shivering man.

With a jolt, Opal realized they had the green camouflage uniforms of the FBI.

What in the world? Is this a government prison?

"The president wants to see you," growled one of them.

Ah, so it is. What would the *president* want with a man like that?

"No!" screamed the man, with a sudden note of hysteria in his voice. "Tell him that I already know that she's looking for me! All the threats he'll make.... It's the most likely timeline!" he screamed. "I know it all!" His eyes widened deliriously. "Please, if I don't make it out of this room, tell my family that I left them beac-" The man's eyes suddenly widened even more. "Oh no, I didn't see this one coming. Stop-" he cried.

A soldier clonked the man over the head with the butt of his rifle, and the delirious man went slamming to the ground.

"Huh. Not very bright, is he?" asked one of the soldiers offhandedly.

"Nope."

What in the world is this?

"The president is getting impatient, I reckon he's going to destroy it, dunno why he doesn't want it getting out; be good for the world." muttered one of the soldiers to the others.

"Don't think like that! He'll have you killed." hissed another one as he dragged the unconscious man out of the cell, slamming the door behind them.

The vision began to fade, and this time, Opal didn't fight it.

Of all the visions Opal had, this left her the most bewildered and confused. She assumed that her visions were all relevant- in one way or another.

The one about Amelia.

The one about Cora's mom.

The one that helped Opal prevent Cora from kissing Tyler.

But this one....

142

It was so strange, a president threatening a delirious old man? And why did that man feel so familiar? Like Opal knew him... Acana Magic.

If these visions were magic like she was beginning to believe...

Was a man like that trapped somewhere in a government facility?

If it was real, then why was the *president* bothering with a delirious nutcase when there was an *apocalypse* going on?

If that's in the future. Is there a future when the world survives this apocalypse?

Who's looking for him?

She.

Timelines.

He talked about timelines.

Timelines of the future?

Does he have Acana Magic?

Am I not alone with Delphina?

Does he know what's happening to me?

Opal awoke, blinking open her eyes. To her great relief, she found that she was no longer in the claustrophobic tank. But her new accommodations weren't much better.

Much like in her vision of Amelia, she was strapped to a metal bed, inclined forward so that if there weren't the metal bands holding her down by the wrists, ankles, and stomach, she would have slid off.

She felt even more exposed out here in the lab, where anything could get to her. The lab seemed deserted, but Opal didn't trust her eyes; she could imagine things hiding behind those metal contraptions, and she could imagine scientists lurking from the shadows.

Opal shuddered; she hated every second in the lab but didn't know how to get out. She couldn't even rely on her family to rescue her.

I should have rescued them first. Then they could have rescued me. Opal thought bitterly.

She could count on no one. No one was coming to save her. And she didn't like to leave things to her own incompetence.

Tyler. Perhaps he will come for me. Perhaps Miranda or Nolan. Not poor Sasha, but I knew they liked me. I helped them get out. Tyler *liked me.*

Opal thought suddenly, warmed by the thought. She couldn't keep back a fierce stab of longing when she thought of Tyler; she wished she was back there with him. *I bet* Cora *will keep him from rescuing me.* Opal thought with a flash of unfair jealousy.

"Hi!" chirped a voice suddenly.

Opal flinched, her heart pounding. She had gotten so used to being ignored.

A boy around her age with dark brown hair swept over his sparklingly green eyes was standing right in front of her. He wore a white lab coat, much like the scientist Opal had seen, but he seemed more like an accessory than a uniform. Opal could see his casual jeans and t-shirt underneath it. This boy was staring at her quite hard, and something inside Opal shivered. There was something about his eyes that unnerved her, something familiar. He was a scientist, no doubt. That wasn't a good thing.

"And, who are you?" Opal asked, trying to keep the quiver out of her voice; perhaps if she was demanding enough, he could tell her where the hell she was.

"I'm Josh!" the boy replied with a grin. "I live here."

"What's that got to do with me?" Opal asked harshly, her mind whirling. What kind of kid *lived* here?

Josh looked bewildered. "Nothing. What's that supposed to mean?"

Is this guy thick? Opal thought, annoyed. "You're a scientist. Why are you talking to me?"

"Oh." Josh suddenly slipped the coat from his shoulders, bundling it up under his arm. "Is that better?" he asked, opening his arms.

Opal rolled her eyes. "No, idiot."

Josh seemed to be determined not to lose his cheery nature as he turned to her. "The scientists here are expected to spend their whole lives here, but they're not restricted from having a family. Do you honestly think with all these people here, two of them wouldn't fall in love? Er, well, not really love, but still."

Opal grunted. Thoughts began to spiral in her mind as gears of curiosity turned inside of her. How many kids were there? Were they being trained to be scientists? Were they all this weird? Had they ever been outside? Could they help her?

Where was she?

Josh smiled again. "I'm the result. I've lived here my whole life with the other offspring. I'm telling you, it's horrible; some kids take a liking to it and follow in their parent's footsteps, but not me. No, I'm trying to help as many people as I can."

Opal felt a flash of sudden hope, dimming all other emotions. "Can you help me? Can you help me escape?" *Or tell me about my family? Please let that vision not be true.* She begged silently as she

145

thought back to the vision of Amelia hovering near death, Delphina's cruel voice echoing through the room.

Josh shrugged. "I mean, I'll try- I've tried lots. No success yet, but still. Nobody here really cares much about me, so I come here a lot. Dad wants me to be a scientist."

"Okay," Opal muttered absentmindedly, thoughts still on her sister as Josh chattered on.

"Yeah, my dad is all about carrying out the family legacy and so on; he makes me do horrible things!" Josh's face darkened, and he looked at the ground.

For the first time, Opal spared a thought for Josh. Perhaps he was just as trapped as she was. "What kind of terrible things?" she blurted.

Josh shuddered. "There was this kid in here earlier; she was about twelve, I think- My dad was so persistent! He kept going and going; it was horrible. He was looking for something he didn't find." breathed Josh as he shuddered. "They moved her, I haven't seen her today. Got you instead." He smiled brightly as if this was a great change.

Opal's throat was coated with bile. Twelve years old- could it be her? What were the chances? No. But if Josh had *dared* hurt her little sister...

Looking for something.

Could these scientists be aware of Acana Magic? And if Opal had it... they could have looked for it in Amelia.

Opal's body constricted when she thought of the ways they would have tried. Torture. *Who were these people?*

If Josh had hurt her...

146

Then, he would be the first one she got her revenge on when she got out of there.

"What was the girl's name?" she whispered, both her hands pressed up against the glass, her body clenched in knots.

Josh looked surprised. "Dunno, I think it was something like... Oliva? Emily? Amelia?"

Opal couldn't think; she couldn't breathe. She imagined Amelia strapped to one of these cold beds as masked strangers-especially Josh moved around her, eliciting agonizing screams.

"Where is my sister!? You lying *snake*!" screamed Opal, emotion bursting out of her body like a tidal wave. Perhaps it was misdirected, but she didn't care. She was furious. She couldn't believe she had missed her sister by a *day*.

Josh looked even more surprised. He scurried back on the floor and climbed to his feet, brushing his hair out of his eyes as he stared at her.

"You know her?" he gasped; he seemed as shocked as Opal was.

Opal's blood boiled. "Yes! Where is she?!" Opal demanded fiercely.

"I don't know! Dad wouldn't t-" Josh started, but a grouchy voice suddenly cut him off.

Delsea stalked into the room. "What are you doing here?!" she snapped at Josh, completely ignoring Opal.

"Where is that girl that Dad brought in earlier?" asked Josh innocently.

Opal's anger at Josh began to fade. It boiled and curdled, moving on from her old target and towards this unnamed force of an organization that kept her captive.

147

"Stop whatever you are doing here, Josh." Delsea snapped again. "We don't have time for your games."

"*I* don't have time for your games." Josh bit back. "That girl. Where is she?"

Opal winced. She didn't care for Josh, but she knew Delsea wouldn't handle that type of sass, and she didn't want to see him pummeled right in front of her. She had seen enough violence for a lifetime.

Delsea seemed to swell like a balloon. Lunging forward, she grabbed Josh by the ear and started hauling him out of the lab as he protested fiercely. "Get out! Go to your room! And I'll make sure to tell your father about your misbehavior!" screamed Delsea as she threw Josh out and slammed the door shut.

Oh dear. I hope Delsea isn't Josh's mother.

Josh shot Opal one last look. *Sorry.* He mouthed.

"Josh!" Opal suddenly called. "My name is Opal."

A ghost of a smile flitted over his face. "Opal," he muttered, trying the sound on his lips.

The door slammed shut in his face.

Opal stared at the spot he had just been. That was one of the strangest encounters she'd had in a while. What would she have done if she was born into a place like this?

Would she hurt innocent girls like Josh was forced to?

To survive?

Maybe.

I would have.

I think anyone would have.

But as Opal stared at where Josh had been seconds before, she found all thoughts of Tyler were driven out of her mind by this new strange boy in front of her, for better or for worse.

"Trying to woo over our young?" Delsea growled, bustling around Opal's prison.

"Where's my family?" Opal tried to push some defiance into her voice, but she couldn't hold back her stutter.

Delsea ignored her. Opal strained against her bonds, but it was like pushing against an iron wall; nothing happened.

Delsea was pounding on the control panel next to Opal's bed, her brow furrowed in concentration.

Before Opal knew what was happening, Delsea clicked a button on the side of her bed, and the whole contraption began to shift, moving slowly until Opal was vertical, as if she was standing up.

A dark yawning hole suddenly opened up by Opal's feet, the floor panels sliding away.

Opal screamed- realizing what was about to happen as suddenly the bonds holding her to the bed hissed and retracted into the metal.

Free! At last!

But just as Opal was realizing she could move again, she found herself crumpling feet first into the dark chute.

Choking in horror, Opal desperately tried to fight and escape- tried to pull herself out of the hole, but Delsea just poked her back in.

Opal lost her grip. She cried out once before she found herself plummeting into darkness.

Opal couldn't see a thing. Air rushed past her, and the darkness pressed into her eyes. She tucked her head in her hands, terror filling her as she imagined what was waiting for her.

She was going too fast- she didn't want to die-

Opal felt a vision coming on to her; she tried to shut it down, but the desire to be brought away from the pain and horror of falling pulled at her, and she felt herself being drawn away into the familiar darkness.

Opal was in a dark and dingy cell, much like the one with the crazy man in it from before, only this one had a black grate fixed into the ceiling.

A buzzing noise filled the cell, and a tall man walked through a large metal door and entered the cell at a brisk pace. His face was screwed up in disgust as he surveyed his dank surroundings.

"What do you want?" growled a voice from the shadows.

"You are needed at the lab, Rose." the man responded coldly. He looked oddly familiar; Opal was sure she had seen him somewhere but just couldn't put her finger on it.

The shadows seemed to flicker and bend as a shape loomed forward, and a voice emerged from the shadows.

Opal couldn't tell if her hair was naturally black or if it was just so matted and tangled that it appeared that way. Her deep brown eyes fixed on the man as she stalked forward, and her faded lips twisted into a scowl of deep hatred. Her jawbones were far too prominent on her pale face; this woman had been here for a very long time.

She seemed familiar as well. Something about her eyes... something about that expression...

That resilience.

Opal had seen it before.

150

"What if I don't want to go to the lab?" snarled the woman with so much venom and hatred in her voice that Opal was surprised that the man didn't flinch.

"You don't have a choice. Move, or I'll kill her." the man responded, his voice dull as if he was used to the same threat rolling off his tongue.

Who is he talking about?

A spark of fear lit up the woman's eyes, and she walked stiffly forward, trying to regain some of her dignity. This girl, Rose, spat on the man's shoes as she passed.

The man's face darkened, and he jabbed her hard in the back, pushing her forward and slamming the cell door shut behind both of them.

Then, the vision did something that Opal had never seen before. It sifted and turned to darkness like usual, but this time, Opal didn't open her eyes back to the present. She zoomed right back into another vision; shape and color materialized before her eyes, and she found herself in entirely different surroundings.

This time, she was in a lab, much like the one she had been trapped in earlier, with the same dark tanks and cold beds.

Strapped to a metal bed was the woman, but something had changed. Her eyes were wild with fear; any shred of dignity that she had managed to cling to was stripped from her body. Scientists in long white coats bustled around her with tools that had twisted metal ends clutched in their hands.

Oh, I don't want to see this. Opal moaned in her mind, trying to wrench her body out of this vision like she did in dreams. But this wasn't a typical dream. It didn't work.

151

The woman fixed her gaze on the clear, white glass screen ahead of her. Behind it, the man from the cell was watching, his expression cold and unfeeling.

"Please," gasped the woman. "My powers are strong enough! Don't do it! Acana Magic can kill you! It can make you delirious!" screamed the woman, and she began to struggle more desperately. "I'm strong! I promise!"

"Just don't forget what's at stake." sneered the man from across the glass. There was no pity in his gaze, no sympathy.

Tears stained the woman's cheeks as more scientists bore down on her, almost covering her in a sea of white.

Opal couldn't see anything through their bodies, and she was glad that they were obscuring her view, especially as the woman's agonized screams tore through the lab.

Little splatters of blood hit the floor, and tools were dropped and exchanged- shimmering with blood.

Rose didn't stop screaming.

Opal felt like crying. She could feel tears streaking down her cheeks.

"Rose. What a weak name, my little puppet." It was the man's voice from the cell, quiet and cold but easy to hear even over Rose's painful screams. "From this moment on. Your name will be Delphina. You will forget everything."

Delphina.

Experiment.

That man...

He has to be the head of the snake. Opal thought, trying to block out Rose's last cries.

152

That was in the past. So was the vision of Cora.

I can see the past.

I can see the future.

Why?

"Well, look at that; she finally joins us." growled a curt male voice.

Opal pried open her eyes, blinking at the harsh light. She was in a brightly lit room with no windows and what appeared to be no door. She was really starting to miss windows. And sunshine. And life.

Her family.

Freedom.

Opal choked back the sob and the wave of helplessness that crashed over her. She couldn't collapse now.

Opal jerked her arms, realizing with a flinch of horror that she was bound to a rickety wooden chair. Her ankles and wrists were clamped to the chair.

In front of her was a crude metal table; two people sat behind it.

One was Delphina. The flash of anger that Opal usually felt staring at her was muted slightly as she remembered Delphina's agonized screams. The following person was a man that Opal had never seen in real life before. But he resembled the man in her vision perfectly, with the same hard lines and dark black hair topped with his ice-blue eyes. The only difference was that he looked many years older, and several streaks of gray shone in his jet-black hair, gelled back in a swirl at the top of his head.

His long, twisted fingers were clenched over Delphina's shoulders as if daring her to make a move.

Opal gasped. Tears were already falling down her face as she stared into the man's eyes. How did she not recognize him from the vision?

She knew who this man was. She's seen him on TV more times than she could count.

But the realization did nothing to calm her spinning head; it only threw her deeper into confusion.

He was behind all this? *Was he* the head of the snake? He couldn't be... He couldn't...

Opal had heard of Allen Richmond practically every day of her life; he'd always been there. A steady presence.

A *good* presence.

But now....

A lab?

Experiments?

How could he?

What was this?

"No," Opal whispered. "It can't be you. What are you doing?" Was there a reason? Because this wasn't supposed to happen, none of this mess was, especially not at the hands of him.

Because Allen Richmond was the president of the United States of America.

13

OPAL

Richmond's face broke into a slow, sly smile. "Yes, I am the president, which makes your imprisonment completely legal."

Opal spluttered and gasped. The air in her throat dried up as she struggled to take in a breath. This was all too much-

Imprisonment? What had she done wrong?!

Opal wanted to cry; she wanted to scream for her parents, for her life to go back to what it was.

"T-that's not possible." Opal choked out.

"Of course it is." Richmond smiled, but there was no warmth in his gaze.

"Then what have you been doing? There is a zombie apocalypse going on! We need a cure! The world is falling apart!" Opal cried miserably. "Why am I here? Why is all of this here when so many people are dying?"

"Opal, Opal, Opal." sighed Richmond, the syllables falling from his mouth in clean precision, sounding every bit like the sly man Opal was beginning to see. "Do you honestly believe that we don't have a plan for these sorts of things? After all, I'm the one who started it in the first place!"

Wait. *What?*

Bile rose in Opal's throat. It was impossible. Yes, she knew the government wasn't perfect, but... Would anyone really start something like this? The hows and whys were stacking up in Opal's mind, threatening to send her tumbling down. People were being driven from their homes, and millions were dying; how could any man be responsible for it? Didn't apocalypse's start because of a freak accident? A bacteria, a parasite... Not a *person*.

"Yes. It's unheard of, isn't it? But a parasite must start somewhere..." Richmond leered. "It was in this very place, actually, where the first human, unknowingly of course, was inflicted with the parasite. Patient zero."

Patient zero.

"Do you want to hear the *story*, Opal?" Richmond leered.

"No." Opal moaned. Who was this creepy man in front of her? Where was the man who swore to protect the constitution of America?

Richmond leaned back. "It's quite *enthralling*, if you know. Like a little *movie*."

"No." Opal moaned again, trying to stop the flow of tears. She was crying so much. For this torture. For this betrayal. But Richmond wouldn't stop.

"We released him, Patient Zero, into the world the next day, and after careful planning, it went well. The man had flu-like symptoms; his throat was raw, and his head hurt. His wife instructed him to stay at home, but when he fell asleep that day while making coffee, his wife had to rush him to the hospital. It's a cloudy day, and he woke up on the freeway and, for no reason whatsoever, leaned over from the passenger side and bit his wife's arm with surprising ferocity for someone so sick. His wife slammed on the brakes and smashed into the car in front of her, which happened to be a police car. The wife was already jumping out of the car, screaming as Patient Zero chased after her. The policeman was forced to detain and taser Patient Zero, but not before he received a bite on the arm. Patient Zero is detained and taken

156

to the police station. This is week one. The wife, confused about her large headache and dry throat, goes to the hospital. The cop, ignoring his slight headache, bandaged his arm with gauze and went home. Sure, the incident is on the news, but it's not entirely unheard of for one man to go berserk. Nobody suspects anything.

"Week two. The wife, who stayed at the hospital, erupts out of nowhere and bites at least ten other people before she is restrained. The cop lashes out and tries to infect his family and his neighbors. Some patients go to the hospital to treat their symptoms, while others stay home. All of which they can't control what is happening to them. And slowly, if they are not detained, these monsters erupt at night, biting at random. It's week three, and these monsters are becoming out of control, taking too many people. Quarantine measures aren't working; they just escape. The city in which it started is practically overrun, as are the neighboring cities. These monster strikes leave behind massive fires, burning cities at whim. These monsters are unstoppable. Monsters that are shadows of people's loved ones and friends. Monsters with no minds or souls. The perfect weapon. These *zombies*. People take to the streets in the quarantined cities, protesting and calling for help. Of course, the *government* is too busy. It's week four. The world is being overrun; of course, there are some survivors. The smart ones who had tornado bunkers or only came out when the sun was out. I estimate a million people around the world will survive by the first year. But of course, that won't last long. Food supplies will weaken. Infections will take in. So many factors. This is America; we live in a pampered era. We need iphones and soft beds to survive. Nobody is fit to survive a *zombie apocalypse*."

157

Opal was frozen, terrified. Here she was, waiting for the government to swoop in and rescue them... And now.

And now what?

Now, she was in their captivity, with strange visions.

At least I'm safe from the zombies. Opal thought miserably. It wasn't a comforting thought. Briefly, her mind flashed back to the friends she'd left behind, Tyler, Miranda, Nolan, and even Cora. How would they cope? How would her mother cope all alone without her daughters?

But why?

There was literally *no motive.*

Why would a president make his entire world a bunch of monsters? He was already one of the most powerful people in the world.

Why would anyone do that?

Suddenly, Opal's mind flickered, and her vision started to go dark.

"Oh, there she goes again." Hissed Richmond.

Opal opened her eyes to sirens; the light was flashing all around as she gazed, bewildered, at her surroundings. It was nighttime; Opal was standing by a large canal; the dark water churned and frothed at least thirty feet below, and the bright city lights of a distant skyline shimmered from across it. Only a couple hundred yards away was a massive dock; a large ferry waited by as hundreds of cars lined and filled the street surrounding the canal.

The night air was punctured by the sounds of thousands of cars honking and police firing back with their own sirens, illuminating the darkness.

158

People got out of their cars, hundreds of them talking forcefully to the police and the armed guards as lines of thousands stretched away from the port.

Opal's vision zoomed in on the entrance to the ferry as at least fifty armed guards were pushing back a clamoring crowd of desperate people.

"Let me in! There's plenty of room!"

"I swear I don't have it!"

"I'm immune, I promise!"

Each guard was whipping out what looked like a gun- pointing it at each person's forehead before they entered the ferry.

Temperature. They were taking each person's temperature. One with a fever was not allowed to enter, even with a one-degree raise, even if they swore it was just a cold.

"NO!" a hysterical woman suddenly shrieked as two guards in full body protection ran forward as she reached a temperature of 103 degrees Fahrenheit.

"No!" she shrieked again, holding onto two smaller children as she was wrenched away. "It's just the flu! I swear! Nobody has bitten me!" but they weren't listening. The smaller children, her children, were crying as they were hustled onto the ferry, sobbing as their mother was led away into a fenced-off pen.

It was pandemonium there.

Some people, like the woman, were crying, sobbing for their families as they hunched over. Others were beyond.

Their eyes were red and wild, skin far too pale for the normal human being, as they stretched out their hands, reaching for someone to bite...

159

"Please, sir! Test me again! I don't have it!" a woman shrieked.

Nobody was listening, nobody cared.

Opal wanted to cry. She wanted to curl up and hide. She was lucky she lived in the country, at least three hours from any major city...

Is this what was happening in the populated areas?

Tokyo?

London?

Chicago?

New York?

She hated it.

But the vision wouldn't end.

The ferry horn suddenly blared, adding to the din of the night; people screamed, yelling at the police. Screaming to be let in. Screaming for space that wasn't there.

People pushed past the guards, ignoring them as they pulled out guns, sprinting for the boat and what they thought was safety. Some people plunged into what was probably ice-cold water, trying to swim the canal, while others lunged for the boat as it pulled away...

They were all trying to escape an infected city.

But they never would.

Opal could see the distant haze of fires crawling over their home,

Opal gasped with horror as she woke up.

"Now that you're back..." sneered Richmond.

Opal gasped. "It was a city, people were trying to get on a boat... people were fighting..." words tumbled from her mouth in a senseless murmur.

Richmond snorted. "Ahh, yes. You'll understand why I did it in time. Why I'm destroying this world. But this is a factor that

160

contributed to it. Humankind. It's horrible. War. Famine. Power. Money. All of this has gotten too out of control. There's eight billion of us. Too many. But.... If you agree to help us, perhaps I will give you back your loved ones and end this plague after it knocked down a few billion. You see. Imagine this. A world devastated. Destroyed. And then. The meager president rises from the ashes and pulls back the last strands of humanity together. *I* will control the world."

"You're *sick*," Opal murmured. "You want everyone dead."

Richmond shrugged. "Why not?"

"You have physiological issues."

"I won't deny."

"Do you have a cure?" Opal demanded. Did these things even have a cure? And if they did. This was the highest level of treason imaginable. The president of the United States of America had a cure, and he wasn't doing *anything* about it? What was this?

Richmond's face crinkled. "A complication," he growled.

Opal's eyebrows shot up. "A *complication?*" she repeated in disgust. "Didn't you make it? If you gave that man t-the p-parasite, wouldn't you have made antibodies? Something to stop it?"

Delphina rolled her eyes. "It's not that *simple*. It is not a *cure*. This parasite infects all your internal organs, your brain, your heart. You can't recover from it. These are antibodies. To save the people who are left."

Opal jumped a little at her voice. She had been so fixated on the president and the cure that she had almost forgotten that Delphina was still in the room.

Richmond tightened his grip on Delphina's shoulder, and for the first time since Opal had known her, Delphina looked frightened.

161

Definitely the head of the snake. Opal thought ruefully. *I just didn't think it would be the president of the United States.*

"What does she mean?" snapped Opal, hoping her voice wasn't quavering.

"Well, Delphina has been doing a little *search,* I'm sure she knows *all* about it," growled Richmond.

"What do you mean?" repeated Opal.

"I've been looking for The Sightseerer." Delphina proclaimed, her chin held high. "And there's nothing you can do to stop me." Her gaze was dark but defiant. She no longer looked like the agonized woman that Richmond was torturing. Still, she also looked far from the sane woman Opal imagined she once was.

"Yes, I know that!" Opal snapped, still confused.

"And outside of my knowledge." hissed Richmond.

"Oh," Opal whispered, so Delphina was still a prisoner like *me.*

The Sightseerer. Acana Magic. He could see the future or the past, like Opal, but more powerfully.

Timelines.

The Sightseerer.

He was the man in my vision! A bolt of lightning suddenly flashed through Opal. It made sense. It had to. He was so powerful... but if Richmond had him in his custody, why was Delphina looking for him?

To keep from Delphina?

Opal lifted her gaze to catch Richmond. He certainly seemed evil enough to do that.

Then, who was the *her* in Opal's vision? Who was the one Richmond threatened to kill?

Why did Delphina want The Sightseerer? To kill him? Or save him?

So many pieces.

In that moment, Opal realized that this wasn't going to be a simple situation anymore; nothing was going to be simple. And somehow, she had gotten tied up in the most messy part.

"Yes, *sir*. We didn't come here to talk." Opal could sense the hatred in Delphina's voice, but she could feel it even more when she spat out the word. *Sightseerer*. She wanted to kill him. Why? Didn't the Sightseerer have Acana magic like Opal and Delphina?

Richmond suddenly stood, circling Opal as she flinched against the ropes that held her down, every fiber in her body craving to be away from him.

"I believe you know Acana Magic, don't you?" he asked quietly, his voice holding a dangerous tilt.

Opal was frozen, petrified. Any notion of defiance was blown from her mind, leaving only the desire to stay alive. Maybe she had done something wrong- and if she just complied, they would send her back.

Maybe without Acana Magic.

"Yes. It's real." Richmond snarled. "I found Delphina when she had powers much like yours. Weak. Out of control."

Opal flicked her gaze to Delphina, who was sitting impassively, her arms crossed.

"Yes. That's right. It comes in visions of the past and future, quite helpful, if I might add. Acana Magic Users are born with an exceptional mental capability, the ability to fight with their minds. Delphina's magic is so fine-tuned that she can actually take over someone else's mind." Richmond hissed.

163

"I assure you, she is much more powerful than you... your abilities are astounding... I can't deny it. But you, Opal. You're more powerful than she ever was; just imagine what we could do if we harnessed those powers! Delphina had become... *difficult*. Together, we could work in a partnership to take control of this world." Richmond's face suddenly darkened. "But if you *don't* comply, the answer is still simple. I will have Delphina take over your mind.

14

TYLER

"HELP!" Tyler cried, panic filling his body like hot tar; Cora faded slowly out of consciousness, her head drooping backward and her body falling limp.

Tyler felt another flash of terror. He couldn't let her die; he couldn't!

The sound of echoing footsteps filled the cave as Tyler looked desperately to find Miranda and Nolan rushing to their side.

Their eyes flicked to Tyler and Casper, both covered in blood.

Then their eyes found Cora, eyes closed, hardly breathing with blood still flowing from her wounds.

"Medicine?!" Tyler gasped; Miranda was already coming back with one of the smallest first aid kits Tyler had ever seen.

Would it be enough?

He hoped so.

It had to be.

Casper was already emptying all their water bottles down on her wounds, Tyler watched in horror as the blood-stained water seeped away, and he could see even more the full extent of the wounds.

Her clothes had done little to protect her, and the large three gashes had stopped bleeding, but the skin was inflamed. Puss oozed from the corners.

Tyler stroked Cora's sopping hair. "It's alright," he muttered. "I'm here. Please be alright."

Casper suddenly shot him a sharp glare. "That's not going to do anything." he snapped. "She can't *hear* you. It's not going to be helpful being *sentimental.*"

Tyler was taken aback at Casper's harsh words, but he was too panicked to take offense. "Just fix her!" he snarled back.

Casper rolled his eyes; moving back to his work, he opened up the kit. It was painfully low. A few sterile bandages, band-aids, gauze, painkillers, and some disinfectant. That was it.

Tyler pulled the disinfectant from the case, trying to ignore his rolling stomach as he dabbed the gel on Cora's cuts. He knew nothing of first aid. *Nothing.* What if Cora died in his hands?

Cora's eyelids flickered weakly, and she let out a soft groan of pain.

Tyler pulled the bandages over her, again and again, until her entire stomach was wrapped in white; hints of blood started to appear in the cotton, but they stopped after a second. She had stopped bleeding.

The little consciousness Cora had gained slipped away as she clenched Tyler's hand before it fell to the ground, slipping into a soft sleep, her chest rising and falling. The painkillers went to work, and she let out a soft gasp.

Tyler crouched down, pressing his lips to her forehead. "Sleep well," he whispered quietly.

Miranda sighed in relief and fell away. "Thank god they weren't too deep; now that they've stopped bleeding, it should be okay."

"Tyler, *what happened*?" Nolan demanded quizzically. "Those are too clean to be zombie hits."

"People," Tyler muttered. "Just came out of the woods and attacked us."

Nolan rubbed his hand through his hair. "Good grief. People are already getting desperate enough to attack helpless kids?"

"We can't keep living like this." Casper suddenly burst out.

Tyler looked bewildered at Casper's dark face and hooded eyes. You *probably can't. Get some sleep, dude.*

"What do you mean?" Miranda asked.

"I mean, Tyler and Cora were this close to getting even more seriously injured. If I hadn't stepped in-" Casper trailed off.

Tyler caught his meaning. Casper had thrown that dagger with deadly precision; without an ounce of hesitation, he'd ended someone's life. Tyler didn't know if he would ever be able to do that, even in the midst of an Apocalypse, even if his friends were in danger.

"My point is we need to learn at least the basics of self-defense, or the zombies will tear us apart like sitting ducks." Casper finished bluntly.

"We *are* sitting ducks!" Nolan muttered. "A little 'self-defense' isn't going to change that."

"Let's see if I can teach you pampered Americans to fight." Casper got to his feet, glowering down at them. "Because in a matter of life and death, it'll make a difference."

Tyler sighed. He was exhausted; the events of the past two days had worn him out. He was sticky with Cora's blood, and the mere idea of fighting made him nauseous. But he didn't want to be caught off guard again.

"Here. Attack me." Casper told Tyler as soon as he had gotten to his feet.

167

"Attack- you?" Tyler asked, bewildered, staring skeptically at the dark-eyed boy. He didn't really want to attack Casper. That boy looked like he could rip him apart.

Casper rolled his eyes. "Yes, pretty boy *attack* me! Imagine I'm a mind-eating zombie coming to chomp on your girlfriend!"

Tyler tried to ignore the sting of insults in that sentence, but his mind still zeroed in on the girlfriend jibe.

Did he mean Cora?

Or Opal?

Stupid! Of course, he meant Cora.

Tyler started forward, confused. Unsure of what to do. He'd never *attacked* someone.

He aimed a punch he knew would be easy to dodge, ready to disapparate his fist if Casper didn't move.

But he did.

Casper's eyes flickered to his for a moment; a burst of dark hatred showed there, but not for Tyler. Memories were flickering through this boy's mind. Dark ones. Tyler was mesmerized for a second, distracted, but Casper wasn't. He lashed out. Grabbing Tyler's wrist that had his hand extended to punch. Casper lurched Tyler forward, causing him to jump into Casper's arms as Casper used his other arm to suddenly and quite violently reach to push his fist into Tyler's stomach.

Tyler gasped, Casper didn't do it, but Tyler could feel the power behind the punch; if he had been aiming to hurt, then Tyler would have laid on the floor, completely incapacitated.

Casper released Tyler, pushing him backward a little bit, and he almost stumbled to the ground.

Casper glowered down at Tyler. "That was weak."

"Well, I'm sorry, I'm not exactly attuned to this sort of thing." Tyler bit, annoyed. How was Casper so unaffected by the fact that he had *murdered* someone only hours before?

Casper rolled his eyes and tossed his silver-tipped hair out of his eyes. "Well, that's going to have to change, isn't it? It's a dangerous world now, and if we even want a *chance* to survive-"

"Casper." Miranda broke in. "How do you *know* this?"

Casper's face darkened. "I grew up in a not-so-great part of London; my father threw both my sister and me onto the streets when we were really young. It was our only option to defend ourselves."

"Sure. Defend." Nolan muttered darkly.

"Alright. So, the only thing that really works on zombies is their head. Elbows, knees, fists. They all work. Now come on, I'll show you."

It was hours before Casper finally called that he was done. The sun was setting, and they tried to stay quiet, away from the prowling zombies that came by.

It was hours, and Tyler's whole body throbbed; he'd been kicked, punched, and thrown around by Casper far too many times.

He didn't feel any safer.

Cora woke up a few hours ago; she was thirsty and hungry. They gave her food and water, but she vomited up the water and refused to take the food. Tyler didn't know what to do for her, Miranda assured him she was healing, but he didn't feel so sure.

The bleeding started up again, but the inflammation and pus had gone down. But Cora still couldn't or wouldn't eat.

Irene poked her head out of her cave to take food but either didn't see her wounded daughter or didn't care.

169

Probably didn't care.

Tyler carried Cora to her cave that night, and as he settled her down, he reached out a hand to feel her too-hot forehead. The ground was too hard for something this injured.

Casper may have been an expert in violence, but he was no medic. Neither was Tyler or Nolan or Miranda. Or Irene.

What were they going to do if these wounds got infected? Who were they going to run to? All of their parents were dead, the military was nowhere in sight, and they were hours from any major city. None of them had a car to get there, anyway. And if they did... What would await them there?

"Tyler. Don't leave me." Cora whispered as she held Tyler's hand tightly. Cora's eyes were glazed- her words half slurred with fever.

"I won't," Tyler promised, too aware of the promise he had made himself. But now he knew, he knew how much it hurt and how hard it was to hurt Cora, even emotionally. He couldn't live without her. He really, really couldn't.

So...

Did that mean he loved her like she loved him?

Tyler gently stroked Cora's hair as he settled down next to her just like they always did... Ready to face the days together.

And with her by his side...

He felt like he could finally face the nightmares.

Tyler flinched awake, immediately looking down to find Cora blinking awake.

His hand immediately went to her forehead, and with relief, he found her fever had broken overnight.

Her bandages were stained red, though; he changed them first, with her smiling tentatively up at him.

"Thanks," she whispered.

"Listen." Tyler started. Cora seemed so much better today. Perhaps it was time to talk to her. "About the whole Opal thing- it was really nothing- were we're just hugging after she had a bad dream-"

Cora raised a hand to stop him. "Relax," she whispered, placing a hand on his chest. "I understand- and I know how you feel about me. It was just my mother twisting things up."

Tyler felt a smile twist over his face as he breathed out in relief. But then... then he could hardly breathe as he placed his other hand under Cora's neck as he leaned in- getting closer and closer as she came just as close-

Was he going to do this?

Was he?

And they were close enough to count each other's eyelashes and-

"Um..." someone cleared their throat behind them.

Tyler, thoroughly startled, jerked back, blushing crimson; Cora's face split into a grin, pleased to be caught.

Tyler turned to find Miranda standing in the entrance to the cave, blushing just as red. "Er- Casper wants to do more training, Tyler."

Tyler turned back to Cora. "Stay here. Rest. Call me if you need anything." he whispered.

"I will, I'm going to sleep some more." Cora sighed, lying back down, but as Tyler suddenly turned to leave, she reached up and softly kissed him on the cheek before falling back down and closing her eyes.

171

Tyler didn't know if his face could physically burst into flames, but it felt like it.

Miranda was smirking all the way out of the cave, glancing at him and waiting until they were out of earshot of Cora to pile on.

"So..... You and Cora, huh? What about Op-" Miranda started.

"Shut up," Tyler mumbled, unable to take her teasing.

Miranda put her hands up. "Alright, alright! I was just wondering."

But Tyler couldn't ignore the ache in his chest. The ache as he thought of Opal, alone with Delphina. She was probably waiting for him to rescue her. And then of Cora, waiting back in her cave, probably waiting for the kiss he almost gave her.

The days passed, and the time passed in which Tyler was painfully aware of how long Opal had been in Delphina's custody. It felt wrong to leave her there, even if they barely knew her. *Someone* needed to rescue her. Slowly, he pressed the idea to the rest of his friends, agreeing once Cora was healed, they would try.

Yet, he still hadn't told Cora. Something inside of him was telling him that Cora wouldn't be too pleased if he suddenly started gallivanting off to find Opal.

They hadn't talked about that moment when they almost kissed- mostly because Tyler didn't want to talk about it, but he sensed Cora would be more than happy to.

But this was beyond some petty drama. This was Opal's *life*. And it was a lot more important than Cora's pride.

And slowly, the days went by.

They trained, ate, and slept, trying not to think about what was happening outside.

On the third day, the group got their first indication that they weren't the only people around. Gunshots vibrated through the forest. Tyler didn't know if it was more gangs or people fighting against zombies. With the sun nowhere in sight behind the thick clouds, the group decided not to take the risk and investigate.

To Tyler's immense relief, Cora got better and better.

Finally, on the fifth day, when she stood up and walked around, eating and drinking fine without any blood and two of her cuts had started to scab over. Tyler decided it was time to breach the subject of rescuing Opal with her.

"Cora?" he whispered, leaning his head into her cave.

"Yeah?" she called back.

Tyler hesitated for a beat as he crawled into the dimly lit cave, illuminated by only one candle that the group was already trying to ration. "You know we can't stay here forever, especially not when-" Tyler took a deep breath. "When Opal is in Delphina's hands."

Cora's face suddenly soured. "You know it's dangerous, even thinking about going after her. Come on, we don't even know where to start. Ty, you knew her for all of a couple hours."

"I know. But we can't leave her, and don't you want to get out in the world to find out what's happening?" Tyler hurried on.

Cora scowled. "But why should we risk our life for her?"

Tyler couldn't help but feel a flash of anger. "Because she's our *friend* and we can't leave her there! We *can't*!" his voice suddenly rose with a flash of emotion.

Cora's face filled with hurt.

173

Tyler sighed, breathing fast. "Look, I'm sorry. But you know we have to go find her. Or at least try; it's not right to leave her with Delphina. And these supplies aren't going to hold up forever, anyway."

Cora hesitated, chewing on her lip. Tyler waited with his breath in his throat.

"Fine," Cora whispered.

Tyler's heart leaped. At last! "Thank you!" he gasped. "We'll leave tomorrow; I can make all the preparations-" he hurried on, but Cora suddenly held up a hand.

"But," she said firmly. "On one condition."

Tyler's heart sank.

What did she want?

Cora reached forward, slipping her hands into his. "I want you to agree to be my boyfriend. I want to be your girlfriend."

Tyler was so taken aback. They'd been whispering about this for months now... He'd expected this was what Cora had wanted, but... He hadn't expected her to suddenly burst out.

But would being her boyfriend really be all bad? I mean, this was Cora. He'd had a crush on her for years... And if this meant saving Opal. Opal's life was a lot more important than any of their feelings.

Cora let out a whisper of a smile as she gently placed her cool hand on the back of his neck. "What do you say, Tyler?"

Tyler could hardly breathe. But this was for Opal. This would mean saving her...

Why was he holding back?

Because of some weird feelings about Opal?

Because Cora scared him to death sometimes?

174

Wasn't that supposed to be love, though? Scary? Unpredictable?

Was he really going to?

Cora's eyes flashed in the dark, Tyler felt her fingers brush up against his, and they interlocked. Cora brought their intertwined fingers up toward his chest.

It felt like Tyler's body had gone into autopilot when he started leaning forward.

After so many years of dreaming of this exact moment, Cora leaned forward, and their lips met.

There were literally no words; the doubts and thoughts of Opal were pushed to the back of his mind as he threaded his hand through Cora's hand.

"What's your problem?!" Suddenly, an angry voice from outside jolted Tyler back to reality, and he burst apart from Cora, turning to face the cave entrance.

Cora, though looking disappointed they were jolted from their moment, raised her eyebrow in confusion.

Tyler stood, helping her pull herself up, and they emerged into another bizarre scene.

Irene had emerged from her cave for the first time in days; she was filthy, even more, filthy than she had been in the bunker; her eyes were half-wild, and her clothes were slicked with mud and filth as she pointed her hands wildly around the cave, finally pointing to Cora and Tyler, with their hands still entwined.

"FOOLS," she screamed. "IT LEADS TO NOTHING."

Cora looked bewildered, glancing at Tyler. "What?" she muttered, averting her mother's gaze.

175

"Love." Irene's words suddenly slowed down, slurring together as if she were drunk. "Love. It'll kill you. All of you. One day, boy, you're going to end up like me, old, filthy, all the beauty drained from your body until you are nothing. *nothing.*" Irene suddenly collapsed on the ground. "He left me. He'll leave you."

Tyler was half terrified, half perplexed. Was she having some sort of mental seizure? Breaking down? Starving?

What was wrong with her?

Tyler glanced sideways at Cora, wondering if she was as scared as he was, but instead, her eyes were shining; she reached up on her tiptoes, pulling Tyler down by his elbow so she could whisper in his ear.

"You love me?"

Tyler smiled; of course, she would take that away from everything her crazy mother would say. And, of course, he loved Cora, he had for so many years, as one of his best friends.

I mean, he'd agreed to be her boyfriend; he'd kissed her. And he did love her. But as what?

Did it even matter?

"Of course I do," Tyler whispered back as Cora released him with a smile.

Irene was shaking now, sprawled across the ground of the cave, her arms covering her head, a horrible half-wailing sound coming from her throat; Tyler cast a worried glance at Nolan as they moved closer, Casper and Miranda following behind.

"S-should we do something?" Miranda mumbled.

"Cora?" Nolan asked.

Cora shrugged, unconcerned. "She's never done this before."

176

"He left me." Irene moaned.

"Ah." Cora winced. "My father."

Tyler glanced at her, shocked. She never ever mentioned the man who had left both Irene and her when Cora was a baby.

Casper inched closer, nudging Irene's shaking and huddled form with his foot.

Irene suddenly froze; she stopped moving and stopped screaming. To Tyler, it looked as if she had stopped breathing altogether.

Casper turned back with a guilty look on his face. "Erm. I didn't do it."

Irene's hand shot out and grabbed his ankle. Casper let out a yelp of surprise, and he tried to jerk away from her, but Irene still collapsed on the ground and kept a tight grip on his ankle. Without warning, she yanked him towards her, and he let out a gasp of shock. Caught off guard, he fell hard to the ground.

"YOU." Irene's voice was wild now. She released Casper's ankle and pulled herself to her feet, stretching herself to her full height.

Casper was struggling backward, still on his back, not wanting to take his eyes off Irene. He slid away on the stone.

"STOP." she screeched; without even hesitating, she swung her leg around and slammed a boot onto Casper's chest, pinning him to the ground as he let out a cry of pain. He groaned, and his head fell back on the stone as he fought to get away.

Tyler let go of Cora's hand, jumping forward. "Stop!" he snapped. "What are you doing?"

Irene turned her leering face to his. "Getting revenge."

"Revenge!" Casper wheezed. "I've never even met you before this! What are you talking about?"

"Y'all won't understand. But that doesn't matter. *I* understand." Irene snarled. "You haven't done anything *yet*."

"You're mad." Casper hissed, struggling under her foot. "Now, will you please let me go?"

"Yeah, Irene. Seriously!" jumped in Nolan.

Some of the anger died from Irene's eyes, and she slowly lifted her leg off Casper. Casper pushed himself into a sitting position, looking bewildered and shaking his silver-tipped hair out of his own eyes, gazing angrily at Irene.

In the beat of tense silence that followed, Tyler nearly screamed for Casper to get away from Irene; she wasn't right. And Tyler's predictions came to pass a heartbeat later. Irene's eyes bulged again, and she lunged forward, not hesitating, as she closed her fingers around Casper's throat.

"*Hey!!*" Tyler gasped, jumping forward and catching hold of Irene's shoulder, trying to wrench her back with all his force, but she didn't budge.

Casper was fighting as best he could, but his eyes were bulging; Irene's hands must have been like steel.

Miranda was already there, wrenching one of Irene's hands away. But the second Miranda pried her fingers loose, Irene shook her off and put her hand back as they wrestled back and forth.

Nolan pulled Irene's other hand as Cora pulled on her mother's shoulders. Irene was fighting with a ravaged strength that seemed so unlikely for someone who looked so frail.

What in the world was driving her?

178

Casper was kicking and kicking, and one of his kicks hit straight onto Irene's face, connecting fiercely with her nose as a thin trickle of blood seeped out. She just kept fighting.

Miranda had wrenched one hand of Casper, Nolan managed the other as slowly all four of them managed to push Irene back until she staggered to the ground, her head hitting painfully on the rock.

Irene lunged forward one more time. Casper was crouching on the ground, but he delivered a swift and staggering kick to Irene, and she fell backward.

Casper got to his feet, rubbing his neck as he coughed painfully. "There's got to be something wrong with her," he growled.

"There ISN'T!" Irene roared, flailing her arms. "YOU'LL KILL HIM. I WON'T LET YOU!"

"I don't plan to kill anyone!" Casper snapped. "Well, unless they deserve it," he added on a second thought, glowing down at Irene. If Tyler had been in Irene's position, he would have started to fear for his life.

"I DON'T CARE! STAY AWAY FROM HIM!" Irene roared again.

"Who?!" Cora demanded.

Irene had broken off, doubling over as she hacked over the rocks; her whole body shook with the force of her coughs.

"I won't let you." she gasped weakly.

"We have to leave her here," Miranda whispered. "She's so dangerous; she's going to try and kill us all! I don't know why she's even here in the first place."

179

Tyler saw Cora wince, and he pulled her close. Miranda didn't mean it, of course, but Irene was here because of Cora; Irene was her mother, after all.

"Yeah, no kidding," Casper muttered, rubbing his neck.

"We should just leave her here, leave her with food, and take off," Nolan whispered.

Cora flipped her hair angrily. "And take off *where*? May I ask?"

Tyler's heart leaped as he squeezed Cora's hand. She had promised. She had.

"Opal. We need to find Opal." Tyler said firmly, trying not to glance at Cora, whose hand had gone slack in his.

"Oh," Miranda whispered. "We could. We could stop this, too. Imagine if we found Delphina and stopped her, we got Opal back, we stopped the apocalypse." Miranda's eyes drifted away, getting dreamy. "We could be heroes."

"We could be," Nolan muttered. "And I agree with Tyler; we can't just leave Opal."

Tyler's heart soared again. Would this really work?

"We could get rid of Irene; give her the slip," Casper muttered. "Go to the mountains. I'm sure that's the way Delphina flew off to."

Tyler risked a glance at Cora; she was biting her lip, a nervous habit but not an angry one.

"Can we do it?" he whispered, probably more to her than to anyone else.

"Of course we can," Cora whispered back. "I promised, didn't I?"

Tyler could hardly believe his luck. Was this real?

"We should leave today!" Cora called out to the rest of their friends.

Miranda and Nolan were already whispering to each other, making plans Tyler guessed or hoped.

"Oh, and we also have an announcement," Cora added quickly, with a glance at Tyler.

Oh god.

Tyler blushed before she could say anything; he could feel the heat collecting in his face as Cora beamed.

"Tyler and I are together now! He's my boyfriend now." she smiled, looking up at him, and Tyler couldn't help but smile back, reaching down so she could kiss him on the forehead.

I'm sorry, Opal. This is for you, you know. He added privately to himself, thoughts that would *never* leave his head.

Tyler turned back to his friends, Casper's face was a mask as usual, but Nolan and Miranda were both beaming.

"Congrats, guys!" Miranda smiled. "Now, as I was saying-" she began, but suddenly Nolan turned to her, cupping her face in his hands before leaning in to kiss her.

Miranda gasped with shock before kissing him back, and they stayed like that for what must have been a minute before Casper cleared his throat. "Alright! We get it. You're all into each other. Now, are we going to do this?" he snapped.

Miranda broke apart from Nolan, beaming happily as she put her arm around his waist. "Right-" she began. "Who's ready?"

"I am," Tyler growled. "Let's go rescue Opal from some zombies."

15

OPAL

"Are you ready yet?" snarled a slippery voice, poking at the edges of Opal's consciousness.

"Quiet!" snapped another voice. "We need her knocked out for more time!"

That got Opal moving. She didn't want to be knocked out! Who knows what they were doing to her? She had to wake up!

She forced her eyes open. Ignoring the pain and dryness of her throat and the way her eyes felt far too heavy than they usually were.

"Look what you did now!" yelled the cruel voice again.

Opal's vision was slightly hazy, but it was getting better by the second. She was in the same room. Richmond and Delphina faced her.

But this time, Delsea waited in one corner, a clipboard clenched in her vice-like grip.

Richmond glared heavily at Opal.

"Have you decided to help us yet?" he growled.

Opal was half paralyzed; what would they do to her if she said no? *Could* she say no? Was she strong enough to? She wanted her mind... she wanted it her own... but she also wanted her life.

"Fine, we'll just show you," Richmond growled flatly and then muttered more to himself. "After this one, I swear to god I'm not enhancing another one of these magic users. It only makes them insufferable."

Opal expected to hear some sort of snide comment from Delphina, but to her surprise, she stayed silent.

182

She's scared. Opal thought with disdain. Delphina was nothing more than a mouse under Richmond's rule. *Well, then, you must be a bug, Opal.*

Richmond nodded at Delsea. Staring flatly at Opal, she went to work pushing and clicking on the far corner of the room, on the sort of command area with an arsenal of buttons, levers, and switches.

Opal felt a bead of sweat drip down her chin; she slowly strained against the bonds that were beginning to cut into her flesh. What was going to happen? The anticipation was probably the worst; her heart was pounding, and her stomach was rolling.

A loud grinding noise filled the room, and Opal lurched as far back as she could in her uncomfortable chair.

The wall behind Delphina and Richmond was *moving;* it shook and turned, slowly peeling back.

Opal tried to steady her breath. There was nothing abnormal about this at all; it was like a garage.

But she didn't want to know what was in the garage. At *all.*

The wall folded back to reveal a thin sheet of glass, probably about a centimeter thick, and inside was a comfortable-looking room containing a hospital bed with emerald green sheets, unlike the steel-cold ones Opal had seen. Around it were heart monitors, brain monitors, and all the machines for a perfectly normal human hospital. A blank TV screen was even set up across from the bed, and clear liquid bags were being transferred into a sleeping young girl lying peacefully on the bed.

Her hair was spread out before her, and her lips were a ghostly pale.

Everything seemed so tranquil. So peaceful.

183

But something seemed off. The girl's brow was scrunched up as if she was in pain, and her expression was far from peaceful.

But the worst fact of all was that Opal knew who this girl was.

Her sister.

Her younger sister was the one in the bed.

"No," Opal whispered, straining to stand up. "Don't hurt her!" Opal cried. "Please! She's just a child!"

Delsea smirked. "I have no problem hurting *you,* and *you're* just a child."

Opal was on the verge of tears. "No!" she cried. "AMELIA!!"

"Quiet!" snapped Richmond, standing in front of Opal.

Opal twisted her head as she tried to keep the sight of her unconscious sister in her vision even as she was blocked by Richmond.

Richmond was there in a flash, gripping the sides of Opal's chair as he hissed in her ear. "We've had her for so long. We can do *anything* to her." he snarled in her ear.

"What are you doing to her?!" Opal gasped. "Please."

"Nothing for now." Delphina hissed. "What!?" she snapped, glaring at Richmond, who glared back. "*I* brought her in. She's *my* charge."

Richmond was pacing behind Opal now. "You know what I want you to do. Delphina is so poisoned. I can't really control her anymore. Nobody loves her. And she doesn't love anybody. All she wants is that poor little Sightseerer."

Delphina flinched.

Richmond moved on, ignoring Delphina's hurt looks. "But you, little Opal. You have so much more to give. And with your visions and a little training, perhaps a little enhancement. Could be *perfect.*"

184

"Enhancement?" Opal whimpered.

Richmond rolled his eyes. "Not as much as Delphina. I ruined her. Just for your visions."

"You didn't *ruin* me." Delphina squawked indignantly.

"Well, I didn't do anything *good* to you!" Richmond snapped back. "Now, will you *shut up*? I'll tell you that The Sightseerer is here in this building if that makes you feel better."

Delphina looked like she had been kicked in the gut. But she kept silent, her eyes wild and wide as she glanced around the room as if the madman would jump out of the shadowed corners.

That man is crazy. It doesn't matter how powerful he used to be; he's gone. Opal thought, thinking of his wild yet eerily familiar eyes.

"Look, girl, I'm only saying this once. You just need to find this cure. We need it in our hands." Richmond smiled at her, but there was no humor behind it.

"Find it? I thought you were the ones who created it in the first place?" Opal blurted.

Richmond's face darkened. "That doesn't matter. What you need to know is that the antibiotics got out of our hands. We need them back." Richmond paused and then added. "We'll give you some time to think about it; just remember- one favor and the world is cured; one slip, and your family perishes." Richmond nodded to Delsea. "She's all yours; bring her back tomorrow."

"Wait!" Opal cried. "My sister! What about her?" Opal cast a wild glance at Amelia, still unconscious and trapped behind that glass.

Richmond waved his hand. "Nothing will happen to her tonight. Not yet, at least. She'll sleep."

And with that, the metal garage doors slowly began to sink down, covering the glass.

Opal's heart cried in dismay. Her sister! "Stop!" Opal cried. "What about Gina? Where is she? Do you have my mother?" Opal cast one last terrified glance at Amelia; for all she knew, this could be the last time she laid eyes on her.

Richmond's eyes flared again. "If this one dies, we still have the other one for leverage. And yes. We do have your mother."

Opal didn't struggle; the numbness in her heart seemed to have spread to every part of her body. She let Delsea untie her and yank her from the room. But when she was pulled out, she became alert.

Opal studied her surroundings with wide eyes. If she wanted to escape before Richmond made her fill out his 'favor,' then she was going to need every scrap of information and knowledge she could scrounge up.

The hallways outside the cells were pitch white. Scientists in long white coats bustled past. Platoons of soldiers in army uniforms marched by without a glance at Opal. Everyone seemed to have a job and a place to be. And they certainly did not appear to be in the midst of a worldwide zombie apocalypse. Shouldn't there be more frenzy? Didn't anyone else know what Richmond had done? Where was this place? How far had Delphina taken Opal? Were they in the mountains? The questions just led to more questions, piling up until Opal's head spun.

Many tall doors lined the walls, and each seemed to have a four-letter combination lock; scientists pressed the correct combination and opened the doors. Opal craned her neck, struggling to see the letters- she could almost make out.

186

Delsea roughly shoved Opal's head down, forcing her only to see the floor; Opal focused on the tile and tried to keep the tears back.

Her poor sister. Amelia was small. Practically harmless, why would they do this? *How* could they do this?

"Here you go," grunted Delsea, snapping Opal out of her thoughts.

Opal raised her head, silently thanking Delsea for not shoving it down again. A small troop of soldiers waited in front of her.

They were army soldiers again, with camouflage uniforms and grim faces. Even on TV, Opal was always scared of them and found them to be robotic. Did they laugh and cry like normal people? Or did their uniformed job bleed into their personal life until they knew nothing else?

But wasn't the army supposed to protect civilians? Against all costs?

Opal looked up into the grim faces of the army soldiers as they reached out to grab Opal by the arms, taking her out of Delsea's hands. She remembered those same faces when she had watched television with her family. Those same people had stood by Richmond's side.

Do you know? Do you know your president is a fraud? Opal asked silently. *Will you follow him while everyone else is dying?*

Did he promise you something? To spare your families?

Something inside of Opal told her that any promise from the president's mouth was as reliable as keeping smoke in your bare hands.

The men didn't talk and just kept matching her along like she wasn't even there.

The grim silence had one advantage. As Opal was being half-carried and half-dragged down the hallways, she spotted the first

187

window she had seen since she had been brought there; it almost brought tears to her eyes. Sunlight. The sky. It physically pained her to see how close she was to everything that she missed and yet how far she was.

But at least she could *see* outside.

Outside, the building was level with the ground, the sky was turning purple, and the sun had just begun to sink under the clouds. Opal coulden't tell if it had been one or several days since she was brought here. Who knew how long she had lost consciousness? Opal pushed away that disorientating thought and tried to focus on the window. She could tell that there were high winds swirling around from the ways the dark pine trees on the distant mountain peaks bent and swayed.

Mountain peaks.

It was a glorious sight. The massive towering peaks stretched out in a bowl-like form with far-out mountain lakes glistening in the setting sun. A few stray snowflakes drifted past the window, a thin dusting already on the bare ground.

Opal knew these mountains well. Skiing with her family and hiking with her friends. She grew up around them; she hadn't traveled far after all.

These mountains were only a few miles from her old home, from where Tyler was.

Where her friends were.

I hope you're alright.

I hope you're alive.

I hope you haven't forgotten about me.

The last thought was an empty one, a sad haunting that had been drifting through Opal's head since the time she had arrived here. The connections she had felt with the people she met in the bunker felt real, especially with Tyler, whatever it was. Was it so wrong to hope that they would try to come for her?

Yes.

One thing that Opal noticed was that the people hustling through the hallways didn't look at her strangely at all.

She was sleep-deprived, starving, muddy, and didn't remember the last time she had changed her clothes; the people didn't even glance at her. It was as if tortured people were dragged through the hallways all the time.

They probably are.

For the first time, one of the army members spoke to her; his voice was gruff, even scratchy. Like he didn't talk very often.

"Here we are; Delsea will be back later," he spoke in his grim, flat voice as if there was no color in the world.

They opened a steel door, just like all the others Opal had seen in the hallway; after shoving her roughly through it, they slammed the door behind her.

Oh. Well. No chains. Just time to think.

And cry.

Alone.

Opal raised her head; the lab was the same as always. Big tanks and weird tables filled with supplies, but this time, all the zombies were absent, and large slabs of metal had been hung on the wall with clamps ready and open.

Opal sank to the floor, hoping for solitude and time to think. Time to plan.

No such time was given; hands were already there, materializing from places and corners Opal didn't know where. She had gotten cocky, gotten her hopes up that they would leave her alone.

No such luck; they wouldn't let her spend the night alone; there were all types of things she could harm herself with or use to escape. Couldn't let the precious captive have that honor!

Opal knew it was frivolous to struggle; of course, it was. What could she do?

"Hold still!" one of the scientists nearly yelled.

"I am." Opal hissed through gritted teeth.

Opal blinked open one eye, catching a glimpse of the scientist's white coats as they dragged her towards one of the tanks.

No.

No, please.

Claustrophobia was so intense suddenly as Opal twisted away; she didn't want to be back in there with the orange haze and the endless helpless feeling.

She couldn't.

She didn't want to go back into one of those. The feeling of being in another world, not being able to interact with the people around her, and, of course, having a sheet of glass all around her had been one of the worst things she had ever felt besides her father dying; these had been the worst couple days of her life.

Opal twisted again; suddenly, a hand was right in front of her, pushing her down, and she didn't think. A new animalistic edge took hold of her body. She bit down so hard the scientist holding her let out

190

a wild shriek as blood welled on his hand, and he staggered away, yelling bloody murder.

Opal yanked free; she was free! Nothing was holding her! No restraints, no people! Nothing stopped her from doing what she wanted to do.

Opal felt so free that she dashed for the door. She was going to escape! She was going to warn her friends! Warn them that it was the president! She could see it! The metal door with the hinge she could pull so it would swing open-

She was getting closer- her feet pumped against the shiny floor, ignoring the shouts of the scientist behind her-

Opal slammed into an invisible barrier and ricocheted backward. Her head exploded with pain as she cried out, falling to the floor.

She landed hard on the floor. "Ouch," she mumbled as the scientist rushed over and grabbed her again. The rush of adrenaline and freedom was gone; they were back, the hands grasping for all her limbs as they yanked her to her feet.

"What the?" whispered Opal as she watched the invisible barrier blocking her from the door sear red and then fade to transparent. It was there, and then it wasn't. The sight made goosebumps erupt over her skin; what sort of secrets lurked in this lab?

There was no way out.

The scientist, thank god, didn't put her in a tube; they dragged her away to one of the tables, pulling it down and forcing her back straight on it.

Clamps were fastened on both of her ankles and hands; one went straight over her stomach, and she cried out, struggling to find a way out.

The scientist flashed her smug smile and strutted out of the room, slamming the door and locking it behind them.

Opal jerked around her hands, only to find them too well secured to do anything.

Opal tried to ignore her dismay. The scientist had left no food or water; her throat was so dry, and her stomach felt as if it were beginning to eat itself. The last time she had any sort of nourishment was at the bunker.

And they left the lights on.

She couldn't sleep either.

Fatigue finally caught up to Opal, no matter how bright the lights were, and her eyelids began to droop. But some distant fear kept her from drifting into a much-needed rest. She was afraid of sleep, afraid of what nightmares would find her; there was no Linea to rush to her side if she started screaming, only cold scientists with long white cloaks.

Mother. How could you do this to your daughter? How could you leave me behind in that bunker?

I need you.

Are you alive?

But exhaustion overcame everything else, and at last, Opal nodded off. Sure enough, the nightmares were waiting for her right there, always lurking in the corners like a beast waiting to pounce and stalk her every move.

Opal dreamed that she was running down a very long road. Whenever she thought she was at the end of it, more roads appeared endless dark concrete as far as she could see.

At last, the road did end, but not in the way she imagined. The road dropped away, and all she could see was pitch-blackness; suddenly, the ground was gone from beneath her feet, and she was falling. It didn't matter if her eyes were open or closed; it was just blackness.

Then the screams started.

"HELP!" it was Amelia's voice, so innocent and so in pain that every fiber in Opal's body wanted to embrace her younger sister.

"I'm coming!" Opal tried to tell her, but it didn't work; nothing came out of her throat. Nothing. She was silent.

Then it was Gina's screaming in the darkness.

Then Linea's.

Tyler.

Miranda.

Nolan.

They all screamed out in pain and were begging Opal to help them. Opal turned in circles and circles, promising she would find them, but never did. She was disappointing them all. Promising it to them all, but she could never find them. They would all leave her.

Opal felt herself falling, falling and falling, reaching out her hands in a silent scream as she fell down the tornado. Nothing was reaching her. Nobody would help her.

She twisted and thrashed in the darkness, but her arms and legs felt like they were being forced to move around in mud. She couldn't move. Fear that she would never get out of this filled her up; she tried to scream, but something was blocking her.

193

Opal felt herself falling faster; it felt as if her body was spinning like a top, and terrible thoughts that she would never land flashed through her mind. But after what felt like an eternity, her feet hit solid ground within the darkness. Her legs almost crumpled, and some of the fear evaporated as she realized she was on solid ground.

Opal looked up, curious to see where she was, and to her bewilderment, she was back in her old house. With the familiar sight, happiness began to ooze into her body. Memories of the tornado started to fade. Everything was so tranquil. It was perfect; she got up in the hallway to go to her room, feeling along the soft baby blue walls she had grown up with. Here was light and peace.

Opal wasn't surprised to see Cora and Tyler sitting on her bed, Cora scowling, and Tyler smiling.

Tyler stood up and smiled radiantly at her. "Hello, Opal! We've been expecting you!"

Opal smiled back. "Me too!"

Opal ran forward; she felt as if she was light as a feather, her heart pounding. She threw herself into Tyler's waiting arms.

She felt his strong arms beneath her as he dipped her down, and suddenly, their faces were inches apart- as he was getting closer.

"Tyler," she whispered and reached forward, her heart fluttering out of her chest. "Wait. What about Cora?"

Tyler shook his head. "It's fine. Nobody cares about her anyway. I like you, Opal."

It was the words she needed to hear.

Opal turned just to see Cora disappear in a wisp of smoke; neither Opal nor Tyler cared; they were already in each other's arms.

"Hi again!"

194

The dream suddenly disappeared in a puff of smoke.

Opal was thrown from her sleep and was forcibly shoved back into the present. All blissful feelings of tranquility that came from the ignorance of dreams disappeared.

Josh was in front of her. His brown hair was tousled as if he had just rolled out of bed, and this time, he didn't wear a lab suit but a simple black T-shirt and pants.

Opal silently ground her teeth; she was unable to explain her frustration with Josh and her anger at being woken up. She wanted to be back in her house with Tyler, where nothing mattered.

"Hi, Josh," Opal replied a little more forcibly than she intended.

"Hey, are you ok?" Josh asked, his brow knitting together to form a concerned expression.

This time, Opal actually was annoyed. "Of course not." she snapped.

"Why?" Josh asked. "Well, other than the fact that you're chained to a slab of metal and about to be experimented on."

The corners of Opal's mouth twitched, but she refused to drop her guard. Maybe she could pry information from him. "Yeah, I guess that. Sorry about me being so crank- wait, Josh, what do you mean 'to be experimented on?'"

Josh frowned. "Oh, I'm sorry. I shouldn't have told you that."

Opal's breath caught in her throat. "Please explain." she hissed through her teeth. "Now," she added as Josh hesitated.

Josh bit his lip. "Opal, I'm really worried. I-I really like you," he blushed and rattled on before Opal could respond. "And I think that

D- the president may just draw your Acana Magic like he did to Rose instead of waiting for an answer."

"Wait, slow down; first of all, how do you know what Acana Magic is?" asked Opal. "I don't really know what it is."

"Man, it's hard to imagine anyone in this building who doesn't know it is!" Josh sighed.

"Thanks, Josh," Opal muttered, getting more annoyed by the second.

"Oh, sorry!" Josh winced. "I'm not very good at talking to kids my own age. Any scientist knows what it is. We're required to study what we know about it and any signs unless it shows up in one of our patients." Josh broke off, seeing the look on Opal's face. "Sorry. Captives. Well, anyway, it's magic in the form of visions. Some people just get one vision in their lifetime and see it over and over again. Weaker power. Others with stronger power get more visions. Acana Magic comes in two families. Irene and Kermana."

Opal started. Those two names were both familiar. Irene. *Irene.* Was it possible Cora's mother went by her surname? That she had magic in her blood? And Kermana... There was no doubt about it now. Opal Kermana had Acana Magic.

"Where does the magic come from? Where do these lines come from?" Opal asked quickly, her breath hitching.

"I have no idea."

"Great," Opal muttered. Opal's breath caught; she had to tell someone, to trust someone, or she might go mad. Could she trust him, though? Could she tell him?

"Josh. Can I trust you?" Opal whispered quietly.

196

Josh's eyes were shining as he stared at her. "Yes," he responded firmly. "Completely."

Opal told him everything. From the moment the zombies came to her house to the second she found out about Richmond, she didn't know how much he knew or anything else, but judging by the absence of shock around Richmond, she guessed he already knew about that. But he did seem shocked when she told him about her having Acana Magic. Opal wondered how hard she was blushing when she had described Tyler, but she couldn't dwell on that now.

"Opal, do you think Irene is part of the Irene line?" Josh asked after Opal had finished explaining.

"I don't know, Delphina claimed that she didn't know anyone named her, but it could be possible." Opal shrugged.

"And you have Acana Magic?" Josh asked.

"Yeah, well, I think so; I have these visions, but that's all," Opal responded.

"Did I wake you up from a vision?!" Josh cried, looking alarmed.

Opal blushed; she wished with all her heart that that *was* a vision, but it couldn't have been. Tyler would never forget about Cora.

"No. No, that was just a normal dream." Opal sighed.

"Opal, do you have any idea what that means?" Josh demanded.

"That I have normal dreams?"

"No! That you have this magic. They won't stop now."

Opal grunted. "I didn't think they were going to stop before this."

Josh shot her an indignant look. "That's not true! We're not all that cruel. I'm not." he added meekly.

As long as you're a 'we' Josh, you are just as cruel as Richmond himself.

"Do you know anything about The Sightseerer?" Opal asked.

"Not really. He's more of a ghost legend than an actual man. His magic was really strong, and Richmond had him in custody for a long time; he might still have him, but he has to be careful because Delphina hates him."

"Why?" Opal asked.
Josh shrugged. "I don't know."

For a moment, it was silent. Josh slid down to the floor, resting his head on the corner of Opal's metal bed.

"Hey, Opal, if you could ask one question, any question, what would it be?" Josh asked abruptly, staring at the ceiling.

Opal knew she should be wary; everything about this place sang of mistrust, but Josh had a sort of innocence about him that suggested he could do no wrong.

"Why?" Opal blurted. "Why are you coming here? Why do you seem to care what's happening to me? Or is this all some sort of joke to you?"

Josh hesitated. "I like you, Opal." Josh started and then broke off, uncertain. "I'm sorry about what happened to your family and to you. Everything about my life seems to suck away happiness. I really just want a friend."

Part of Opal wanted to scream at him. Scream that she didn't want anything to do with this facility or him. But another part could hear the sadness behind his words, see the human in this boy.

And she could use a friend in this empty place. Opal hadn't had friends in so long; she had had one friend, a tough girl so unlike Opal. Named Emily, someone who Opal could slip into the background with but yet fiercely loyal to her. She still missed her; ever since she'd moved to LA years ago, Opal had been friendless, and now, suddenly, she had made so many more! *Nothing like an apocalypse to push you together.* Opal thought ruefully.

Opal realized for a second that Josh was waiting for her to answer; he was biting his lip as he glanced at her.

"I like you too, Josh. And I could really use your help."

"I want to help you, Opal. I really do-" Josh began but was suddenly cut off.

"You want to do *what* exactly, Josh?"

A prim and proper voice suddenly rang out, jolting Opal back as Josh's eyes went wide with terror.

"Uh, oh," muttered Josh.

"What is it!?" hissed Opal; she heard the sound of boots against the tile and the door being opened, but she couldn't see beyond where her table was angled. It didn't matter how much she craned her neck. Her bonds were simply too tight.

Josh opened his mouth, but for once, he seemed at a loss for words.

Six people bustled into Opal's vantage point. One was Delsea, and the other five were scientists Opal hadn't seen before.

Opal's eyes glanced over four of the scientists. They were unremarkable, walking with their heads down, clipboards in their hands, waiting for orders, but it was the one who walked in the lead that caught Opal's eyes. He was a man with a long auburn ponytail slicked to the back of his head, green eyes, and a scowling face that he had hidden behind a fake smile. He wore dark brown leather boots and brown pants with a button-up shirt underneath his lab coat; he clutched a pen like a dagger as if he was ready to wield it anytime.

Josh grimaced, glancing a regretful look at Opal as he moved to the man's side.

Is that his father?

"Why don't you tell your new *friend* who I am." snarled the man as he gripped Josh's shoulder, digging his fingers in so hard that Josh winced.

Yikes.

"T-This is Adax, oh, Opal, I'm so sorry." moaned Josh, eyes on the ceiling.

Opal's stomach twisted and churned. What was this? Who were they? What were they going to do with *her?*

"Yes, hello, *Opal.* My name is Adax, Delsea's boss ." Adax smiled his fake smile with a glance at Delsea. Opal hated the way her name rolled off his tongue, hated that this evil man even knew it.

"What d-do you want?" growled Opal, hating herself as the words came out with a stutter.

"Please be nice to us. We're trying to help you escape the pain." Adax snapped, exchanging a whispered word with Delsea.

"Don't listen to a word he says-" Josh whispered. He opened his mouth to say more, but Adax shot him a glare, tightening his grip on Josh's shoulder, leaning forward to hiss something into his ear. Opal didn't catch what he was saying, but she watched as his eyes widened and he closed his mouth.

Adax's brow furrowed. "We've received new orders," he growled. "Change your clothes and eat something while we discuss." With that, he was beckoning to Delsea and the rest of his crew as they went off to one of the doors. Opal could only see the hint of a white coat; Delsea chucked a bundle of clothes and a packet of dried food to Opal before following.

She was alone with Josh, who glanced at her miserably. "I'm sorry," he muttered.

"For what?" Opal hissed; she didn't bother trying to hide the anger in her tone. She wished Josh would stop *apologizing* and actually start doing something. Her heart was pounding. It was everywhere, the darkness. It is happening more often now. Ever since she was a little kid, Linea would find her curled up on her bed or curled up in the middle of the day, wailing. For a few minutes, she would be unresponsive, crying out to the world. It was because the darkness shrouded her. Panic attacks. Her breath would be too fast, and her heart would speed up.... And it was the terror of having those attacks that brought them on. But it was a more profound terror than that.

Dying.

How could she explain it?

The fear that she would be in a black world forever...

That nobody would come for her, that she would be trapped.

Now, what was going to happen?

Opal felt the panic attacks coming; she'd fought them off *so well*, but now she couldn't help it. It was too much.

When the zombies came- when Delphina had taken her family- it had been different. Because she could run. She had hope.

Here.

201

Here, there was no hope. No hope beyond this pathetic little boy.

She couldn't run.

She couldn't plead.

They would do anything they wanted to her.

And she wouldn't be able to stop it. She would stay bound to this bed.

Darkness shrouded the edge of her vision as her breath became hard; she collapsed in her binds, breathing shallowly.

"Opal! Opal?!" The voice was far off, as if echoing from a long tunnel.

Suddenly, arms were around her as the binds fell away, and she collapsed, shaking like a leaf, into Josh's arms.

Her limbs felt so strange after being trapped for so long she could hardly move, but she was able to weakly hug Josh back as he rubbed her back.

"It's alright," he whispered.

"It's *not*." Opal choked through her tears.

"Well, how about I make it alright?" Josh's lips brushed Opal's ear as he leaned into hiss in her ear. "I'll help you. I'll help you escape. Whatever it takes, I promise."

16

OPAL

Opal glanced up at him, eyes disbelieving.

"You will?" she demanded. "But isn't your family here?"

Josh shrugged. "They don't care about me. I'm not a scientist. I'm just a disappointment."

Opal didn't know how to respond. So she didn't. Instead, she pulled herself to her feet and wiped the tears from her eyes. "Thanks," she muttered; after the heat of the moment, embarrassment began flooding her as she imagined herself crying and screaming on the ground.

"Turn around," Opal muttered as she unwrapped the bundle of clothes, swallowing the dried chicken in three bites and downing the water in the plastic water bottle in one breath. Even after dreaming of food and water for so long, it tasted like sawdust on her tongue. She quickly changed out of her old clothes, trying to ignore the slight pangs as she let go of her only connection to her old home and pulled on a standard-issue pair of slacks and a t-shirt.

"Will you come see me tonight?" Opal asked Josh as he turned back around. "If I'm still alright after t-this." Opal's voice broke at the end, quavering as she tried not to let her eyes tear again. At first, she had meant the words as a feeble attempt at a joke, but it was too serious for her.

Adax would be back, and Delsea would be back. It wouldn't end. She had to be strong. Didn't she?

What could she do but wait?

Josh suddenly reached forward, more of a lurch, really, and grabbed her hand. "Of course I will. I promise. We'll get through this *together.*"

Opal shot him a bitter smile, trying not to note it wouldn't be much of a *together,* but it was sweet. Who cared? Though the bitterness started to sweep over her. He was a talker, wasn't he?

She'd like to see how excited he would be to help her escape when *his* life was on the line.

Sure, his life here was probably miserable, with no purpose, love, or fun. But he was *safe.* And that's all that mattered. Didn't it?

"Josh!" Adax suddenly swept into the room, his eyes dark, his absent smile gone from his face, and his lips twisted in a sour pout.

Josh turned quickly to face Adax, dropping Opal's hands.

"Get in line, kid," Delsea growled, hunching over the control pad, working the levers and switches, looking just as sour and angry as Adax.

Josh suddenly turned back to Opal, his face serious. He leaned in to kiss her on the forehead.

Opal felt a jolt of shock as he leaned away, smiling weakly at her. "For luck," he whispered.

Words dried up in Opal's throat as she stared at Josh. What was she supposed to say? That felt like something more than just a little token of luck.

And she didn't know how to feel about it.

"Josh!" Adax's voice was fierce, and he lunged forward, striking Josh across the face and grabbing him by the arm to yank him back to his side.

204

"Wait!" Opal protested for a moment; blank concern for Josh outweighed everything else, and she jumped forward. In an instant, hands were on her, pulling her away from going to Josh's side. Opal watched him cry out in pain, cupping his cheek with his hands as Adax shook him fiercely, hands on his shoulders.

"*Never* get involved with a *patient*." Adax snarled.

Involved?

I just agreed to be his friend.

The way he looked at me.

Friends don't do that. They don't.

But why was she focusing on this now? Opal screamed out as the other four scientists pulled her backward, yanking her toward somewhere she didn't want to go.

"Please! Just stop this!" Josh cried. "Please!"

Adax glowered at him. "Since I am the *forgiving* type, I will give you the honor of assisting me in this experiment," he rumbled.

Josh moaned. "Oh, come on."

"Strap her in," Adax ordered, stomping towards her, hauling an unwilling Josh with him.

"Wait!" Opal protested, but she was ignored. Delsea shoved her onto the metal bed, and bonds slowly came up from the bed and wrapped themselves over Opal, one on each ankle, one on each wrist, and one over her stomach.

Opal tried to keep her breathing level. This was so much worse, so much worse than any zombie or any fire. She was trapped, literally. She could run if there was stuff chasing her. She couldn't run here. She could hide if things were stalking and searching for her. She couldn't even fight as if they were attacking her. All she could do was wait. Wait and let them do whatever they want.

"Josh!" Opal's voice was wild as she locked eyes with him. "Please. If we are friends. Don't do this. Stop them."

Josh's eyes were just as wide as hers as he glanced at her with helpless horror, opening his mouth to say something.

"Josh?" Adax barked a laugh as he hauled Josh in front of him. "Josh can't do anything to stop us. He'll assist us. Or be punished. *Severely.* Care about those limbs, Josh? Help us out." Adax added darkly.

Josh paled. His gaze was desperate between Opal and Adax.

He won't help you. The voice was a morbid whisper in Opal's mind, but she was right.

"Let's see, orders, orders, orders," mumbled Adax. He rifled through his papers. Seemingly unaware of the threats he had just made to the young boy. "Ah! Here we are. *Just find out what she can do. Don't hurt her that much; push her till she shows any power.*" Adax read from his papers. He looked up at Opal, his eyes glinting.

"You see, the line between 'finding out what she is' and 'hurting her' isn't very clear, and I think we can bend it a little." laughed Adax.

Josh lurched forward. "*No!*" he yelled.

Adax stopped him. "And you will prove your loyalty by helping." he snarled.

Please, Josh. Help me.
I can't do this alone.
I can't do anything.

Delsea walked down the lines of tools past the metal bed on which Opal was strapped. They looked like dentist tools, sharp, metal, and long, glinting in the odd light. Opal had to fight back a whimper.

"Get the blue syringe. Yeah! That's the one!" called Adax.

Delsea happily lifted a large needle and fitted it onto a vial, twisting it shut.

"No!" Opal protested weakly. "I'll do anything, please! Don't do that to me!"

Nobody was listening. Shouldn't they have been listening? At that moment, in that fear, she would have happily agreed to find any cure. Destroy any cure. Do *anything*.

The anticipation.

The fear.

It would make the strongest human crumple.

"Ready," Delsea growled.

"Wait," ordered Adax. He turned on Josh with a leer. "He'll do it,"

Josh's eyes widened pathetically, and he tried to back away. He turned to Opal with tears shining in his eyes.

I like you, Opal. Josh's words echoed in her mind as Josh approached her.

Opal imagined him as his lips brushed her face.

Please.

Adax watched with a content expression on his face. "Go on," he growled, poking Josh roughly in the back.

Josh moved to put the syringe in Opal's arm. "I'm sorry, Opal." Josh suddenly hissed in her ear. "I'll owe you forever. I have to do this. I have to. But I'll come back. I promise. I'll come back, and I'll rescue you."

Opal's fingers twitched; still in the binds, she twined them with Josh. "Come back, and I'll forgive you," she whispered. *Maybe.*

With shaky hands, Josh tested the needle against Opal's arm.

She was shaking, her stomach cramping with helpless fear as she thrashed her head just to have more hands on her, holding her down.

She felt something splash on her cheek and realized it was a tear from Josh's face, still warm.

Josh plunged the needle into Opal's skin and staggered back in horror at what he had just done.

Opal felt the top pierce through the layers of her skin in the ordinary point of pain, like a little flu shot. But the similarities stopped there. After the needle was withdrawn, then came the pain.

Fire was filling Opal.

All thoughts of Josh were driven out of her head as she thrashed and screamed in agony.

She wanted it to stop. She wanted it to end. "Josh!" she yelled, crying, pleading. But there was no response.

A monster inside of her awakened; it clawed at her insides and seemed to want to engulf her, tearing through her, through her veins, skin, and bones. Everything. To the tip of her hair and to the tip of her toes, Opal was in pain.

She thrashed; she tasted blood in her mouth from where she had bit into the side of her mouth.

She wanted it to end. She tried to get away, to crawl from her own skin.

208

Then she felt a new pain in her arm, a pricking sensation, and the fire inside her began to subside. It retreated inch by inch as Opal gasped in relief, her chest rising and falling with ragged breaths.

She drifted back into the world and saw the hazy faces of Delsea, Adax, and Josh staring down at her.

Adax's face was calm and delightful, as if he took pleasure in watching people suffer. Delsea's face was pinched up, and she was muttering to herself. Of course, Josh's face was tear-stricken, and his hands were shaky as he took Opal's hand.

"Oh, Opal, I'm so sorry!" he wept.

Opal's throat was raw and scratched; she couldn't respond but wanted so badly to tell Josh that the fire was gone. It had left. Was she safe?

"Hmm, I think she responded well to that one; maybe try this one." mused Delsea and handed Adax a vile filled with sloshy red liquid.

"Well?" snarled Josh. "She almost *died!*" he yelled in Adax's face.

Adax shrugged. "It's all part of the experiment."

"Experiment? What are you *doing*?" Opal choked, finally finding her voice.

"Acana Magic." Josh sighed. "Under stress, it is one of the most powerful."

"A wonderful way to find out what you can do, dear Opal." Adax smiled.

"Under stress." Opal choked. "No."

209

"I think this is starting to get out of our hands; bring him in."
sighed Adax suddenly. He snapped his fingers again, and Delsea trotted
off.

Opal didn't want to be a xenophobe, but she was petrified of
what or who the next person would be; she didn't know how to stop
them. Acana Magic was *visions*. Unless it was enhanced... How could
she stop metal and tools? Even The Sightseerer... In her visions, he
couldn't fight metal holding him or fight the people torturing him.
These visions were smoke and fog. They were true. But not helpful in
captivity.

She wasn't special.

She was helpless.

Moments later, a man strode into the room at a brisk pace; he
just seemed to appear. But Opal didn't question it for longer than a few
moments. She had seen more than enough magical things in the past
weeks; they could have been doors anywhere. People could be watching
her through glass screens, and she didn't know.

The man had crisp brown hair flattened onto his head. He was
neither tall nor short, perfectly average. He had sharp emerald eyes, but
they were a great deal kinder than Adax's piercing glare. He wore a
white lab coat with a whole collection of ballpoint pens tucked away in
one pocket. His high leather boots clicked on the floor as he walked
towards Opal.

"So this is the one that Richmond is so excited about," he
sighed. His voice wasn't at all as slippery as Adax's or Delphina's; it was
warm, but there was nothing comfortable about it.

"Yeah, not much to look at." Growled Delsea from behind
him.

"Hello, Opal, my name is Silas Jones; I am your head scientist." the man reprimanded.

He wasn't as sinister as Opal was expecting, but he certainly wasn't friendly. Silas's eyes swept around the room. His eyes rested on Josh, and a surprised and concerned look flitted across his face. "Josh, what are you doing here?" he demanded, not to crossley.

Josh didn't respond, eyes downcast.

"Well, get out of here! This is no place for children!" Silas snapped.

Opal desperately wanted to point out that, strictly speaking, if Josh was a child, then she was definitely a child, and they were holding her captive, but she bit her tongue. Making Silas mad wasn't going to help her problems. It was like adding wood to a blazing fire in an attempt to quench it.

"No," Adax growled firmly. "He stays; we need to teach him... A *Lesson*," the mire tone of Adax's words made a drip of sweat slide down Opal's face. "He's become *infatuated* with this patient."

Silas shrugged. "Where am I to argue? We all work together here, after all. If this helps his er... Feelings, then why not."

Lies. Lies. Lies. Opal's brain hissed.

Keep talking. Keep talking. Opal silently prayed. Was it done?

"Well then," Silas chirped as he snapped on large blue gloves. "Let's get started, shall we?" He smiled.

"Delsea, get the lights," Adax ordered.

Darkness?

No.

Please no.

Opal's heart nearly tore open as she tried to keep the whimper away. She couldn't be left in darkness, not when they were walking around her with the metal in their hands.

But she couldn't do anything as Delsea obediently flicked off the leading lights, plunging the room into a state of temporary complete darkness, only to the sound of dripping liquid and shallow breathing, Opal felt a slow crawl of terror start to fill her, and she opened her mouth to scream just as another light was switched on, near Opal's face blinding her. Just like in the room where Delphina had questioned her, the light slashed through her mind until she couldn't see.

It was all a haze.

Sharp white light.

Josh's terrified face.

Adax's sneer.

Silas's fake smile.

Syringe.

Liquid.

A scream.

Who's?

She didn't know.

Pain.

Sudden pain.

She was losing herself in her head, losing herself in the white light.

Nothing but pain and light.

Opal was sweating now; she lost sight of everybody, even Josh. It was all light in her mind now. All voices with no bodies as she felt more and more things enter her body.

Silas didn't take his eyes off Opal; they were looming high above her. Always there. "Yes, Josh," he sighed. Then he looked at the terrified boy before him, and his face softened. "It may be a bit frightening to watch someone be experimented on at first, but don't worry, you'll get used to it."

So that's how it's going to be, old man?

You wait until someone's been trapped in this hellhole long enough, and then the screams won't reach their heart anymore? Until their hearts are sealed with iron and metal?

You wait until the scientists of this place are cold-hearted murderers?

Silas's words didn't seem to comfort Josh at all. She could feel his fingers on hers, but everything was too numb.

Stop.

Stop.

Stop.

STOP.

They were everywhere; she could feel them. The monster. The pain. The metal. It was all merging until there was no more Opal left in this foreign beast's body. Somewhere inside of her, she knew that part of this. All of this pain wasn't to find out how strong her Acana Magic was. No.

Richmond wanted to break her spirit.

Until he could use her powers for his own evil.

He was succeeding.

Someone let out a cry of pain as the monster strapped to the bed dug its fingernails into someone's hand and drew blood.

It was a tornado, coming faster and faster and faster until it was all swept up in a swirl of pain, light, blood, metal, and tears.

It was reaching its peak, waiting to topple over like a wave. It hovered on the edge, spinning with energy. Pulsing and trashing- moving and hurting-

And- it was all quiet. The pain suddenly drifted away. It was gone. The blackness, the light.

It was so quiet.

Thump.

Thump.

Was that her heart? Why was it so slow?

And where had the pain gone?

She was retreating, retreating into the very dark corners of her mind, into the hallways she couldn't come out of. It was a labyrinth. A labyrinth with no escape. But that was alright. There was no pain. No apocalypse. No monsters. No enemy girlfriends. No disappointed mothers or angry scientists.

Opal sat down.

It was cold down there on the floor, with the towering shelves making way for an inky black sky.

Thousands of towers stretched in all directions. A maze. A labyrinth that she could never find the exit to.

And honestly, she was alright.

If she was never found.

Thump.

Thump.

214

"Opal?" he came out of the shadows, just as Opal had imagined.

Her father. With the same deep brown eyes and gentle smile as he emerged from the shadows, dusting off the same brown pants he had worn... he had worn them the last time Opal had seen him.

The day he had died.

"Father?" Opal whispered.

Thump.

Thump.

"Opal. My Hylight." His voice was just like he remembered, and Opal couldn't stop the tears that ran down her face as she jumped up to embrace her father.

He was warm, sturdy as ever, as he hugged her tight. "It's time to go now," he whispered in her ear. "It's time to follow me."

Thump.

Thump.

"Follow you?" Opal whispered. "Follow you where?"

"I know you're afraid, my Hylight, but it will be alright."

The day he had died. He looks the same as the day he died.

Opal pulled away. "I'm dying?"

"Of course you are. It's time now. It's stalked you for so long; it's only been your will that's held you on. Now come." her father slipped her hand into his, pointing with his free hand towards the dark, winding hallway in front of them.

No.

Thump.

Thump.

Her father smiled at her, but suddenly, it wasn't comforting.

215

She would keep walking. She could see it in her mind now. She would follow him into the darkness, but it would end. Death.

No heaven or underworld was waiting for her. Only darkness. "No," Opal whispered. "I won't."

Her father's face suddenly creased. "But you *must*. I-I'm sure this is the path you take." he started forward, taking her hand. "Come with me."

"No." Opal tore her hand away. "I won't die! I won't!" she suddenly started running, getting faster and faster. She turned just to see her father staring after her, his face nothing but sadness.

But she couldn't. No matter how much her heart twisted or how much she cried to run back to her father, she wouldn't. She *couldn't*.

Her father wasn't worth giving up life, not while she still had fight left in her body.

Thump.

Thump.

Opal was running faster now. Into the labyrinth, she screamed again and again as it started to come down on her.

Every turn, every twist. It led nowhere. No escape.

Everywhere.

Nowhere.

Opal screamed; dust and stone blocked her on every corner as she tried to claw her way out, desperate to stay ahead, to fight the darkness...

I won't.

I won't.

I won't go into the darkness.

216

I WON'T

It was her plea. Her promise, as Opal screamed to the world, was suddenly a tangible thing she was fighting. A darkness she was working to claw her way out of... she would get out.

Because her life depended on it.

"There, all finished."

It was one more blast of pain, and then it cooled.

Everywhere, a calm blanket was spreading around the monster, clothing and comforting it. Its sensation swept back into its body, and with it, Opal returned bit by bit.

The labyrinth was gone. Her father was gone.

But what was left of her?

The light was gone. The metal was gone. The bags of liquid were gone.

Adax was there.

Silas was there.

Josh was there.

She had cheated death.

How long could she cheat it for?

Thump.

Thump.

Thump.

"Thank god you're ok!" Josh cried.

"Don't get it comfortable; this was just the easy part," growled Adax. "I think we need more blood samples," he added.

No.

How could she go back to the maze? To the never-ending corners. To the blackness. To the death.

217

"Nonsense!" chided Silas, and Opal breathed a sigh of relief. "We just need to test a few things."

Josh inhaled as Opal tried to come back; slowly, her mind came back to her body, but she knew. She knew that a part of her would always be trapped in the darkness with her mournful father waiting for a daughter who would never return.

I'm sorry Daddy.

I'm just not ready.

"First, let's test for antibodies to the virus." snarled Silas.

Delsea and Adax grumpily moved to a control station as if they took more pleasure in watching Opal suffer than in actually obtaining any helpful information. Probably did.

Delsea tapped a button on a table, and a computer popped up on a desk.

It was a large metal desk with two computers that issued odd beeping noises. There was also a strange device that resembled a hunk of metal, but it was stimulating a green line across the top.

Delsea clicked onto the computer with Adax hovering by her shoulder.

"Ok, scanning, now," Delsea remarked in a flat tone.

Silas stared intently at Opal as Opal tried to calm her breathing, Josh was by her shoulder, and Opal hadn't realized until now that he had been stroking her hair. He jumped back with a startled expression as he realized she was awake. He leaned forward, resigning to whisper comforting things in her ear that soon became nothing but background noise in her fear.

"Boss, I think it's unlikely that she had any antibodies." whined one of the scientists.

"Yeah, maybe you're right, Stefan." agreed another one with the nameplate: Rubert.

"Hmph, I don't even know why the president is making us research her!" put in the last one with the name tag: Eijahn.

"Stop whining!" roared Adax. That shut them up, they muttered to each other, making excuses and glancing at the floor.

Delsea's brow furrowed. "Silas, you may want to take a look at this,"

Silas trotted over. Josh tried to look, but Silas shoved him down. "No, it's not for your eyes," he growled. "We already need to have a talk about..." he paused, glaring fiercely at Opal and then at Josh. "About you *mingling* with your father."

His mysterious father.

Silas stared at the screen and stared at it some more; his eyes popped, his brow furrowed.

"That can't be right!" he exclaimed. "Check it again!" He demanded. "This is none of the standard responses to the tests!"

Delsea nodded to one of the scientists, and he got out a creepy-looking vial; Opal's mind didn't even have time to whip herself into a frenzy before the shot was in her and out, pulling out a thin stream of blood with it. Adax collected the blood and slipped the sample into the computer.

There was a moment of tense silence, then the computer drawled in an animated voice: ***antibodies detected.***

17

TYLER

"You've already packed everything, Mandy!" Nolan cried, annoyed as Miranda wrung her hands around at the five packs they had packed for their trip, leaving a good week or so of food and clothes with Irene, who was still unconscious.

Miranda turned to Nolan, her face a mask of terror. "B-but what if something happens? I mean... come on. It's dangerous out there."

Nolan laughed, swinging Miranda around until she laughed, too. "What could dare hurt you when I'm around?" he demanded, kissing her softly.

"Are you sure about leaving Irene?" Cora whispered.

"It's the best, isn't it?" Tyler muttered back.

Cora sighed faintly. "I know. But she was home. She reminded me. Reminded me of... before."

Tyler clenched her hands. "*I'll* remind you."

"If this is what's going to be the rest of this *adventure*, I'm opting out to stay back with the crazy lady." Casper suddenly growled, sweeping his silver-tipped hair out of his eyes as he strapped his backpack on. "I'm seriously going to be sick."

"Of course not." Nolan smiled, still twirling Miranda.

Cora beamed at Tyler, batting her eyelashes. "Of course not." she echoed.

Casper rolled his eyes, tossing backpacks to each of them.

Tyler strapped on his, the frayed straps of his knapsack, the one he had grabbed before rushing away to find Cora-

A bolt of lightning struck suddenly in Tyler's mind.

Irene.

She had saved his life.

In a way.

She had been so foul to Cora the night before in a drunken rage that she had driven Cora from the house, causing Tyler to run after her at the break of dawn; the fire that had swept across the village had missed them both. And Irene conveniently.

Conveniently.

Irene seemed to be in a drunken rage half the time, bellowing things about the future and the past to Cora and him half the time, but he had always dismissed it.

But the night before, when she had almost killed Casper and screamed at him and all of them.

That wasn't a drunken rage.

What did she know?

Or did she know anything?

Tyler sighed. He was whipping himself up into a frenzy for nothing. Irene was just plain crazy. She'd been crazy for years, slipping farther and farther away from the world ever since Cora's father took off.

She's gone. Tyler thought sadly. There was no point in thinking that Irene knew anything because she didn't.

"Are you ready?" Nolan asked quietly.

Everyone's gaze suddenly drifted to Irene; she was still slumped like she had been the night before, with a pack of supplies for a week sitting next to her.

Only a week.

"I-I didn't think about what it would be like. What it would be like when we left her." Miranda whispered. "She's an adult. No matter how she is."

Cora was deathly pale as she stared at her mother. Tyler couldn't even begin to wonder what she was thinking.

"Guys. Be strong." Casper growled, stepping forward.

Tyler shot Casper a glare; no matter how prickly he was or how tough his gang life had been, it didn't offer any excuse. Cora was leaving her *mother*.

Casper's face softened under Tyler's glare. "I know it's hard, but she'll get us killed. We're going to find Opal in the mountains where an old woman can't keep up; she doesn't know defense like we do, and she'll just die in front of us."

Silence greeted his words, everybody glancing at Cora, waiting for her reaction.

Cora suddenly stiffened, squaring her jaw as she looked up. "You're right. She will slow us down; she's been horrid to me for years, and in a way, this is *my* revenge."

Tyler couldn't beat back his smile as he glanced at her.

That was her.

Not the jealous, clingy, ditzy girl most people saw. No, the Cora *Tyler* knew. The strong, brave, courageous girl who was afraid of nothing.

222

Was Opal scared up there? In the mountains? Was she waiting for him?

I'll come. I promise. Wait for me. Tyler thought quietly.

Irene suddenly jerked in place; one bloodshot eye opened wide as she stretched, pulling herself to her feet. "So." Her voice cracked, and Tyler jumped at the sound of her voice; all his friends were slowly backing away from her, scooping up their supplies and moving towards the exit if they had to make a fast retreat.

"So." Irene snarled again. "You're trying to give me the *slip,* aren't you?"

Nobody moved. Nobody said anything; all eyes flicked to Cora.

Cora raised her chin as she stared her mother dead in the eye. "Yes. We are. There are supplies, and I'm sure there are shelters you can go to, and the government will take care of you. We won't anymore. We're going to rescue... our friend." Cora's voice hitched, but Tyler pretended not to hear. "I'm done." there was so much more meaning behind those two words. Tyler could almost feel the history pouring from the simple syllables, hear every cruel word Irene had ever yelled at Cora, hear every night Cora had spent curled up and sobbing.

Irene sneered; Tyler wished nothing more than to wipe the smile off her face once and for all. "Go then. Let's see if you can do it."

Tyler clenched Cora's hand; they were all ready. They could walk out of here and be on their way... yet it was *so hard.*

"A disowned daughter. A boy who can't make up his mind. A clown. A murderer and a girl destined to die. Good luck." Irene snarled. "My stupid daughter with only fluff behind ears. No courage, just a pretty face that nobody will look at twice, nonetheless love."

223

Cora suddenly turned on her heel, rushing away from her mother, sliding down the rock face and out into the sunlight.

Tyler shot one last glare at Irene, at the woman who had saved his life, hunched over and snoring. A last look at the cave that had saved his life.

But he had to move on.

He had to survive.

He was coming.

Hold on, Opal. He thought grimly. *I'm coming.*

A disowned daughter.

A boy who can't make up his mind.

A clown.

A murderer.

A girl destined to die.

No.

It can't be.

Cora isn't disowned.

Nolan's more than a clown.

Okay, Casper could be a murderer, but that doesn't matter anymore; he's with us now, and we'll guide him.

Miranda. Destined to die? How?

I-I can make up my mind. I can.

Tyler slid after Cora down the rock to find her curled up, shaking.

Tears hadn't spilled out yet from her eyes, but her eyes had the glossy look of someone who was about to. She stared up at Tyler.

"Is it wrong that I still want her to love me?" she asked quietly.

Tyler was frozen for a second, unsure of what to do. How could he relate to her at all?

But when she held out her arms, he didn't hesitate to pull her up in a hug. "No." he breathed into her hair.

Nolan and Miranda were both by her shoulders seconds later, patting her back or whispering words of comfort.

"It's time to go." Casper suddenly called gruffly.

Tyler turned to face him; his face seemed a shade paler than usual as if he was just as shaken by Irene's murderer taunts as Cora. No matter how much time Tyler spent with Casper, he still couldn't quite get a read on him. At first, he had seemed just the aloof and angry boy that he projected, but then.... He'd saved both Tyler and Cora's life. There was definitely more to him than what met the eye. Tyler couldn't decide yet whether that was good or bad.

"Let's get high up," Casper muttered. "Any zombie would freeze before they get us." Casper pointed a pale finger towards the distant, towering peaks before them; a swirl of cloud suddenly started to drift across the dark rocks; Tyler could just imagine the load of snow it was carrying.

"And we won't?" Cora demanded skeptically.

"Bundle up, princess," Casper smirked, tossing her a bundle of clothes.

Tyler gripped his torch tighter. The sun was still shining brightly, but the twisting trees of the forest before them were just too dark for his liking; according to Nolan and Casper, the zombies were repelled by fire, but looking at the flickering light at the end of his stick Tyler wasn't sure that would even make a dent in an attack.

225

And the zombies had been perfectly content to attack the villages while the fires raged.

Tyler's heart beat faster and faster as they got farther and farther away from the caves, stopping by the place Cora and he had gotten attacked to drink and splash water on their faces. Tyler shot a dark glare at the trees around him, his mind flashing to when the water had run red. Tyler glanced at Casper, but he seemed unconcerned about the fact that he had committed murder there. Not wanting to probe any deeper into the forest across the bank, the group followed the river until it started looping uphill, the current, of course, going down the hill.

"Up?" Miranda asked tentatively.

"It's a big mountain range," Nolan said doubtfully. "How will we find where Delphina is?"

"The chances are low..." Cora added quickly.

"Guys!" Tyler protested. They weren't going to back down now, were they? "Come on. We can't leave her with Delphina!"

"I know... but how will we find her?" Cora demanded.

Tyler paused, his heart thumping. Suddenly, the snowy peaks seemed all the more dark and ominous. How would they find Opal? How would they find her before freezing to death in a swirl of snow?

A sudden idea suddenly flashed through Tyler's mind. A smile curled over his lips as the idea turned over in his mind. "I know someone we can go to to reassess. They live in the mountains, and their father is a wilderness buff- always talking about conspiracy theories and apocalypse. If anyone knows where a supervillain is, it's him." Tyler smiled, glancing at Cora, whose eyes had widened.

"Are you *serious*?" She growled. "I'd rather go out into a storm."

Tyler took her hand in his. "Come on, it's alright. We were *five*, and you'll see Lida."

Cora sighed again.

Tyler smiled again, flattening his hands against hers so they entwined.

"Guys! Fill us in!" Casper snapped. "I'm *really* not doing this if the whole time all y'all are just making moony eyes at each other." His gaze was so dark Tyler flinched.

"Right!" Tyler snapped out of his thoughts. "This family lives in the mountains. They used to come down to the lake with us every summer, with me and Cora, and they're great. Though er- Cora doesn't like them much- or specifically Violet."

"Or *at all*." Cora hissed.

"Really? *Cora* not liking someone?" Nolan gasped. "*Impossible.*"

"Shut up," muttered Cora.

"Erm. Violet told everybody Cora would turn into an ogre and eat them all if anybody talked to her." Tyler tried to stifle his laugh. He recalled how Cora had barely tolerated Violet ever since; it probably didn't help that Violet was his best friend and really pretty.

They had been friends almost as long as he and Cora were strictly friends. Cora got along fine with Violet's twin sister; however, funny enough. Probably because Lida despised him.

"Well then! Let's go there." Nolan clapped his hands. "Sounds great."

227

"Hold on!" Cora held out her hand. "They could have been driven out, all of them. Or go to the government's shelters. Nothing is telling us that they are still at their house. They could be dead."

Tyler tried not to flinch at how matter of fact Cora spit out those words; even the thought of finding his best friend mangled with clear glassy eyes like Sasha made him sick.

"Really? *Logan*? He had a full *tornado* bunker on the side of his house. He literally *lives* for these kinds of things." Tyler responded quickly. "And he wouldn't trust the government enough to go to one of their shelters."

Miranda glanced uneasily up at the sky. "Well, let's go quick then, it's getting dark... How do we know where to find them?"

"We'll just follow the river; they live right by this same one. Use it to get fish and stuff." Tyler replied promptly, pleased that he had retained at least one helpful bit of information.

"Come on." Casper started forward, wielding his torch in the dim light of the forest as they entered. They tramped for what must have been a mile, going through the foggy forest, only catching glimpses of the sun that was slipping farther and farther down the sky. Slowly but surely, the terrain began to change as they got higher. The trees dwindled away and were replaced by rocks. Soon, the only constant was the winding river. It must have been at least ten miles.

Tyler was drenched in sweat, his chest heaving and his legs aching as they finally came to a sheltered part of the river bend where it turned sharply, cutting off a large sandy bank with an overhanging rock ledge. They wouldn't be fully covered, but it was better than nothing.

"Let's stop here," Casper called; Tyler turned for the first time since they had started climbing in elevation; they must have traveled

228

even farther than he had thought. Below them, he could only make out the tips of the fuzzy trees of the valley; they were much, much higher now, and it was a lot cooler. Tyler was already pulling on more layers, and he shivered, listening to the wind swirl up around him and his friends.

He tried not to look towards the dark, snow-covered peaks that they still had to travel to.

If Tyler remembered correctly, the Daltons lived where the snow was still thin enough for it to be habitable in the winter and where the house was at least a few miles up in the mountains to be found.

It meant a long hike tomorrow. Up, up, and up into the clouds.

Cora collapsed on the ground next to Miranda, breathing loudly. "That was so *long,*" she whined. Tyler could almost feel the foul mood coming off of her in waves.

"Move over," Casper grunted; he was building a wall of fire. *Literally.* He was gathering sticks and kindling to create a line around the entrance to the rock overhang, blocking them completely from the zombies but still allowing a cleft of air to let the smoke escape; it would shelter them from the monsters and keep them warm from the cold that was starting to creep in.

We must be closer to Violet's than I thought if it's this cold. Tyler thought, rubbing his arms.

That's when the first flakes started to fall. They started out small, drifting into the river and landing on the ground, melting at contact. Still, it wasn't long before a thin dusting of white started to cover the ground. At that moment, Tyler was so grateful for Casper; he already had a roaring wall of fire going, with a giant stack of kindling next to it.

"Get in," Casper called. "Before I seal it up."

Tyler squeezed in with Cora; with all five of them, it was a tight fit, but it was alright. It was warm.

They stayed as close to the rock as they could, with the final result about ten feet from the flames, not daring to go any closer in the worry one of them would turn over in their sleep and roll into the fire.

Food was passed out with half-frozen fingers, warmed by the fire.

"You know. I'm really starting to miss fruit with *water* in it." Nolan sighed, turning over a dried plum before sticking it in his mouth with a sour expression.

"I never thought I'd *miss* vegetables," Miranda muttered.

"Or my annoying little brother." Nolan sighed.

"Good night," Casper said abruptly, dropping his head to his knees.

Nolan looked surprised, but his eyelids were already starting to droop. "I can keep watch..." He began.

"No need," Tyler responded briskly. "It's too cold for them, and besides, we have fire."

"Hot and cold," Nolan muttered before drifting off.

Tyler watched the flakes drift down faster and faster behind the hazy bit of smoke and fire.

"Good night," Cora whispered, curling up; Tyler smiled down at her, at her and her gorgeous face, with her blonde hair spread out like a cloud.

230

He laid down next to her and closed his eyes, even though every part of his body ached from the long trek.... Nightmares went hand in hand with sleep.

It started out with his brother.

Just him and his brother sitting in Calico's room. Calico's red walls and messy bed almost brought tears to Tyler's eyes as he stared around. He could practically feel fond memories radiating from these walls.

"So." Calico suddenly turned to him. "I'm dead."

"What? What a thing to say, bro. Of course, you're not dead! I wouldn't let that happen to you." *Tyler felt a sudden shock hit him. What was Calico talking about? Who would say such a thing? But for some reason, it felt so* real. *Like that did happen.*

Did it?

He couldn't quite remember.

"Yes." Calico hissed, suddenly standing up. "You left me for your girlfriend. *You should have burned along with us. That's what a real brother would have done. Or maybe you would have saved us."*

Tyler felt paralyzed with shock. Yes. Yes, he remembered. He'd gone to find Cora that morning and came back to find Calico and h-his parents being consumed by the heat and flames.

"Now you lie next to the flames that killed us and next to the girl that killed us! How dare you?!" Suddenly, Calico was on him, his eyes blazing with such a fury that Tyler had never seen in his younger brother before.

Tyler stumbled backward, and suddenly, the whole room was crumbling and falling before him until all he could see was his brother's dark, leering eyes, staring at him with such hatred, such betrayal.

"I HATE YOU!" he roared before the debris came thicker. Dust *and smoke fell from every possible patch of air, covering him completely.*

Tyler gasped awake, flinching away from Cora, who had her arm flung over his side. He jumped to his feet, cursing silently as he banged his head on the rocky ceiling and fell back to his knees.

It was still night; he must have slept for a couple hours because he felt rested, but he also felt terrified.

Irene might have saved his life, but she killed Calico and his parents.

A burst of hatred suddenly surged through Tyler.

I hope the zombies get her.

It wasn't my fault, Calico. It was Irene's. All hers.

Tyler tried to stem the flood of emotions, but he couldn't. Not the hatred that seemed to be consuming him these days, that strong feeling that he couldn't resist. How long before he took it out on someone? Before he lashed out at Cora? Or Miranda? Until the hatred in his brother's eyes was reflected in his own?

Tyler sighed. It wasn't really Irene's fault. No. It was the zombies. And the one who controlled them. The one who had Opal locked away in her clutches.

Delphina.

Tyler sighed again and resigned to stare out into the darkness; a few stray flakes still floated down. It felt a lot colder than when he had fallen asleep, though.

Was the fire burning down?

The fire.

232

Tyler's gaze tore across the kindling that circled the rocky cave. Snow dusted across the fire line. The fire had burned down while they had slept. And so had their protection.

It was gone.

Relax. It's too cold for them. Tyler thought uneasily.

But yet, as he stared out into the darkness, he felt a lot more worried. Those swirling depths of the night weren't dangerous a few months ago, but they were now.

It wasn't just coyotes and bears that could get them.

Yet what was that noise?

Tyler glanced around at his sleeping friends. He didn't want to wake them... especially Cora, who was exhausted after the hike and with her wounds that were still healing from the attack.

But.

He might just be paranoid.

Maybe he was just hearing the swirling and howling wind...

But suddenly, it sounded much, much more clear.

The sky was dark.

The night was dark.

And he heard it.

Marching.

Footsteps.

Dragging footsteps.

Hundreds of them, disorganized, lumbering noises. As if the creatures were half-deformed. The first groans splintered the night air. They were moving. A crowd of them. Thousands of them.

And he and his friends had no protection. They had to run. They had to get to Violets.

233

Or die.

He heard them before he saw them.

Zombies.

Energy jolted through his body. "Wake up!" Tyler hissed frantically, shaking his friends with all of his might. His hands shook with cold and fear as he pulled on their supplies, trying desperately to run against time.

In a moment, he was eye to eye with bleary Nolan, and he shook him fiercely. "Zombies!" Tyler half shrieked. "Hundreds! They're coming! I can hear them!"

Surprisingly it was Miranda who reacted first, her eyes going wide with fear and her head cocked, no doubt listening to the noises of the horde getting closer and closer.

All five of them were awake now, blearily wiping sleep out of their eyes as they worked to pack up their stuff.

"We need to get out of here before they corner us!" Tyler gasped. "Cora!" he half-wailed.

"Come on!"

"Hurry!"

"Do you have everything?"

"What are we waiting for?"

"Run!"

"Go!"

"Get out!"

It was half chaos, bundling everyone up, pushing and yelling out the enclave and into the snow, slipping in the wet grass, and pushing each other forward as they ran half-blind up the mountain.

"We have to go straight to Violet's!" Tyler cried. "Don't stop!"

234

It was pure madness, with darkness and snow surrounding them and the dark, roaring river swirling unfathomably by their sides. Terror, adrenaline. Monsters.

They were running blind up the mountain face, over rocks, bushes, and trees. Branches wiped Tyler's face as he held on tight to Cora's hand. He made the mistake of looking back, just one glance, but the sight filled him with dread. About two hundred feet behind but slowly gaining were hundreds of zombies.

Eyes glinting, mouths open, feet dragging. They were running on all fours like some sort of rabid animal; some of them even got trampled in their attempts to get forward.

They were inescapable.

Cora was sobbing as she ran. "We can't escape! It's miles to their house!"

"I'm not giving up!" Tyler snarled, reaching to pull Miranda along. But how could he keep running? They were running from the dead and didn't need to rest or stop.

And slowly, their own bodies gave way; it was a mile before Tyler's chest started to heave and contract, before his legs began to stumble, Cora falling farther and farther behind. The adrenaline was failing. *He* was failing.

"Wait!" Tyler cried to Casper, Nolan, and Miranda in front of him. "Cora." he gasped, paralyzed with fear. He couldn't lose her; at some point in the run, she had slipped from his arms, and now, he saw her fifty meters behind them, clutching her chest where two dark slashes of blood had appeared. Her wounds had been reopened with the strain, and now her face was chalk white with fear and blood loss.

"I'll get her." Miranda cried, darting back down the slope to Cora before Tyler or Nolan could protest, throwing her arm over Cora's shoulder and pulling her along.

How were there *more?* Where did all of these zombies come from?

If it was this bad in the middle of the mountains... What was it like in the populated cities?

"Cora!" Tyler called out; he couldn't take it anymore. He darted down the slope towards Cora. But something was wrong with Miranda; she was fighting wildly, pulling herself forward; her foot and pant leg were entangled hopelessly with a tree root, and her face creased with effort.

"Go!" Miranda called in a strangled gasp. "I'm fine! Give me a second; I'll be right there!"

Tyler didn't move; they were right behind him; Cora was bleeding heavily, sinking into him. She couldn't move; he had to get her out of there.

"Go!" Miranda shrieked.

He had to. He caught one last glance at Miranda's terrified face and of the monsters boring down on her before he scooped up Cora and ran up the slope.

"Where's Miranda?" Nolan demanded. He and Casper were hovering near the tree line. Nolan's face twisted, and Casper's face shone with sweat.

"S-She's coming. I-I had to get Cora." Tyler panted. But he knew. He knew Miranda would never come; it was too late.

Dreading what he would see, Tyler slowly turned back and watched the scene unfold.

236

Still struggling with the root, Miranda screamed as loud as she could. "*Nolan! Help me!* PLEASE!" she shrieked.

Nolan's face went white, and he ran forward; Tyler didn't hesitate to throw himself in front of Nolan, pushing back the smaller boy with his shoulder as Nolan pushed himself against Tyler.

"No! You'll die!" Tyler cried.

Miranda's face was twisted in horror, and it was only moments before she was swallowed in a mass of moving limbs and shrieking bodies. The sickening crunch and rip was enough for Tyler to know that Miranda was dead.

For a moment, everything was silent, frozen in shock as snow swirled around them.

"Go! They won't stop with her!" Tyler yelled, pushing a numb and shocked Nolan forward, helping Cora up the mountain as he tried to ignore the guilt scoring through him.

She was dead.

She was dead.

She was dead.

And it was his fault.

His fault.

His fault.

He couldn't keep running, not when he was practically holding two other people and when his chest felt like it was going to burst, his vision was fading in and out, his breaths coming in wild gasps.

But the sky was getting lighter; they'd been running for an hour, and it had paid off. It started with the clouds slowly burning away, and small streaks of pink began to crease the sky.

Dawn.

He could see his friends muddied, terrified faces now, see Cora's blood-streaked body, and see his own pale white hands, frozen with the cold.

But still no sun.

They ran. They didn't dare hesitate, not with the zombies biting at their heels.

But finally...

The sun came with a bolt of warmth and light.

It came with the shrieking of the zombies.

It came with freedom.

With salvation.

The sun crested the tips of the mountains, rising into the sky as Tyler let out a cry of happiness. The monsters scattered, running anywhere but towards Tyler and his friends, diving for cover.

He fell to the ground, Cora collapsing next to him as sunlight tore across the snow-topped trees and rocks.

All four of them collapsed, limbs throbbing, chests heaving.

"W-We s-survived." choked Cora.

"N-No." Nolan gasped. "We *didn't*." And suddenly, he was on his feet, his eyes half wild with grief and shock.

"Miranda." Cora collapsed, her shoulders heaving.

They laid there. Snow blanketing their bodies. All but Nolan who stood, staring off into the distance, slow tears trickling out of his ghost-white face. Casper had his head in his hands, and Cora curled up with Tyler wrapped around her.

It must have been another hour before they moved when Tyler felt his lips crack with cold, and his fingers began to shake.

"We need to move. Before we freeze to death." Casper snapped. "We can't be far from your friend's house."

"I'd rather freeze to death than continue without Miranda." Nolan cried bitterly.

"She's *gone,* Nolan," Casper said roughly. "And she doesn't want you to freeze to death."

Nolan turned his head away, his eyes shining with tears. "No, but I do," he whispered.

Tyler felt a flash of fear. Was Nolan so far lost in his mind? Lost in his grief that they would lose him?

"No," Tyler said firmly, helping Cora to her feet. "No. We keep going. We can grieve later." *We have to.*

The food was frozen solid; no matter how much they tried to warm it up, it didn't melt. Tyler began to wonder if his body was freezing in the same way, but they didn't stop. They hiked higher and higher. They didn't bother with fire, not that they could with their frozen fingers, but there was no use. It was too cold.

Dark thoughts began to creep into Tyler's mind, leaving behind little seeds of doubt. What if he was wrong? What if the Daltons didn't live by the river? What if they'd already passed them? The river still gurgled next to them, winding up to where Tyler could see the distant source of the half-frozen waterfall.

Tyler felt hopeless; he couldn't help it. So much had happened. He missed his family; Miranda *and* Sasha were dead. They were freezing to death in snow that was endless, with no hope of seeing Opal or even Violet.

Nolan was pushing grimly on, but his eyes were hollow, as if he were only there in body, his mind far, far away.

239

Tyler wanted to collapse, his footsteps getting weaker and weaker... until-

"Look!" Casper choked.

In a sea of white and wind, Tyler's eyes caught a glimpse of a strange structure, but it looked so different than what he remembered; instead of being the stone cottage he recalled, hidden snugly next to the roaring river. It was now a metal contraption, with metal walls and blackout shades covering the entire house except for the chimney, which was billowing smoke.

Logan. Tyler thought wirily. Of course, he seemed to be the only one who could survive in the middle of an apocalypse in the middle of the mountains. Logan and his wife had built this place themselves, hoping to raise their children in the beauty of the natural world rather than in a city like they had both grown up in. They went down to the town often enough but always had a large stack of supplies on hand in case a blizzard would wipe through the mountains and snow them in.

Half frozen, the four friends stumbled towards the house, now hopelessly protected by metal.

"Where do we get in?" Nolan muttered.

Cora was already banging on the metal. "Lida! Logan!"

"There should be a tornado bunker entrance around here..." muttered Tyler, shifting uselessly through the snow; the cold was getting to his brain. He was so cold now; it felt like sharp spikes of pain in his torso and chest, but something scarier was happening to his face and fingers and toes; they were numb, completely numb, even when he pressed his fingernails into his cheeks, he couldn't feel a thing, his fingers were a scary blue.

240

"We need to find it before we freeze to death!" Casper snapped, hitting the metal harder.

"Logan! Lida! Aleesha! Violet! Conner!" Cora screamed again and again.

It was silent, with no noise except the howling wind.

Until-

BANG.

Snow flew everywhere as a snow drift suddenly burst apart, revealing a tall, middle-aged man who stared gruffly at the kids on his doorstep, standing on the steps to the tornado bunker he had just opened, which Tyler had been searching for frantically. The first thing that Tyler noticed was that in his thick hands, he held a heavy gun.

Tyler's heart seized, and he raised his hands above his head, praying Logan would recognize him.

"Tyler?" Logan demanded disbelievingly.

"Help us." breathed Tyler.

Logan stared them up and down, his skittishness battling with his compassion; they waited for a heartbeat; Tyler could almost feel the cold spreading through his body.

"Fine. Come in. And *quickly!* We're losing heat." Logan snapped, stepping back to let them gratefully stumble down the wooden steps.

Tyler glanced at Logan as they went past; he looked older, a few more lines stained his face, highlighting his dark green eyes, and a hint of stubble lined his jaw, but his bald head was as shiny and bare as ever, his strange pink scar the shape of two fingers was still as prominent as ever.

241

Tyler remembered asking the scary man about how he got his scar when he was younger.

"I wasn't paying attention while climbing a tree and disturbed an eagle's nest; it got me in the head."

"What happened to the eagle?" little Tyler had gasped.

Logan had fixed him with a steely glare. "It didn't survive."

Logan was wearing his usual combat-style clothes: dark green pants, combat boots, and a brown shirt as if he was about to jump right into war.

Tyler stumbled down the stairs, his legs still numb from cold and unused to the blast of warmth the bunker provided; it was as habitable as usual, always ready to be moved in. Stacks and stacks of canned food, dried herbs, and vegetables crowded the small, earthy space; illuminated by a single light, a set of wooden stairs led up to their house.

Tyler pushed past a flood of claustrophobia as he remembered what had happened the last time they were in a bunker and how Opal had nearly died in his arms. But looking around, the walls were dirt, not metal, and it couldn't have been airtight. Plus, there were exits and no frenzied mob of people trying to escape.

"Let's go upstairs; Aleesha can take care of you," Logan muttered, his eyes sweeping over their bedraggled, frozen group.

Tyler's whole body was tingling as the warmth of the earthy air swept over him. He felt like he was thawing.

Tyler let out a breath as slowly he relaxed; it was going to be alright. An adult could take care of them now; they weren't wandering out in the snow. And he could see Violet! It had been too long since he had seen his best friend, Tyler glanced sideways at Cora.

242

And there have been some developments.

Tyler smiled as he went up the stairs and pushed open the door to an even warmer blast of warmth.

He only caught a glimpse of a well-lit room, with a fire crackling merrily in the hearth and a well-looking woman with chocolate-colored skin tossing away her book with a smile as she saw her guests before a wave of black hair whipped him in the face and he was tackled in a hug.

Tyler couldn't help but smile as he hugged his friend back, swaying back and forth until they broke apart.

Violet tightened her grip on his shoulders as she smiled at him. "It's so good to see you!" she gasped. Violet had caramel-colored skin, wavy black hair, and warm brown eyes that crinkled as she smiled at Tyler.

Violet's gaze moved from Tyler to Cora, and she smirked. "Oh, it's good to see you too, Oger."

Cora rolled her eyes. "*Hilarious.*"

Violet shrugged, moving on to introduce herself enthusiastically to Nolan and Casper.

Tyler glanced around their house; it seemed the same since he had visited a few months ago, the same dark red and brown bricks stretching up to the wooden rafters on the ceiling to make the outside of the house and the same gigantic crackling hearth, always blazing with flame. Couches and armchairs were arranged in a semicircle around the fire and in the common room, with separate hallways leading off to the kitchen and bedrooms.

Aleesha Dalton, Logan's wife, smiled as she embraced Tyler. "It's so good to see you! I'm so glad you're alright," she whispered.

243

Aleesha was a pretty woman, with eyes just like her daughters and short black hair. Logan had met his wife in an exchange program in South India nearly twenty years ago.

Lida, Violet's twin sister, came out of the kitchen, wiping her hands on a towel, Cora moved to hug her tightly. Lida didn't share much resemblance to Violet. Instead, she had Logan's green eyes and brown hair.

"Tyler, my man!" Conner came out of his bedroom to slap Tyler on the back, just like he did every time they saw each other. Conner was twenty, having just returned home from college in California for a few weeks. Tyler guessed he had just stayed with his family when the fires hit. Conner was tall and gangly, with light hazel eyes—a mix of green and brown—and spiky black hair.

It was a few minutes before Tyler and his friends were settled into couches and chairs, wrapped in blankets, their hair still dripping from recent showers (with running water from the river outside, of course), and holding steaming cups of hot chocolate. Cora had a fresh bandage around her stomach, and to Tyler's relief, it had stopped bleeding.

"So what's going on?" Aleesha asked, curling herself up on a chair. "What brings you here?"

"Well." Tyler began- glancing at his friends.

"It's a long story," Cora added quickly.

"Well, good thing, boy. We have all the time in the world." Logan grunted gruffly.

Tyler glanced around, looking for permission before he began. "Well, it started with the fires..."

"Well, you're safe now. No need to go running around in the snow again." Lida sighed when Tyler had finished.

Tyler shot her a look. How did *nobody* understand? Understand that Opal was still alive! It wasn't like she was bitten or something; she was a *prisoner.*

But what use is she?

Why would someone like Delphina, who is simply so powerful, want a teenage girl like Opal?

"Nonsense!" Aleesha cried. "As soon as this blizzard dies down, we should, of course, go find your friend!"

"We, Aleesha?" Logan growled from the shadows.

"Or them." Aleesha sighed. "But we can't stay here forever."

Logan rolled his eyes. "We probably could."

Aleesha opened her mouth to begin to argue but then stopped as Nolan suddenly nodded off, falling asleep right into his cup of hot chocolate.

"That's right. You guys have been running practically all night; why don't you show Casper, Tyler, and Nolan somewhere to sleep, Conner?" Aleesha asked. "Actually- there's probably only room for three-?"

Tyler caught Cora's panicked gaze, and he added quickly. "I'll stay with Cora."

Conner shrugged. "Suit yourself." Conner shook Nolan awake, taking him and Casper away to one of the hallways.

"Wow, he's handsome." Violet suddenly sighed.

Tyler looked at her in surprise. "Who, Nolan?" he asked, trying not to wince at the thought of Violet taking a liking to Nolan just after his girlfriend died.

245

"No, silly, the moody one!"

"Casper?" Tyler tried not to laugh. "Casper's an... interesting... choice."

Violet hit him hard on the arm. "Tyler! He's *mysterious* and *perfect* for me."

"Okay..." Tyler muttered. "You're crazy..."

"Oh, shut up," Violet grumbled. "You're getting in the way of my *romance*."

Tyler tried not to laugh, trying and failing to imagine bubbly Violet with the moody and dark Casper.

"I want to sleep, too," Cora said abruptly. "Lida?" Cora's friend jumped up, and the two girls left, arms linked as they whispered together, heads bowed.

Tyler watched them go. Trying and failing to understand what Cora was thinking right now. Violet's parents moved to the kitchen, talking in hushed voices.

"So." Violet's voice suddenly became dead serious. "What's up? How are you?"

"I'm f-fine-" Tyler suddenly froze. What was he saying? He was most decidedly *not* fine. But by habit, he'd forced out the word anyway. And now he was choking on it.

"Hey," Violet whispered. "It's okay not to be fine. None of us are, really."

Tyler tried to force a smile on his face, but it went flat. "Yeah. I'm really not. Calico- my parents... they're *dead*, V. I couldn't do anything to stop it, and now Miranda is gone too- and even though I just met her, I feel as if..."

"It's okay," Violet repeated. "You don't have to understand it all."

Tyler managed to choke back his sobs, taking a huge gulp of air instead. He had to change the subject, or he would start crying again. He didn't want to talk about this. "What about you guys? I haven't seen you in months."

"Well, our town is a little bigger than Duxbury. Things weren't as peaceful as what happened to you guys..." Violet began.

"Peaceful?!" Tyler bristled, his mind flashing to all the countless people who had died.

"That's not what I mean." Violet backtracked. "What I'm saying is *after* the fires hit, not everybody could fit in the provided shelters, and suddenly it was mayhem; people were looting left and right and even killing each other. I feel like Dad knew what was coming for months between the murders and the disappearances. We lost nearly everything in the fire, but Dad packed up what we had and brought us here, to the mountains. The zombies can't come up here; it's too cold. They'll freeze to death. So Dad told us that we were safe and we've just been here. But it goes double ways; we can't go out for long, or we'll freeze to death. So, I haven't gone out much in the past few days. I know it's better than being dead, but... it's still hard."

Tyler felt a flash of pity; he couldn't imagine poor Violet being holed up for days on end in this house, as comfortable as it was. She needed people. More than just her family.

"I know-" Tyler began but was suddenly cut off by the sound of a wild banging.

Tyler jumped upright, Violet at his shoulder as the house filled with the same violent and wild banging.

247

The zombies.

Could they have found us?

No.

Impossible.

"Dad! Mom!" Violet cried, terror making her voice crack as she glanced at Tyler.

Logan was already tearing into the main room, Aleesha by his shoulder; this time, Logan had his long, dark black rifle strapped to his shoulder.

Tyler didn't think it was for show as Logan pulled it from his shoulder, gripping it tight in his hands, finger sliding off the safety and closing around the trigger.

Cora was suddenly right behind him. "Who is it?" she whispered softly.

Tyler gave her a helpless shrug.

Logan pounded down the stairs to the bunker, Tyler right on his heels as they creeped down the stairs.

Logan's face was dark, and with the butt of his gun, he slammed open the door to the bunker.

The sky was light outside, the air slightly warmed by the mid-day sun, but snow still spiraled down in drifts, and Tyler was hit with the howling wind.

But there was somebody out there.

Somebody he knew.

Someone he never thought he would see again.

Somebody he hated.

Cora gasped behind him.

Looking frozen, bedraggled, bleeding, and spitting mad, Irene leered down at them. "Did you *really* think I was going to let you go that easily?"

18

OPAL

Opal nearly choked on her own spit, mixed emotions of fear and relief crashing through her but then filled with uncertainty.

Antibodies of *what?*

"What do you *mean* 'antibodies directed?'" Opal nearly screamed. "Of what?"

Her mind was spinning. Her head was spinning. Spots danced up in her mind. She was too tired to think clearly; her body felt like it had been pushed through a shredder and pulled out. She knew. She knew in that labyrinth she had nearly died. Now, she was thrown out of the frying pan and into the fire.

Joash rushed up to her. "I'll find out more," he promised quietly. "I will."

Adax spotted him. He dragged him back to where they were standing. "No, you will *not*," he growled fiercely. "Do we have to take you out of here?"

Josh shut his mouth.

Adax shoved Josh into a chair. "Stay here until the next test," he ordered forcefully. "Or we'll tie you down."

Josh shot Opal an apologetic look, and to Opal's relief, he didn't argue with Adax.

Good. Opal sighed inwardly. She couldn't bear the thought of another person she cared about getting hurt.

I care about him? When did that happen? Opal thought, bewildered.

250

Suddenly, an image of Josh reaching up to kiss her lightly on the forehead flashed in her mind.

He was cute, but he was no Tyler. She cared about him but as a friend.

Right?

If she liked Josh that way, then didn't that mean she was fine with Cora being with Tyler? With them kissing?

No.

Silas hustled up to Opal. "Do you know anything about this?" He demanded forcefully.

"I swear I don't," Opal whispered. *Please believe me.*

Adax growled in frustration. "It's a response to the tests. Her Acana Magic or whatever, but I've never seen this before. Nobody has refused these viruses... they should have killed her. I don't know how she survived or how she fought them off."

Adax's words had immediate reactions. Or at least with Josh and Opal.

"*Killed* her?" Josh cried.

"*Virus's?*" Opal snapped.

"Relax!" Silas hissed. "We had cures for them all, but clearly, you didn't need them."

Delsea nodded to one of the scientists, Stefan.

He plucked a syringe with purple liquid in it and reached for her arm in one brisk movement. "It seems under a lot of stress, her body, her magic more like it, simply kicks in and protects her. Should we test this fact?"

Opal gasped, jerking away. Unimaginable terrors were already racing through her mind as her imagination ran wild. It could be fire through her veins, ice, or pain - anything. All designed to hurt her.

Silas didn't take any notice of this; he was too busy riffling around with his papers, ignoring Opal's cries.

Adax slammed the syringe into her arm before Opal could scream.

But it wasn't fire.

It was something strangely worse. No pain. No hurt. Just *numbness*. Because she didn't want to fight it. Why would she want to fight it? She wasn't fading into darkness, just into light. Into sleep. She couldn't move her body. Everything felt so sluggish. Blurry shapes danced across her vision.

"Josh?" she muttered.

"Opal!" he shouted back. "Hold on!" he yelled.

She felt herself drift away, drift away into the light. *It's okay, Josh.* She wanted to whisper. *I need some nothing right now.*

"You killed her!" yelled a fractured voice, maybe Josh's.

"Relax! She's just knocked out while we move her."

And she was gone.

"Opal, Opal, can you hear me?" a man spoke, puncturing the darkness that had started to creep in.

It was a vision; she was sure of it. The same feeling, the same sort of darkness on the edges... but... the people in her visions couldn't usually hear her or see her. So what was this?

Dream?

But it was so vivid...

The blurry view of a man came into shape. He resembled the man Opal had seen in her other vision or the crazy man in the cell. His wizened white hair was wilder than ever, and his hands were twisted with worry as he wrung them in front of her; it seemed like an old video camera, his body glitching in and out of sight. *The Sightseerer. The one with the timelines. The mad one. The strange one. Who was he?*

Opal tried to speak. "You can hear me?" she asked, and to her amazement, it worked; the words flowed easily from her mouth.

"Oh, Opal, you have grown into a wonderful young woman." sighed The Sightseerer.

"How did you do this?" Opal responded she didn't know why the man's eyes shone with pride when he looked down at her, but it was really starting to creep her out.

The Sightseerer's gaze turned serious. Opal still couldn't see her surroundings, but the man was staring at a spot over her shoulder, as if in anticipation when someone would walk towards them.

"We don't have much time," he breathed.

"How did you do this?" Opal repeated, more demanding this time.

"Opal, my powers are a little more advanced than yours; I can make a measly projection of two Acana users' minds! "Oh, be quiet, 82!" muttered the man.

He's delusional. He might be powerful, but he's crazy. He's hearing voices in his head. Opal regarded the man skeptically as he wrung his hands again and again.

"You're The Sightseerer, aren't you?" she asked scathingly.

The Sightseerer smiled. "You were always a bright young woman," he remarked.

253

Does he know me? I don't know him. Do I? *His brown eyes were awfully familiar; Opal just couldn't place where she had seen them.*

The happy look melted from his face. "I don't have much time, Opal," *he whispered.* "I am captured; my Acana Magic is weaker than ever; ask me one question; that is all we have time for," *The Sightseers gasped.*

Opal wanted to shake him in frustration. She had so many questions! Why couldn't he keep the connection longer? What was Richmond's story? Why was he doing this? What were her powers? Where is my family? Are they okay? What was Delphina's story? Where were her friends right now? What was Josh's story? How could she stop this apocalypse? Where was her family? How could she find them? Does Tyler like me? *The last question wasn't allowed on the list.*

"Where is the cure? Or the antibodies? Is it here?" *her voice quivered at the weight of her question.*

A ghost of a smile fluted across The Sightseerer's face. "I know where it is. Trust me. I'll get the information to you in time."

"That's useless!" Opal cried.

The Sightseerer's face fractured, and he came out of focus.

Opal opened her mouth to say something, but he cut her off.

"No, Opal, listen to me; there's a plane coming. A big one. You must get to L-L-L-o-os Ange-" *his voice fractured and cut out before coming back in.* "-find the cure there-" *The Sightseerer was cut off, and his face swam.*

"Timeline three is shifting," *the man muttered, his face clouding over and his eyes glazing over, something Opal recognized; the man was going into a vision. To Opal's surprise, he glitched back.*

The Sightseerer suddenly fell to his knees.

254

"Opal, listen to me," he choked. "Do not judge Delphina too harshly; she is- well, it's my fault," he rasped.

Opal just stared at him in confusion. "Child, say her name! Your powers will know what to do!" he called to her.

The man's face started to dissolve like sand in the wind. "Remember! The cure!" he called.

"No! Don't go!" yelled Opal; she struggled forward and tried to hold onto the man before he faded away, but he was going too fast. "Say, who's name?!" Opal felt herself being pulled out of the vision, out of information, out of the dream world, and back into reality. Cold, cruel reality.

"Opal! Opal!" someone kept repeating her name; someone was nudging her.

Opal opened her eyes.

Silas, Delsea, and Adax were gone. So was the lab, with its weird tanks and the pain. It was gone.

She was in a hospital bed, the thin sheets laying over her bruised and battered body, the mattress thin yet a million times more comfortable than the metal bed her back had gotten used to. She had no metal binds holding her to the bed. Her bed was tilted up so she could see the rest of her room. It resembled a white box; her bed was the only furniture besides a chair. Opal didn't even need to try the door to know it was locked.

Josh was on the chair next to her, his head bent in his arms as if he were praying.

Opal's mind was spinning from her vision. What had The Sightseerer meant? Say whose name? What was going on? She was only sure of one thing: The Sightseerer was crazy powerful; she didn't even know someone could project an image of themselves into others' minds. Powerful but crazy.

I wish I could do that. She sighed, wishing for anything more than to jump into Amelia's mind. Or Tyler's. Or even her mother's.

"Opal?" Josh asked tentatively. He looked pale as he stared at her. "Are you awake? Are you okay?"

"I'm fine," Opal responded quickly, her voice dry.

Without warning, Josh leaped up and embraced her when she was still in the bed.

"I'm so glad you're alright!" he breathed. "Seriously, I thought Adax was going to blow when you went unconscious! Silas stepped in and told him that you had enough; bless him."

"I'm glad *you're* okay," Opal responded. "You were seriously pushing the line back there. I'm surprised they let you back in here."

Josh chuckled, his innocent nature peeking through. "Well." He smiled sheepishly. "Each of the residents here has something that can open all the doors from the outside, not the inside." Josh sighed with a grimace. "And it didn't take much for me to ask for a favor from one of my friends once Adax took mine."

"So welcome to my home, Opal!" Josh said suddenly. "You're in Area 50! I never really got to tell you the name of the facility, did I?"

Opal couldn't help but laugh. "Is that a joke?"

"Well, Area 51 is in Nevada, so they named this one Area 50!"

Opal snickered. "Nice. Classy. So you live here?" Opal tried to ignore her slight horror at the thought of being trapped in these windowless rooms for her entire life.

256

Josh sighed. "I don't go out a lot, but I visit a lot of people in different rooms. You're the first kid, well, first teenage girl I've seen before, though."

Opal flashed him a smile. "I'm one of a kind."

Josh ducked his head. "You really are."

Opal's mind drifted back to her vision. Had the whole vision been a figment of her imagination? A hope? But it seemed so real... but it wasn't the future... How could it be? It was like a video call... in her mind.

Say her name! That's what The Sightseerer had told her. But whose name? And what was he talking about when he said he knew where the cure was? The cure and him were connected somehow. He was the key... yet it was so confusing, too many loose ends.

"Opal? You okay?" Josh asked.

"Josh, I can trust you, right?" Opal asked absentmindedly.

Josh offered her a half-hearted smile. "You already asked me this, and I'm pretty sure I said yes."

Opal felt the words on the tip of her tongue, her story, all the small secrets she had been building up over her days at this lab. It was all there. A large part of her desperately craved to confide in someone, to puzzle out her terrible circumstances. But a small persistent part of her also protested that she didn't know this kid; he could turn on her in a second.

But eventually, the loneliness and confusion won out. She just had to pray that she could put her trust in him. And did she have that much to lose?

As the lonely thought slipped out, Opal's mind flashed to Amelia lying on that bed in the hands of Richmond. Yes. She did have a lot to lose. But she wasn't going to get anywhere without help.

At first, the words came slowly, but then Opal was blurting everything out. She told Josh about her vision with the Sightseerer and then about every other vision she had; she told him about her family and how they got kidnapped, and then about how she got kidnapped. Every theory, every question she laid out at her feet, desperate for any sort of answer. Opal watched as Josh's expression got more and more confused, but she kept talking.

"That's probably the most confusing thing I've ever heard," he confessed. "So The Sightseerer was breaking up at the end, and you didn't hear him?"

"Yeah, you can say that again," sighed Opal. "And yes."

"So you think Irene is part of the Irene line?" Josh asked.

"I mean, that's not a common name, is it? And Delphina kind of looks like Irene, so what if they're related?" Opal asked.

Josh was nodding along. "There's definitely a lot of secrets in this facility; I don't know even a fraction of them. I can't believe this apocalypse actually happened."

Opal hugged her knees to her chest. "I hope my sisters are okay." She paused. "How was she when y-you know-" Opal broke off.

"When Richmond brought her in?" Josh finished and shuddered as he relived the memory. "Not good," he admitted honestly. "But, she was okay when they took her back."

"Are you certain she's here?" asked Opal, not daring to let hope seep through her voice.

Josh slowly nodded. "Yeah."

"Josh, can I ask you something?"

"Ask away."

"Who are your parents?" Opal asked tentatively, hoping it wasn't something big like Delsea or Adax.

Josh flopped back on her bed near the end, his expression sour. Opal sat down next to him. They both laid across the bed, their ankles brushing. Side by side, they stared up at the ceiling; it was cracked and frayed, the paint peeling, just like Opal's mind and body.

Just like Opal's story, the words seemed to pour from Josh's mouth, far overdue. "My mom was the most amazing person on earth, and I loved her, but my dad didn't. I don't know if he ever loved her, or it just faded over time, or if this facility and this life corrupted him. He just wanted a kid. Some sort of heir junk and found the first woman who loved him. " Josh hesitated, his voice cracking; Opal paused awkwardly before gently laying her hand on his.

Josh breathed out for a second before continuing, his eyes on their intertwined fingers. "Dad worked with the government; he was so involved that he turned a blind eye to the people's suffering, including my mom's. This was before the apocalypse, but we still lived in this facility. We hardly left, and I don't think we could have. Mom tried to give me a normal childhood, but it was getting harder and harder. We watched as he experimented on people, yearning for something, but we didn't know what. I know now what he was looking for: a way to get that virus out into the world. We suffered in silence, staying quiet and out of the way, staying together. Until one day, my mom had had enough. She stood up and told him that they were leaving. My dad didn't protest; he hardly saw us, and we hardly saw him unless he stopped by in a drunken rage after something had gone really wrong.

259

My mother always protected me from it and took the brunt of the hits. But seeing the marks on her was just as bad. But it was too much to hope that we could escape this hellish life. The night we planned to leave, my dad stopped us. He told us that we knew too much and couldn't be permitted to leave. I was so frightened. I was only seven when it happened. I didn't understand what they were talking about, but it sounded like they said my mom said that she wouldn't be part of experiments to unleash a plague that would wipe out mankind. I didn't know what it was; for years, I didn't know... Then my dad grabbed her wrist; I was crying and trying to follow. But he led her away, and his guards held me back. I never saw her again. My father killed my mother. I just know it. I asked my dad about it, and he just shrugged. He *shrugged* and said that I'll forget even her name in time. It was just a sacrifice for the greater good."

Josh finished his story, his eyes shimmering with tears as he stared mournfully at Opal. "But I didn't forget her name, and I never will. Pamela. There is no greater good for me, only for him and his selfish needs."

"I'm so sorry," whispered Opal. The tragedy of Josh's path didn't seem like it could be cured with words; what could she say after all?

"Don't be sorry; there is only one way to make me feel better, to avenge my mother, really."

"How?" asked Opal eagerly, hoping with all her heart that she knew what Josh was about to say.

"Opal, we escape and burn the place down."

19
OPAL

"Josh, trust me, if I would have known to escape before I would have been long gone." Opal sighed, but the hope of his words were starting to eat their way into Opal's heart.

Josh sighed. "I know, I wanted to escape badly too, but I never had the courage to do it alone."

"Do you know where they are keeping my sisters? And my mom?" Opal said. Whatever anger Opal had been harboring towards Linea for not taking more care of Opal in the bunker was forgotten in the lue of the danger, all Opal wanted was her mother back with her.

"I think it may be in ward seven, but all the doors are locked," admitted Josh. "And I mean the security's pretty high, and even if you could get out of *this* room it's like ten more levels until the ground floor and the elevators are always under guard. They moved you out of the lab areas."

"Ugh..." moaned Opal, dropping her head into her hands. There were so many obstacles, so many places where she could fall again. So many places with darkness.

"Oh, no." whispered Josh. "Here they come, *again*."

Opal could hear the faint click of boots on tile, coming and coming and always coming.

"Hide!" she hissed viciously, shoving Josh under her bed. She couldn't let them know that Josh was visiting her, they would lock him up and she would lose her one shred of hope.

Well it's not much hope when one little boy is your only chance of escaping. Opal thought thinly. She was much too tired and much too angry at the world to chide herself for her unfair thoughts.

"We'll talk about this later." Opal hissed to Josh, who was curling up and making himself as small as possible in the dark shadows under her bed.

Four grim faced guards marched into her cell. They wore high black polished boots and gray uniforms, they all wore dark shiny helmets like the top of insects that dipped down below their eyes, casting a shadow over half of their faces and making it impossible for Opal to distinguish them.

"Who are you talking to?" one demanded fiercely.

Opal didn't respond, her throat going dry, it was flashing in her eyes now. The light, the pain, the questions. She couldn't do it again. But what choice did she have?

It wasn't even torture because of what they were doing to her, it was torture because she coulden't stop them. She couldn't control it.

I'm immune. My magic saved me.

Immune to viruses.

Not knives.

Or fists.

Or anything else.

My magic can't save me.

"You're wanted in an hour," one of the soldiers told her gruffly while slamming down a tray of food before turning on their heels they all marched out, slamming the cold door behind them and with the twitch of a lock they were gone.

Wanted. *Like I'm invited for* tea.

262

"They lock all the doors, but we may be able to steal a key." whispered Josh, sliding out from underneath the bed.

"But then wouldn't they just raise the alarm? Then we wouldn't be able to get my family *or* The Sightseerer out." Opal hissed back.

"True."

"Can we get down the doors?"

"They put sensors on the doors."

"Fine." Opal snapped. "How about I just go through that torture again and *you* find out where my sister's and The Sightseerer is and tell me later?"

Josh winced at her angry tone. "I mean I don't know what else we can do."

Opal tried to breathe, tried to keep the darkness from pressing into her mind.

Any magic for me? Opal thought skeptically, almost wishing she could slip into a vision and find something out. Maybe disappear for a bit.

"Opal. Opal. don't drift off just yet. Here, why don't we meet someone." Josh's voice seemed strange, reality seemed strange but Opal was too curious to care. Something about her was slipping, like her sanity was moving through her fingers and she couldn't catch it. She didn't know how much longer she could try and grab it for. The darkness. It was too strong.

And she knew.

She knew that a little part of her would always be lost in that labyrinth and on that bed with the too bright lights.

"Who?" Opal asked softly, her voice sounding strange.

263

"Come with me," he responded, smiling.

Josh led Opal to the far side of the room where there was another door.

"If that's unlocked and we never went there-" Opal began, starting to get frustrated at his forgetfulness. He might be able to go where he pleased, but she certainly couldn't. Who knows what they would do to each other?

"Relax! It doesn't lead anywhere, in Area 50 all the kids and patient rooms are connected in one long block and the doors are never locked to each other unless of course for some other greater reason that never happens." Josh led the still hesitant Opal towards the door on the opposite end of the room, and to her surprise it opened easily. They walked through three empty rooms that looked like a copy and paste version of hers. When they got to the fourth room a sheet of glass prevented them from going any farther but Opal could see inside of it just fine.

Inside it looked much like Opal's room, but nicer. There were two brass beds and a pattern of little butterflies filled the walls. Two girls sat at a small table moodily picking at a tray of food, whispering quietly to each other.

"Huh. I guess they don't want you in here." Josh muttered, pressing his fingers against the glass. "Hey! Raven! Bree! Over here!" hissed Josh through the glass.

Both girls looked up, surprised. "Josh?" one girl asked disbelievingly. "I thought you were locked up?"

The two girls got up, pushing away their chairs as they slowly walked towards them.

"Who's that?" asked one of them, arching her eyebrow.

264

"This is Opal. Opal this is Raven-" Josh pointed to the girl on the left, she had silky black hair and emerald eyes. Her legs were long and agile, it made her look like she had been stretched by a large machine. "And the other one is Bree, short for Brieena, of course," Bree had short black hair that went up to her chin, angled in a bob, she wore fishnet stockings and had the same emerald green eyes. Sisters. Opal guessed. If it wasn't for the severe expression on Bree's face then Opal wouldn't be able to tell them apart.

"Hi." Raven gave a shy wave.

Bree pursed her lips. "Hi."

"Hi, so how long have you been in Area 50?" asked Opal, carefully choosing her words, in case she offended them.

Bree's expression became increasingly sour. "Our parents are Silas and Delsea, we grew up with Josh." Bree shot a smile at Josh loaded with a strange emotion Opal couldn't place.

Opal was taken aback. "They're together?" she'd had no hint on that at all, no glance between the two of them as if they had any connection to each other outside of the lab.

"Not really." Raven trailed off, glancing at Bree.

"We're lab rats. They just had us so we could be tested with all their viruses." Bree spat, Opal sensed the sheer venom and hatred in her voice. Opal thought that she was mad but her anger felt like a lit candle next to Bree's inferno.

Opal tried to keep back her shivers, sure it was terrible what Bree and Raven were talking about, but the venom in Bree's voice sounded as if she would willingly shoot her own parents in the head and drag down their home brick by brick.

"It's horrible." shuddered Raven.

265

Opal squinted at both of them, now that she was opening her eyes up a little she could see marks, the long criss cross patterns of scars, some knew that marked all the way from Ravens neck and crept through her sleeves to the blue and black bruises on Bree's wrists and ankles suggesting her viciously trying to free herself of shackles.

"I'm sorry." Opal whispered.

"It's fine." Bree suddenly rolled her eyes. "We had Josh to lead us through it all." She smiled flirtatiously at Josh who looked flustered, glancing at Opal.

Oh dear. Another Cora. Opal thought, annoyed. *At least I won't be fighting her this time. I couldn't care less who Josh dates.*

She paused for a second, realizing it wasn't true, the thought of this venomous girl dating sweet Josh sent shivers up her spine, and she didn't know why.

"We're used to it by now, but we're desperate for fresh faces." Raven smiled gently at Opal. "And a chance to leave. Perhaps."

Bree suddenly turned on her sister. "Raven!"

"What!" Raven yelped as her sister hit her hard on the side.

"Don't tell the *prisoner* about our plan!" Bree snarled.

"No-no! It's fine. I-I want to escape to." Opal jumped in quickly.

"And we will." Josh added.

"I know." Raven sighed dreamily. "We're going to bust out of this place one day, Opal."

"Bust out and kill some people on the way out." Bree added viciously.

"It'll be alright, Opal. I know you're terrified but I talk with Josh a lot and-" Raven began looking sympathetically at Opal.

266

"Raven!" Bree suddenly turned and with a sharp motion slapped Raven hard across the face. "Go away! I'm talking to Josh!"

Opal gave a little yelp of surprise as Bree shoved her sister in the back, pushing her away from the glass.

Oh my god. Bree's just as bad as Silas and Delsea.

Who was this girl?

Raven shot a glum look at Josh, Both of their faces seemed years older, filled with years of sorrow and disappointment as Josh watched Raven slink away to the bed, sitting there with her hands in her head.

Bree slowly turned her head from her sister's slumped form and pressed both of her hands against the glass. "I'm so sorry about Raven, it's hard to live together. If only I could live with you... Josh."

I take it back. Cora is fifty times better than this girl. Yikes.

Opal watched with a half bemused expression as Bree batted her eyelashes at Josh through the glass.

"I-I'm going to come back." Josh muttered, his face red.

"Alright! I'll wait for you." Bree smiled with no happiness in her face as she watched Josh leave.

They were three rooms away, back in Opal's room before Opal dissolved in a fit of giggles. "Oh my *god,* Josh. Why did you never tell me about *Bree.*"

Josh was still red in the face as he glared at her. "Shut up! There's nothing to tell. She's just very... persistent."

"Oh my god you're *so* lucky there's a sheet of glass between you two." Opal laughed.

"I feel worse for Raven." Josh muttered.

The smile and laughter slowly melted out of Opal's face. "Is it always like that?"

"Let's just say she doesn't get all of those scars from her parents." Josh muttered darkly. "Bree inherited her mothers cruel streak and her fathers deception."

"Are they the only other kids here?" Opal asked.

"That I know of. Ravens great but Bree is always around, it's hard to get a word in." Josh shook his head.

"So why did we go to see them?" Opal said quizzically.

"Well I was hoping Bree would be asleep, Raven is actually really smart. She's really good at picking up small hints and usually knows where everyone is and I thought she'd know where your family would be. I'm sorry but I can never stay there for long." Josh shot her an apologetic look.

Opal felt a flash of pity for him and Raven, with the shadow of Bree over them all. "That's fine, of course. We can always go back anyway-"

The sound of a clicking lock jolted Opal out of her words.

"Hide!" she hissed to Josh, and he leapt back under her bed.

The same six men marched into the room. They carried rifles and their faces were grim as they stared down at her.

"Come with us." growled one of them.

Another grabbed Opal's arm and tried to march her out of the cell, but she wrenched her arm out of his grip.

"I can walk on my own, thanks." she snapped.

The other guard didn't say anything but moved enough to slam her back with the butt of his gun. "I don't think so." he growled, seizing her by the back of her neck and forcing her forward.

268

Opal ducked her head, miserable as she imagined Josh watching her from under the bed. Humiliation sparked through her but she tried to lift her chin.

The guards hustled her out and into the hallways. The hallways were plain white and boring, but most of the doors were made of glass. When Opal looked closer, shucking in breath and hoping that they didn't have locks on them, she saw the normal four key lock that was on her door, leaning back in disappointment, she looked around.

Lots of scientists ran around, all of them looking like they had a purpose, they wore oxygen tanks strapped to their backs and breathed unearthly through large masks. Opal felt a flash of fear for her own breath whistling in and out of her mouth without an oxygen tank. Did they know something she didn't? Why were they walking around with those huge and probably heavy things if the air wasn't dangerous?

The guards hustled her towards a dark grove in the floor, marking the end of the hallway, it jutted out just enough to let a full grown person slip through.

Opal's feet slipped as she stared at the dark tunnel going down and down into nothing.

"Come on." sneered one of the men. "Not scared are you?"

The jibe hit Opal hard as she imagined the darkness of the labyrinth and the fear of the pain that would follow her in death.

Her breath was shallow as she stared at the dip, it looked like a tunnel that she would fall right down.

Fall down into nothing.

"Come on!" one of the men snapped, prodding her hard in the back. "Do we need to taser you?"

269

Opal took one stiff step, calming her breathing. *It's just darkness. You'll feel silly when you're out. There's nothing down there. Nothing.*

What if it's the nothing *I'm afraid of?*

But what other choice did she have?

Opal, only with a slight trace of hesitancy stepped onto the darkness.

For a few moments everything was black, then a slight trace of light flickered at the end of a tunnel, Opal tried to keep her vision on it, trying not to imagine the darkness pressing in on her. She tried not to imagine it caressing and getting closer to her.

It was the only light Opal could see, so she followed it. She carefully placed her feet as she went towards it, the last thing she needed was to face plant.

You're doing it.

She was painfully aware that the guards around her were bristling and alert, as if waiting for her to bolt.

I won't. Opal didn't even know where this stroke of resilience was coming from but she liked it. She liked the feeling of defying them, even if it was the most inconsequential thing.

"In here." growled one of the guards.

Opal looked up, surprised, the light was coming from a door, a steel one with a glass window and a soft white glow haloing the space inbetween the frame and the door.

The soldiers on either side of her wrenched it open and with a shove in the back she stumbled through the frame and out of the darkness.

You survived.

270

The feeling of happiness filled her up for a second, as she let out the breathe she didn't even know she was holding. The light was so blissful that for a moment Opal closed her mind to the fears that waited for her in this room. But she couldn't stay in the bliss forever.

It was a large room. With searing white walls that seemed to blind Opal. No windows. There was a simple white table and three iron chairs. But one of them... Opal's breathe caught in her throat. Shackles were waiting at the arms and legs, open. Like little smiling bugs. Waiting to seize her.

Opal squeezed her eyes shut, trying not to remember what had happened last time she was tied down. She tried not to let the memories suck her down as she bit back tears.

Sitting in two of them, across the table from the shackled chair were Delphina and Richmond.

"Good for you to join us," sneered Delphina like it was her choice whether she wanted to meet with them or not.

"Leave us." ordered Richmond and with a nod the guards left but not before two of them shoved her hard into the chair, the chains snapped shut on impact and Opal tried not to wince and whimper as she was locked in again.

"I hope you weren't offset by our little experiments." Richmond said calmly, his voice dripping with venom and his smile not meeting his eyes.

"I survived didn't I?" Opal managed to choke out.

"Yes you did." Delphina sneered. "For now."

"So. Have you thought about our proposition? To help us?" Richmond asked. "Find the cure and guard it?"

A bolt of realization suddenly flashed through Opal's body, her first clear thought in days.

Opal could be saved if she had those antibiotics in her system, her Acana Magic could fail at any point. Falter. It was only under stress that it seemed to work... so if she had this cure inside of her... she would never be a zombie.

And if she played along long enough she could slip away, find Tyler. Maybe rescue Josh and Raven. She couldn't imagine leaving them in such a cruel place.

"W-would you release my family?" Opal asked tentatively.

"Of course," Delphina answered, Opal could almost hear the fakeness oozing off her tone.

"Will you release The Sightseerer?" asked Opal, he was the key. She needed to know more... she doubted they would say yes but perhaps they would play along? She expected them to play along and say yes, but to her surprise, Delphina leapt up and snarled "Never!" she screamed, with a hint of hysteria in her voice as she stared daggers down at Opal.

Richmond glowered at her and forcefully pushed her back into her chair by the shoulders. "You will *not,*" he growled, then turned to Opal, smoothing his face down to a pleasant grin. "Certainly."

Delphina stayed silent but the way she was glowering at Opal made it all too clear that she had no intentions to do what Richmond said.

"Then we are in an agreement," Opal lied, making sure that her voice didn't quaver. "I-I'll do this for the g-good of h-human kind." her voice broke on the lie.

I don't care about the rest of these humans.

272

I just want those antibiotics.
I just want my family and friends safe.
I just want to survive?
Is that too much to ask?

20
OPAL

The beat of silence that filled the room after Opal agreed was so tense she felt like she could touch it. She waited for her enemies to speak, her leg tapping nervously against the ground. Her mouth dried as Richmond turned his dark gaze to hers.

"You honestly think you can fool us, Opal?" Richmond said slowly. His voice sounded lethal, slippery with danger, his face dark.

"W-what? I-I don't know what you're talking about!" Opal stuttered, but fear seeped into her tone. Had they figured out her plan? Was she that obvious?

Richmond glared heavily at her. "It was honestly very obvious you just wanted those antibiotics for you. You're cowardly, and your selfishness is so plain."

Opal flinched. That wasn't true. Was it? And even if it was... she could change. Could she?

And do I want to?

I mean, this has gotten me this far...

I'm not a coward.

Opal took a deep breath. She had to hold herself together.

Richmond suddenly flipped open a metal phone from his belt and rasped into it. "Bring her in," he growled.

Opal froze with fear. Who was her? Not Amelia surly.... Was it? Or Gina? All the girls Opal knew flashed through her mind, anticipation mixing with fear, making her feel sick.

The door clicked open, and Delsea and Adax melted into the room; suspended in their hands was Raven, with Bree walking beside her, her head hung low. Adax leered evilly as he passed her. One person was missing. If Raven and Bree were here...

There must have been cameras in the rooms. Of course! They were so stupid.

"Where's Josh?" demanded Opal quietly.

"Learning," Richmond replied.

Opal felt sick. What were they doing to him? He thought he could escape... he was willing to help her. He was her only hope.

If anything happened to him.... Opal began to think worriedly, her mind swirling. Josh. He'd been so kind to her. He was a good person, right down to the heart, no matter what this facility was doing to him.

"I am VERY disappointed in my daughter. Being dragged into Josh's plot. *Conspiring* with the patients. About *escaping*." growled Delsea. As she glared heavily at Raven and Bree.

"You don't even *care* about us!" Bree suddenly exploded, raising her head just a little to reveal angry eyes as she stared around and locked gazes with her parents, eyes flashing with pent-up anger. And the thirst for revenge. Opal remembered with a shiver the violent words that Bree had spewed back at the rooms. Who knew who she would turn her anger on once she took it out on her parents?

Delsea paid no mind to her; she completely ignored her daughter.

"What do we do with the boy?" growled Delsea.

275

Adax stepped forward, a sneer frozen on his face. "You and Silas have always been too soft on him; I told you he would betray us one day, I told you, and you didn't listen!" Adax snarled at Richmond.

Delsea looked shocked, her mouth hanging open slightly at Adax's direct challenge to the president's leadership.

Opal would have been shocked as well, but she was too worried about Josh for room in her mind for Richmond's and Adax's leadership quarrel.

"The only person I am being soft with is you." Richmond hissed quietly, his voice dripping with silent threats.

"Well, I think it is high time that we have a little change around here!" retorted Adax, Richmond's quiet demeanor giving Adax strength and confidence. Adax turned back to Delsea, raising his arms. "The only good idea you had was the plague, and since then, everything has fallen into hell."

"You think that?" Richmond inquired quietly, and Opal recognized the cold, hard tone hidden deep inside his voice.

"Yes! This place needs to be run with purpose! And I'm just the person-" Adax stopped midway because he was blasted across the room by a large flash of purple light.

He crashed into the wall and slid down, unconscious.

Delphina stood next to Richmond, her finger extended. She looked almost bored, her eyes shifting around as if she did this every day.

"Are there any other questions about my leadership?" Richmond demanded, his voice dangerously quiet.

When nobody said anything, he continued in a prompt voice that showed no discussion. "Good, then let's proceed."

276

The room seemed silent for a second, eyes flickering to Adax's unconscious form.

Delsea was the first to snap out of it.

From her thick clothes, she pulled out a remote and pushed the largest button on it.

Not to Opal's complete surprise, the largest wall she was facing started to rumble, just like a garage door pulling back.

With Delsea, Richmond, and Delphina all watching the wall intently, Bree, Raven, and Opal had no one watching them.

"Are you ok?" Opal whispered across the room, straining ever so slightly in her chair.

"Nope. You?" responded Raven out of the corner of her mouth.

The corner of Opal's mouth twitched. "Nope."

"Shut up!" hissed Bree. "I want to see where Josh is!"

Raven caught Opal's eye, but they didn't argue. Further conversation was cut off because the wall had finished its course.

The sight that had been concealed by the door was a plain room devoid of anything except a large metal bed, just like the ones in the labs. But it also had another connection. It was the same metal bed that Delphina, or Rose, had been in Opal's vision when she had been enhanced by Acana Magic; Opal recognized the crude sharp edges, unlike the one she had laid on.

Opal swiveled her head to Delphina to watch her expression. Her face was pinched and white, and her eyes were widened in surprise. She must have recognized the bed, Opal stared at her, soaking up the small flash of humanness in her face, but it slowly melted back into her usual bored mask.

277

Richmond was watching Delpina with a cruel leer on his face.

Opal was driven out of this thought by another when she realized someone was on the bed.

Josh was almost unrecognizable; his face was a deadly white as if all the blood had been drained out of it, his body deathly still. The joy was driven from his kind face.

Bree let out an intake of breath when she realized who was on the bed. "Oh my god," she whispered.

So, she actually cares about him.

"Don't tell me that's Josh," murmured Raven.

"As a matter of fact, it is," proclaimed Delsea cruelly, staring down at her daughters.

A scientist, dressed in a large lab coat and a metal mask, appeared in the cell through one of the heavy doors. He had large metal oxygen tanks strapped to his back.

Is there no oxygen in there?

Is that why Josh looks like that?

Opal's stomach twisted with horror.

Memories flashed through her mind, adding to the growing pile of trauma. Her mind turned back to those minutes in the bunker... when she could feel her life slipping away. When the air left her... was that happening to Josh? Did they slowly drain the oxygen from the room until he was gasping? And then continued until he was pale and lifeless?

Opal recognized the scientist as one of them who had performed the test for antibodies on her, Stephen.

"Um, sir, was General Adax supposed to oversee this test?" asked Stephan cautiously, his eyes flickering all over the room.

278

Richmond's face curled up in a sneer. "The *traitor* Adax is no longer general and shall await trial, General Stephan."

The newly appointed general silently accepted his position. His eyes flickered to Adax's unmoving body, and he gave a brief nod; Opal could almost sense gears in his head turning. But he didn't protest; he didn't even make a comment.

"Then began," growled Delphina.

"Began *what*?" screeched Opal, unable to hold it back.

She and Raven exchanged a momentarily terrified look.

Stephan bent down to the metal floor and pulled a lever; the floor rose, revealing a control panel that spiraled up in a circle until it stopped at Stephan.

"Ok, starting now," reported Stephan. His fingers lingered over a bright red button, and then he pressed it.

Immediately, a foggy mist began to fill the room. It swirled around and filled every tiny nook and cranny.

Josh jolted awake, his eyes wide with fear. The momentary relief that filled Opal at seeing her friend alive was swept away in light of what happened next. The second Josh took a breath, he began to cough, his lungs unable to process the smoke.

"Stop it!" cried Opal. "Enough!"

"What are you doing?!" Bree cried.

Josh looked straight at them; his eyes were wild from fear, and he was bent over, coughing. "Help me!" he yelled.

"Raven!" Opal hissed. "Unlock me!"

Raven's eyes bulged, but she didn't hesitate to run forward and slam the button on the back of Opal's chair. Her arms and legs relaxed as the shackles hissed open.

"What are you doing?!" Bree snarled suddenly, coming up behind Raven, shoving Opal back into the chair, and pushing her sister back.

"You'll get us all killed!" Bree yelped.

Opal stiffened, glancing between the two sisters as Raven's eyes suddenly blared with a wave of familiar anger. "I don't *care,* I might as well die fighting."

Opal clenched her fist as she stood up, watching a vein twitch in Bree's temple, switching from Josh choking in the smoke to Opal.

"We don't have time for this." Bree suddenly snapped. "Raven. Come on. Get the remote." Bree shoved her sister hard in the back towards Delsea, kicking her roughly in the back of her legs. "I'm not going to wait to save the day because of your stupidity. I want to save Josh, not your pathetic excuse for a person."

Raven made a quiet hissing noise in the back of her throat. "One day," she whispered, so quietly Bree couldn't hear it.

Opal tried not to shiver; the venom between these two sisters was so real and so tangible Opal could almost taste it in the air.

One of them is going to kill each other. Opal thought ruefully.

Richmond, Delphina, Delsea, and Silas's eyes were all trained on Josh, watching with a sick sort of fascination.

Josh's pained eyes suddenly landed on Opal's. *I'm coming.* She thought fiercely. Nobody was watching as Bree and Raven crept up on Delsea, eyes flashing with undisguised hatred.

Opal steadied her breath, her eyes glancing at the door.

There's no time to be a coward. I'm not going to let Josh die. I can't.

I'm going to do this.

280

Opal tackled Richmond from behind, her arms knocked over his legs, and he crashed to the ground; he let out a bellow of surprise and rage. Out of the corner of her eye, Opal watched Delphina react. She seemed to turn around in slow motion, her face twisting as she watched the two of them roll on the cold ground.

Bree and Raven suddenly lunged at Delsea. Raven wrenched back her mother's hand and made a grab for the remote clutched in Delsea's squat fingers while Bree pulled back her mother's head, her face twisted in a half-evil smile.

"DELPHINA! Help me!" screamed Richmond suddenly from underneath Opal as he surged upwards to try and throw off Opal.

Opal kneaded him on the head and tried to get him to stop struggling, but Richmond was twice her size and was much stronger; he wrenched one of her hands away from him as Opal struggled to hold on and keep him down. She could only last a few more seconds.

"DELPHINA!" he bellowed.

Opal didn't know what she would do if Delphina joined the fight; she didn't know how she could fight her magic.

Words?

I can't fight with words.

But I can try.

I can always try.

"Please, Delphina! Hasn't he been cruel enough to you already? Please help us." Opal pleaded quietly, her gaze fixed on the dangerous woman. "Please."

Delphina seemed to consider this, her gaze flicking from Opal to Richmond. Was it too much to hope for? Would the hatred Delphina harbored for Richmond outweigh her fear?

281

"Don't you *dare!*" Richmond growled. "I-I'll kill him. I'll kill The Sightseerer! I will!"

"No!" Opal cried. "He won't. Because The Sightseerer is the only one who knows where the cure is."

Richmond growled softly. "How do you know that?"

"Why else would you want to keep him alive?" Opal answered softly. It made sense; that was the answer she was looking for, the reason she needed him.

"I don't need your permission for anything, *Mr. President.* I'll find that *Sightseerer* and kill him myself before that grubby girl gets her hands on him." Delphina turned away. "It's been too long since I walked free."

"NO!" roared Richmond underneath Opal's hands. She kneed him again and heard the sickening crack of his head against the stone floor. Delphina sneered, her face twisting in a grin.

"Thank you." Opal gasped. "I won't forget this."

Delphina suddenly turned her strange eyes on Opal, her face hardening. "Don't think we're on the same side, girl; if you cross my path again, I will kill you. I may not help the president now, but that is *my* choice, but it doesn't mean I won't help him in the future."

Delphina turned as if she was about to walk away.

"Delphina! Wait!" cried Opal. Wasn't she going to help them? They still had scientists to escape from, and it was getting harder and harder to hold Richmond down...

Delphina turned back on Opal, her eyes blazing with a quiet fire. "That's not my name, my name is Rose. And don't do well to forget it."

With that, Delphina raised her finger to the sky. There was a beat of tense silence before a large burst of purple fire flew from her hand, the ceiling erupted, and Opal saw starlight for the first time since her capture. It disappeared in a second. The rubble rained down hard on all of them, filling Opal's lungs with dust.

Opal let out a yell and rolled off Richmond, covering her head with her hands. She tried in vain to look for Raven and Josh but couldn't see anything over the falling debris.

For a moment, the only thing she could think or feel was plain panic. How was she ever going to get out of this alive? But as the last drops of dust rained down, she was met with abrupt stillness. Opal cracked one eye open and found herself staring up at the night sky.

That's what hope looks like.

Delphina stood amongst the rubble, head thrown back as she stared at the stars.

"Don't you dare!" Roared a very disheveled Richmond from the ground, a vein pulsing in his forehead.

Delphina shot a sly smirk at him before closing her eyes and levitating off the ground, hovering with concentration before soaring through the hole into the night sky. She was gone without a glance back.

Opal was too busy watching Delphina to bother with Richmond, and it came back to bite her when he suddenly tackled her and threw her to the ground, pinning her down.

"Let me go!" Opal screamed as she threw herself around, determined to wrench herself out of Richmond's iron grip.

"Let her go, or we'll release the zombies!" someone suddenly screamed.

283

Richmond slowly turned his head to stare at Bree as she clenched the remote tightly in her hands, her face leering with triumph.

"Let her go," she yelled. "Let us *all* go."

Instead of looking worried, a sort of pleased expression flitted across Richmond's face.

Nonetheless, he let go of Opal and stepped back. His hands raised high in the air. Opal didn't stop to question his strange response; she just scrambled to her feet.

"Now let's do this very carefully, girl," whispered Richmond.

Bree's grip didn't waver on the control. Opal edged around to stand next to Bree and Raven, her heart pounding.

"Get that smoke out of Josh's air." Bree snarled.

"As you wish." Richmond dipped his head in a sort of mockery, nodding at Stephan, who looked shocked yet submissive and pressed the red button again, sending the smoke out of the room in a long hiss. The glass sheet separating the two rooms suddenly shifted away, and Josh came stumbling out, collapsing at Opal's feet.

Opal gasped, crouching down to check his pulse, to shake him, to make sure he was alive.

"Josh," she whispered. "Come on."

Josh's eyes flickered, his hand weakly raised as he grasped hers. "Opal," he muttered.

"I'm here," Opal whispered. Was he alright? What was happening?

"Out of my way! Out of my *way!* He wants *me!*" Bree suddenly tossed the remote to Raven, who caught it with a startled expression and fell dramatically against Josh's side, shoving Opal and Josh's hands apart.

284

"I might vomit." Delsea snarled, staggering up; a cut on her head was bleeding, trickling into her hair and crusting it with blood as she stared at her daughters.

"Delsea. Be careful; after all, our little friends here hold the remote to the zombie quarters." Richmond called to his scientist, a hint of humor laid thick into his words.

Would he give up so easily? Opal could hear the mocking tilt to his words. This was a trap.

Raven still held the controller; her face was shining triumphantly, but Opal couldn't shake the lingering feeling that Richmond wouldn't give up so easily. What was he doing?

"Your friend needs medical help. You see, Opal, if you help me, I can save him." Richmond hissed, his gaze fixing on Bree crouching over Josh, who was breathing weakly.

"We don't want any help from you!" Bree spat viciously. "We're going to be *heroes* when we take you down."

"Mistake," warned Richmond.

Opal turned her back on him. "I don't think so."

"Then you won't help me?" Opal sensed the danger in Richmond's voice, the threat.

Opal opened her mouth, unsure of what to do. So what if they managed to leave the facility? Josh could just die in the mountains; they could all be hunted down.

"No, we *won't*." Bree snapped.

Bree no!

I wasn't ready!

Opal felt a sudden flash of foreboding, a flash of warning, a flash of fear churning deep in her gut. Something was coming.

285

Something big. Something to destroy them all. It wasn't a vision. It was something she knew.

"GET DOWN!" she screamed. She pulled Josh under her, shielding him as best she could. She screamed at Bree and Raven to get down, but not fast enough because then the room exploded.

Opal flew backward in a haze; everything was thrown out of focus.

Opal slammed into what she thought was the wall. But there were no walls anymore.

The walls had crumbled. The room was now completely open to the solid white hallways, the dingy light spilling into the pristine, clean place.

Scientists stopped and stared at the room and its inhabitants, covered in dust and out in the middle of the facility with no walls and a giant hole in the ceiling.

Opal coughed again; her vision blurred, and all she saw was a haze of white and dirt. Everything was unclear; everything hurt.

"Josh? Raven?" she coughed. "Bree?"

No response came out of the dust. Was she alone?

The silhouette of a person appeared through the haze, cautiously picking their way through the rubble. "Josh? Raven?" Opal called again, but she got no response. She was alone. Alone again. Alone to die. Alone to die in misery.

Alone.

Alone.

Fear threatened to submerge Opal like a tidal wave, threatening to push her under.

"Opal, Opal, Opal, I *told* you that there would be consequences if you didn't cooperate." Opal would recognize the distinctive leer of Richmond's voice anywhere.

Swallowing her fear, she struggled to her feet; she had to get up; she had to stop him from pinning her down like he had earlier. She had to stop him.

Her mind seemed fogged because out of the corner of her eye, she swore she saw *eyes* blinking out at her from the gloom. Big ones. Inhuman ones.

The lights were still shining outside in the hallways, but they did little to illuminate the former room.

Her hand brushed something large and bulky. She leaped back in fear, but it was only Delsea's unconscious body, splayed next to Stephan's.

Opal squeezed her eyes shut and opened them again.

A growl rumbled through the darkness. Chilling Opal to the bone.

Then, something pulled itself from the darkness. It was a creature. Unlike any creature, Opal had seen. That was not human. That was not of earth. That was as earth as zombies were. This was no animal, reptile, or any creature born underneath the sun.

H-how?

It was a great snarling beast, at least three times the size of a normal wolf, with dark, impenetrable gray fur and bristling shoulder spikes that jutted unnaturally out from its pelt.

Its jaws parted slightly to reveal jet-white fangs; its beady eyes flinted with menace. Muscles rippled under its glossy gray coat...

287

But it was also strangely beautiful in a way. At first glance, she thought it was a stocky beast, but instead, it was more lithe and agile than she realized.

Also dotted on its muzzle were flecks of white that burst out on her solid gray pelt.

To Opal's surprise and dismay, Richmond was atop the beast. Leather straps were wound under its belly and fastened between its four legs as if this inhumane thing was nothing more than a common horse.

He sat quite comfortably on a leather harness strapped onto the beast's back.

Is that some sort of mutation that Richmond cooked up in one of the labs? Like the zombies?

Richmond looked *way* too smug, and then that's when Opal realized he was clutching the control that Bree was holding just moments ago.

What happened to them?

"Where is Bree?" Opal demanded.

Richmond frowned as if Opal was a displeasing child.

"Move, Sierra," ordered Richmond.

It took Opal a few moments to realize that Richmond was talking to the beast.

Sierra tipped her head obediently and moved aside.

Can she think? I wonder if she's scared of Richmond. Opal thought for a second but then shook herself. Beasts couldn't *think*. No matter how gorgeous or intelligent it looked. *She.*

Her thoughts had distracted her from what Richmond was trying to show her.

Underneath Sierra's body, lying in a heap, were her friends. Josh coughing feebly, Bree lying over him, and Raven collapsed by Josh's side, her face terrified.

"Guys?" Opal called, worry creasing the lines in her voice.

Richmond took this as a moment of weakness and pounced. Literally.

Sierra leaped forward and effortlessly pinned Opal to the ground with her large paws. Her claws were sheathed and didn't slice into her, but the weight threw her back, knocking all the air out of Opal as she gasped out loud.

Opal struggled, but she wasn't strong enough to throw off the beast, not strong enough to do anything but be pinned.

What could she do? She was nothing. Nothing but a little girl who happened to have these strange visions.

She was someone with fear.

She was someone who was chasing after a boy ten times better than her.

She was afraid of everything.

Nothing could help her.

Except?

Did she have something that set her off from the rest? Something that edged her a little higher than them all? Something that could save her?

Opal closed her eyes. Richmond laughed a little- thinking she had given up.

But this time.

This time.

She was far from it.

289

And instead of drifting off into nowhere- instead of simply letting the world happen-

Instead, she reached through to her powers.

Powers.

Confusion.

They were wrong half the time.

But they were her only hope.

Josh was lying on the ground, incapacitated.

He needed help.

Tyler wasn't going to save her.

Her friends weren't coming.

She couldn't do it.

Perhaps her subconscious could do it instead.

I need a vision of how to escape. Just give me a vision. I need a vision of the future that shows me how to escape. I need a vision of how to escape. Opal whispered to herself.

Nothing happened. Opal felt herself stay rooted in the present, in this hellscape. Disappointment swept over her, accompanied by another wave of fear. She had failed.

But yet-

Very, very slowly, the familiar darkness began to take over; it felt hotter than usual as it gripped her tightly and pushed her under. Opal didn't struggle; she didn't fight it. She let her mind go numb as hope filled her body. She let her mind drag her down down down...

Sierra was leaning over her, her claws digging into Opal, lips curled to reveal sharp teeth.

This felt different from the other visions; instead of simply observing Opal, she found that she was actually the Opal trapped beneath Sierra's claws. When that Opal blinked, so did she.

Richmond suddenly leaned down, shoving his metal phone into his pocket and wrenching the unconscious form of someone up. It was Delsea, with her head lolling and her eyes closed. From his belt, Richmond withdrew a small syringe, barely bigger than Opal's pointer finger, filled with clear liquid.

Richmond didn't hesitate. He jammed it into her arm with no particular gentleness. Delsea awoke with a jolt, her eyes popping open, her body going through a small series of spasms before she straightened up. For a moment, her beady eyes widened with surprise at the sight before her, but she didn't ask any questions.

"Go guard her; if she escapes, I'll torture your daughters to death," Richmond ordered Delsea carelessly.

Delsea's eyes widened even more; it would probably be a lot to watch your own daughters die in front of you, no matter how little you care about them. Or whatever was going on in Delsea's mind got her moving.

Delsea crouched by Opal. Her beady, inquiring eyes fixed upon Opal; she could almost feel her gaze burning into her body.

Opal pretended to pass out, her head lolling to one side, slipping her eyes closed, evening her breath.

Richmond snapped his gaze to Opal; upon seeing her unconscious body, he whistled, and Sierra leaped off her; Opal almost sighed with relief as the weight was lifted.

Was this really the future? It felt exactly like the present...

Richmond moved around the room with Sierra next to him. He revived Stephan, who pulled Josh, Raven, and Bree to the other side of the room to wait to be revived with the clear liquid.

He also revived Adax, but only to lock him in cuffs and a large metal band around his neck. Stephan took charge of Adax and escorted him out of the room, where scientists took him from there. Their curious eyes darted across the room, from Sierra to Opal to Richmond. When they spotted Richmond, Opal could see a spark of fear alight in their eyes; they hastily moved away and went back to their business.

Opal was still pretending to be unconscious; her mind was twisting with ideas on what to do next. Delsea turned away from her, thinking she was no threat, when she was unconscious, hissing quietly to Stephan.

Everything was hanging on a thread.

Even in this dreamlike vision —no matter how vivid it was —Opal could feel the tension.

Something tugged deep inside of her stomach, like a wrench in her gut. Telling her to... do something. To act. Like the moment was right now, right here, and she wouldn't have another chance.

Opal tried to resist, but the urge became too great. It just felt... right. This was the reason she had this vision in the first place. It almost felt like she was being guided by a greater hand.

And she moved. Her body felt agile, more in control than she ever felt in real life. Because this wasn't real life, was it? This was the future. She sprang up, and with her left leg, she spun and smacked Delsea hard in the nose. The impact shocked her a little; Opal could feel the power radiating from her body. She felt something she hadn't felt for a long, long time.

292

Power.

Hope.

Courage.

Strength.

The emotions were coursing through her body, fueling her.

With a cry of pain, Delsea sprang backward, crumpling to the floor.

Richmond's head jerked up, alerted by the noise. Before Opal could move, Sierra darted forward and knocked her to the ground. Pinning her arms beneath her, Opal struggled to no avail.

Josh, Raven, and Bree had been revived, but they were too groggy to do much; Josh looked like he was ready to pass out again. And Raven's eyes were flickering from Josh to Opal, not sure who to help; Bree's face was twisted in a sneer. As if Opal deserved this to happen.

Bree didn't make a single move to help. Instead, she knelt by Josh's side, laying a hand over his arm. The meaning was clear. He's mine.

Even in the heat of this moment, of this battle. Bree was such a selfish person she couldn't look past her own stupid love life.

Opal couldn't keep back the strong surge of anger, even though it hadn't even happened.

Go to hell, Bree.

Opal felt Sierra's body relax, her muscles relaxing. She must be thinking that Opal had given up.

But Opal hadn't given up. That same feeling was fueling her body, giving her strength. What did she have to lose? With a twist of her body, Opal wriggled out of her hold and jumped up.

Richmond's face crumpled into a figure of shock as she leaped up, running towards her friends- running to escape-

But she saw it.

With a twist of her head, she caught Richmond's extended hand- she saw the flash of metal that he had emerged from his belt.

She couldn't move fast enough. She had no warning. She had no time.

Time.

Opal screamed as the knife whizzed through the air, thrown from Richmond's hand, and embedded itself into her back. Blood flowed. It was too late.

Time had run out for Opal Kermana.

21

OPAL

Opal blinked. Her heart was beating so fast, from her vision, it took her a few moments to calm herself down and to piece together what was real and what was the future. What was reality?

But it will *be a reality. I can* make *it a reality.*

And I won't get stabbed in the back.

That was a warning.

It was time to take action.

I won't die.

I can do this.

"Go guard her; if she escapes, I'll torture your daughters to death." Richmond was ordering Delsea carelessly.

My powers aren't just a nuisance anymore. They're a weapon. Opal realized softly. *The same thing is happening.*

Delsea walked over to Opal; just like her vision, she crouched down beside Opal's unmoving body.

The following events happened just as they had in her vision.

Adax was bound.

Josh, Raven, and Bree were dragged to the other side of the room.

Stephan and Adax left.

Opal pretended to be unconscious.

Then the time came.

Opal didn't even know she could do it. She could see it. But how could she do it? How could she do it knowing that it would end with a knife in her back?

What choice do I have?

So, with a small burst of energy, she sprang up and twisted her body sideways; flinging her leg up, she kicked Delsea in the nose.

Opal knew what was going to happen next. On cue, Richmond sent Sierra hurtling towards her.

Opal sidestepped easily, sending a smirk Richmond's way and seeing his eyes widen ever so slightly in shock. She watched out of the corner of her eye Josh's pleased and slightly awed face and Bree's bitter one.

She started to run towards Josh, her heart pumping.

Time seemed to slow down.

Now.

It's happening now.

Opal didn't have to look back to know what was flying from Richmond's hand.

Now!

She twisted as she ran.

She saw Richmond's hand extended, the knife hurtling through the air at fifty miles per hour, his face extended in a silent scream.

Opal dipped her back as if she was doing the limbo, letting the knife soar and whizz over her, clattering to the cold tile ground far, far away from her.

Opal didn't pause to celebrate her victory. "Do we run now?" asked the hoarse voice of Josh in front of her as Opal slid down to meet him.

Opal was almost ready to burst with joy that her friend was alright as she smiled at him.

He smiled back; it was a weak smile, but there was something in his eyes that made Opal feel like she was made of gold.

"Yes," Raven interjected. Not a second too late. Richmond and his cronies were just recovering from their shock, and they would be after them. Richmond may have lost Delphina, but he was still powerful, and he still had Sierra.

"Come on!" Bree snapped, swiping at her sister and clenching Josh's side, pushing him up.

But they couldn't get far; they were in the hallway, hobbling forward, but Richmond had already recovered; he brandished his finger at them, and in a heartbeat, the sound of pounding paws filled Opal's mind. Sierra was on them; with a swipe of her giant claws, she sent Bree and Josh tumbling one way and Raven and Opal the other way.

"Ouch!" Raven roared as she went tumbling over the floor, slamming into one of the larger pieces of rubble.

"I hope you're ready to die, you infernal children!" Richmond snarled; his voice was hinged with hysteria. Opal and her friends were trapped at the end of the hallway; the only door was too far away for them to reach. Sierra growled in front of them, her eyes narrowed in undisguised hate.

Opal gasped; she half-pulled and half-dragged Raven out from where she'd fallen over to Bree and Josh. The three of them huddled away from Sierra. There had to be a way to escape-

Richmond was a ghostly pale with dust, and his face was full of rage; his calm demeanor had cracked. He reached into his suit pocket and drew out a short handheld pistol; he didn't hesitate as he aimed it right at Bree's head.

Bree shrieked, moving away and covering her head with her hands.

"Don't struggle, girl. Or I'll kill them all and make you watch." Richmond snarled. "My patience is worn out."

Josh moaned weakly, pushing himself up into a sitting position.

"Wait!" Bree cried. "Please!"

Raven suddenly gasped in shock as Bree scooped her forward, pressing her against Bree's body in a headlock. Raven scraped uselessly against Bree's iron lock of her arms and cried out in horror.

"Bree!" Opal yelped. "What in the world?!"

"Stop! What are you *doing*?!" Josh choked.

"Saving you," Bree said. She turned to Josh with a smile, one filled with twisted emotions. The undisguised want for Josh was clear... but who knows what that would make her do? And then she turned to Richmond. "I'm going to give her to you. I'll kill my sister. I don't care. I'm loyal, I promise. Just let me live."

Richmond raised his eyebrows, his mouth twisting in a pleasantly surprised way as he regarded her. "Is that so?"

Bree nodded frantically. "But Josh. I want Josh. He has to live with me."

298

Josh's eyes widened. "Bree-" he began.

Richmond shrugged, lowering his pistol ever so slightly. "Who am I to argue? Go ahead. Kill your sister." With that, Richmond leaned over and slid the pistol across the shiny metal floor. Opal tried to make a lunge to grab it, but Bree was quicker, and she grasped it with her free hand.

Opal didn't dare try to wrench the pistol from Bree's grasp, not when she had Raven pinned.

Richmond knows Bree won't turn that pistol on him. He knows her soul is rotten.

It took a second for Opal to register, to even get what was going on. Bree a *traitor.* What?

But yes. She could see it.

That mad girl could do anything she thought was right.

"Bree!" Josh cried, lunging forward to grab her wrist. "What are you *doing*?"

Bree suddenly released Raven, nearly jumping on Josh, she pressed her lips against his, holding him still for a moment while the pistol dangled in her free hand.

Opal's mind flashed to her vision of Cora and Tyler doing nearly the same thing. *Oh god. Has Tyler forgotten about me? What if they've already kissed? Cora's just another Bree-*

No.

She's not.

Opal watched in horror as Josh pushed Bree off him, looking flummoxed as Bree, now with a smile fixed on her face, turned from him and extended her arm, clutching the pistol at Raven's shocked face.

299

"Looks like it's the end of the road, sister," Bree said with a smile. "I was always going to kill you after all." Her fingers slipped off the safety and onto the trigger.

Opal glanced at Richmond, horrified, unsure of what to do, crawling towards Josh.

Richmond was watching them with an almost pleasant smile on his face.

Raven stared at her sister. "Bree. Come on. It's me. It's Raven."

Bree suddenly lowered her pistol, staring her sister dead in the face. "I know." she hissed slowly.

Opal felt another flash of foreboding, so unsure of what to do.

Raven smiled hesitantly, lifting her arms as Bree lowered her pistol completely. "Yes. It's me."

A flash of iron shot over Bree's face, and without hesitation, she punched her sister in the face.

Raven yelped as a thin stream of blood trickled from the corner of her mouth where her lip had split open.

"I know it's you, and that's why I'm going to kill you!" Bree snarled, jumping on her sister and wrestling her down until she had the gunpoint on her head.

"No!" Opal cried, jumping forward, but Richmond's hands were holding her back as he snarled at her. "This is between the two of them."

"No!" Opal shrieked again.

Raven struggled against Bree, whose face was half mad.

"You're going to *die*, little sister, because you're always in the clouds. Halfwit. Idiot. You're going to die." Bree snarled. "Never smart

300

enough to beat me. Were you? You little coward. You little *rat*. Hissing with Josh when he's MINE."

She's crazy.

What is it with these two?

Raven's eyes glistened with tears as she stared at her sister. "Bree. Bree, I loved you. I loved you even after every hit, after every jibe. I loved you after you punished me for seeing Josh. I loved you even when you sent me to my death chasing Delsea for that remote. I did all this. I obeyed you because I loved you. You were my sister. We were supposed to be best friends, companions." Raven closed her eyes, letting a slow teardrop from the corner of her eye. "Bree. I'm letting you go. I've been angry at you for sixteen years. We'll see if any of that anger pays off." Raven slowly opened her eyes. "I don't love you anymore, Bree."

Bree froze as she stared down at her sister, going still beneath her. Something changed in Bree's voice. It was as if she always expected Raven to be that meek little mouse, and suddenly, she wasn't.

Suddenly, she had feelings of her own.

And Bree didn't like it.

"No, I don't love you," Raven repeated. "Bree," she whispered. "*I hate you.*" It was so vicious and unplanned that Bree was taken aback.

Raven surged up, throwing Bree off her as Bree let out a gasp of surprise, her pistol flying high into the air. Raven didn't hesitate, lunging forward and snatching it out of midair. She slammed her foot down on Bree's chest and threw Bree to the ground, pointing the pistol right at her chest.

"Sixteen years. Every night. Every morning, I promised myself that one day, my love for you would fade to hate, and one day, I would be strong enough to finally get the revenge I wanted. To watch the light die from your eyes as you realize the assassin has been hiding here all along." Raven whispered. "So now."

Bree gasped. "Raven?"

"So now," Raven repeated. "I'm strong enough."

Bree let out one last yell, grappling at her sister's foot. Screaming out-screaming for Josh- screaming for her parents- for Richmond-

"So now. It's *my* revenge. Goodbye, Bree." Raven whispered and pulled the trigger, shooting a bullet through her sister's skull.

Opal was paralyzed with shock. Josh was still beside her, his wide eyes switching frantically from the two sisters he had grown up with. They were all silent as Richmond released Opal, and she fell to the ground.

Raven dropped the pistol as all three of them crawled together in Sierra's shadow.

"Well. That was *entertaining*," grumbled Richmond. "But not entirely productive."

Opal felt something snap. The events of the last few minutes had been traumatic. Terrifying. But that wouldn't stop Richmond.

Nothing would.

"Run," Opal whispered. "RUN!" she screamed, grabbing her friend's hands and sprinting down the hallway, pushing past scientists and pushing them aside.

She tried not to look back. Because she could see the dim shape of Bree's body. No matter how toxic she was.

302

She could see Bree still twitching her fingers feebly while scientists crouched over her.

She saw blood trickle from her forehead.

"STOP THEM!" bellowed Richmond.

It all happened at once.

Sierra leaped forward, determined to fill out her master's bidding, but she slipped and fell, her paw catching on a vent, yanking it open. The air filled with smoke, making it nearly impossible to see.

It was the perfect cover.

The fog billowed out into the hallways, blanketing them in a white, fluffy fog.

"This way," whispered Opal.

Opal felt her heart beat faster and faster as they inched away from Richmond and towards what she hoped was freedom.

"We need somewhere to hide." breathed Josh.

"There!" Raven pointed to the only door that they could see that didn't seem to be locked; at least there was no bolt on it.

But as they inched forward, Opal spotted the four code combinations that had been on her cell.

"It's *locked*," moaned Opal. Despair poured into her like cement.

A loud noise suddenly filled Area 50 like a loud siren, blaring into her ears.

She clamped her hands over her ears, and her eyes watered in pain as the siren continued to blare through the compound.

Then the voice started.

"Area 50 is now fully locked down. I repeat: Area 50 is under full lockdown."

The voice repeated this sentence another couple of times, and then it issued a whole new sentence.

"The zombies will be released for the hunt at dawn. Be warned. Three dangerous criminals are roaming the halls. They have already attacked the president. The fugitives are Josh Richmond, Raven Canbell, the daughter of scientist Silas and experimenter Delsea. Last, and probably the most dangerous of the criminals, is Opal Kermanna. She has Acana Magic.

Find them and return them to the president's corridors. Stay inside at dawn when the zombies are released."

Opal shivered at the announcements. Trying to fix her mind, Raven slammed her side into the door again and again.

But as the announcement repeated several times, the one thing that stuck in Opal's mind, and refused to leave, was the word: *'dangerous criminals'*

She hated it. She didn't want to be a criminal, but yet, in many people's eyes, she was.

The voice sounded again, carving out hollows into Opal's mind.

Distantly, Opal started to hear the noise of clanking boots on tile.

Opal frantically wiggled the door, but it wouldn't budge.

"Pray this works," murmured Raven suddenly.

From her hair, she withdrew a small bobby pin about the size of her pinky finger. She inserted it into the lock and wiggled it for a few moments while Opal and Josh waited with bated breath. Finally, the lock gave a little click, and the door opened just a crack.

Without warning, all the lights in the hallways dimmed red, and a warning siren went off. It was like a pulsing heartbeat, that siren. The entire world was thrown off as the red sent strange glows through the whole corridor. It stained their skin an eerie color, and Opal could barely make out anything at all.

Opal, Josh, and Raven bolted into the room just before a squadron of soldiers dressed all in black ran by. Their feet slammed into the floor in ominous synchronization as they marched, guns slammed against their hard clothes.

"Shut the door!" Raven snarled. She slammed the door shut behind them and fumbled with the lock until it clicked.

They were plunged into darkness. Opal gasped out loud- she should feel safe, Richmond was behind a locked door, but the thought did nothing to stop the flood of panic attacking her.

Suddenly, she was back in that chair.

She was trapped.

Death was looming over her.

Death was coming for her-

She suddenly felt Josh's hands close around her wrists as he stumbled over some sort of object.

His touch grounded her back to reality. She took a deep breath and focused on his warm fingers closing around her cold skin; slowly, she came back to the present.

"Are there any lights in this place?" Josh muttered after letting out a string of curses when he slammed into an object.

There was a noise like someone was fumbling around, and then Raven switched on the lights.

Opal gasped in relief as the light swept over the formerly dark room. The shadows beaten back. And this wasn't harsh light. Warm light. Yellow light. Safe.

Opal's breath quickened as her gaze swept over the small room. *About the size of my old room back at my house in Duxbury.* Opal realized with a little twinge of sadness.

There were four steel walls, with large glass cabinets filled with thousands of tiny glass bottles, each labeled with its own unique label.

One of the walls had a six-by-six-inch window plated and covered by a white screen.

On the other side of the room was a metal cage with twisted iron bars that formed the shape of a leaf. On the floor was just a bundle of rags or an old dress, by the looks of it.

In the very middle of the room, there appeared to be a table where an experiment had been going on. There was an assortment of tools scattered across the table.

But Opal's relief was short-lived.

"*Who are you?*" demanded a speculative voice. It had an odd accent.

They weren't alone.

Opal nearly jumped out of her skin at the noise, exchanging a panicked glance with Josh. This person could jeopardize everything if they turned them into Richmond-

Opal glanced around in bewilderment for the person who had spoken but could find no one.

"I *said*, who are you!" the voice demanded again.

It seemed to come from the cage, but Opal couldn't see anyone in it.

Until the dress raised its head.

It was a girl around Amelia's age but so thin that she looked much younger. Her skin was pale and seemed to glow dully in the odd lighting. Her strawberry-colored hair was short and uneven as if someone had cut it off with a chainsaw.

She stared at them with her large green eyes. Her dress was torn and muddy. The girl staggered to her feet. The cage was tall enough for her to stand but not large enough for her to stretch. Opal wondered how long she had been trapped in this place. Was she an experiment? An Acana user?

Opal noticed for the first time that she had large, heavy shackles on her feet, bolting her to the ground and holding her in place.

"Um. We come in peace?" Raven tried.

"We're running from Richmond," Josh added.

The girl tilted her head as if confused. "Oh. Well, if that's the case, then I guess you're welcome here," she told them. The girl's voice did have a strange accent. But it wasn't one Opal recognized. It sounded almost Jamaican but different.

The girl put her hands on the bars as if she was trying to squeeze through them. "My name is Celeste, by the way,"

Suddenly, a headache like nothing before splits through Opal's head like a knife. Her knees buckled under her, and suddenly, her legs couldn't support her weight anymore, and she fell to the ground. Her eyes watered in pain as the headache cleaved through her skull.

"Opal?! Opal!" a voice was shouting her name. Maybe Josh, but she couldn't hear him. She was fading into the blackness.

A new scene unfolded before her like ink on a page, unlike anything she had seen before. Ice stretched out in every direction. A frozen

307

wasteland of snow-covered ice, the wind swirled and blew snow into the air. And the ice... the ice was stained red with blood.

Two races of people fought on this wasteland. One were men. Men with hands wrapped tight around guns and their clothes instantly recognizable as those of the army. But the other was completely unfamiliar.

They were people... but people unlike Opal had ever seen. Their skin was puckered and frozen. A pale blue shade. Frostbite. But it seemed as if this was completely normal. Their eyes were narrowed in concentration as they stretched out long hands and shot blasts of ice out into the air and towards the army. They were cloaked in white.

But Opal's vision wasn't focused on the fight; her vision zoomed in on two figures outstretched on the ground, a little bit away from the action.

One was older than the other; she lay stretched on the ground, her eyes glazed over in pain. It took Opal a few seconds to realize that the growing patch of red around the older girl was blood.

Tears were staining the younger girl's face as she cupped the older girl's hands in hers.

"I'm not leaving you! You're going to be fine." she was shouting, her voice stained with fear. Opal felt her heartbreak for the young girl, who was most likely Indigo's sister, crouching beside her and sobbing.

Then, with a jolt, Opal realized who the young girl was: Celeste, younger but with the same hair and the same build. The same determination in her eyes.

"Save your strength, sister. I'm already gone." Indigo rasped.

"Stop talking, Indigo." Celeste cried, burying her face in her sister's blood-stained chest.

308

"I love you." Indigo breathed. Then, her eyes became distant, and she was gone.

Celeste leaned her face against her sister's lifeless body and began to sob.

Then, like smoke, the vision dissolved.

In its place, there was a new scene.

It was a forest, but it was enclosed within a boundary. There was a high wall of woven-together branches around the perimeter to keep things out or to keep them in.

"You're as slow as roots! Climb!" a voice with no particular gentleness was screaming.

A small crowd of people was waiting under a large tree, as wide as five people and as tall as a skyscraper.

There was an angry-looking man. Maybe a teacher, waiting at the foot of the tree and yelling up at a girl, to Opal's surprise, was clinging to the tree's bark. Her face was furrowed in concentration as she gripped onto the bark. Her fingers were doing little good as she slid down a little. The man furrowed his dark eyebrows in disappointment.

Her face was pinched in concentration, and she looked like she was about to fall.

Opal felt a rush of fear for her. Just as someone threw a pinecone at her, it bonked her neatly on the nose and fell to the ground again.

It hit Opal again. This girl climbing the tree was Celeste. *Her short red hair was tangled and filled with dirt and small twigs, and her pale face was smudged with so much dirt that it nearly obscured her freckles.*

Opal saw Celeste's eyes widen in fear; her arms loosened around the trunk, and she began to slip.

309

"Hurry up, you sloth!" jeered the teacher.

Opal saw Celeste's jaw harden with determination as she edged up the tree, but it was too much for her.

Celeste slipped, ungracefully sliding down the rest of the tree trunk. She scratched and ripped her clothes on the way down, landing with a hard thump on the mossy ground.

Opal could feel her humiliation and pain; she wanted nothing more than to run over and hug the girl as Celeste scrambled to her feet, her eyes blazing with defiance.

The crowd didn't try to comfort her or even see if she was alright. They just stared at her with grim disappointment, even though they had been egging her on.

"You're useless, Celeste. The only child in this realm who can't climb a simple tree. I swear if you don't pull yourself up, I'll expel you myself."

The other kids cheered. Actually cheered. *Stamping and clapping, roaring with support.*

Opal winced. This was terrible.

Opal felt like she was out of the vision, but the room where she was wasn't coming back into focus. Which meant one thing: her powers weren't done with her.

Who is Celeste? That was the one question in Opal's mind; she'd never tried asking her visions something, but perhaps it'd work. She was getting more powerful... right? It was worth a try.

She imagined her powers as a person, a woman. Someone inside of her. Her subconscious.

WHO IS CELESTE?

WHO IS CELESTE?

WHO IS CELESTE?

It was silent, no darkness, no helpful visions.... until.

As if a switch was turned on, a loud voice in the back of Opal's head began to speak:

Accessing all known information about Celeste.

Opal nearly has a heart attack. There was a voice *inside* her head. And it wasn't hers.

She must be going berserk. But yet, some part of her felt like the voice was just part of her and that she shouldn't panic. But embrace it.

H-hello? Opal's conscious voice whispered. When she received no response, she concluded that she must have imagined it; it was strange, probably a part of her visions.

Hello, Opal. I'm glad that we're finally being introduced. The voice whispered pleasantly, just whispering like it always had been.

What. The. Hell??? W-Who are you?

Was it a person? Trapped in her mind? Could it hear all her thoughts? Hear what she dreamed about?

Visions of her life started flashing before her eyes: holding hands with Amelia, a hug with Linea, a laugh with Josh, a glance with Tyler, and so much more.

I am your personal assistant; all Acana Magic Users have them.

B-But, w-why-

Why didn't I come into the picture earlier? Why? Because you didn't give me an order that I could follow.

Er. Can you hear my thoughts? Opal asked tentatively.

311

Only a direct thought addressed to me; at any other time, I will just be a helpful voice, staying silent unless called. I'm so pleased you've finally activated me!

Well, I wasn't trying to do that. Opal thought thinly. So many strange things had happened to her. Her powers. This strange magic. It was growing. So why not this?

Look. Um- do you have a name?

You can call me: number FSO-3489625-4532.

FSO-34879- what?

FSO-3489625-4532,

No way am I going to call you that.

It's my name.

I'm calling you Fso.

Hm, Fso, I like that.

Alright, Fso, can you give me all the possible information on Celeste?

I will be happy to.

Opal's mind was whirling; she couldn't think straight. Opal tried to calm her beating heart. She didn't want a robot in her head! She didn't want her! She wanted her mind to be her own! Wait. Could Fso hear her? *Well, she's not responding...*

Fso?

Yes?

Did you hear that?

Not unless I was called.

Oh, thank god. I'm safe

Then to Fso.

I think I'm going insane.

I think you're perfectly sane. She commented. (Opal decided that Fso was a she)

Opal couldn't help smiling a little bit. Now that she thought about it, having a voice in her head and giving her advice was actually pretty cool when she was called, at least.

Did you find anything?

Not yet. This might take a few moments.

Um, is the information going to come as a vision?

Yes. Fso answered. **I have gathered all possible information about Celeste. Information that your vision could provide you. Would you like me to share it with you?**

Yes, please.

Alright. Get ready; this may be a slight override.

I'm ready.

It all came at once. Opal was overlapped with the information, flashes of everything, flashes of the world coming at awkward angles. Flashes of Celeste's life.

Laughing with her sister.

Sitting alone in a room, her face in her hands.

Practicing magic, blasting roots from her hands.

Spitting mad and yelling at a red-headed boy.

Screaming at her parents.

Hugging a younger black-haired girl.

Shooting out into space.

Sobbing to the sky as she tried to stop the flow of blood coming from her sister's broken body.

Splattered in mud as she raced after a boy years older than her on an obstacle course she could never win.

313

It was so overwhelming that Opal could feel a large headache coming on, trying to splinter through her skill.

Before she could cry out in pain, Fso's voice entered her head.

Celeste is from the eleven realms. Fire. Shadow. Water. Earth. Ice. Air. Plants. Sky. Coal. Smoke. Gas. She is from the Earth realm. She struggles with her magic, unable to control it. She claims it is not strong enough for her to do anything with it, but she is wrong.

Her magic is so strong that it could destroy the entire world. Her teachers and mentors realized that. Because Celeste has a past. A long one.

What?

It is unsaid.

To guarantee that she never realized what she was, they decided to crush her spirit.

They ensured that she faced the most difficult challenges, nearly impossible challenges.

Celeste was hiding in a hall. Her shoulders shivering. This time, Opal could feel her fear.

Three men stomped into the room.

They immediately spotted Celeste stomping over and hauled her to her feet. Their loud, harsh voice seemed to penetrate Celeste like small shards of ice.

"Useless. Will never be anyone!" a teacher shouted at Celeste as a large animal made out of earth crumbled to the ground.

Opal's head was throbbing. She was so confused.

What are the realms?

314

The realms are what you humans call space. They perch on the bridge of existence. Humans don't know of their existence, and they don't know of their existence.

Richmond found out about them; in his desperate struggle for power, he didn't view the realms as a peaceful race of people who minded their own business. He just saw more people to crush under his control.

He sent Delphina to conquer them; that's how Celeste lost her sister. Indigo. The only person she ever loved.

Since Richmond's army killed Indigo, Celeste has promised to kill him. And destroy what he has been creating.

But what has he been creating? Wondered Opal. A seed of fear growing deep inside of her. She was worried she already knew the answer to that.

An army of zombies to take over the realms and earth.

The words sank deep into Opal's heart. She already knew that. But some childish part of her had always hoped that if she escaped... life could just go back to the way it was before. But that was impossible. She always knew it.

But before Opal could spiral away, Fso's voice spoke again.

Celeste had been in Richmond's custody for the past four years, as you can imagine, that had made her very mad. She wants to destroy Richmond even more now.

Why does Richmond want to do this?

Richmond has been troubled since he was very small. He lost someone he loved to one of his best friends. He lost his family. His brother was always better than him. He wants revenge.

Opal wanted to disappear. She wanted to be sucked into a whirlwind. This was *not* happening.

Oh, Fso. What am I going to do?

We. What *we* are going to do. We are a team, Opal.

Um. Thanks?

You weird voice. Opal added silently to herself.

You're welcome. Should I continue?

Opal sighed inwardly. She would rather do anything than listen to Richmond taking over his home world. But if she wanted to stop him and survive, this was the best way.

Please do.

Richmond wants to release the zombies on the realms, but he must first find the cure, which he has yet to discover. The Sightseerer won't tell him. Perhaps it is being moved around. Nobody knows.

Opal shuddered. Then, a new question popped into her mind.

But then, where would the cure be now?

The answer is not available yet.

Opal wanted to groan with frustration. She wanted to yell it to the heavens, but she kept it inside.

Fine. Then how do I find it?

The answer is not available yet.

Come on!

I am sorry, Opal, but my resources are limited.

Apologized, Fso. **just as your powers are limited. For now.**

Ok. fine.

Opal didn't really know what to ask Fso next if her sources were as limited as Fso had assured Opal. What she really wanted to know was who The Sightseerer was; he seemed to know her, but how?

A distinct memory popped into Opal's mind. *Say her name.*

Fso, can you give me all possible information about Delphina?

Now, that is something I can do.

Delphina was captured by Richmond when he discovered that a young girl was living with her parents and sister. This family — at least her mother, sister, and herself — was rumored to have strange abilities by their neighbors. They were rumored to have the ability to see into the future. Know things they shouldn't have from the past. Or even know things yet to come. Acana Magic. This was the Irene family.

He stormed their house and killed their husband and father. He took Delphina, her sister, and her mother into his custody. Richmond had been working on an experiment since he first discovered Acana Magic. He decided to test it on Delphina, who was previously an Acana Magic user with her sister and mother but nowhere as powerful as Richmond wanted.

Naturally, Delphina refused, so he used the threat of killing her mother and sister to make her cooperate.

Unfortunately, it worked. Delphina now has Acana Magic more powerful than anyone else's except The Sightseerer.

It also came with many other powers. Including heat that radiates from her hands and warms her blood, she can levitate, and like all of Richmond's high generals, she can control the zombies.

317

Shortly after Delphina was enhanced, the three Irene women made a dash for freedom. The three of them managed to escape Richmond's custody, but when they were on the run, things came to a startling halt in a forest. Delphina's mother was killed. Her sister disappeared. And Delphina went right back to Richmond.

Opal shivered; the story made ice drip down her spine. She also felt a large amount of pity start to make its way toward her. Perhaps she *had* judged Delphina too harshly, and maybe she was just misunderstood.

Some of the pity evaporated as she remembered Delphina's cruel face and her last words to Opal. *I'll kill you.* The words were a whisper against Opal's skin, a caress like Delphina was still with her, ready to make real on her threat.

How did Delphina's mother die anyway?

If Fso has a face, Opal could imagine her frowning. **The answer is not available yet.**

Opal sighed.

I do know that Delphina's mother was named Lily.

Still, I wish we knew more. That's not very helpful.

Wait. Opal, I'm gathering more information. I know more. I have it. I have the information.

Um, great. Can you tell me how Lily died?

Yes. The Sightseerer cares about you a great deal, I am not quite sure why yet, but I am certain I shall find out soon. Well, The Sightseerer looked into the future, and he saw Delphina hurting you.

318

Opal had never felt more confused in her life. Why did The Sightseerer care about her so much? Care about her enough to want to stop something in the distant future? Was it because she had Acana Magic? Was he from the Kermana line, and they were distantly related?

Opal began to feel light-headed, and the darkness started to creep in; she knew this could only mean one thing: she was getting a vision.

She was in a dark forest; tall trees reached the sky, blocking all the light that would have come through. There was a small gap in the trees, and Opal could see patches of a starry sky blinking merrily down at her.

Opal turned in a slow circle, addressing her surroundings, watching the fog unfurl from around the dark bark of the trees and wind around her legs.

Before long, she heard a loud noise blundering through the undergrowth, smashing across plants and branches. It was something large and coming right her way.

Opal tried to steady herself, reminding herself that she was safe. Whatever came through those trees wouldn't be able to see or hear her, much less hurt her.

Then Opal remembered the vision of all those people on the docks. This vision might not be able to hurt her physically, but the mental scars would be just as deep.

A woman suddenly ran out of the bushes. Her face was smeared with dirt, and she looked as if she was running from something for quite a while. Her clothes were in tatters, and her long brown hair looked like it had been through a shredder.

319

She whisked past Opal and disappeared into the dark trees; soon, she was only a shadow, lost to the forest.

Only a few seconds passed before a man jumped out from the space she had just emerged from.

Opal recognized him almost instantly as The Sightseerer. He seemed several years younger than when she had seen him in her vision. His eyes weren't as wild and crazy as they had been when she first saw him, and his hair still had a few streaks of light brown in it; the rest had already melted to silver.

He scanned the forest, and his eyes landed on the distinct shadow of the woman.

"Delphina," he murmured, his voice low.

Opal wasn't so sure that it was Delphina, though. The women she had seen hadn't looked like Delphina much; they had shown some resemblance, the same build, but yet. Not quite. Not the same eyes. Not the same anger in their movements.

Perhaps it was because Delphina hadn't been changed yet.

But The Sightseerer wasn't close enough to see that. Or maybe he didn't want to

Opal's breath stilled in her chest as she realized what The Sightseerer was doing. From his large coat that he was wearing, he withdrew a silver pistol that gleamed in the starlight.

Opal didn't need to see the future to know what was going to happen next. Her heart cried out. She knew- she knew that the woman wasn't Delphina.

The Sightseerer was going to shoot the women. Was that Lily? Delphina's mother? Opal wished with all her heart that she could stop him - this was all because of her? Why?

320

She watched in horror as he raised the pistol, his eyes squinting into the gloom.

She wanted to scream. To go back and change the future, stop the cascading of events that would crash down on The Sightseerer's head, land him in a dirty cell, and land Delphina as a monster under Richmond's thumb.

"NO!" *Opal cried.*

Then he fired.

The bullet seemed to shoot through the forest in slow motion. It whizzed past Opal, disappearing into the gloom.

Have it miss. Have it miss.

Please.

Opal prayed, but she knew it wouldn't. It never would.

This had already happened.

The shadow in the depths of the forest suddenly let out a blood-curdling scream and collapsed against the mossy floor. The bullet that would change everything had hit its mark.

The vision faded, leaving Opal with a terrible feeling of dread.

The reason Delphina hated The Sightseerer so much was because he had killed her mother.

The Sightseerer had written his death sentence the second he shot that bullet in that forest. Delphina would hunt him mercilessly now.

It felt thrown upside down. Delphina had been bad. The Sightseerer had been good, or at least that's how Opal had seen it. But it was all wrong, wasn't it?

Is it my fault?

Why did The Sightseerer do that because of *her?*

321

Why?

Delphina's sister escaped back to civilization. But Delphina and The Sightseer both went to Richmond for different reasons. Delphina, because she knew Richmond was the only one with enough resources to continue her search for The Sightseer because she couldn't find him. The Sightseer went to Richmond because, in his visions, he saw the only way to avoid Delphina would be to hide with the devil himself. Richmond.

It's so twisted.

It is. There's a long, long history with Acana Magic, Opal. And I think we're just scratching the surface.

Opal was surprised to see the room coming back into focus.

She had learned so much in just a couple minutes; she felt like she was years older as she returned to the room with a splitting headache, the new information filling her to the brim.

Opal inhaled. She was glad to be with her friends again. Or as close to a friend as she could get. Josh, yes. Raven... Opal shuddered as she remembered with a distinct flashback, Raven's eyes glinting as she pulled the trigger on her sister.

I can't say I'm sad that Bree's gone, though. Opal thought ruefully, remembering the girl's vicious passion and cruel demeanor.

And maybe Raven and Bree are only connected in name.

"Opal! Oh my god! Stop *doing* that!" Josh cried. "You literally just collapsed!"

Opal laughed weakly with him as they clasped hands.

Raven was looking at her eagerly. "What did you see?" she demanded.

322

Before Opal could answer her, she needed to make sure that Fso was real and that she hadn't just imagined her, that she was not just another voice in her head.

Fso? Are you there?

Yes, I am. Your friends care deeply about you.

Opal smiled inwardly; Fso was still there.

Apparently, they do.

"Well? What did you see?" Raven repeated.

Opal looked into their eyes. "I understand,"

22

TYLER

Cora gasped softly beside Tyler, and Tyler felt her go rigid. He knew how she might feel, how she'd prepared herself over and over that she was never going to see her mother again, to leave everything safely in the past with the horror of the apocalypse and now to see her again, bleeding and bruised on the doorstep of where she had assumed she was safe.

And every feeling, every flash of terror in Cora's eye as she curled her hands into fists, was right. It was all right. Irene was horrible from the time Cora was so young.

Aleesha's face creased.

Tyler knew she had recognized Irene immediately; they all knew who she was, the poor widow who had lost her husband, not in the way Tyler and Cora knew her.

"Aleesha," Tyler whispered, keeping his eyes trained on Irene in case she made any sudden movements. "She's vile. I'm telling you, be careful of her, alright?"

Logan lowered his gun as he took in Irene's bedraggled state; with no bite marks, she was unaffected and practically harmless. Or that's what Logan assumed. Sometimes, the emotional scars were just as deep.

"I won't let her hurt you," Tyler promised quietly to Cora, but she was too stiff to respond.

Irene stamped down the steps, each foothold coming down harder and harder.

"Hope there's an extra room for me, eh Loggy?" Irene sneered.

Logan nodded stiffly, glancing at his wife, who shrugged. "We can't just leave her out in the snow," Aleesha whispered, shooting an apologetic look at Tyler and Cora.

Cora was shaking, her hands still balled up, eyes flashing as she stared at Logan and Aleesha. "She's going to ruin everything!"

Aleesha shot a quick glare at Cora. "Don't talk about your mother like that."

Cora snapped her mouth shut; her eyes, however, continued to blaze. Despite her angry interior, Tyler could see that she was practically shaking on her feet; the poor girl was terrified, and the other adults in the house had just let in the devil.

"That's right, *daughter*. I am your *elder*, and you must *respect* me." Irene suddenly snapped; she swayed on her feet.

Cora flinched under her mother's scrutinizing gaze, shrinking away.

"Aleesha, just take her into the kitchen and clean her wounds. She can stay. For now." Logan nodded at his wife, his voice ringing with finality.

Aleesha nodded in response, locking eyes with Logan. It was as if an entire conversation passed within them in one glance, but then Aleesha had broken their gaze and was ushering Irene away into the kitchen and shutting the door behind her.

"Look, kids, I know you all want to rush into the world and rescue your friend, but we can't do anything tonight. Why don't you get some sleep, and we can discuss this again in the morning?" Logan said, somewhat awkwardly, once Aleesha and Irene had disappeared.

"So, is that a yes on rushing into the world?" Tyler jumped on the chance, and Logan shrugged.

"No promises, kid," Logan muttered.

Tyler's heart sank. What was Opal doing right now? Was she in danger?

Was she-?

He couldn't think of that.

Did she think he had forgotten about her, that they all had?

Opal's own family had been kidnapped; who was supposed to rescue her? She probably felt so alone-

"Come on! I'll show you around!" Violet offered, maybe trying to break the silence. "The bunker was very unpersonalized when we first came here, basically just a hollowed out divet in the ground with a few walls. Logan and Aleesha got the best room, but I managed to get the second biggest."

"You mean *our* room." Lida snapped. "We worked on it *together*, V."

Violet rolled her eyes and tugged on Tyler's sleeve- starting to lead him away, but Cora caught his hand.

"I'll come *with* you." she smiled through gritted teeth.

Tyler had to stop himself from rolling his eyes as he somewhat forcefully smiled at her.

Talk about awkwardness.

But Cora had every right to do that now, after seeing Irene.

Lida joined them, and they walked to the next room through the darkened hallway.

Tyler was acutely aware of how Cora was clinging to him and how Violet kept rolling her eyes at her whenever Cora snapped at her.

326

Why won't they just get along?

Tyler could almost understand Cora's reactions when he was around Opal, but with Violet, it was just unnecessary-

Wait what? Did he really just think that? So he was saying that Cora's pettiness towards Opal was justified because he liked Opal? More than a friend-?

Who was he kidding? Some part of him, a part that was growing bigger each day, liked Opal, more than a friend.

The next room, Tyler could tell, was just as makeshift as the rest of the bunker. It was a nice room nonetheless, with smooth dirt walls that had tiny divots in them for storage.

Someone, probably Violet, had strung tiny fairy lights into all of the divots and around the whole room, giving it a lived-in feel and chasing away the shadows with warm light.

There was no furniture, just piles of pillows, soft fabrics, and sleeping bags on the floor to almost make a sort of carpet.

Tyler saw little signs of Violet everywhere, not just in the fairy lights but also in the family photo she must have had carefully pinned onto the wall. For a moment, Tyler imagined himself as her, thrown out of her home and into this new one, desperately trying to make it seem like what she had lost by adding all these tiny details.

"This is beautiful, V." Tyler smiled, and for the first time in a while, it felt genuine.

Violet beamed back. "Sorry you're stuck with the girls; there was no room with Conner," she added.

"Ah, it's okay." Tyler shrugged. Though he would have liked a break from squabbling, it wasn't like he was going to confine in

Casper, Nolan, or Conner. And Conner was just going to tease him the entire night anyway like he did every time they saw each other.

"I'm going to go say goodnight to my mom; I'll be right back," Violet whispered and slipped away.

Tyler felt her absence the second she left; now, it was just him, Cora, and Lida. Lida was shooting daggers at him, and he didn't even know why; he felt heat rise in his face. Cora just looked sad. He had to get out of here.

Tyler made a hasty excuse for the bathroom and stumbled over several pillows in his eagerness to leave the now stifling room; it wasn't until he was out in the darkened hallway that he realized he had no idea where the bathroom even was.

He was wandering around for a few minutes, moving down a long dirt hallway before he slammed head-first into someone else.

Tyler had to stifle a scream of surprise as he jumped backward, every nerve on his body becoming alive with fear.

"What the hell is wrong with you? Don't you look where you're going?" snapped an irritable voice.

Tyler relaxed; he knew that voice, even if it wasn't particularly his favorite person. "Casper. Sorry. What are you doing?"

Now that Tyler's eyes had adjusted to the dim light of the bunker after the vibrant fairy lights, he was able to make out the form of Casper leaning away from him and against the nearby wall, arms crossed and eyes dark.

"Both Nolan and Conner snore," Casper responded shortly. Tyler waited a beat for more of an explanation, but Casper offered none.

"So…" Tyler tried to prod more of an answer out of Casper, but it felt like pulling teeth. The only time Casper had really looked at him was when he had been beating Tyler to a pulp back in the caves.

"*So* pretty boy, I'm going to find another place to sleep! God, why are you so thick?" Casper's words were sharp, and Tyler flinched.

"On the floor?" Tyler couldn't help but ask.

"Yes, *on the floor*! This conversation went on far longer than it needed to." Casper growled, and with that, he brushed past Tyler and kept moving toward the main room.

Tyler felt a flash of anger; the first thing he was going to do when he saw Violet again was to tell her to stay the hell away from Casper.

It didn't take him much longer than that to find the bathroom after that.

He stayed in front of the mirror in the bathroom for a long time.

He let out a shaky breath. His reflection seemed paler than usual. This whole thing was catching up with him. The apocalypse. Cora. Opal. He was losing the race.

He breathed again and cupped his hands under the running tap. The water was ice cold when he splashed it over his face, and it felt good. He felt a whole lot calmer when he finished. He walked back-ready to face whatever Cora or Lida had to throw at him until he heard them talking.

Talking about *him*.

Tyler stopped dead in the entranceway, right outside their room. He felt like a complete sneak, but he couldn't move; it was as if his feet had rooted to the ground.

329

"I just don't get it!" wailed Cora.

"You got to give him *time*," Lida responded calmly.

"I did!"

"He'll come around."

"I bet that Opal's going to ruin this; he likes her! I can tell! And he likes your sister! Am I not enough!?" Cora grumped. "Ughh."

"He already promised to be your boyfriend," Lida resonated.

"I know! But I feel like he's.... I don't know..... not committed? I mean, I feel like he's ignoring me or something? I don't know; maybe Irene showing up just threw me off."

"Hey." Lida's voice was calm. "You're not imagining; Tyler has always been the kid who could never make up his mind; it's not you, it's him."

Tyler felt sick. What the heck? What was this? Was this how Cora thought of him? He liked her! *Was* he ignoring her? He was friends with Violet, that was all! And Opal... well, he had already told Cora that he would be her boyfriend! It was just getting ridiculous. Really ridiculous.

It's not you, it's him?

Thanks, Lida.

"Tyler's shy! He's not outward with his affection like you, and he holds your hand all the time." Lida explained patronizingly slowly.

Oh, thanks, Lida.

Tyler felt a flash of anger sear through him; he wished nothing more than to run in there and show Lida he wasn't *shy*.

There was the sound of ruffling blankets, and Tyler could imagine Cora leaning back on the ground and sighing.

"I know. That's one of the things that I like about him, he's so modest! And we would be the perfect couple! Why doesn't he see that? I just need someone right now; I almost want to show Irene that I'm not like her; I can be loved. Is that wrong?"

"It's not wrong, Cora," Lida said softly. "The only wrong thing is Tyler not committing. But I'm telling you! He'll come around."
"Well, it's taking forever!" Cora complained.

Tyler felt hurt as if Cora had physically pushed him down. Was this how Cora saw him? A stubborn boy who wouldn't return her affection? And what the heck? Was this what people were talking about him behind his back?

Tyler was already flushing with embarrassment, and nobody could see him. All the work he had done to calm himself down in the bathroom vanished in one second.

"My god, though, Cora." Lida suddenly giggled. "He got *hot*. Are you kidding me? Like what?"

Cora laughed with her. "I know! It's insane."

The two of them laughed together, making Tyler feel even more miserable and alone.

Girls. Tyler thought, disgruntled.

"Well, it's getting late. We should probably go to bed. I'm going to try and find Violet." Lida suddenly sighed.

It took Tyler a moment to realize that Lida was walking right out of the room. Lida passed him, eyeing him coolly, her blue eyes narrowed as she put two and two together that he had been listening in on everything.

"Um, do you know where Violet is?" Tyler asked, feeling guilty about asking for Violet instead of Cora, and then he felt guilty about feeling guilty.

Why can't anything *be simple!?* Tyler thought angrily. He had initially intended to go back into the room and get some sleep, but he did not feel like seeing Cora right now, especially after hearing their conversation; he didn't know how he would handle it. He knew he should be comforting her right now after Irene burst in on them, but... He just couldn't right now.

Lida looked him up and down suspiciously. "She's in the main room. Why?" she demanded, her gaze already flicking back to the bedroom as if the second he walked away, she would go report back to Cora.

"I just want to talk," Tyler responded. *Is that a crime? Wanting to talk with another girl?* He added silently.

He didn't wait for a response; he moved past Lida and walked purposefully toward the main room, trying to ignore the feeling of her eyes on his back.

Tyler half expected not to find Violet, but there she was, sitting on the ground with her head held skywards, towards the little smoke skylight he had seen earlier. The fire was off, and the glass was shut to keep the cold away, but it was a cloudless night, and he could just make out a little bundle of stars.

He let out a small breath of relief that he had found her. Slowly, he sat down next to her and turned his gaze skyward as well. The stars glittered like diamonds, so far away, basking in the beauty of the world while Tyler sat trapped down here. Trapped by an apocalypse. Trapped by a girl he loved and trapped by the thought of Opal far away, scared and alone.

Violet quietly accepted his presence with a nod.

"You alright?" Tyler asked after a beat of silence.

Violet grimaced. "I'm just thinking. It's my father. He loves us so much- but he just shows it by protecting us, shielding us from the world. It's getting harder." Her voice was soft, strained. "I think if I stay much longer in this house, I'm going to go insane. I need to *do* something, Ty."

Tyler didn't know what to say. He couldn't say he related. He'd been staggering around since the day the fires raged. A little bit of annoyance flared inside of him. He would have loved to be safe in that house like Violet. But yet- he could sense that crushing feeling of cabin fever coming off her.

For a second, he was worried he was going to just sit there, gaping like an idiot because no words would come, but slowly they did like they were pouring straight from his heart. "When my family died, I thought I couldn't go on or survive, really. All these changes, I thought it would kill me, but you always find a way to keep going. It's human nature, you know."

Violet sighed and leaned against him. "Yes. But how strong is human nature against the will of the world?"

Tyler opened his mouth, unsure of what to say to counter her words, to make her feel better. Eventually, those words failed; he couldn't make her feel better. Nobody could, but maybe he could tell the truth. "It isn't," he said finally. "But shouldn't we keep going because we owe that to the people that died? We owe a chance to make the world better because they couldn't?"

333

"The world's better because you're in it." Violet sighed; her eyes were drooping as if she was about to fall asleep against Tyler.

"Please tell me that was *not* you proclaiming your undying love for me. I have enough of that from Cora." Tyler joked, feeling a slight pang of regret as he poked fun at Cora.

Violet laughed. "Nah. Sorry, Tyler, but I've really never had any feelings for you. Well, I mean, I love you. But not like Cora."

Or Opal.

No.

Opal doesn't love you, idiot. You knew her for like two hours. Stupid.

Tyler almost laughed. "Me neither, little bug."

"Besides." Violet continued. "I got eyes on someone else."

Tyler couldn't help but jump at the mystery, a small distraction from this terrible situation. "Really?! Who is it? Do I know them?"

Violet laughed. "Yeah! Can't you guess? I met him like four hours ago, but I know... we're destined for each other-"

"Oh no. It's not Casper, is it?" Tyler demanded, looking down at her.

"Of course it is! I don't like your skeptical tone."

"Hm. I won't get in your way, but are you *sure*? He seems like someone who would never fall for anyone." Tyler thought of the dark British boy with his untouchable personality and then his biting words when Tyler had run into him in the hallway.

"Ah, but Tyler, you see, I'm not just anybody," Violet smirked. "He'll fall for me with a little work. I'm confident."

"Right. Tell me when he does." Tyler muttered.

"I understand your skepticism, but look *closely* at him, Ty! Okay, besides being weirdly handsome, he also has this kind of wise air around him. Like he understands everyone. He also has this strange dark humor around him. It's kind of funny." Violet trailed off. Her eyes were misty, and she seemed lost in thought.

Tyler tried for a second, really tried to see Casper the way Violet was describing. And try as he might, he simply couldn't. It sounded like Violet was describing an entirely different boy. "Fine. Tell me if you still feel this way after a couple days with him."

Violet rolled her eyes. "You have no faith. Well, enough about me! What's going on with you and Cora?" Violet added excitedly, eyes flashing, eager for drama.

Tyler sighed. "Oof." He winced, a thousand thoughts flying through his head. He had been wanting so badly to explain his hurricane of thoughts, but now, staring at the opportunity, he felt his words dry up, even with his best friend. "I don't know. She's mad at me. Again." He sighed. The words felt dry, empty. But how was he supposed to explain this whirlwind of feelings that felt so deeply tangled?

Violet winced. "Eeh. That doesn't sound good. Did you guys fight?"

"N-No, not really. It's- this is going to sound strange, but there's something about Opal I can't shake in my mind. And I think Cora picked up on it." Tyler's voice stumbled over the confession. Even though he knew Violet wouldn't tell anyone, admitting his feelings out loud felt like admitting it to himself.

"Oh." Violet made a face. "That's tough."

"Yeah. I just heard Lida talking to Cora about it. Cora said she didn't think I was *committed.*"

Violet raised her eyebrows. "Well, if you're thinking about Opal that way-"

Tyler couldn't help but flinch. "That's not what I meant!" he protested. "It's not fair to Cora to think that I think about Opal that way when I hardly know her-"

Violet raised her eyebrows, cutting Tyler off. "Can you control how you think about her?"

Tyler sighed, considering her words for a moment. "No," he muttered after a pause. "Not really."

"But you want to be with Cora?" Violet prodded.

Tyler didn't know what to say to that. He was frozen, speechless. A few weeks ago, he would have responded with a resounding yes, with all the certainty in the world... but now. He didn't know what to say.

"Geez, you're confusing," Violet muttered, breaking the awkward silence that had enfolded. "I can't imagine living in your head."

Tyler smiled, thankful for the lightheartedness that had returned to their conversation.

He was about to open his mouth to tease her with a reply when he realized she had fallen asleep against her shoulder; she looked so peaceful, with her breath whispering in and out of her lungs, that he didn't bear to move her.

He hadn't meant to fall asleep, only to close his eyes for a second, but before he knew it, he was falling into the comforting darkness of a sleep without dreams.

336

Tyler woke up stretched on the floor, his leg digging uncomfortably into the coffee table. Violet was still fast asleep next to him; his arm was curled over her head, which she was using as a pillow.

It was peaceful, laying on the floor in a silent bunker with moonlight wafting into the common area to make it less eerie, but something told Tyler that he should probably not spend the entire night on the floor, and nor should Violet.

As gently as he could, he scooped Violet into his arms; she stirred but didn't wake.

His back hurt from sleeping on the floor for who knows how many hours as he carefully walked through the silent hallways back to Violet and Lida's room.

To his relief, both Cora and Lida were sleeping peacefully in the mess of blankets and pillows. They didn't wake up to confront him about why he was carrying a sleeping Violet back to their room.

Tyler tried to deposit Violet as gently as he could on the blankets before moving to make an attempt to fall asleep next to her.

"It's late." A familiar voice behind him breathed out the words.

Tyler jumped, his heart hammered unnaturally against his chest as he turned slowly and fought to control his breathing. "Jesus, you scared me," he muttered.

Cora crossed her arms. "I just woke up and saw you cradling Violet."

Tyler had to fight back an eye roll. "That was nothing. We just were talking in the main room and fell asleep. I just woke up." Tyler carefully stepped over Lida and moved to sit by Cora.

Was she shying away from him, or was that his imagination?

337

"Look, I'm sorry I couldn't sleep!" Tyler burst out; he couldn't help it when Cora was staring daggers at him. He felt like a bug squirming under a microscope.

Cora didn't respond.

Tyler opened his mouth to say something more, but Cora stopped him with a short remark of her own.

"This has to end," she growled.

Tyler felt a flash of annoyance. What had to end? He wasn't doing anything! He liked Violet as a *friend,* nothing more! It wasn't his fault that Cora was so jealous! And being friends with another girl wasn't a crime.

Opal.... Opal was another matter.

"What has to end?" Tyler vacillated softly. "You don't own me."

Cora scowled at him, clearly hurt. "I'm not trying to."

"Well, you seem like you are." Tyler bit. "She's my friend."

"I need to know what's going on. I'm your girlfriend. Not Opal's, not Violet's, only me. You're your own kid, of course, but I can't keep tiptoeing around. It's exhausting. I feel like every second, you're saying oh, that's nothing. But what if it is? I'm not a fool."

"*You're* tiptoeing around *me*?" Tyler couldn't help but exclaim. *Of all the stupid things to say-*

"Tyler," Cora whispered and suddenly lifted her hand up to cover his mouth, silencing his words. "Just tell me, and I won't bother you again. Do you want to be with me? Because if not, we can call this whole thing off. I won't stop you."

Despite her strong words, Tyler caught the quiver in her lip and the way her eyes were glossy with unspilt tears. He was hurting her, and he couldn't stand it.

Tyler was frozen, unable to speak, and not to mention she still had her hands pressed over his lips, which was very distracting.

But why was he hesitating?

Was he *really* that cocky and arrogant to think that Opal might feel the same about him after only knowing him for a day or so?

Why was he holding out on this near-invisible hope? It didn't make sense.

Why was he acting like it was some big choice? These feelings for Opal didn't make sense. Cora made sense. *Being* with her made sense.

Cora was staring at him expectantly. One of her eyebrows arched. To anyone else, it would look like she was completely indifferent, but Tyler knew her; he knew the fragile girl behind her stone walls.

And he loved her for everything she was.

Tyler swallowed his breath. He squashed any doubts.

Just because he was throwing away any romantic feelings for Opal didn't mean he didn't care for her as a friend; they could still go to rescue her.

"Of course, I choose you, Cora. I always have." Tyler whispered finally. *That's a lie. That's a lie.* Tyler forced the ugly thoughts out of his head and focused on the girl he had just promised.

Cora let a slow smile break over her face. "Really?"

She sounded so happy in that moment, so unlike the sour, vengeful girl that everyone else seemed to see that Tyler couldn't help but smile back at her.

"What did you think I was going to say?" Tyler chuckled.

"Not that," Cora responded truthfully. And then she pulled him close and kissed him.

Tyler laughed and kissed her back; in that moment, everything felt *right*. He was being ridiculous, feigning feelings for Opal when he hardly knew her; Cora was the one who was always there.

She was the one he wanted.

It wasn't hard to feel that way when her hands were tangled in his hair, and when they pulled apart, her cheeks were flushed, throwing her face into a sort of breathless beauty.

"Goodnight, Ty," Cora murmured. She leaned forward again, and for a heartbeat, Tyler thought she was going to kiss him again, but instead, she looped her arms around his neck and shoulders and pulled him into a tight hug. "Thank you," she whispered into his ear as he held her tight.

Tyler felt his eyelids get heavy, but he knew he was a long way from sleep, not when all he saw when he closed his eyes was Opal.

How does she have such an effect on me? Tyler wondered sadly.

When he kissed Cora, everything felt *right*. There was no doubt in his mind that he loved her, but in the aftermath, he couldn't stop the regret from attacking him.

Some of the comments Cora made... Were downright controlling and mean.

How long could he take it for?

340

Tyler tossed back and forth next to Cora that night, drifting in and out of a dream where Opal cried at him for betrayal.

"I've been holding out for you!" she sobbed." How could you?"

"I'm sorry!" he tried to tell her. "But it's Cora!"

Opal's face became angry, her mouth twisting in a snarl as she lashed out her hand, fragmenting the dream as if it were shattered glass.

After an almost sleepless night, Tyler awoke to the sound of breaking glass, shattering through his mind and jolting him out of the dreamless cloud he had been stuck in.

Leaving Cora sleeping peacefully, he crept out of the room to see what was happening, his heart pounding. Lida and Violet were both gone from their sleeping bags.

Nolan, Conner, Aleesha, Violet, Casper, and Lida were standing in a ragged circle around Irene in the main room, watching her with half-confused and half-horrified expressions.

She was sitting with her head in her hands, blubbering nonsense, talking as if nobody was listening.

Tyler walked up and grabbed Violet's shoulder.

"What's going on?" he asked.

Violet shrugged helplessly. "I don't know! I woke up, and she was like this!"

Tyler watched as Irene sobbed into her hands.

"I never should have agreed. Rose, you idiot! Richmond. Rose. President. TOO MUCH! TOO MUCH! I wish I never had a stupid sister! Delphina, what a stupid name. It fits her!"

Tyler felt a bolt of shock shoot through him like lightning.

Cora suddenly popped up next to him. Violet cast her a suspicious look, but Cora was either too tired or too confused about her mother's behavior to snap at Violet.

"Delphina, the stupid name! I hate you, sister! He'll kill him! Adax. I can't let that happen!"

Cora's eyes widened.

"Is she saying what I think she's saying?" Tyler gulped.

"I think so," murmured Cora, her eyes wide with horror.

"Oh no." Tyler watched Irene. She didn't even seem to notice the people watching her.

"Does that mean that Delphina and Irene are *sisters?*"

"*Delphina* is my Aunt?!" Cora exclaimed disbelievingly, her eyes wide.

"What's going on?" Casper demanded, reaching forward to shake Irene forcefully on the shoulders. "Irene. What do you know?"

Irene raised her dirty head; her eyes were bloodshot and red, her face twisted in a dark leer. "Listen, kids, cuz I'm only saying this once. I'm gonna help you out of the goodness of my heart, but that doesn't necessarily mean I won't ask for anything in return. My real name is Raya Irene. I come from the second line of Acana Magic, right? You idiots don't know what that is. Fine. Acana Magic is what your little friend Opal had, being able to see the future and, on some occasions, the past. Delphina is my sister. Her real name is Rose, but when Richmond- w-when he experimented on her and enhanced her Acana Magic, it made her delusional! But he changed her name to Delphina. The reason I almost killed you, Carter-"

"Casper."

"Whatever! *Anyway,* boy- you know what I'm not going to tell you! Chew on *that!*" Irene snarled, her eyes wide and her mouth opened; a little bit of spit dribbled out, making her look even more crazy.

"You can't do that!" Tyler protested, his mind spinning from information. Who was Richmond? Could he be Allen Richmond? The president of the United States? Tyler pushed his thought away. That was *not* possible; sure, the president hadn't been heard of since he issued directions on how to survive when the plague started, but that didn't mean anything! The president had important things to do. Did t-this *Richmond* have anything to do with Opal kidnap? The head of the snake, as Opal would say?

"Says who?"

"Says me!" Tyler retorted fiercely.

"Shut your mouth! I *told* you I'm only saying this once! The president is evil. My family is riddled with holes. My mother is dead. My sister is not far off. The president created the apocalypse. He wants to take over the world." Tyler tried to keep up with the slur of words falling from Irene's mouth.

Tyler choked, and his world spun. Allen Richmond? The beloved president of the United States..... *created the apocalypse?* How was this possible? What? What?

Tyler wanted a sinkhole to swallow him up; he never wanted to hear the word zombie again.

He wished that Calico was still alive.

He wished that this plague didn't exist.

But from experience, he knew that wishing something away never helped.

The rest of his friends didn't seem to be taking it all that well. Cora let out a nervous laugh, her voice high and delirious.

"You're lying!" Nolan suddenly exclaimed.

Irene let out a hoarse laugh.

"I've been many things in my life, and a liar isn't one of them." Irene hissed.

"But that's not possible! How could *Allen Richmond* be responsible for this?!" protested Logan. He looked strained, and his knuckles were white on his gun.

"It's a long story," Irene growled. "I sense my mind slipping already. It happened to the killer of my mother. It happened to my mother. And it's happening to my sister. Acana Magic takes its toll."

Tyler glanced at Violet- uneasy. He thought Irene had been losing it for years, but to hear her say it herself was a whole other deal. Nonsense words were already coming out of her mouth, and the way she acted towards her daughter showed that she wasn't right in her mind. But was that really because of this... magic? That *Opal* had? Was that why she would collapse?

Why didn't she tell me?

"We have a long time, Irene." Casper hissed. "And you're going to tell us everything."

"No. Nobody has a lot of time." Irene snarled back, her eyes narrowed with hate as she stared at Casper.

"Just tell us!" he demanded.

"Your time will run out just like everyone else." Irene's voice was veiled with threats, but Casper didn't flinch.

"I'll *make* your time run out unless you tell us," he growled menacingly.

Okay, we're making death threats now.

But weren't we ready to leave Irene behind in the caves? Where she surely would have died.

Casper is just being more direct... Sort of.

Tyler glanced sideways at Violet. This was the boy she liked so much?

And Violet's gaze was on Casper- but she seemed to be staring right into him. Right into who he was. She was definitely transfixed.

Irene glowered, but under Casper's heavy gaze, she began. Her voice went low. Everyone was transfixed; nobody moved as Irene started to speak. And as she started to speak, years seemed to melt from her body. Suddenly, she wasn't the old drunken mother. Suddenly, she was years younger.

Emotions.

Real emotions flashed through her face as she closed her eyes and let memories wash over her. She began to speak. "It was the dead of night. Witching hour. I lived with my family at about twenty years old or so. My parents and my sister. I was jolted awake that night because someone had entered our home. My father, Sam Irene. My mother, Lily Irene. And my sister Rose Irene. Dark men rushed into our house- they ransacked it, and we could do nothing to stop them. My father laid down his life when he ran in front of my mother. The men killed him with no hesitation.

"I thought they were about to do the same to us. But no. We weren't that lucky. The three Irene women in that household were bound and subdued. We were prisoners.

"They took us to the mountains- far from my home in LA. They took us to a man. It was his first year of presidency, but his

345

popularity was growing. Allen Richmond. Richmond was a troubled soul as a young boy. His parents were killed when he was young, and they both had cancer. Richmond was bounced from orphanage to orphanage and treated horribly at all of them. He was used to being hungry, and soon, he developed a new hunger: a hunger for *power*. This festered inside of him for a long, long time until one thing tipped him over the edge.

"Richmond had plans to take over the world with a zombie apocalypse and control the zombies so he would have the ultimate army.

"But he didn't stop there. He found magic. *Real* magic on this earth, he developed an entirely new obsession; he began to hunt down Acana users. Acana Magic. The power to see the future. He enhanced my sister's and Rose's magic and turned her into his own personal weapon. A monster. Delphina."

"Our family was crumbling. My mother died at the hands of the most powerful Acana user of all. The Sightseerer. He can see all possible futures- not just the most common one. Timelines, he called them, but years of seeing the future riddled his brain, and like many other Acana Users, he started to go mad. The killing sent Delphina into a rage. She dug her grave bigger than it already was by chasing blindly after him. Until she couldn't get out. Her mind is long gone. Just like my mother."

"I escaped Richmond's clutches but not alone. I met my love. He was one of Richmond's highest generals. I escaped that facility with your father, Cora. I was pregnant with you a year and a half later. We lived together for about five years, but I knew he would never stay; he wanted to return to Richmond to fight for power. No matter how

346

much I pleaded with him and no matter how much I told him not to, it fell on deaf ears. I loved him. And I thought he loved me too. But he went back to Richmond and broke my heart. I guess he didn't love me." Irene sighed, closing her eyes briefly before continuing.

Cora looked stricken. After hearing for years about how it was her fault that her father had left... This was probably a shock.

He pushed his fingers into her hands and squeezed. He tried not to think about Lida's words. This was just him and Cora now.

"Who's The Sightseerer?" Casper demanded, enthralled by Irene's story.

Irene let out a musty cough. "Rick Kermana."

"Wait." Tyler's breath caught in his throat. "Isn't that *Opal's* last name?"

Irene smiled. "Yeah. He's Opal's father."

23

TYLER

"*What?*" Tyler burst out, his eyes stretched wide.

"How is that *possible?*" demanded Nolan.

No way. Tyler gasped in his mind. But yet- of course, Opal would be related to one of the most powerful people ever.... Did she know? Or did she think her father was dead?

Irene leered, enjoying their confusion. "Opal was convinced her father died when she was very young, but she *didn't* know that he had left his young daughters and his wife because he looked into the future and saw that Opal would be threatened, he didn't study one of the timelines, and he thought that if he left them, Opal would be fine, well he was wrong!"

Tyler was so confused. So utterly bewildered, and Irene wasn't helping. This was a whole other world. This was a world of magic. If they weren't in the middle of a zombie apocalypse, Tyler would have never believed her...

"And then he was captured by Richmond, but not before he looked into the future and saw Delphina hurting Opal.

"He looked for her, but he tracked down my mother instead; he killed her when she ran through a dark forest, and he mistook her for my sister. He shot her, and my mother was gone."

For the first time, Tyler felt like he could detect a trace of genuine regret and sadness in Irene's voice, but before long, her expression hardened like she was pouring concrete over it. Any trace of human-like emotion was wiped away.

"Well, that drove Delphina into a rage; she searched for The Sightseerer everywhere, intent on getting revenge; her mind was lost by Richmond's enhancement and the visions. Delphina chased after him with a bitter hatred even I couldn't counter.

"But she didn't know that The Sightseer was in Richmond's custody.

"Richmond didn't get much out of The Sightseerer except about a certain place.... A place where Delphina was sent to conquer. And he got one more thing.

"The Sightseerer had three daughters, but only one of them had the gift of Acana Magic; the Sightseerer told him that that daughter's magic would be the strongest of all and would be able to defeat him once and for all, why she would be the strongest we don't know.

"Opal. Opal is the key to unlocking the plague." Irene finished on a grave note.

Her speech was met with silence.

Finally, Cora broke in, "So you'll help us?"

Another moment of silence.

"No, no, I won't because I called Richmond here, and he'll be here in minutes," Irene growled suddenly, fixing her daughter with a beady glare.

Tyler's blood froze. "You didn't," he breathed.

"I did. And he told me he would release Rose if I did so! So all I need to do is keep you here!" Irene roared; in one fluid motion, she rose from the ground and threw herself at Tyler.

The room erupted in chaos.

349

Tyler cried out in shock as Irene barreled him over, knocking over the coffee table in the process.

Wood dug into his back as Tyler desperately shoved off Irene's heavy body- he felt her fingers reach for his throat, and he called out.

Casper jumped to his aid- with one hand, he grabbed Irene's shoulder and flung the old woman off Tyler.

Tyler scrambled to his feet as he watched Irene cackle and cough- sprawling on the floor.

Was Irene's threat true?

W-Was *Richmond* coming?

Why?

Why did he bother with them?

B-because.

We're going to rescue Opal. And Richmond has Opal.

He.

He's the head of the snake.

Aleesha and Logan were wasting no time trying to decipher Irene's words- instead, they were scrambling around, throwing bags and supplies around as they tried to pack their entire house in minutes.

"To the truck!" Aleesha screamed.

"Truck?" Nolan gaped.

"Come on!" Lida called.

Tyler abandoned Irene and sprinted after Aleesha and Lida as they made their way towards the separate room, down the stairs to the garage. Irene let out a furious wail and raced after him, but she tripped over the overturned coffee table and fell on the ground, flat on her face.

He was inches away from the threshold of the other room; he could just make out a large gray truck with massive snow tires; Aleesha and Logan were throwing supplies into the bed of it.

He was nearly there when the first bomb struck.

Something large crashed against the ceiling. A yell burst its way out of Tyler's lips as the impact shook the entire house. Dust showered down from the ceiling, but the bomb didn't puncture the house... Yet.

Tyler looked around wildly- he had to find Cora and Violet before another bomb struck-

"Cora!" Tyler screamed, catching sight of her by the truck. He ran forward, but that's when another bomb struck. This time, Logan's beautifully engineered house couldn't hold on any longer; the bomb punctured the roof and crashed into the Dalton's living room.
Tyler was thrown back with the impact, the wind was knocked out of him in one fatal move, and dust flew everywhere as the meal groaned and gave way.

Tyler tried to sit up, but he realized that one of his legs was caught on a piece of rubble, pinning him to the ground, sending waves of impact and pain all over his body as he screamed out loud, in pain and panic.

BOOM! BOOM!

Two more large objects crashed through the ceiling, sending rubble everywhere, dust caking Tyler's body as he screamed again.

Tyler jerked his leg, but it was too stuck.

He could hardly see two inches in front of him; with all the particles of rubble around him, he could smell the acrid scent of smoke as the fireplace was crushed and the flames started licking toward the carpet.

351

Suddenly, he wasn't in this house anymore; he was back in Duxbury, his parents pleading with him to run as his childhood home went up in flames-

But he couldn't fall into memories now. This was do or die.

There was a faint ringing in Tyler's ears, muffling the world as he groggily screamed until his throat was hoarse, screaming for anyone to hear him. He felt tone-deaf, staring at his perspective from an outsider. He was even numb to the pain, the adrenaline still seeping through his body and hiding everything.

But then one thing cut through the haze.

An ominous ticking becomes louder by the second.

Bomb ticking. The house was going to be wiped off the map.

Richmond didn't want prisoners this time.

He had to move. He owed it to his family to survive this, even if fate was determined to take them all the same way. He had to survive. With a large pull that nearly dislocated his leg, Tyler wrenched himself free, ignoring the sound of his pant leg ripping. Then, a searing sensation as blood started to trickle.

His lungs were clogged with dust, and he found it increasingly hard to breathe. Using his now dust-stained shirt, he covered his mouth and ran for the garage.

He couldn't stop the flashbacks crippling his body- nearly sending him to his knees.

Calico.

Mom.

Dad.

Struggling to escape- dust clogging his veins- had his luck run out this time?

352

More bombs.

Every time they threw big craters in the house- sending debris everywhere- Tyler didn't know how he was alive- if he even was alive.

He was nearly there- he could see the truck, blissfully unharmed. For now. He could see Cora screaming at him; Conner was holding her back from running towards him.

"I'm coming!" he wheezed, but he knew there was no way they could hear him over the bombs.

But that's when he heard a weak voice cry from behind him.

"Wait. Boy. Help me!"

Tyler didn't need to turn around to know who was talking.

He turned. Irene was pinned under rubble. Her face was white and pinched.

"Help me!" She cried again.

Save her and possibly die. Save the devil and then face the consequences. Or he could leave her to die and live. Hadn't they tried to leave her to die? In a brief second, Cora's eyes caught his through the dust and the pain.

"Tyler. It's okay." she mouthed. "Go."

And suddenly Irene wasn't Irene anymore. She was Calico.

"Boy. Save me." His brother cried. "Don't leave me!"

Tyler shook his head fiercely. That wasn't his brother. That was a woman who had caused pain to Cora. Caused pain on them all.

They'd tried to kill her once before, and it hadn't worked.

He made his choice in the blink of an eye.

"Goodbye, Raya Irene," he whispered. "I'm sorry."

It felt like the sky was falling with all the rubble crashing down on the house, and Irene's gaze filled with rage, hatred, and betrayal.

He would remember that forever, her gaze.

"I'm sorry," he said again, backing up more and more before turning one last time to run.

Irene's bellow shook skies and gouged oceans; she screamed with such anguish and hate that it almost made Tyler's feet stop.

No. He ignored it.

As more bombs crashed down, an automated voice filled the now-destroyed house.

Countdown to complete obliteration.

Thirty seconds.

Tyler ran.

He ran, only glancing back to see Irene, still fighting, getting buried alive. There was no way she survived this. The cat with nine lives was dead.

The truck waited for him, and it looked ready to take on the apocalypse.

It had large, heavy-duty wheels that looked as if they could crush anything. The windows were made of five-inch glass, bulletproof, he guessed by the way they were surviving getting pelted with debris.

God, I love you, Logan. Tyler thought, a grin splitting over his face.

Ten seconds

Tyler didn't need to tell twice.

He ran to the door and leaped in.

"Tyler! Where's-" Aleesha started, but Tyler cut her off.

"No time! We got to go!"

Logan, who was sitting in the driver's seat, hit the gas.

354

The car made a full 180-degree turn until it was facing a very sturdy-looking dirt wall.

"Wait!" Cora intervened. "Where's the door!?"

Logan started the engine. "This is a zombie apocalypse, girl." The car zoomed towards the wall. "We don't need doors."

"Are you *kidding* me? Hell no, dude!" Casper screamed.

Tyler covered his head, half expecting the car to slam into the wall and break apart. But it must have been as sturdy as it looked because it did indeed slam into the wall, and the wall broke apart with a spray of dirt.

Dirt. Dust. Rubble. Freedom.

They hit snow, grinding down the mountain at a speed Tyler could never achieve in a normal car, snow soaring away from their tires as the car plowed its own way through the drifts.

Tyler couldn't help but scream, cry out not only at his terrible fear but also because they were losing all the height they had gained on Opal. They were going back to square one all because of one crazy old lady.

In minutes, the snow began to fade from the trees, and the few patches of ice in the river disappeared. The terrain that had taken Tyler and his friends hours to climb up was done in minutes. The landscape was a blur as they soared down the steep incline. Suddenly, they passed by the water tower, which was located down the cliff.

And they hit the road.

Well, it was more of a ruined road, but the car got on just fine; cracked and ruined cement tumbled under their wheels as they soared across the tar and skidded to a halt in Tyler's old city.

Tyler's heart seized. His town was very different. The roads were cracked and broken up. The houses were deserted and smoking. The fires had swept out all the greenery, and the forests looked blackened. The houses were crumbling and falling. It scared him.

The car was still shaking from the tumbled descent, and for a moment, the only noise in the car was labored breathing and Casper's mumbled curses.

He was crammed next to Cora, who was clutching his hand so hard it hurt. On his other side was Nolan, with Lida next to Cora and next to Lida was Violet.

Then fear melted to exhilaration.

They had survived!

"I'm sorry about your house," Nolan said tentatively, breaking the silence. "It was really nice."

That's when they started laughing. Tyler didn't know if it was from the relief or simply the aftershock of the fear, but at that moment, he was just happy to be alive.

"Don't worry about that, boy. Let's just try and put as much distance between us as we can so that the president doesn't attack us again." Logan said gruffly.

But their excitement was short-lived.

They should have decided on a better place to shelter than in the middle of an abandoned city on a cloudy day. Or maybe they had just forgotten what it was like to live with the zombies.

Because out of the blackened forest came the undead. Waves of them. Drones of them. They ran on all fours like rabid animals against the pavement, zeroed in on the car and seemingly the only live humans in miles.

356

And nothing was more terrifying than a thousand zombies chasing a car with limited gas.

Logan wouldn't accept defeat, though.

When he found that the zombies had blocked their escape route, he jerked the wheel and sent the car skidding sideways, the wheels protesting loudly against the tarmac.

Tyler screamed because he realized that they were about to plunge off a cliff.

Yearning in front of them was a cliff; fifty feet away was the safety of a forest on the other side of the cliff. Roughly a hundred feet down roared a fast-moving river and sharp rocks.

So, they were faced with death. Death from jumping off a cliff or death by zombies.

Logan jerked the wheel again; instead of plunging off the cliff like Tyler expected, the car jolted and ran down the cliff horizontally, hitting hard against the steep slope, just barely holding on, fighting against gravity.

Tyler couldn't scream; he was too terrified, the air was sucked straight from his lungs.

The car was shaking and tumbling, almost groaning as it hit the sandy ground again and again with sickening thuds.

They were going too fast. Rocks waited for them at the bottom; the river churned ahead of them.

Tyler yelled this time, and he wasn't the only one. The car lurched again, flying faster than ever as it soared into the air and suddenly leveled out.

357

They smashed into the ground with such force that Tyler's head hit the ceiling. Water splashed over the trunk, but they managed to land hard on the ground on the other side.

And then it was over.

The car skidded to a halt, the wheel groaning in protest as it tossed up water and mud.

Tyler could hardly believe it.

They were alive!

But yet again, there was no time for celebration.

The zombies didn't care if they got hurt; they only wanted to kill.

So, in droves, they rolled down the cliff like stones.

Tumbling one after another.

Some of them just jumped. He watched their bodies fall when they hit the bottom- impaled by stones. But some got up; they ignored the useless, hanging limbs, and some even tore them off. And they moved forward.

Tyler saw it happen in the rearview mirror; he saw them collecting each other up to run. Everyone was panting, laughing at their survival. Nobody saw them coming towards them.

"L-Logan! D-Drive!" he screamed.

Logan caught sight of the rumbling horde behind them and went pale. He hit the gas, and the car lurched in the mud. It didn't go anywhere. The car's engine groaned some more.

Cora screamed.

Logan cursed under his breath and hit the gas again. The wheels blew up mud, and the engine sputtered in protest. They didn't move.

Panic was starting to set in now. What were they going to do? Tyler's heart was thudding out of his chest. Was this really where it was going to end? The zombies weren't slowing down; they were gaining.

Just when Tyler thought that the car would be overrun, Logan slammed his foot one more time on the gas, and with a ferocious sucking noise, the car jolted out of the mud.

The car sped towards the forest, knocking down the zombies that got in their way. All Tyler could see out the window trees whipping against the glass, again and again in a merciless pattern.

Mud splashed the windows, and zombies scratched at them.

Every time a tree cracked against the windshield, Tyler thought it would be over.

The glass held.

Cora was screaming like crazy; everyone was screaming and yelling until Tyler's ears just became endless halls of screaming, the ringing from Dalton's house coming back to plague him.

And finally, they made it out of the dense crowd of trees.

They sped onto the open road, churning up dust and spinning out of control until they came to a stop.

There was a brief pause.

They had emerged from the forest by a canal, the Fort Longsworth Canal, if Tyler could remember correctly.

The shimmering water glistened in the sunlight; far to the south was a small bridge that allowed cars to travel across it.

The road along the canal wasn't damaged badly and would be a smooth ride; the houses looked deserted, just like everything else.

Glittering fifty feet away on the other side of the canal was Fort Longsworth Island. If any place would be safe from the zombies, it would be there. The island was small, no doubt, and on the other side was the open lake, or Lake Wachusett.

"Where to?" asked Logan, breathing heavily.

"The mountains?" Tyler offered.

"We need to cross the bridge!" Nolan jumped in.

"Why?" Violet asked.

"Because zombies can't swim! Don't you *know* that? I mean, it's *obvious*." Cora responded cruelly.

Violet stuck her tongue out at Cora.

Tyler ignored their squabbling.

"I guess we could wait at the island for a little....."

And the decision was made; the car sped towards the bridge, but it looked painfully far away, and the undead were already circling around to head them off.

"Aleesha, try to see if you can get some of the firecrackers out," Logan ordered.

Tyler glanced at Nolan.

Firecrackers?

"What does he mean?" Cora demanded as if Tyler had the answers.

Tyler shrugged wordlessly; his heart was pounding too loudly for him to make sense of anything.

Aleesha was rummaging around in her bag, and a few minutes later, she withdrew a pack of basic firecrackers, bundled and red.

Cora looked at Aleesha as if she were crazy. "Who keeps firecrackers in their *purse?*"

"Zombies are afraid of them. Don't you think they would be handy to have in the middle of an apocalypse, dear?" Aleesha asked,

360

smiling. Suddenly, Tyler could see even more why Logan had married her.

Cora shrugged. "Just get them out!" she screamed, glancing at the pile of creatures coming up behind them.

"Since when did you keep firecrackers in your purse, Mom? I could have used some to make a huge splash at my Halloween party!" Conner exclaimed.

Aleesha gave him a wry smile. "The police came to shut it down for a reason; I didn't need to add anything to it."

"Pff. They don't know how to have fun!" Conner smirked.

"Your party wasn't the biggest *I've* been to!" Lida snapped. "Now shut up!"

Aleesha's face turned serious. "Logan, hand me a lighter."

TYLER

"Cover your ears!" Aleesha screamed.

Tyler bent down, nearly on top of Cora, with his hands clamped firmly on his ears, blood pounding through his body as he tried not to yelp.

There was a startling crack, and the firecracker exploded outside the window from where Aleesha had thrown it.

Then there was the loudest bang that Tyler had ever heard next to the noises of the bombs hitting the Daltons house. It made his ears pop and his head ring.

He glanced out the window.

Outside, the firecracker had exploded in a flurry of light. It sparked and popped, creating brilliant fireworks that glowed dimly before fizzling out, and a new burst of light would erupt from the firecracker, dimmed by the sunlight through the clouds.

The zombies had halted, Tyler couldn't tell if they were truly frightened away, but they were hanging back. The noise had jolted them back. They were cowering- scrambling away and scattering in all directions.

Even if it only worked for a couple moments, the distraction was enough.

The car sped forward until they were only meters away from the bridge, so close; Tyler's breath caught in his throat as he watched the red metal get closer and closer. But-

"How will we stop the zombies from just crossing the bridge?" Cora demanded, voicing every single one of Tyler's doubts that were printed into his mind.

"We break the bridge?" Conner called back, his answer sounding more like a question than an answer.

"How?" Violet put in. "That thing is solid metal!"

"Tell me you have some explosives or something in that bag!" Tyler exclaimed. He hadn't meant it as a joke, but Cora laughed shrilly anyway.

He could see that it wasn't made for cars; it was narrow and rickety. Since there were no roads on the island and the population was zero, the only reason they would have a bridge was for people coming to look at the scenery or for a quick lunch by the beach and then heading back to the mainland.

There were no cars on the island.

And no reason for cars to cross.

Tyler watched the bridge sway under the cars' weight; as they got closer, he realized that the whole thing was made of wood. It was *not* meant for this.

Fifty feet down was the canal, glittering menacingly, as if whispering for the car to plunge into its depths, as if waiting for it to meet a watery death.

"Wait, what if we don't have to *destroy* the bridge?" cried Casper suddenly.

"What do you mean?"

"I mean, this bridge isn't meant for a lot of weight, right?"

"Sure."

"Then when the zombies come, and they come in herds, the bridge may topple!" Casper finished excitedly, his dark demeanor cracking as the plan came into focus in his mind. "We don't have to do anything except get across."

His words were met with a stony silence.

Cora was the first to break it.

"Sorry to break it to you, but that will *never* work." Cora proclaimed she tossed her hair to her shoulder in a shimmer of gold, nearly blinding Tyler as it swished by his face. "You see, if the bridge is strong enough, they'll come and kill us all, and we can't just risk everything on one small chance. Right, Tyler?"

Cora looked at Tyler expectantly.

He didn't know what to do; he was caught off guard from watching the zombies chase them in a herd, kicking up dust as they went. "Er, um, well... I mean...." He stuttered nervously. He felt the car jostle back and forth as the bulky frame weaseled its way through the narrow bridge, splinters flew from the side. He didn't like how much this bridge was swaying.

Cora widened her eyes slightly, and Casper narrowed them at Cora.

"Well, okay, Casper had a *good idea*, and Cora has a point too." Tyler tried to be as fair as possible, sweat dripping down his forehead as he watched the undead creep closer. *Why* was this bridge so long? He caught Cora looking at him disgruntledly, her arms crossed.

Why does she have to make everything so difficult! Casper's idea is great!

"Er, how bout we vote?" Tyler's voice came out squeaky and small, not at all how he wanted it to.

364

Cora shrugged, probably sour at not getting her way.

"Ooo, who died and made you a leader?" Chuckled Nolan.

Tyler flushed slightly and punched Nolan in the arm. This wasn't him! It was Cora.

"Ow!" He complained and shielded himself.

"You deserve it!"

"No, I don't!"

"Do two."

"Do not!"

"Boys!" Aleesha intervened sharply.

"Brace yourself!" Logan suddenly yelled, and in a flash, Tyler knew why.

The slant of the bridge that led to the other side of the island had broken away and decayed with time. There was no clear path taking them to the other side, just open air with glittering water far behind.

"Logan!" Tyler yelled. "What are you doing? Slow down-!"

"I can't, son. We're going to have to jump it." Logan said gruffly, eyes focused on the road.

"We're dead." Lida hissed. "Dead."

Tyler felt Cora reach for his hand, and he took it, their disagreement forgotten as he held on tight.

The bridge swayed under even more weight as the first zombies jumped on.

Logan hit the gas with a new power, and the car shot forward like a bullet.

Just like before, they were airborne; for a moment, Tyler felt free; maybe all the terror in his body had been leeched out. He was floating out of his seat, held in place only by his seatbelt.

He felt like he could fly away into that cloudy blue sky and disappear into freedom.

But then the car slammed down into the opposite bank with such an impact that the teeth in Tyler's skull rattled. The back tires skidded against the water, but Logan jammed the wheel, and they managed to skid into the sand.

"We don't have time to do anything else, so we're going to have to try Casper's method," Logan growled fiercely.

Casper shot Cora a smug look.

"Get to the other side of the island; even if it doesn't work, we need to have a head start." Aleesha gasped. "We'll swim if we have to."

It felt so strange having adults in the car, having people who were supposed to be so experienced and know everything simply trying not to die. How the tables had shifted.

The car veered; it rumbled forward along the sand.

The island was large enough, but it was clearly uninhabitable. It was coated with a beach on the edges, and the rest was forest. On the other side of the canal, on the opposite side of the island, was a lake; it stretched as far as the eye could see, but very distantly, he swore that he could make out the distant shapes of trees and destroyed houses, still flickering with smoke. The mountains, of course, were behind them, making way for flat-out land.

It's all gone. The fires. Across the world.... How many people did it kill?

Richmond.

366

Could it have been him?

If Irene was lying...

But why would she lie?

I killed her.

Left her to die.

Just like my parents.

A rumble came from behind the car.

Tyler jerked around and saw the herd of zombies climbing onto the bridge; they were attacking it from all sides, scaling the top and bottom. The bridge was entirely consumed by their rotting bodies. The wood swayed and churned under their weight.

Every minute or so, there would be a splash, and one of the zombies would fall into the water, sinking below the current.

The zombies inched closer.

Cora let out a shrill scream. "You'll be the death of us, Casper!" Cora screamed.

Casper let out a stinging reply, but he didn't look too sure, his gaze fixed on the toppling zombies, his skin paler than usual.

The bridge was quaking, it rumbled, it swayed, and finally, with a defining crack, it broke. The support bands snapped away, and large chunks of wood fell into the water with a giant splash, dislodging a giant amount of water. The entire bridge sank into the water with the zombies still clinging to it. Their moans were silenced by the wave of ice water that washed over them.

Slowly, their group tumbled out of the car and stared at the horror they had just escaped.

Cora was shaking like a leaf, her mouth half open. As soon as her feet hit the sand, she sank to her knees.

367

Tyler wrapped his arms around her and tried to calm her down. Sure, they had seen a lot of action in the last few days, but it didn't make it any more tolerable.

This was no exception.

Tyler tried to stop the wave of guilt as he thought of fragile Miranda.

Oh god, I killed her too.

So, how many people have I killed?

Calico.

Mom.

Dad.

Miranda.

Irene.

"They can't *swim*, c-can they?" Cora whimpered.

Tyler tried to comfort her in the calmest way, even though his own heart was pounding. "No, I don't think so."

Cora pressed her face into his chest, Tyler heard her sobs, and he wondered if she was thinking of her mother and if he could have saved her.

Suddenly, he was there, he was there in the bunker with the walls collapsing over him and Irene reaching out her hand...

But it wasn't Irene- suddenly it was Miranda- then Calico- then his parents-

How much more blood would be on his hands by the time this was over?

"Get the hell away!" Casper suddenly screamed, his voice hoarse with panic.

"What?!" Tyler demanded; not more terror? He caught a glimpse of three zombies staggering out from the shore; somehow, they had managed to escape the collapsing bridge. Tyler wrapped his arms around Cora and pulled her backward, shielding her behind him the best he could.

Logan quickly blew a hole through two of the zombies' skulls, and they crumpled to the ground, but the third one took a massive leap and slammed into Logan, pinning him to the ground and knocking his gun straight from his hand.

Tyler was frozen in horror as he saw the zombie unhinge its jaw, ready to sink its rotting teeth into Logan's flesh-
BANG.

The gunshot rattled through the air, and Tyler flinched. The zombie went limp and fell off Logan as its head lolled off its neck.

The group's eyes shifted towards Aleesha. Her fingers were curled around the gun, eyes narrowed and determined, face pale.

The group held its breath, waiting for another zombie to jump out from the water, but none did. For the first time, Tyler felt like he could breathe; they weren't being chased; they were *safe*.

Stranded on a deserted island, but *safe*.

For a second, Tyler was overwhelmed.

Delphina. Richmond. The Plague. Zombies. All too much.

Oh, Opal, where are you?

"Well, I guess we should get ready to spend the night here," Logan growled dejectedly as he kicked the zombie away. "And throw these bodies into the canal."

"And *then* we make a plan," amended Casper fiercely. "I'm not sitting on an island until we starve."

369

He kicked off his shoes and let his toes sink into the cool sand. "Take off your shoes!" He urged Cora.

Cora half-heartedly tugged them off, glancing around nervously.

"We need a place to sleep," growled Logan, already marching around. He looked around the island, blinking at the light.

The beach ended after a few feet; the sand gave way to dirt, and then trees sprouted from the ground, making up a dense forest with moss lining the ground.

Behind the trees, Tyler could see the sun dipping lower and lower in the sky; it wasn't long before it would disappear completely.

They can't reach us. Tyler whispered to himself, the thought becoming a mantra to keep his beating heart at a normal pace.

Tyler sighed. How many days had it been? He felt as if the hours of sunlight were precious few. The hours of the moon were many.

Aleesha helped her husband collect supplies from the truck. Tyler put his shoes back on and went to help them.

Cora sat on the beach watching the sun dip lower and lower, her gaze always fixed on the mountains, not glancing at anything else. She didn't bother to help. Tyler swallowed his annoyance and turned back to his work.

They pulled their supplies into the forest, where they would be sheltered from the wind.

They only had one tent. Which meant that a couple of people would have to sleep outside; Tyler stared down at the misty moss-covered ground with a shiver.

The camp was situated in a clearing in the middle of the woods but still close enough to the beach. Thick trees surrounded him; it was unnerving, and he had to keep reminding himself that he was safe. But when you're surrounded by gloom, it's hard to say that.

The hoot of an owl set him off; he rummaged through a bag until he found a lantern; the light eased his fear a little bit, but only a little.

They had sleeping bags and pillows, food, a large map, lanterns, rope, medication.... Anything you might need. But only enough to last a group of their size, even a week on the island.

And they were stranded there. So, how long before they started running out?

And there were. So. Many. bugs.

Tyler swatted at a clump of mosquitoes who were making a buffet on his arm, spit out a gigantic gnat-like fly- and pulled a caterpillar inching up his leg away from him. He could already feel the other bugs getting closer to him. As if to eat him alive.

"Hey." Logan suddenly emerged from the trees on the other side of the camp, nearly making Tyler jump out of his skin.

Logan carried a bundle of firewood, dumping it down on the ground as he grinned at Tyler.

"H-hi," Tyler stuttered; a bit of his fear leaked into his voice; he just couldn't pin down the crawly feeling creeping across him.

"Scared, eh?" Logan asked, not unkindly. "Dark forest. I feel perfectly at home."

"Yeah. I guess," Tyler didn't feel that comfortable confessing his fears to an adult, most of all Logan, but what choice did he have?

"Ever been camping, kid?" Logan asked.

"Yeah."

"Well, think of it like that."

Tyler nodded wordlessly, thinking of the half-disastrous trip he took with his family, which landed them in a hotel room for the last night with poison ivy. But even that seemed so happy, especially when he thought about Calico and his parents-

Alright. Now, that was too *painful.*

Logan scrapped a pit in the ground; he held up a stick and stuck it in the ground around a thirty-degree angle. "Your friend over there seems to like the dark." Logan nodded over at the shadowy shape of Casper, perched on a rock and his face towards the sky.

"Yeah. I wouldn't really call him my friend." Tyler muttered. He placed timber under the support stick and more sticks around it; finally, he withdrew a match from his pocket and set it ablaze.

Tyler watched the flames rise; he felt the heat wash over him and felt a flash of relief as the light beat away the shadows and the smoke started to work on the bugs.

"So, you like my daughter?" Logan asked, not suspiciously, but he turned to look at Tyler.

Are you kidding me?!

"No!" Tyler told him immediately, putting his guard up. "I like Violet as a friend! Nothing more! Ask her, I promise you."

Logan let out a slow chuckle. "Yeah, that's how it starts," he smiled knowingly.

Tyler was getting tired of this; why couldn't he just be friends with a girl?

I mean Opal's only my friend! Right?

That's different.

372

Don't compare Opal to Violet.

"Come on, Logan, that's not true!" Tyler protested.

Logan chuckled. "Sure, she likes you, can't you tell?"

Tyler felt a surge of anger. "Yeah, as a *friend*,"

Logan didn't answer; he just kept setting up the camp, smirking ever so often and chuckling to himself.

Tyler tried to smooth out his hands that he had curled into fists; he felt so angry, so annoyed, really.

Conner blundered into the camp. "Hi, peeps." He smiled nonchalantly.

"Hey, Conner," Logan responded quickly.

Tyler didn't say anything; he was still feeling a bit prickly towards Conner, matched by his annoyance at half the Daltons and Cora. Conner didn't seem to notice anything; he winked at Tyler and smiled secretly like they had a secret between them that made Tyler's skin crawl.

Violet and Lida emerged from the trees, talking quickly but shut off with a sharp glance from Violet before dumping their firewood on the ground.

Logan nodded approvingly. "We need enough firewood to keep it going all night."

Lida dumped her load on the ground and disappeared back into the trees, breathing heavily.

"Why don't you look for some fresh food? Don't eat anything before showing it to me. Berries, maybe some plants you recognize." Logan called.

Violet nodded. "Come on, Tyler, let's look for some," Violet motioned for him to join her.

373

Tyler didn't really have anything better to do, so he followed her back into the forest.

He caught Conner's eye, and he winked again at him.

Tyler refrained from rolling his eyes but only barely, trying to grit his teeth.

Tyler was on edge. The forest was full of sounds, and he couldn't bear having almost no light; he almost felt as if the tendrils of smoke and darkness were starting to wind around him, mixed with his frustration. They had been *so close*. Now, they were just thrown back again.

Desperate to break the silence, Tyler turned to Violet. "Where did you learn all this stuff?"

"Girl scouts," she answered promptly. "They teach you a bunch about survival and stuff. And Dad, of course."

A hoot of an owl lanced through the forest.

Violet didn't flinch, but Tyler jumped almost a foot in the air, stumbling backward.

His heart beat wildly, and he had convinced himself that they were about to be attacked, just the *fear*. The on edge.

Violet looked at him, and for a second, he thought she was crying, but she was *laughing* instead.

"You better watch out, Tyler! The owls are planning an invasion!" she laughed some more and helped him to his feet.

Tyler's cheeks were burning, and Violet was doubled over from laughing.

Suddenly, a scream pierced the air, quicker and much louder than the owl, a *human* sound. Tyler jumped up.

High-pitched and scared.

374

"Oh no." Whispered Tyler. He *recognized* the scream.

"Cora." he gasped. Tyler tried to pinpoint the scream, listening desperately, his heart pounding with terror for his friend.

"It's coming from that way!" Violet snapped.

He pelted into the forest, his heart beating out of his chest. He didn't care what Cora was to him; he loved her, and he couldn't stand her screaming.

"Can we go *three* minutes without trouble?" he growled half to himself.

The trees opened up, and he found himself on a cliff on the complete other side of the island; he skidded to a halt, a few stray stones tumbling down. He couldn't see Cora anywhere.

It dropped off at a sheer angle; if he had taken two more steps, he would have fallen to his death. He could see the beach far below him. The cliff was an eroded side of the forest, and he could see a clear path down if he was careful.

They were on the lake side of the island; wherever he looked, crystal clear water awaited him.

His mind was racing with terror. Had she fallen off? Was he going to find her broken body somewhere down there?

Violet skidded up next to him, her eyes wide. "Wow. It's pretty." She whispered.

Tyler felt his heart seize. He couldn't care less about the scenery right now. "Where's Cora?"

Was she hurt?

Did she need help?

"We're going down." Tyler hissed, gaze scanning for an easy way down the steep slope. He slid downwards almost on his back, sand scrabbling against the incline as he slid ungracefully down the lesser steep side until his feet hit the sand.

Tyler caught sight of the distant form of Conner, standing by the water's edge, crouching over something.

Or someone.

Tyler raced forward; his chest was burning from their run through the forest, but he didn't care.

To his relief, he found that Cora was facing Conner, her eyes burning with anger; she was sitting down in the water, her clothes drenched and her hair wet and sandy but unhurt.

Conner was standing innocently next to her, biting back a laugh.

Cora didn't hear Tyler coming, and when Conner acknowledged him, she whirled around to face him, her hair flying as she pushed herself up.

"Tyler!" she cried.

"What's going on?" he asked, calming his breath.

Cora pointed an accusing finger at Conner. "He pushed me into the water!"

Tyler's face burned. It was just Cora being Cora.

He glanced sideways at Violet, who was smirking, her arms crossed over her chest.

Tyler heaved a sigh; that was embarrassing; he'd torn through the entire island thinking Cora was hurt or something.

He pulled Cora into his arms. "I thought you were *dead*, Cora. Don't do that again."

"I wouldn't be dead if I was screaming. And you would rescue me anyway." Cora whispered in his ear.

376

Tyler froze, her faith in him rippling over him like a blanket of pressure as he stared down at her serene face. She believed it. She believed *him*. No matter what she whispered to Lida, she still believed him.

But do I believe her? Tyler sighed.

"Guys!" Lida's voice suddenly split over the beach; Tyler looked up to see her shining face as she stared at them, outlined on the cliff. "We're leaving."

"How?" Conner demanded. "We just got here."

"You should come see this. Somehow. We got a plane."

"*A plane?*" Tyler demanded.

He didn't waste a second. The five of them were already tearing back through the greenery and the forest. The night suddenly didn't bother him; he was too alight with curiosity. And finally, they tore into the clearing.

There really was a plane.

It was parked in between the trees (having flattened quite a few in the process). It was large and metal —a huge, great gnat landing among the green. Logan's car was shadowed in comparison.

A flood of light came down from the open ramp off the plane. A girl about their age waited on the threshold with two other adults behind her.

"Hey. My name's Emily," she called.

Tyler exchanged a bewildered glance with Violet. "Er- who are you?" he demanded.

The girl walked purposely down from the plane ramp and came to a stop right in front of him.

377

She had light skin and wild red hair tied back in a bun, but a few strands were already flying out. Her eyes were a brilliant green, and she smirked at all of them. She wore high combat boots and a green jumpsuit.

"My family and I are from LA. We got up on the plane after the fires started striking. People were talking about it being safe up north. Canada- you know? We were flying there when I remembered my old friend back in Duxbury. I wanted to see if she was alright. We went to her old house, but it was burnt up, so we were flying up when we saw you guys get stranded on the island. Um. Do you need help?" Emily finished her story with a glance around them.

"Who's your friend?" Tyler asked hesitantly. Who was this girl?

"Opal Kermana. Name ring a bell?" Emily asked, raising her eyebrow.

No way.

How are we this lucky?

Tyler felt his hopes sore with his mind as he smiled at her. "Yeah, it rings a really big bell."

Emily had come with her father and mother. Luke and Elise Sans. It had taken a bit of time for all the new families to warm up to each other, Logan especially. But they caught Emily up to speed on their position, and Elise offered to fly them all up to the mountains.

"But not tonight." Luke yawned. "It's been a long flight. I'm going to hit the hay."

"Can I sleep on the plane?" Nolan asked hopefully, glancing around at the small tent.

378

"Uh, sure. There's room for twelve, I think." Luke glanced around, taking numbers. "Sorry for four of you. For four of you. Huh. for four."

"Dad, stop," Emily muttered, embarrassed.

Tyler felt a spark of pain go through him as he saw their easy mingling. He missed his family. He missed everything.

"I'll sleep outside." Casper offered.

"Me too," Tyler muttered. He didn't really want to sleep in the same area with the happy family. They might have lost their home, but at least they had each other to support them. He also didn't particularly like the thought of being trapped there. He just needed some air tonight.

Cora looked at him, alarmed. "Fine. Me too. I guess."

Tyler half laughed at her. "You don't have to."

She grimaced. "Yeah, I really don't want to sleep outside."

"Then don't." Tyler pressed. He didn't know why he was pressing, really; maybe he just wanted a second space from Cora.

"I'll sleep outside." Violet offered.

Cora scowled. Her hatred for the great outdoors battled against her pettiness as she finally relented. "Fine. Don't do anything funny, Ty," she muttered.

She hugged him quickly.

"Don't worry so much," Tyler whispered in her ear.

Cora gave him a bittersweet smile when she pulled away. "Tyler, you should know by now. If *anyone* has you as their boyfriend-even for a second. They should *always* be worrying."

Tyler stared at her open-mouthed. What was that supposed to mean?

379

The more Tyler seemed to look at her, the more she seemed like a stranger. He never knew she thought this way.

Cora must have sensed how dumbfounded he was because she kissed him quickly and then offered him another half-smile before hurrying away into the plane.

"Damn, Ty, she got you on a short leash," Violet muttered behind him. "You guys are torn up over a night away from each other?"

"Oh, shut up," Tyler growled, his face burning. "I don't know what goes on in her head."

"Trust me, I don't either."

Tyler ducked his head and pulled back the flap of the tent.

It was large, but the ceiling stooped so low that Tyler had to get on his hands and knees to enter. Just entering the tent sent a wave of nostalgia and sadness through him as he thought of the failed camping trip he had with his family.

"Night," Casper muttered. He retreated into the shadows, pulling blankets and pillows from the center of the tent where they were heaped up.

Tyler shared a frozen chicken and prune with Violet before they both laid down, side by side, in the stuffy tent.

"I almost wish we were outside outside. So we could see the stars." Violet whispered.

"Yeah. But outside, it's scary. And there's so many bugs." Tyler whispered back. He felt childish saying scary, even though he knew so many of them were probably thinking it... He just... He wished he could be strong.

"Tyler. We live in a scary world now." Violet murmured. "It's our reality."

380

"Yeah, I've never much liked reality," Tyler mumbled. He waited for a response, but Violet's breath had evened out. She had fallen asleep.

Tyler sighed. He didn't know what the feeling inside of him was. Restlessness, maybe, annoyance? But at who?

He wished he could be happy.

They were going to rescue Opal! Violet was at his side; they had found new allies, and he guessed things were alright with Cora, and yet...

He had never felt more miserable.

Tyler awoke to the sound of screaming.

He bolted upright in the tent, his head grazing the poles and sending blankets and pillows scattering.

Violet was also up, her hair a mess as she scanned the tent for the source-

Tyler looked around for Casper, and to his immense surprise, it was Casper who was screaming. His eyes were wild- as he jerked himself up from a sleeping position.

It looked like he was desperately pulling himself from sleep.

Casper stopped screaming immediately as soon as he realized that Tyler and Violet were watching him, and he realized he was back in the real world.

"S-Sorry. It's nothing. Nightmare." Casper muttered, his tone cool as if he wanted to let it roll off.

But Tyler saw in his eyes that it really wasn't nothing for him. He had a bad nightmare.

"I-I'm going to get some air." Casper let out a shaky breath and got to his feet. The next second, he was out of the tent and leaving it strangely empty.

"Well, that was strange," Tyler muttered, turning back to the ground, his head still hazy from sleep. He wanted to keep sleeping- to tune out the world for a little more-

"I'm going after him." Violet jumped up.

"Violet wai-!" Tyler started to call, but she was already gone. He sighed and stuck his head out of the tent.

The cold air stung his face as the fresh air swirled over him. It was very relaxing. He could tell it was still very much night- many hours from dawn.

The world was strangely beautiful; the forest was cloaked in darkness, yet it shimmered with the light of the stars shining brightly overhead. The moon shone out in all its glory, basking in the cloudless night. Tyler didn't remember the last night when the world was so clear, without the haze of electricity from the cities.

Tyler scoured the forest in front of him until he found Violet.

Casper was walking forward, one hand at his side and the other on his forehead, rubbing his face again and again as if to expel the dream that was lodged there.

From Tyler's spot right outside of the tent, he couldn't see any of the details of the two figures- instead, he could only see their silhouettes, cloaked in darkness.

Violet hurried after Casper, and when she caught up to him, she reached out and grabbed his free hand.

Wow. I would not have the courage to do that.

Casper whirled around at her touch- his gaze was wild as he turned to face her. He jerked his hand out of her grip.

"Casper-" Violet started.

"W-who are you?" he demanded.

Ooh, burn. Does he really not know who she is?

Tyler could almost sense the hurt flashing across Violet's face. "Y-you don't know who I am?"

Casper sighed, leaning back, recognition dawning on his face. "Violet. Sorry. I'm a little... Confused right now."

"What was your dream about?" Violet asked cautiously and patiently.

"I-It was nothing," Casper mumbled, turning away from her and sweeping his hair out of his eyes.

"Yeah, it didn't look like nothing," Violet muttered back. "Care to share?"

"Wow, you're quite relentless, aren't you?" Casper smirked, but his usually biting words didn't have the same edge; they sounded almost... joking. Violet waited patiently, and after a beat of silence, Casper continued hesitantly. "It was about my sister, alright? She died of illness back in London. She just keeps coming to me as a zombie, that's all." Casper finally relented. "We all have them."

Violet touched his shoulder. "But that doesn't make them any easier." She smiled at him.

For the first time since Tyler had known him, a ghost of a genuine smile pricked the corner of Casper's lips as he ducked his head to look at her. "Thanks. For that and for coming after me. I-I think I'm going to sleep out here tonight. Maybe down at the beach."

"Alright, be careful," Violet warned softly.

383

"Yeah, I'm not much of the careful type, but maybe just tonight I'll try."

"Okay. I'll see you in the morning then." Violet's gaze seemed to burn into his as she turned away as if she wanted to say more, but she held back.

She was walking back to the tent when Casper called after her. "Hey, Violet!"

She turned, smiling. "Yeah?"

"I won't forget who you are next time."

She smirked. "You better not."

He dipped his head and walked farther into the trees until the shadows swallowed him.

Tyler fell back into the tent, processing what he had just heard and said when Violet collapsed next to him.

"Oh my *god*, Tyler, did you *see* that?" she gasped, her eyes alight with excitement as she stared at him.

"Yeah... He's weird." Tyler laughed as she jumped on him, rolling over to his side.

"No. That was like a serious, romantic conversation in the dark." Violet whispered. "He has this cute little accent when he says my name, you know."

"Yeah, he's British." Tyler laughed.

"I wanted to kiss him so badly," Violet whispered.

"I'm pretty sure he would have punched you, considering he didn't know your name for the first half of the conversation...." Tyler teased.

"Oh, shut up." Violet punched him. "One day."

"Yeah. You do that." Tyler laughed again as she punched him again.

That little ember of melodramaticism inside of him from the night before started to vanish. He should be grateful. He was alive. And tomorrow...

Tomorrow, they would finally take on the world. They wouldn't hide.

I'm coming, Opal.

And we're coming for you, Richmond. We're going to reveal to the world just how much of a snake you are.

25

OPAL

Raven still looked confused.

"What do you mean you *understand*?" she demanded. "Understand *what*?"

Opal didn't answer immediately, still trying to catch her breath as the images Fso had shown flashed in her mind's eyes.

She got to her feet, helped up by Josh, and looked Celeste in the eye.

"You're from the realms, aren't you?" she asked. The words seemed strange even to her, flipping from her tongue like an unwelcome food.

Celeste nodded, her head cocked to one side. "How do you know that? Most of the people that I have talked to don't believe me."

Tell them about me; it's alright.

Opal almost nodded, but she stopped herself, a voice in her head. Perhaps she was crazy. And they would think she was crazy.

But what other choice did she have?

She couldn't do this on her own.

So she told them everything.

***

After the entire story had been spilled, they stared at her like she was insane.

Opal shrugged. "What? It's true; I know you don't have to believe me, but I'm telling you that it's true. Nobody believes Celeste is from the realms."

"I believe you!" Josh exclaimed almost immediately. His eyes are wide.

Opal smiled gratefully at him; he had been avoiding her eye a little since Bree had kissed him. She hoped he wasn't embarrassed; she didn't want to lose his friendship. Or his knowledge.

And, plus, whatever Bree did —that wasn't his fault. No. That girl was insane.

Opal tried to blink back the image of Bree lying- broken on the floor, the scientist swarming around her.

Was it out of their control to heal her?

Could the scientist somehow nurse Bree back to life?

No.

She took a bullet to the head. There's no way she's coming back from that.

Raven stood abruptly. "This makes no sense. I don't believe *any* of it! I don't know what to do. I need to find Richmond."

"Richmond?" Opal exclaimed, standing quickly. "What do you mean?" her stomach clenched as she stared at the girl.

Raven was shaking slightly; her eyes were wide and half-wild. "I-I need to go back to my old life; it was fine. Perhaps he'll let me..."

"Raven!" Josh protested, also standing. "What on earth do you mean? You *hated* it. I know you did."

Raven shot Josh a glare. "Don't pretend you knew what my life was like from the whispers we managed to steal together."

"But you want to go back to *Richmond*?" Opal exclaimed shrilly. "You can't. W-we won't let you."

Calm yourself, Opal. Raven is grieving. She doesn't know what she's saying.

387

Fso whispered in Opal's mind.

Grieving?! She's the one who shot the bullet! She had no right to grieve.

I hope you don't mean that. Of course, she has a right to grieve. This is the most her life has changed in years.

Opal breathed out once, ripping her gaze back to Josh, who looked just as flummoxed as her.

"Let's be *honest,* Josh." Raven snapped, walking in tight circles around him. "You're not the innocent boy you want people to believe you are."

Josh looked pale.

"You always liked all the attention my sister gave you." Raven spat.

"Come on." Josh protested. "I haven't liked her in *years.*"

"But you're the one who started it!"

The two of them stopped moving, glaring at each other.

Opal could almost feel the history radiating between them, the grudges, the years trapped together in time in which they didn't get closer, only got farther.

Does Raven like him, too?

Don't ask me.

"It *is* your fault, Josh, and I'm not going to follow you!" Raven snarled. "I'm leaving!"

Josh seemed taken aback, his eyebrows raised in surprise.

"But Raven, they'll catch you! You can't go!" he protested.

"I'm the daughter of two of the highest generals! I'll survive!"

Opal caught Josh's arm; she didn't want him to leave her. Go with his lifelong friend. Raven was half delirious from guilt and, like

388

Fso had said, probably grief. Love just didn't turn to hate that quickly; in the moment, it would fuel you, but later, it would creep in.

Opal didn't want to be alone with only Celeste from the realms as her companion.

Josh won't go; he likes you too much.

Opal didn't really dwell on what Fso had meant because Raven started speaking again.

"I'm not going to let you find happiness, though, Josh. Not after letting my sister live strong for all those years. You let her *torture* me."

"Raven!" Josh protested. "There was nothing I could do, and she wasn't exactly docile to me-"

"Oh, please." Raven hissed. "She was practically throwing herself at you, and you did nothing to discourage it-"

"I did nothing to *encourage* it!" Josh cried. "You're not being fair- she had us all imprisoned in some way-"

"I got my revenge on Bree, Josh. Perhaps it's time I took my revenge on *you.*"

Raven suddenly turned on Opal, her eyes flashing.

"And one more thing, Opal, there's something your little *friend* has been hiding from you." Raven hissed.

Opal froze, her mind racing. What could Josh be hiding? Something with her family?

"Yes, he's never told you about his parents, has he?" Raven cooed.

"Oh, come on," Josh whispered, his gaze pleading as he glanced wildly from Raven to Opal.

389

"Who," Opal whispered. "Who is his father?" she already knew the answer; she knew it in her body. She felt like ice. Why did it have to be him? Maybe some part of her knew it the second she saw them in the room together. Now that she focused on it, their resemblance was uncanny.

"You already know, don't you?" Raven smirked, and in that moment, she couldn't have looked more like Bree. "Yes. Josh's father is Allen Richmond."

There was a crackle of light, and Raven collapsed, falling to the ground.

Opal hardly noticed she was too busy staring at Josh. Opal knew Raven had spoken the truth; she knew by the way he ducked his head. But a part of her wished with so much power that it was wrong. It had to be wrong. How could Josh be related to that monster?

Please deny it. Deny it. Opal whispered in her mind, but Josh wasn't exactly jumping out of his seat to say it wasn't true.

"Look, Opal-" Josh began.

Opal shook her head. "No. No. I *trusted* you!" she screamed. Maybe it was a little harsh, but she felt too angry, too betrayed.

How could this young, innocent boy be the devil's son himself?

"You can still trust me!" Josh was reaching out with his hands now, tentatively brushing her hand.

Opal shoved him away. "Your *father* has done too much; he captured my family! For god sake, Josh! He's imprisoning the *world!* He's caused the death of millions of people!"

Opal felt light-headed with anger and grief like she was almost drifting away.

390

Relax. Whispered Fso calmly.

Relax? His father is like the biggest enemy I've ever had!

That doesn't mean *he* is. Fso answered, once again saying cool logic.

Well, I guess.

Josh must have seen the changed look on Opal's face because he reached out again.

"Please, you *have* to trust me!" pleaded Josh again. "I'm nothing like him, I promise."

"I never said I'll exactly trust you, but I can try," Opal whispered. It was true, wasn't it? She couldn't let this no longer innocent boy creep into her heart. Only Tyler could go there.

Josh smiled a bit; it wasn't a full smile but a hopeful one as he glanced shyly at Opal.

"Veeeeerrrrryyyyy touching; when I get out of this cage, son of Richmond, I'm going to kill you," Celeste whispered. "I'd watch your back. He's hurt a lot of people."

Josh ducked his head. "You think I don't know all of this?" There was a definitive edge to his voice as he glanced up, and Opal saw a small fire burning there. "You must know it's me included. He's hurt me. He killed my mother. I hate him just as much as you guys do."

Opal looked away for a second, noticing the quiet plea for empathy, even some pity.

Opal glanced over at Raven. She was face down with her arms spread eagle, not moving, sprawled over the ground.

"What happened?" demanded Opal; she glanced at Celeste, her throat dry.

391

Celeste shrugged; the chains around her shoulders let off an ominous clank. "I filled her blood with earth; it's temporary; you don't have to be very powerful to do it."

Opal almost shuddered; she had a strong feeling that Celeste could be very powerful if she wanted to be. She imagined her or Josh on the floor, immobile. What would stop Celeste from doing it to all of them in an instant? How had Celeste not escaped by now?

Remember the vision I gave you? Celeste *is* powerful; she just doesn't know it. Her biggest issue is confidence.

I'll keep that in mind. Opal whispered.

"We need to get you out of these chains," Josh interrupted briskly. "We'll help you get out, of course."

Celeste looked at him like he was a cockroach, one to be squashed on. "I'm good, thanks. I don't want anyone with Richmond's blood touching me."

Josh shrank back, wincing.

Opal opened her mouth but closed it sharply; thoughts of defending Josh drifted away. Celeste was *right.*

Suddenly, Opal heard the distinct clank of boots outside the door, coming closer and closer.

"Hide!" she hissed viciously, her heart seizing. She grabbed Raven's feet and dragged her behind one of the tables, pushing her into one of the large cabinets before closing the door. She desperately glanced around for more cabinets, but the only one she could see was the one Josh was already climbing into.

Opal tried not to groan and swallowed her pride as she squished in next to Josh.

It was strange; Josh was pressed close to her in the darkness with nothing but the sound of their shallow breathing. Opal was acutely aware of every part of her body that was pressed against his.

Josh pressed a finger to his lips before opening the cabinet door a little so they could see.

"I'm sorry," Josh whispered suddenly. "I'm nothing like my father. I promise."

Opal's breath caught as she stared at his sincere eyes.

"What happened between you and Bree?" Opal whispered back. She had to know; it was killing her.

Josh ducked his head. "She used to be great."

"Used to? I thought she was perfectly pleasant when I met her." Opal muttered dryly.

Josh chuckled. "She was my first crush, of course. We were kids, and when we were thirteen, she was my first kiss, dated for a few months... But Delsea took her away for a week, and when she came back, she was... different."

"Different, how?" Opal asked; she felt pushed into the story, watching Josh's chest rise and fall. "How?" she whispered.

"She was suddenly possessive, she wasn't sweet and innocent anymore, she started talking about killing.... I don't know what Delsea made her do or what Delsea did to her, but I think it changed her. Anyway, she was perfectly pleasant to me, but when I went over there, I could see how she was to Raven." Josh winced. "She'd hit her when she thought I wasn't looking; she'd take all her food. Yell and punch her if Raven so much as talked to me." Josh shuddered. "I couldn't take being with Bree, so I cut it off."

"D-did she hurt you?" Opal asked quietly.

393

"No. No, it was more a quiet sort of anger. She promised she would get me back as her boyfriend." Josh sighed, rubbing the back of his neck. "I don't know. It's been years. I just can't imagine being Raven."

Opal sighed. "I can't imagine being *you*. And growing up here. It must have been hard."

Josh cocked his head. "Hard enough to forget my parentage?"

Opal laughed a little. "Maybe." Opal was silent for a moment before another question popped up in her mind. "D-did you ever like Raven? Or did she ever like you? Was that why Bree hated her so much? "

Josh let out a quiet laugh. "Hah. No. Definitely definitely not."

For some reason, Opal found it hard to believe. "Really?" she asked skeptically, raising an eyebrow at Josh. "Handsome fellow like you?" She meant to sound joking, but somehow, the words wouldn't fold that way.

"I'm flattered," Josh smirked playfully before his face became serious again. "No. Er- she doesn't like boys, or maybe she likes boys and girls. I'm not sure. But we've never been a thing."

"Oh," Opal whispered.

"I-I actually think that's the seed of Bree's sort of hatred at her." Josh ducked his head. "Sorry, oversharing."

Opal was silent for a moment, a rush of anger surging through her. How *dare* Bree hate someone because of *that*. That was horrible. "Really?" Opal whispered.

The door suddenly buzzed open, and people filled in, their boots clunking ominously on the tile floor, causing Josh and Opal to jump back. Josh pressed his finger to his lips, urging Opal to be still and quiet.

Josh stiffened next to Opal, and she realized that one of the men entering was Richmond, his *father*. She thought with a slash of spite.

Richmond's deep voice echoed through the room.

"I want a full report when I get back; I'm going to find that wretched girl and *kill* her Acana Magic or not!" Richmond growled, leaving Opal shaking. He marched out, slamming the door behind him.

From the small vantage point of Opal, there were five scientists left in the room. One was Delsea, the other Stephan, and three more with the names (she could tell because of their ridiculous name tags pinned to their coats): Renald, Jalen, and Sofia.

Renald was a tall man with a jet-black goatee and small beady brown eyes, darting around the room; for a moment, Opal's breath caught as his gaze flicked over their cabinet but then moved away.

What will they do to us if they catch us?

Visions of metal tools and blinding light flashed through Opal's mind, matched with Delphina screaming in pain, strapped to the metal bed.

Opal felt sick.

Jalen was the opposite of Renald; he was short and squat with a messy mop of red hair and light blue eyes.

Sofia was a middle-aged woman with a permanent squinting face, short green hair that was poorly dyed, and thick glasses that obscured her brown eyes and clashed horribly with her green hair. For a moment, Opal imagined what it would be like to be in their shoes. Did they like their jobs? How did they even get here? Did they have families like Delsea and Silas?

Sofia had dragged a large wooden wagon into the room and shoved it next to six beds that had used to be one table but split into six different parts.

They had metal bands on the armrests, footrests, the middle, and the head.

Delsea marched over to the cage where Celeste was kept; Opal saw Celeste's face steel over. Years of practice rolled off the young girl in waves as she crossed her arms. Delsea unlocked the cage and Celeste's ankle and arm shackles, pulling her out by the arms. She shoved her roughly towards one of the beds. Celeste snapped at her and wrenched her arm free; she staggered for a moment as if she hadn't walked in a long, long time.

And she probably hasn't.

Opal felt fear rising in her throat as she watched the bands fasten around Celeste's neck, hands, feet, and stomach.

The bed rose up to make a slanted chair, like in the dentist's office, but Opal doubted that the worst thing that could happen here was that Celeste got a cavity filled.

Jalen moved towards the wagon with the iron bars above it, shifting his hands over the iron door until he opened it and pulled out four people with the help of Delsea, Sofia, and Renald.

No way.

It can't be that easy.

This has to be a trap.

Emotions swelled in Opal's chest, and she had to press a fist against her mouth to stop the sobs slipping from her lips.

Out came Amelia, looking tired and hungry, bending her head away from Delsea.

Gina, looking defiant as always, snapped angrily at her captors.

Linea, glancing worriedly at her daughters.

Opal's eyes roved over her family, desperate to memorize every detail of their beings in case they were taken from her again.

I'm right here. Opal wanted to wail; they were so close to being together again, so close to everything being fixed.

Opal felt Josh wrap his arms around her in the darkness; the quiet support melted any lingering betrayal Opal harbored toward him.

Finally, the last person to be pushed from the wagon elicited even more of a muffled gasp from Opal.

He looked even worse than he had in their visions. His eyes were foggy and unfocused as he stumbled around, his wild white hair tousled and erratic. He looked like a shell of a human. Opal wondered if he even knew the damage he had caused.

Will he even help me? Does he even remember where the cure is?

They looked horrible, with dirt on their faces, bags under their eyes, clothes in tatters, and cringing away from Delsea.

Her mother. Visions of Linea staggering away from Opal in the bunker... What would Linea think if she saw her daughter now? If she knew what she'd gone through... How much she had survived.

I feel stronger. Opal thought quietly.

You are. Fso whispered.

Her sisters. She'd failed to save them. Would they be angry? Had they missed her?

And The Sightseerer! He was the answer, the answer to her questions. He had to be. He could help her learn to control her powers. To understand who she was.

If he could even collect his thoughts far enough to do that.

She missed all of them so badly, mixed with worry for all of them and her.

What were the *chances*? They managed to stagger into the room with all the most important prisoners. They must not have wanted to move Celeste far if they brought the other prisoners to her.

Or was this a trap?

Josh squeezed her arm, his lips by her ear as he whispered words of comfort to her, but she didn't hear them. She could only stare.

The Sightseerer didn't even acknowledge his captors; he waved them away like they were flies and walked over to Celeste's cage; as he passed Opal and Josh's hiding place, Opal could have sworn that he had winked.

Her heart seized. Was he so delirious he was going to give them away? Or was he just proving his power? And if he was so *powerful*, why hadn't he gotten himself out of this yet?

The Sightseerer sat down comfortably in Celeste's cage and let the scientist bolt him down with heavy chains. He watched them do it as if he were watching a pleasant play.

Gina was pulled onto the bed, snapping angrily; she hadn't lost her spirit.

They're alive.

And I'm getting them out of here.

Opal believed her words. The Sightseerer could help them, and now, with her and Josh, though he was weakened by the smoke Richmond had put on him, surely they would be able to do something by now.

Linea had tear marks on her face, and she didn't struggle as they strapped her in.

Amelia looked pained as she was tied next to her sister and mother.

Soon, they were all strapped into painful restraints and facing the scientist as they bustled around with clipboards and dragging machines closer to the beds.

"Why are you doing this?" whispered Linea, obviously not the first time she had said it; her voice seemed raw.

The scientist ignored her.

Opal's joints were on fire. She didn't know how to feel. She wanted to be with her family, to feel safe again...

If I leave here... Opal was careful to close off her mind to Fso, to let her unfiltered thoughts range free. *It's helpful to have a robot in my mind, but not all the time.* She thought spitefully. *If I bust out of here and try to save them, they'll just take me again; they'll take me back to the lab. They'll strap me down until I can't move.*

Is anybody worth that?

Is anybody?

And suddenly, people she loved were flashing through her mind. People she'd known her entire life and people she'd just met but people she loved, who trusted her, and she trusted them. Visions were flashing in her mind, things that had never happened but were simply who these people were, the people to whom Opal had given her heart a

399

little bit; no matter how hard she tried to lock it away, some people still held the keys. These were visions of the people she loved and why she loved them.

It was Amelia, laughing, her eyes sparking with defiance as she raced Opal across a wide-open field.

It was Gina leaning down from her bed to talk to her younger sister on the floor after a long day of school.

It was Linea curled up with Opal on the couch, whispering in her ear words of comfort.

It was suddenly Tyler, his hair sparkling as he reached out an arm for her to take, pulling her close to him.

It was Josh, his head bent and his hands clasped in front of him as he smiled at her.

Opal gasped, jerking out of her thoughts; her eyes were sparkling with tears.

She would risk anything for these people. There was no choice. She would die if they died. They would be together until the end.

The finality of Opal's thoughts raced through her body like a fast-moving current. The world had suddenly become crystal clear.

I don't want to watch this. Opal whispered as she watched through the crack of the doors, Delsea wheeling a cart full of metal tools and four oddly shaped hunks of metal closer to her prisoners.

The clanking of chains came from behind them. The Sightseerer was standing up in his cage and pulling lightly on the chains, his gaze mild, but his body vibrated with a sort of intensity Opal couldn't place.

Sofia moved forward, jerking The Sightseerer back until he was sitting flat on the floor.

400

Delsea came forward with the metal hats, placing them with no particular care on each of her prisoners' heads, strapping them tightly under their chins.

One by one, the helmets were lowered onto their heads, and the reaction was visible.

Every one of them stiffened and stopped struggling; they went limp, and their head lolled to one side.

Opal's blood went cold as she watched her family go limp, falling spread eagle.

"Josh. Josh. Josh!" Opal repeatedly touched her friend's arm, not taking her eyes off her family's.

"What?" he hissed in an undertone.

"Help me! Stop this!" Opal hissed back.

"Stop what? It's already begun!" Josh whispered back and gestured to the tables, his expression wild.

Opal's family's bodies were jerking slightly, hitching up and down as if they were in pain.

Jalen had run over to one of the weird machines and was frantically pushing buttons.

Delsea stood before them, calmly twirling her thumbs, glancing ever so often at Jalen.

Sofia was holding a clipboard and jotting down notes with a red pen.

Renald was adjusting the metal helmets so they were hooked to the wall with long metal wires.

Fso, what do I do? Opal thought wildly; her terror for her family was matched by her terror for herself.

Seeking help was the best thing Opal could do, and I hope that someone else jumped in.

Wait until the right moment.

Opal took the advice to heart; she waited, she waited, pressed against Josh as they stared at Opal's family. Every second that ticked by felt like a little knife in her heart. She had to *do* something.

She watched as Renald removed the helmets from the prisoner's heads; he unclipped Celeste and shoved her towards the door, roughly pulling her by the hair to make her go faster.

Something triggered inside Opal, a fire. She was so mad. So very mad, she felt like a fireball, heaving to its full extent and then exploding in a million balls of fire, just watching Renald push Celeste around roughly, striking her in the face when she resisted.

Celeste fell to the ground, crying out as Renald kicked her swiftly in the side; she curled up her body away from his foot.

Renald shoved Celeste to the ground; he did it like she was a rag doll, forcing her hands under her. He pushed her under a table, being careless of the odd angel that she landed in, chaining her to the floor since The Sightseerer had taken her cage. She was so young, Amelia's age.

Amelia, Linea, and Gina were unconscious, but The Sightseerer was staring at Celeste, his eyes wide, his gaze flickered to the cabinet where Opal and Josh were.

The Sightseerer suddenly burst from his cage like he wasn't bound at all, knocking Sofia out of the way as he snarled angrily, swiping his hands as if to dare anyone to come closer.

Act!

Opal burst from the cupboard; with all of the scientists distracted by The Sightseerer, she had just enough time to run over to Gina's bed and pull open her restraints.

"Opal?" Gina gasped, unable to believe it. "What are you do-"

"No time to explain! Free the others! We're leaving!" Opal responded hastily.

Gina clambered off her bed, rubbing her sore wrists.

"Hi! I'm Josh!" Josh introduced himself; he was busy helping Amelia and had turned his head to nod at Gina.

"Who's the cute guy?" Gina smirked at Opal, not losing her flirtatious gaze as she winked at Opal.

Opal hoped her cheeks were not as pink as she thought they were.

"His name is Josh! He's saving your life, so be nice!"

"Likewise," Gina smirked.

The Sightseerer had knocked over Delsea and had her pinned to the ground with her arm stuck to one side so she couldn't summon help, but their screams were bound to attract someone soon.

Delsea was strong, and she struggled fiercely, but despite The Sightseerers frail looks, he was stronger and bigger; he kept her down.

Linea and Amelia were released, Celeste had crawled out from under the table, and soon, they all were facing the remaining three scientists.

Opal had forgotten what it had felt like to be near her family; she had forgotten how comforting it was. But yet, it was strange; something was off. It was so different, and they were all so different now. They had all gone through so much and had their own experiences now. Opal glanced sideways at Linea.

403

I don't know what to say to her.
But I'm glad she's alright.
That we're all alright.

Don't celebrate so soon; you still have to get out of the facility. Fso warned quietly.

Opal quickly embraced her little sister, shielding her from Sofia, Jalen, and Renald's hands that were reaching for them.

Gina swiped at Sofia's legs, but Sofia jumped out of the way and seized Gina by the hair, dragging her through the room.

Jalen leaped on Linea and pulled her towards one of the shelves, slamming her against it; bottles fell and shattered into a million pieces on the floor.

"No!" Opal screamed. She watched as the tiny shards cut into her mother's skin, leaving behind slashes of red.

Opal felt a flash of white-hot pain coursing through her body and paralyzing her limbs. She tried to move, but she was stuck, alarmed. She tried to flail but to no success.

She glanced at her arm and realized, with a bolt of horror, a feathered dart sticking out of it, a paralyzing dart; it was sinking through her, attacking her. The paralyzing feeling spread to every inch of her body, sinking through tissue, blood, and bone until she couldn't move. She was helpless. She was in the custody of Richmond now.

Yet again.

As everything faded to black, Opal's heart slowed down to the effect of the dart, and she fought back the tears pricking in her eyes.

Everything was messed up.

In just a few short weeks, her entire life had changed. This apocalypse, Tyler, Josh, Richmond, Delphina, The Sightseerer, Fso, Everything.

Her family.

Her life.

Her love.

But she couldn't give up.

She *couldn't*.

She might have been a coward, but Opal knew she was *not* going to give up.

She was going to fight with everything she had, her magic, her allies. Her courage.

She was going to fight Richmond until he was on his knees and until the scum of the apocalypse was washed from the earth.

Get ready for the next installment in this thrilling trilogy!

APOCALYPSE

THE BEGINNING OF THE END

PART TWO

Eleanor Leiva

Survive. Surviving. Survivor

Acknowledgments

Writing a book is no easy task. This book has been a long-running project for nearly five years, and I am thrilled to finally bring it to the world. There were many times when I wanted to give up on this story, and it would have remained an unfinished document on my computer if not for the tireless support of many people.

First of all, I would like to thank a few of my friends who were the first to read this story, all the way back in fourth grade: Charlotte, Aster, Siena, Melody, and Maddy. The support you gave me, even back then, was enough to carry this project to the finish line.

Another one of my friends I'd like to thank is Savannah; each time we see each other, you've always asked how my book is going, and it means so much to me.

I would like to thank my family for supporting me through each book I've written and being understanding as I hit roadblock after roadblock. It can't be easy having a young child with so many ambitions, but thank you for helping me anyway.

Thank you to Steve for helping me build my first-ever website; I never would have been able to do that on my own.

I give thanks to my two schools, Riverbend and Rivers, which provided me with the education I needed and the opportunities to pursue my dreams. To all my teachers and friends, your support has meant so much!

Last of all, I give the biggest thanks to my readers. If you've made it to the end of this book, then that is the greatest gift you could ever give to me, and I am grateful for every one of you.

About the Author

Eleanor Leiva is currently fourteen years old and lives in Massachusetts. She attends the Rivers School in Weston and lives with her older sister and parents. This is her third novel, her first two being *The Stanchess* and *Fireborn and the Three Essentials,* written under the pen name E.M. Leiva. Writing has always been her passion, and she hopes to continue publishing many more books throughout her writing career. She enjoys reading, spending time with friends and family, and being outdoors as much as possible, especially when playing sports. You can visit her at eleanorleiva.com